Selected Stories of

Mary E. Wilkins Freeman

Conscience

Selected Stories of
Mary E. Wilkins Freeman

Edited with an Introduction by

Marjorie Pryse

W. W. NORTON & COMPANY

New York   London

MARY E. WILKINS FREEMAN
Pencil portrait by Glaspern
Courtesy of the Manuscript Department, University of
Virginia Library

Printed in the United States of America.

Library of Congress Cataloging in Publication Data
Freeman, Mary Eleanor Wilkins, 1852–1930.
   Selected stories of Mary E. Wilkins Freeman.
   Bibliography: p.
   I. Pryse, Marjorie, 1948–   . II. Title.
PS1711.P7 1983   813'.4   82-21179

ISBN 0-393-01726-5
ISBN 0-393-30106-0 {PBK.}

W.W. Norton & Company, Inc.
500 Fifth Avenue, New York, N.Y. 10110
W.W. Norton & Company, Ltd
10 Coptic Street, London WC1A 1PU

2 3 4 5 6 7 8 9 0

Contents

Introduction

A COUNTRYSIDE OF HER OWN

Historians have described the brief half-century following the Civil War as an interlude during which a "New England in decline" lost its ascendancy in American life and letters. Mary E. Wilkins Freeman and other writers who lived in New England, with the exception of William Dean Howells and Henry James, are generally acknowledged as the recorders of the decline, as popularists of a waning past who have little of enduring significance to say to succeeding generations.[1] The historians look to masculine themes—manifest destiny, the challenge of the wilderness, the flight from domesticity, and the American Adam's heroic innocence[2]—in their attempts to characterize American literature both during its so-called "renaissance" of the antebellum period and again in the twentieth century—after a great leap over those writers categorized and denigrated as "local colorists" and "regional realists."

In the case of Mary Wilkins Freeman, the critics' neglect has kept us too long unfamiliar with one of the finest short story writers in our literature—a writer who disproves the historians' assertions. Far from suffering from what Van Wyck Brooks described as "New England Indian Summer" (his phrase for the dying of literary culture during the period 1865–1915), the region that claimed not only Freeman but also Harriet Beecher Stowe, Elizabeth Stuart Phelps, Rose Terry Cooke, Sarah Orne Jewett, and Alice Brown in fact witnessed the burgeoning of women writers' contributions to American literature—surely a cause for celebration, not lament. Yet the critics' neglect has enforced our ignorance—until The Feminist Press issued a slim collection of Freeman's stories in 1974.[3] I owe my own reacquaintance with her fiction to this out-of-print volume and am now delighted to pass along the joys of rediscovery to other readers with the publication of the present collection.

For the first time in American peacetime history, the women of an entire region were left in a world transformed into a quasimatriarchal one both by the casualties of the Civil War and by the departure of a substantial proportion of the region's remaining young healthy male population.[4] They became "New England nuns," to cite the title of one of Freeman's stories—abandoned on the Vermont hillside, and in New Hampshire and Maine. The world they found themselves inhabiting, characterized by its depressed economy and partly stripped of its masculine point of view, exposed a reality—the lives of women in nineteenth-century New England—that had only just begun to find its way into American literature.[5] This reality became the subject matter of much of our earliest fictional realism and of Freeman's best fiction.

The vision that emerges from the work of the New England regionalists presents a more comprehensive view of American cultural identity than we have previously recognized. In her portraits of New England village life, Freeman in particular establishes alternative paradigms for American experience, different from those that until recently have dominated our national self-portrait. Masculine themes seem diminished or disappear from the fiction; and that fiction expands our perception of our national literature. For example, Louisa Ellis of Freeman's "A New England Nun" rejects rather than embraces the concept of manifest destiny when she chooses her solitary life over marriage to Joe Dagget, her fiancé who returns after fourteen years in Australia. And Sarah Penn of "The Revolt of 'Mother'" establishes domestic power and vision as a countervailing force to the theme of flight from domesticity that appears throughout nineteenth-century fiction in the works of Washington Irving, James Fenimore Cooper, Mark Twain, and other male writers.

In my introduction to the Norton edition of *The Country of the Pointed Firs and Other Stories,* I describe the way Sarah Orne Jewett invents new myths of female paradise in the New World. In Jewett's greatest fiction, her characters find consolation in the face of inner anxieties by joining again a community of women capable of redeeming the fallen world in which "mother" has lost her power.[6] If Jewett's mythical contribution to the dialectic of American intellectual and literary history may be characterized as "reunion with mother," Mary Wilkins Freeman's must certainly be described as the "revolt of mother." Yet both Freeman and Jewett make it clear, through some of their male characters, that these myths include the experience of American men as well as women. The stories in this volume and those included with Jewett's *The Country of the Pointed Firs* form companion collections. Together they offer the reader a double perspective on an alternative American cultural identity that antecedes these reprints by a full century.

In Freeman's depiction of nineteenth-century America, her characters find in domestic life a source and a form for their vision. They also discover the symbolic and emotional role women play for their society as well as for each other—when they are portrayed as real people rather than idealized or romanticized figures. And specific stories reverse the dominant historical theory that in the move westward, the strong and adventurous left New England while the weak and conservative remained.[7] Freeman's strong New England women make us realize that one mark of independence and free thinking, in a century in which many were followers, was to remain behind, with the challenge of rebuilding a postbellum world.

The vision of nineteenth-century American life that Freeman offers suggests that in collaborative, cooperative, and
communal endeavors we have found symbols most conducive
to supporting human life. Instead of man alone against the
wilderness, Freeman depicts two women or women in small
groups (and in one story, "A Solitary," two men) facing life
together. Such sisterhood threatens the patriarchal structure
of American society and further marks Freeman's protagonists.
Instead of romanticizing the image of the independent, self-
sufficient pioneer and the "lonesome cowboy"—which the
Frederick Jackson Turner theory of American history has
given us—we ought to look to the community Freeman's
women created in the wake of the westward movement. Only
one among the eighteen representative stories collected here
concerns a woman who truly lives alone, without the support
of other women. Yet even in that story, "A New England
Nun," Freeman suggests by her choice of title that the protagonist participates at least symbolically in a sisterhood.

Freeman shares with Jewett the single theme that both
writers find universal as well as characteristically American:
she emphasizes the presence of marked or stigmatized characters as receivers and creators of vision. Throughout her New
England stories she depicts old and poor women discovering,
in the way they come to possess social difference because they
are solitary, eccentric, or unconventional, previously latent
strength and power. However, not all of her women protagonists combat convention successfully—as the stories in this
collection demonstrate. Some of them ruin their health in the
process, like Candace Whitcomb of "A Village Singer" or
Betsey Dole of "A Poetess"; others manage to mask their
deviance, like the women friends in "Up Primrose Hill" or
the Shattuck sisters in "A Mistaken Charity." But most of
them achieve their vision and find consolation for their social
stigma in the affections of other women and in their choice to

lead independent lives, as do Jenny Wrayne of "Christmas Jenny" and Hetty Fifield of "A Church Mouse."

Critics may have relegated Freeman to second rank because, in writing about women, she has chosen characters who are marked and therefore not representative (in the way our culture has recently insisted that the word "man" can include "woman" but that "woman" excludes "man"). If so, then like our Puritan forefathers we have searched only for what is manifest in examining the markings of our American destiny. The Puritans controlled metaphysical uncertainty and inner anxiety by withholding church membership and full citizenship from women, young men, and heretics; and certainly the Puritans would have considered heretical such sympathy as Mary Wilkins Freeman reveals for the stigmatized.

Yet in presenting characters whose vision results from social exclusion, Freeman actually joins other American writers for whom marking also leads to vision—writers who preceded her, like Hawthorne in *The Scarlet Letter* or Melville in *Moby-Dick;* those who were her contemporaries, even after she stopped producing her best work—Stephen Crane in *The Red Badge of Courage,* Edith Wharton in *Ethan Frome,* Henry James in *The Beast in the Jungle,* and Sherwood Anderson in *Winesburg, Ohio;* and many others, especially William Faulkner in *Light in August,* Ralph Ellison in *Invisible Man,* and Toni Morrison in *Sula.*[8]

Although Freeman's early stories rank with the best in American literature, in her total production over the course of her long lifetime the subject matter and themes of her early fiction may seem unrepresentative. In later stories and novels, men appear more frequently as protagonists, courtship plots abound (even though she retains many independent women characters, including some who, she implies, have formed homoerotic attachments[9]), and she tries her hand generally unsuccessfully at historical fiction, ghost stories, and more successfully with two collections that experiment with narrative form.[10] Her weakest fiction coincides with the period of her marriage and move away from New England and, in some of her later novels, deals with middle-class and suburban life.[11]

What we need to keep in mind, as we reconsider Freeman's accomplishments, is what represented her most significant work, not the flawed fiction. In the present volume, I have included the best of fifty-two stories that originally appeared as *A Humble Romance* (1887) and *A New England Nun* (1891), universally accepted as her finest collections.[12] Throughout her career, whenever she addressed the themes of rebellion and revolt, in the village fiction that focuses primarily on women, she wrote her most successful work.[13] Therefore, even though at the statistical level of numbers of words and volumes conventional themes appear to dominate other concerns in her life's work, in writing about rebellion—whether personal or social, manifested as mere eccentricity or more disruptive social behavior—she was best able to sustain combined strengths of prose style, character development, realistic plot, and regional subject matter.[14] In the specific stories in this collection—which represent, in effect, the best of her best—the reader can evaluate the combined effects of form and theme that produced Mary Wilkins Freeman's most enduring contribution to American fiction.

One of our greatest literary critics must receive credit for early, if unheard, recognition of Freeman's significance. Writing in 1931 shortly after Freeman's death, F. O. Matthiessen captured the response to her stories that many of us, fifty years later, share:

> Her vision is uncompromising; her extraordinary power comes from the unflinching directness with which she sets down even the harshest facts. Unlike Miss Jewett she is never the detached spectator watching what is going on about her; she and her characters are one. She can present

all the essential elements of a situation in a few blinding sentences the very blunt and awkward shortness of which intimates the kind of life she is creating.[15]

And for Matthiessen, the value of both Sarah Orne Jewett and Mary Wilkins Freeman "is greater than that of simply providing a link with the past. They not only reported life; each of them created, if not a world, at least a countryside of her own, the permanent endurance of which has enriched the American soil." [16]

For us, that "countryside of her own" becomes a symbolic region of gender that helps us understand how to reinterpret our own geography. Freeman puts women on the American map by demonstrating a way of seeing that Puritanism, and its heirs, obscured. Just as Adoniram Penn's trip to buy a horse in "The Revolt of 'Mother'" gives his wife her chance to move into the new barn, the economic decline of New England and the abdication of its young male population provided the historical opportunity for women to express their experience in literary form. Mary Wilkins—she did not take the name Freeman until 1902—intimately lived and observed the reality she portrays in her stories. Reading them allows us to reestablish similar intimacy with women who, except for her fiction, might have been irrevocably forgotten.

The publication of this edition marks our wider recognition of Freeman's contribution, and in making her work more accessible to readers it creates the possibility that Freeman's perception may become our own. In her mature vision, she transformed the experience of social stigma into art. In embracing her vision, we share that transformation and can understand how her fiction teaches us. Unlike her contemporaries Howells and James, who believed in a realistic fiction that reflected the nature of reality, Freeman makes us see that a literary realism that challenges conventional perception can actually transfigure reality itself.

A BRIEF BIOGRAPHY

Mary Ella (later, Eleanor) Wilkins was born October 31, 1852, in Randolph, Massachusetts. She moved to Brattleboro, Vermont at the age of fifteen, when her father went into partnership in a dry goods shop. After graduating from high school she attended Mount Holyoke for a year, then returned to Brattleboro. Biographical legend associates her with a Naval Academy graduate from Brattleboro, Hanson Tyler, whom she would see infrequently in her youth, who would die before she married, but whom she apparently remembered into her old age. The deaths of her seventeen-year-old sister in 1876 and her mother Eleanor in 1880 marked her young adulthood, and her biographer, Edward Foster, describes her as being "much dependent" upon her mother. (Her love for her mother apparently led her at some point to change her middle name.) During the same period she was beginning to write and submit her work to magazines—publishing her first significant story, "Two Old Lovers," in the March 31, 1883, issue of *Harper's Bazar*. In 1884 she moved back to Randolph to live with an unmarried childhood friend, Mary Wales. For almost twenty years this friendship primarily sustained her emotional life.

In 1892 Mary Wilkins met Dr. Charles Manning Freeman, a New Jersey physician (who did not practice) with a reputation for drinking, driving fast horses, womanizing, and eluding marriage.[17] After a decade of acquaintance and three years of broken and then renewed engagements and postponed wedding dates, she married Freeman on January 1, 1902, and moved to his house in Metuchen, New Jersey. Since no letters to Charles appear to have survived, it is difficult to understand Mary Wilkins's decision to marry him. Her letters from this period do document her fear that in marriage she might lose her own identity. This fear may explain the series of postponements—along with her uncertainty that she would be able to control Charles's fondness for alcohol—but the approaching marriage itself attracted a lot of attention in the newspapers, and a reader of her letters might speculate that in the end she married in part to elude inquisitive reporters who had invaded her privacy. The *New York Telegraph* wrote: "The public is really tired of the love affairs of the literary old maid, and the sooner she marries the doctor and takes him out of the public view the more highly will the action be appreciated." Shortly before the wedding took place, the *New Brunswick Home News* ran a story under the headline "Please, Miss Wilkins, Marry Dr. Freeman." [18]

The marriage appears to have worked well enough for a few years, but by 1909 Charles had begun to enter sanitariums for drinking, and by 1919 Mary committed him to the New Jersey State Hospital for the Insane to be treated for alcoholism. During the next four years he escaped from the hospital and returned home for brief periods, but the marriage broke up in a formal separation. By the time of Charles's death in 1923, he had written a will leaving one dollar to his wife. (She and her sisters-in-law later successfully contested the will.)

Mary Wilkins Freeman's circle of friends and acquaintances included Hamlin Garland, William Dean Howells, Rudyard Kipling, Julia Ward Howe, Lucy Larcom, Thomas Bailey Aldrich, Mrs. Margaret Deland, Francis Marion Crawford, Octave Thanet, and Lafcadio Hearn. She also exchanged letters with Sarah Orne Jewett and met her on several occasions. [19] She sat next to Mark Twain at a banquet given to honor his seventieth birthday, and in April 1926 received the Howells Medal for Fiction from the American Academy of Arts and Letters. Later that year, she and Edith Wharton were among the first women to be elected to membership in the National Institute of Arts and Letters.

On a recent visit to the academy on West 155th Street in New York, I saw the bronze doors at the entrance, installed in 1938, which bear the inscription "Dedicated to the Memory of Mary E. Wilkins Freeman and the Women Writers of America." (The inscription has outlasted her literary reputation, as I discuss more fully in the Afterword.) In reading the Freeman file at the academy, I discovered that her election to membership came much later than it was originally proposed. In 1917 she received a letter from the secretary of the National Institute of Arts and Letters asking whether or not she would be willing to be considered. The secretary added that although there was no clause in the society's constitution limiting the membership to men, he imagined that the membership would be divided on the question of admitting women. Freeman replied, in a letter of October 25, 1917:

> I shall not fail to understand if I am not admitted because of the division among the membership as to the advisability of admitting women. Why not an honorary membership which would really not be so great an innovation if I may ask? Please be very sure that I shall not be in the least disturbed if women are not admitted. I can very readily see that many would object.[20]

The self-deprecatory tone of this letter is characteristic of Freeman. Her correspondence reveals that she held a slight opinion of her own poetry,[21] and she rarely consented to appear before an audience. She suffered chronic headaches for many years and declined numerous public appearances on the grounds that her voice was weak, or, as she expressed it in one letter, "not suitable for public reading."[22]

Over the course of her life Mary Wilkins Freeman became one of the first women writers to support herself fully by her writing, and the 1931 value of her estate, even after public auction, totaled over a hundred thousand dollars.[23] She died March 13, 1930, of a heart attack, having published in her lifetime fourteen collections of stories, thirteen novels, a play, two novels and a prize-winning detective story in collaboration with other writers, eight children's books, several articles, poems for children and adults, and dozens of uncollected stories.

NOTES TO THE INTRODUCTION

1. See Fred L. Pattee, *A History of American Literature Since 1870* (New York: The Century Co., 1915), *Sidelights on American Literature* (New York: The Century Co., 1922), and *The Development of the American Short Story* (New York: Duffield & Co., 1923); V. L. Parrington, *Main Currents in American Thought, Vol. III: The Beginnings of Critical Realism in America 1860–1920* (New York: Harcourt, Brace, 1930); and Van Wyck Brooks, *New England: Indian Summer (1865–1915)* (New York: Dutton, 1940). The phrase "New England in decline" belongs to Pattee.

2. See, for example, Henry Nash Smith, *Virgin Land: The American West as Symbol and Myth* (Cambridge, Mass.: Harvard Univ. Press, 1950) and R. W. B. Lewis, *The American Adam: Innocence, Tragedy, and Tradition in the Nineteenth Century* (Chicago: Univ. of Chicago Press, 1955) for two works that document these theories of American history and literature; see Page Smith, *As a City Upon a Hill: The Town in American History* (New York: Knopf, 1966) and Annette Kolodny, *The Lay of the Land: Metaphor as Experience and History in American Life and Letters* (Chapel Hill: Univ. of North Carolina Press, 1975) for alternative theories.

3. Michele Clark (ed.), *The Revolt of Mother and Other Stories* (Brooklyn, N.Y.: The Feminist Press, 1974).

4. The best source for information on the region's economy and demographic change is Harold F. Wilson, *The Hill Country of Northern New England: Its Social and Economic History* (New York: Columbia Univ. Press, 1936). Many young women also left the farms for the milltowns of Massachusetts; see Wilson.

5. Harriet Beecher Stowe must receive credit as the first major writer to fictionalize the lives of nineteenth-century American women, as well as the first to write in a regionalist mode. See in particular her novels *The Minister's Wooing* (1859), *The Pearl of*

Orr's Island (1862)—which Sarah Orne Jewett would claim as one of her earliest literary influences—and *Old-Town Folks* (1869).

6. See my introduction to Sarah Orne Jewett, *The Country of the Pointed Firs and Other Stories* (New York: W. W. Norton, 1982).

7. For one of the best challenges to the Frederick Jackson Turner thesis of westward expansion, see Page Smith, *As a City Upon a Hill,* especially the opening chapters and pages 44–52.

8. I have written elsewhere about marked characters in Hawthorne, Melville, Faulkner, and Ellison. See *The Mark and the Knowledge: Social Stigma in Classic American Fiction* (Columbus: The Ohio State Univ. Press, 1979).

9. Perry Westbrook (*Mary Wilkins Freeman* [New York: Twayne, 1967]) cites Sylvia Whitman of *The Shoulders of Atlas* (1908) as a woman "of indomitable volition" and describes her attachment to another character, Rose Fletcher, as "unmistakably homosexual" (pp. 156–57). The ending of *By the Light of the Soul* (1906), in which the protagonist Maria Edgham ends in an alliance with a woman dwarf, also reflects Freeman's fascination with homoeroticism between women.

10. *The Heart's Highway, A Romance of Virginia* (1900); *The Wind in the Rose-Bush and Other Stories of the Supernatural* (1903); and *Understudies* (1901) *and Six Trees* (1903).

11. *The Debtor* (1905), *"Doc" Gordon* (1906), and *The Butterfly House* (1912).

12. The eighteen included in this selection represent about one-third of the original volumes and form a larger collection by far than any subsequent single book of Freeman short stories, except for *The Best Stories of Mary E. Wilkins* (New York: Harper & Bros., 1927), selected and with an introduction by Henry Wysham Lanier.

In all, Freeman published close to 200 stories, only about 150 of which were collected. See Edward Foster, *Mary E. Wilkins Freeman* (New York: Hendricks House, 1956), for a complete list of stories in collections and uncollected stories.

Even though critics have agreed that her later fiction does not consistently match the quality of the two earliest collections, there are later stories, particularly those in which Freeman returns to the New England subject matter and region of her early work, in which she approaches her own standard of excellence. The reader who wishes to pursue her later work should begin with *Pembroke* (a novel available in College and University Press paperback) and the stories collected in *The Best Stories of Mary E. Wilkins.*

13. *Pembroke* has a male protagonist along with many strong women characters, some of whom "revolt" against society's proscriptions.

14. Her biographers speculate that the more popular her writing became, the more she discovered that financial success lay in conventional plots and writing for her market. Brent L. Kendrick, in "The Infant Sphinx: Collected Letters of Mary E. Wilkins Freeman" (unpublished Ph.D diss., Univ. of South Carolina, 1981), writes that Freeman's

> willingness to subject her creative impulse to editorial demands carried over to her longer fiction as well. It became clear why holiday stories figure so prominently in her canon. In a way, she approached writing just as practically as her father had approached his building or dry goods trade: gauge the consumer's need and meet it, always with an eye toward pleasing him (p. 46).

15. F. O. Matthiessen, "New England Stories," in John A. Macy (ed.), *American Writers on American Literature* (New York: Horace Liveright, 1931), p. 405.

16. Matthiessen, p. 413.

17. This description of Charles Freeman is Edward Foster's (p. 113); I have drawn heavily on his biography throughout, except where I have noted other sources.

18. Kendrick describes the history of Freeman's and Wilkins's courtship, pp. 389–95. He notes that both quotations are from "Newspapers Urged Wedding on Him," *New Brunswick Home News,* September 27, 1939.

19. See Kendrick, who includes several letters to Jewett.

20. Kendrick, letter 437, p. 672.

21. Kendrick, letter 260, p. 429.

22. Kendrick, letter 163, dated January 13, 1895, p. 319.

23. Kendrick, p. 48.

From *A Humble Romance* (1887)

TWO OLD LOVERS.

LEYDEN was emphatically a village of cottages, and each of them built after one of two patterns: either the front door was on the right side, in the corner of a little piazza extending a third of the length of the house, with the main roof jutting over it, or the piazza stretched across the front, and the door was in the centre.

The cottages were painted uniformly white, and had blinds of a bright spring-green color. There was a little flower-garden in front of each; the beds were laid out artistically in triangles, hearts, and rounds, and edged with box; boys'-love, sweet-williams, and pinks were the fashionable and prevailing flowers.

There was a general air of cheerful though humble prosperity about the place, which it owed, and indeed its very existence also, to the three old weather-beaten boot-and-shoe factories which arose stanchly and importantly in the very midst of the natty little white cottages.

Years before, when one Hiram Strong put up his three factories for the manufacture of the rough shoe which the working-man of America wears, he hardly thought he was also gaining for himself the honor of founding Leyden. He chose the site for his buildings mainly because they would be easily accessible to the railway which stretched to the city, sixty miles distant. At first the workmen came on the cars from the neighboring towns, but after a while they became tired of that, and one after another built for himself a cottage, and established his family and his household belongings near the scene of his daily labors. So gradually Leyden grew. A built his cottage like C, and B built his like D. They painted them white, and hung the green blinds, and laid out their flower-beds in front and their vegetable-beds at the back. By and by came a church and a store and a post-office to pass, and Leyden was a full-fledged town.

That was a long time ago. The shoe-factories had long passed out of the hands of Hiram Strong's heirs; he himself was only a memory on the earth. The business was not quite as wide-awake and vigorous as when in its first youth; it droned a little now; there was not quite so much bustle and hurry as formerly. The factories were never lighted up of an evening on account of overwork, and the workmen found plenty of time for pleasant and salutary gossip over their cutting and pegging. But this did not detract in the least from the general cheerfulness and prosperity of Leyden. The inhabitants still had all the work they needed to supply the means necessary for their small comforts, and they were contented. They too had begun to drone a little like the factories. "As slow as Leyden" was the saying among the faster-going towns adjoining theirs. Every morning at seven the old men, young men, and boys, in their calico shirt-sleeves, their faces a little pale—perhaps from their in-door life—filed unquestioningly out of the back doors of the white cottages, treading still deeper the well-worn foot-paths stretching around the sides of the houses, and entered the factories. They were great, ugly wooden buildings, with wings which they had grown in their youth jutting clumsily from their lumbering shoulders. Their outer walls were black and grimy, streaked and splashed and patched with red paint in every variety of shade, accordingly as the original hue was tempered with smoke or the beatings of the storms of many years.

The men worked peacefully and evenly in the shoe-shops all day; and the women stayed at home and kept the little white cottages tidy, cooked the meals, and washed the clothes, and did the sewing. For recreation the men sat on the piazza in front of Barker's store of an evening, and gossiped or discussed politics; and the women talked over their neighbors' fences, or took their sewing into their neighbors' of an afternoon.

People died in Leyden as elsewhere; and here and there was a little white cottage whose narrow foot-path leading round to its back door its master would never tread again.

In one of these lived Widow Martha Brewster and her daughter Maria. Their cottage was one of those which had its piazza across the front. Every summer they trained morning-glories over it, and planted their little garden with the flower-seeds popular in Leyden. There was not a cottage in the whole place whose surroundings were neater and gayer than theirs, for all they were only two women, and two old women at that; for Widow Martha Brewster was in the neighborhood of eighty, and her daughter, Maria Brewster, near sixty. The two had lived alone since Jacob Brewster died and stopped going to the factory, some fifteen years ago. He had left them this particular white cottage, and a snug little sum in the savings-bank besides, for the whole Brewster family had worked and economized all their long lives. The women had corded boots at home, while the man had worked in the shop, and never spent a cent without thinking of it overnight.

Leyden folks all thought that David Emmons would marry Maria Brewster when her father died. "David can rent his house, and go to live with Maria and her mother," said they, with an affectionate readiness to arrange matters for them. But he did not. Every Sunday night at eight o'clock punctually, the form of David Emmons, arrayed in his best clothes, with his stiff white dickey, and a nosegay in his button-hole, was seen to advance up the road towards Maria Brewster's, as he had been seen to advance every Sunday night for the last twenty-five years, but that was all. He manifested not the slightest intention of carrying out people's judicious plans for his welfare and Maria's.

She did not seem to pine with hope deferred ; people could not honestly think there was any occasion to pity her for her lover's tardiness. A cheerier woman never lived. She was literally bubbling over with jollity. Round-faced and black-eyed, with a funny little bounce of her whole body when she walked, she was the merry feature of the whole place.

Her mother was now too feeble, but Maria still corded boots for the factories as of old. David Emmons, who was quite sixty, worked in them, as he had from his youth. He was a slender, mild-faced old man, with a fringe of gray yellow beard around his chin ; his head was quite bald. Years ago he had been handsome, they said, but somehow people had always laughed at him a little, although they all liked him. "The slowest of all the slow Leydenites" outsiders called him, and even the "slow Leydenites" poked fun at this exaggeration of themselves. It was an old and well-worn remark that it took David Emmons an hour to go courting, and that he was always obliged to leave his own home at seven in order to reach Maria's at eight, and there was a standing joke that the meeting-house passed him one morning on his way to the shop.

David heard the chaffing of course—there is very little delicacy in matters of this kind among country people—but he took it all in good part. He would laugh at himself with the rest, but there was something touching in his deprecatory way of saying sometimes, " Well, I don't know how 'tis, but it don't seem to be in my natur' to do any other way. I suppose I was born without the faculty of gittin' along quick in this world. You'll have to git behind and push me a leetle, I reckon."

He owned his little cottage, which was one of the kind which had the piazza on the right side. He lived entirely alone. There was a half-acre or so of land beside his house, which he used for a vegetable garden. After and before shop hours, in the dewy evenings and mornings, he dug and weeded assiduously between the green ranks of corn and beans. If David Emmons was slow, his vegetables were not. None of the gardens in Leyden surpassed his in luxuriant growth. His corn tasselled out and his potato patch was white with blossoms as soon as anybody's.

He was almost a vegetarian in his diet ; the products of his garden spot were his staple articles of food. Early in the morning would the gentle old bachelor set his pot of green things boiling, and dine gratefully at noon, like mild Robert Herrick, on pulse and herbs. His garden supplied also his sweetheart and her mother with all the vegetables they could use. Many times in the course of a week could David have been seen slowly moving towards the Brewster cottage with a basket on his arm well stocked with the materials for an innocent and delicious repast.

But Maria was not to be outdone by her old lover in kindly deeds. Not a Saturday but a goodly share of her weekly baking was deposited, neatly covered with a white crash towel, on David's little kitchen table. The surreptitious air with which the back-door key was taken from its hiding-place (which she well knew) under the kitchen blind, the door unlocked and entered, and the good things deposited, was charming, although highly ineffectual. " There goes Maria with David's baking," said the women, peering out of their windows as she bounced, rather more gently and cautiously than usual, down the street. And David himself knew well the ministering angel to whom these benefits were due when he lifted the towel and discovered with tearful eyes the brown loaves and flaky pies—the proofs of his Maria's love and culinary skill.

Among the younger and more irrevent portions of the community there was considerable speculation as to the mode of courtship of these old lovers of twenty-five years' standing. Was there ever a kiss, a tender clasp of the hand, those usual expressions of affection between sweethearts?

Some of the more daring spirits had even gone so far as to commit the manifest impropriety of peeping in Maria's parlor windows ; but they had only seen David sitting quiet and prim on the little slippery horse-hair sofa, and Maria by the table, rocking slowly in her little cane-seated rocker. Did Maria ever leave her rocker and sit on that slippery horse-hair sofa by David's side? They never knew ; but she never did. There was something laughable, and at the same time rather pathetic, about Maria and David's courting. All the outward appurtenances of "keeping company" were as rigidly observed as they had been twenty-five years ago, when David Emmons first cast his mild blue eyes shyly and lovingly on red-cheeked, quick-spoken Maria Brewster. Every Sunday evening, in the winter, there was a fire kindled in the parlor, the parlor lamp was lit at dusk all the year round, and Maria's mother retired early, that the young people might "sit up." The "sitting up" was no very formidable affair now, whatever it might have been in the first stages of the courtship. The need of sleep over-balanced sentiment in those old lovers, and by ten o'clock at the latest Maria's lamp was out, and David had wended his solitary way to his own home.

Leyden people had a great curiosity to know if David had ever actually popped the question to Maria, or if his natural slowness was at fault in this as in other things. Their curiosity had been long exercised in vain, but Widow Brewster, as she waxed older, grew loquacious, and one day told a neighbor, who had called in her daughter's absence, that "David had never reely come to the p'int. She supposed he would some time; for her part, she thought he had better; but then, after all, she knowed Maria didn't care, and maybe 'twas jest as well as 'twas, only sometimes she was afeard she should never live to see the weddin' if they wasn't spry." Then there had been hints concerning a certain pearl-colored silk which Maria, having a good chance to get at a bargain, had purchased some twenty years ago, when she thought, from sundry remarks, that David was coming to the point; and it was further intimated that the silk had been privately made up ten years since, when Maria had again surmised that the point was about being reached. The neighbor went home in a state of great delight, having by skilful manœuvring actually obtained a glimpse of the pearl-colored silk.

It was perfectly true that Maria did not lay David's tardiness in putting the important question very much to heart. She was too cheerful, too busy, and too much interested in her daily duties to fret much about anything. There was never at any time much of the sentimental element in her composition, and her feeling for David was eminently practical in its nature. She, although the woman, had the stronger character of the two, and there was something rather mother-like than lover-like in her affection for him. It was through the protecting care which chiefly characterized her love that the only pain to her came from their long courtship and postponement of marriage. It was true that, years ago, when David had led her to think, from certain hesitating words spoken at parting one Sunday night, that he would certainly ask the momentous question soon, her heart had gone into a happy flutter. She had bought the pearl-colored silk then.

Years after, her heart had fluttered again, but a little less wildly this time. David almost asked her another Sunday night. Then she had made up the pearl-colored silk. She used to go and look at it fondly and admiringly from time to time ; once in a while she would try it on and survey herself in the glass, and imagine herself David's bride—a faded bride, but a happy and a beloved one.

She looked at the dress occasionally now, but a little sadly, as the conviction that she should never wear it was forcing itself upon her more and more. But the sadness was always more for David's sake than her own. She saw him growing an old man, and the lonely, uncared-for life that he led filled her heart with tender pity and sorrow for him. She did not confine her kind offices to the Saturday baking. Every week his little house was tidied and set to rights, and his mending looked after.

Once, on a Sunday night, when she spied a rip in his coat, that had grown long from the want of womanly fingers constantly at hand, she had a good cry after he had left and she had gone into her room. There was something more pitiful to her, something that touched her heart more deeply, in that rip in her lover's Sunday coat than in all her long years of waiting.

As the years went on, it was sometimes with a sad heart that Maria stood and watched the poor lonely old figure moving slower than ever down the street to his lonely home; but the heart was sad for him always, and never for herself. She used to wonder at him a little sometimes, though always with the most loyal tenderness, that he should choose to lead the solitary, cheerless life that he did, to go back to his dark, voiceless home, when he might be so sheltered and cared for in his old age. She firmly believed that it was only owing to her lover's incorrigible slowness, in this as in everything else. She never doubted for an instant that he loved her. Some women might have tried hastening matters a little themselves, but Maria, with the delicacy which is sometimes more inherent in a steady, practical nature like hers than in a more ardent one, would have lost her self-respect forever if she had done such a thing.

So she lived cheerfully along, corded her boots, though her fingers were getting stiff, humored her mother, who was getting feebler and more childish every year, and did the best she could for her poor, foolish old lover.

When David was seventy, and she sixty-eight, she gave away the pearl-colored silk to a cousin's daughter who was going to be married. The girl was young and pretty and happy, but she was poor, and the silk would make over into a grander wedding dress for her than she could hope to obtain in any other way.

Poor old Maria smoothed the lustrous folds fondly with her withered hands before sending it away, and cried a little, with a patient pity for David and herself. But when a tear splashed directly on to the shining surface of the silk, she stopped crying at once, and her sorrowful expression changed into one of careful scrutiny as she wiped the salt drop away with her handkerchief, and held the dress up to the light to be sure that it was not spotted. A practical nature like Maria's is sometimes a great boon to its possessor. It is doubtful if anything else can dry a tear as quickly.

Somehow Maria always felt a little differently towards David after she had given away her wedding dress. There had always been a little tinge of consciousness in her manner towards him, a little reserve and caution before people. But after the wedding dress had gone, all question of marriage had disappeared so entirely from her mind, that the delicate considerations born of it vanished. She was uncommonly hale and hearty for a woman of her age ; there was apparently much more than two years' difference between her and her lover. It was not only the Saturday's bread and pie that she carried now and deposited on David's little kitchen table, but, openly and boldly, not caring who should see her, many a warm dinner. Every day, after her own house-work was done, David's house was set to rights. He should have all the comforts he needed in

his last years, she determined. That they were his last
years was evident. He coughed, and now walked so slowly
from feebleness and weakness that it was a matter of doubt
to observers whether he could reach Maria Brewster's before Monday evening.

One Sunday night he stayed a little longer than usual—
the clock struck ten before he started. Then he rose, and
said, as he had done every Sunday evening for so many
years, " Well, Maria, I guess it's about time for me to be
goin'."

She helped him on with his coat, and tied on his tippet.
Contrary to his usual habit he stood in the door, and hesitated a minute—there seemed to be something he wanted
to say.

" Maria."

" Well, David ?"

" I'm gittin' to be an old man, you know, an' I've allus
been slow-goin' ; I couldn't seem to help it. There has been
a good many things I haven't got around to." The old
cracked voice quavered painfully.

" Yes, I know, David, all about it ; you couldn't help it.
I wouldn't worry a bit about it if I were you."

" You don't lay up anything agin me, Maria ?"

" No, David."

" Good-night, Maria."

" Good-night, David. I will fetch you over some boiled
dinner to-morrow."

She held the lamp at the door till the patient, tottering
old figure was out of sight. She had to wipe the tears from
her spectacles in order to see to read her Bible when she
went in.

Next morning she was hurrying up her housework to go

over to David's—somehow she felt a little anxious about
him this morning—when there came a loud knock at her
door. When she opened it, a boy stood there, panting for
breath; he was David's next neighbor's son.

"Mr. Emmons is sick," he said, "an' wants you. I was
goin' for milk, when he rapped on the window. Father an'
mother's in thar, an' the doctor. Mother said, tell you to
hurry."

The news had spread rapidly; people knew what it meant
when they saw Maria hurrying down the street, without her
bonnet, her gray hair flying. One woman cried when she
saw her. "Poor thing!" she sobbed, "poor thing!"

A crowd was around David's cottage when Maria reached
it. She went straight in through the kitchen to his little
bedroom, and up to his side. The doctor was in the room,
and several neighbors. When he saw Maria, poor old David held out his hand to her and smiled feebly. Then he
looked imploringly at the doctor, then at the others in the
room. The doctor understood, and said a word to them,
and they filed silently out. Then he turned to Maria.
"Be quick," he whispered.

She leaned over him. "Dear David," she said, her
wrinkled face quivering, her gray hair straying over her
cheeks.

He looked up at her with a strange wonder in his glazing
eyes. "Maria"—a thin, husky voice, that was more like
a wind through dry corn-stalks, said—"Maria, I'm—dyin',
an'—I allers meant to—have asked you—to—marry me."

AN HONEST SOUL.

"Thar's Mis' Bliss's pieces in the brown kaliker bag, an' thar's Mis' Bennet's pieces in the bed-tickin' bag," said she, surveying complacently the two bags leaning against her kitchen - wall. "I'll get a dollar for both of them quilts, an' thar'll be two dollars. I've got a dollar an' sixty-three cents on hand now, an' thar's plenty of meal an' merlasses, an' some salt fish an' pertaters in the house. I'll get along middlin' well, I reckon. Thar ain't no call fer me to worry. I'll red up the house a leetle now, an' then I'll begin on Mis' Bliss's pieces."

The *house* was an infinitesimal affair, containing only two rooms besides the tiny lean-to which served as wood-shed. It stood far enough back from the road for a pretentious mansion, and there was one curious feature about it—not a door nor window was there in front, only a blank, unbroken wall. Strangers passing by used to stare wonderingly at it sometimes, but it was explained easily enough. Old Simeon Patch, years ago, when the longing for a home of his own had grown strong in his heart, and he had only a few hundred dollars saved from his hard earnings to invest in one, had wisely done the best he could with what he had.

Not much remained to spend on the house after the spacious lot was paid for, so he resolved to build as much house as he could with his money, and complete it when better days should come.

This tiny edifice was in reality simply the L of a goodly two-story house which had existed only in the fond and faithful fancies of Simeon Patch and his wife. That blank front wall was designed to be joined to the projected main building; so, of course, there was no need of doors or windows. Simeon Patch came of a hard-working, honest race, whose pride it had been to keep out of debt, and he was a true child of his ancestors. Not a dollar would he spend that was not in his hand; a mortgaged house was his horror. So he paid cash for every blade of grass on his lot of land, and every nail in his bit of a house, and settled down patiently in it until he should grub together enough more to buy a few additional boards and shingles, and pay the money down.

That time never came: he died in the course of a few years, after a lingering illness, and only had enough saved to pay his doctor's bill and funeral expenses, and leave his wife and daughter entirely without debt, in their little fragment of a house on the big, sorry lot of land.

There they had lived, mother and daughter, earning and saving in various little, petty ways, keeping their heads sturdily above water, and holding the dreaded mortgage off the house for many years. Then the mother died, and the daughter, Martha Patch, took up the little homely struggle alone. She was over seventy now—a small, slender old woman, as straight as a rail, with sharp black eyes, and a quick toss of her head when she spoke. She did odd housewifely jobs for the neighbors, wove rag-carpets, pieced bed-quilts, braided rugs, etc., and contrived to supply all her simple wants.

This evening, after she had finished putting her house to rights, she fell to investigating the contents of the bags which two of the neighbors had brought in the night before, with orders for quilts, much to her delight.

"Mis' Bliss has got proper handsome pieces," said she—"proper handsome; they'll make a good-lookin' quilt. Mis' Bennet's is good too, but they ain't quite ekal to Mis' Bliss's. I reckon some of 'em's old."

She began spreading some of the largest, prettiest pieces on her white-scoured table. "Thar," said she, gazing at one admiringly, "that jest takes my eye; them leetle pink roses is pretty, an' no mistake. I reckon that's French caliker. Thar's some big pieces too. Lor', what bag did I take 'em out on! It must hev been Mis' Bliss's. I mustn't git 'em mixed."

She cut out some squares, and sat down by the window in a low wooden rocking-chair to sew. This window did not have a very pleasant outlook. The house was situated so far back from the road that it commanded only a rear view of the adjoining one. It was a great cross to Martha Patch. She was one of those women who like to see everything that is going on outside, and who often have excuse enough in the fact that so little is going on with them.

"It's a great divarsion," she used to say, in her snapping way, which was more nervous than ill-natured, bobbing her head violently at the same time—"a very great divarsion to see Mr. Peters's cows goin' in an' out of the barn day arter day; an' that's about all I do see—never git a sight of the folks goin' to meetin' nor nothin'."

The lack of a front window was a continual source of grief to her.

"When the minister's prayin' for the widders an' orphans

he'd better make mention of one more," said she, once, " an' that's women without front winders."

She and her mother had planned to save money enough to have one some day, but they had never been able to bring it about. A window commanding a view of the street and the passers-by would have been a great source of comfort to the poor old woman, sitting and sewing as she did day in and day out. As it was, she seized eagerly upon the few objects of interest which did come within her vision, and made much of them. There were some children who, on their way from school, could make a short cut through her yard and reach home quicker. She watched for them every day, and if they did not appear quite as soon as usual she would grow uneasy, and eye the clock, and mutter to herself, " I wonder where them Mosely children can be ?" When they came she watched their progress with sharp attention, and thought them over for an hour afterwards. Not a bird which passed her window escaped her notice. This innocent old gossip fed her mind upon their small domestic affairs in lieu of larger ones. To-day she often paused between her stitches to gaze absorbedly at a yellow-bird vibrating nervously round the branches of a young tree opposite. It was early spring, and the branches were all of a light-green foam.

" That's the same yaller-bird I saw yesterday, I do b'lieve," said she. " I recken he's goin' to build a nest in that ellum."

Lately she had been watching the progress of the grass gradually springing up all over the yard. One spot where it grew much greener than elsewhere her mind dwelt upon curiously.

" I can't make out," she said to a neighbor, " whether

that 'ere spot is greener than the rest because the sun shines brightly thar, or because somethin's buried thar."

She toiled steadily on the patchwork quilts. At the end of a fortnight they were nearly completed. She hurried on the last one morning, thinking she would carry them both to their owners that afternoon and get her pay. She did not stop for any dinner.

Spreading them out for one last look before rolling them up in bundles, she caught her breath hastily.

"What hev I done?" said she. "Massy sakes! I hevn't gone an' put Mis' Bliss's caliker with the leetle pink roses on't in Mis' Bennet's quilt? I hev, jest as sure as preach-in'! What shell I do?"

The poor old soul stood staring at the quilts in pitiful dismay. "A hull fortni't's work," she muttered. "What shell I do? Them pink roses is the prettiest caliker in the hull lot. Mis' Bliss will be mad if they air in Mis' Bennet's quilt. She won't say nothin', an' she'll pay me, but she'll feel it inside, an' it won't be doin' the squar' thing by her. No; if I'm goin' to airn money I'll airn it."

Martha Patch gave her head a jerk. The spirit which animated her father when he went to housekeeping in a piece of a house without any front window blazed up within her. She made herself a cup of tea, then sat deliberately down by the window to rip the quilts to pieces. It had to be done pretty thoroughly on account of her admiration for the pink calico, and the quantity of it—it figured in nearly every square. "I wish I hed a front winder to set to while I'm doin' on't," said she; but she patiently plied her scis-sors till dusk, only stopping for a short survey of the Mosely children. After days of steady work the pieces were put together again, this time the pink-rose calico in Mrs. Bliss's quilt. Martha Patch rolled the quilts up with a sigh of relief and a sense of virtuous triumph.

"I'll sort over the pieces that's left in the bags," said she, "then I'll take 'em over an' git my pay. I'm gittin' pretty short of vittles."

She began pulling the pieces out of the bed-ticking bag, laying them on her lap and smoothing them out, preparatory to doing them up in a neat, tight roll to take home— she was very methodical about everything she did. Suddenly she turned pale, and stared wildly at a tiny scrap of calico which she had just fished out of the bag.

"Massy sakes!" she cried; "it ain't, is it?" She clutched Mrs. Bliss's quilt from the table and laid the bit of calico beside the pink-rose squares.

"It's jest the same thing," she groaned, "an' it came out on Mis' Bennet's bag. Dear me suz! dear me suz!"

She dropped helplessly into her chair by the window, still holding the quilt and the telltale scrap of calico, and gazed out in a bewildered sort of way. Her poor old eyes looked dim and weak with tears.

"Thar's the Mosely children comin'," she said; "happy little gals, laughin' an' hollerin', goin' home to their mother to git a good dinner. Me a-settin' here's a lesson they ain't larned in their books yit; hope to goodness they never will; hope they won't ever hev to piece quilts fur a livin', without any front winder to set to. Thar's a dandelion blown out on that green spot. Reckon thar *is* somethin' buried thar. Lordy massy! *hev* I got to rip them two quilts to pieces agin an' sew 'em over?"

Finally she resolved to carry a bit of the pink-rose calico over to Mrs. Bennet's and find out, without betraying the dilemma she was in, if it were really hers.

Her poor old knees fairly shook under her when she entered Mrs. Bennet's sitting-room.

"Why, yes, Martha, it's mine," said Mrs. Bennet, in response to her agitated question. "Hattie had a dress like it, don't you remember? There was a lot of new pieces left, and I thought they would work into a quilt nice. But, for pity's sake, Martha, what is the matter? You look just as white as a sheet. You ain't sick, are you?"

"No," said Martha, with a feeble toss of her head, to keep up the deception; "I ain't sick, only kinder all gone with the warm weather. I reckon I'll hev to fix me up some thoroughwort tea. Thoroughwort's a great strengthener."

"I would," said Mrs. Bennet, sympathizingly; "and don't you work too hard on that quilt; I ain't in a bit of a hurry for it. I sha'n't want it before next winter anyway. I only thought I'd like to have it pieced and ready."

"I reckon I can't get it done afore another fortni't," said Martha, trembling.

"I don't care if you don't get it done for the next three months. Don't go yet, Martha; you ain't rested a minute, and it's a pretty long walk. Don't you want a bite of something before you go? Have a piece of cake? You look real faint."

"No, thanky," said Martha, and departed in spite of all friendly entreaties to tarry. Mrs. Bennet watched her moving slowly down the road, still holding the little pink calico rag in her brown, withered fingers.

"Martha Patch is failing; she ain't near so straight as she was," remarked Mrs. Bennet. "She looks real bent over to-day."

The little wiry springiness was, indeed, gone from her

gait as she crept slowly along the sweet country road, and there was a helpless droop in her thin, narrow shoulders. It was a beautiful spring day; the fruit-trees were all in blossom. There were more orchards than houses on the way, and more blooming trees to pass than people.

Martha looked up at the white branches as she passed under them. "I kin smell the apple-blows," said she, "but somehow the goodness is all gone out on 'em. I'd jest as soon smell cabbage. Oh, dear me suz, kin I ever do them quilts over agin?"

When she got home, however, she rallied a little. There was a nervous force about this old woman which was not easily overcome even by an accumulation of misfortunes. She might bend a good deal, but she was almost sure to spring back again. She took off her hood and shawl, and straightened herself up. "Thar's no use puttin' it off; it's got to be done. I'll hev them quilts right ef it kills me!"

She tied on a purple calico apron and sat down at the window again, with a quilt and the scissors. Out came the pink roses. There she sat through the long afternoon, cutting the stitches which she had so laboriously put in—a little defiant old figure, its head, with a flat black lace cap on it, bobbing up and down in time with its hands. There were some purple bows on the cap, and they fluttered ; quite a little wind blew in at the window.

The eight-day clock on the mantel ticked peacefully. It was a queer old timepiece, which had belonged to her grandmother Patch. A painting of a quaint female, with puffed hair and a bunch of roses, adorned the front of it, under the dial-plate. It was flanked on either side by tall, green vases.

There was a dull-colored rag-carpet of Martha's own

manufacture on the floor of the room. Some wooden chairs stood around stiffly ; an old, yellow map of Massachusetts and a portrait of George Washington hung on the walls. There was not a speck of dust anywhere, nor any disorder. Neatness was one of the comforts of Martha's life. Putting and keeping things in order was one of the interests which enlivened her dulness and made the world attractive to her.

The poor soul sat at the window, bending over the quilt, until dusk, and she sat there, bending over the quilt until dusk, many a day after.

It is a hard question to decide, whether there were any real merit in such finely strained honesty, or whether it were merely a case of morbid conscientiousness. Perhaps the old woman, inheriting very likely her father's scruples, had had them so intensified by age and childishness that they had become a little off the bias of reason.

Be that as it may, she thought it was the right course for her to make the quilts over, and, thinking so, it was all that she could do. She could never have been satisfied otherwise. It took her a considerable while longer to finish the quilts again, and this time she began to suffer from other causes than mere fatigue. Her stock of provisions commenced to run low, and her money was gone. At last she had nothing but a few potatoes in the house to eat. She contrived to dig some dandelion greens once or twice ; these with the potatoes were all her diet. There was really no necessity for such a state of things ; she was surrounded by kindly well-to-do people, who would have gone without themselves rather than let her suffer. But she had always been very reticent about her needs, and felt great pride about accepting anything for which she did not pay.

But she struggled along until the quilts were done, and no one knew. She set the last stitch quite late one evening; then she spread the quilts out and surveyed them. " Thar they air now, all right," said she; " the pink roses is in Mis' Bennet's, an' I ain't cheated nobody out on their caliker, an' I've airned my money. I'll take 'em hum in the mornin', an' then I'll buy somethin' to eat. I begin to feel a dreadful sinkin' at my stummuck."

She locked up the house carefully—she always felt a great responsibility when she had people's work on hand—and went to bed.

Next morning she woke up so faint and dizzy that she hardly knew herself. She crawled out into the kitchen, and sank down on the floor. She could not move another step.

" Lor sakes!" she moaned, " I reckon I'm 'bout done to !"

The quilts lay near her on the table; she stared up at them with feeble complacency. " Ef I'm goin' to die, I'm glad I got them quilts done right fust. Massy, how sinkin' I do feel! I wish I had a cup of tea."

There she lay, and the beautiful spring morning wore on. The sun shone in at the window, and moved nearer and nearer, until finally she lay in a sunbeam, a poor, shrivelled little old woman, whose resolute spirit had nearly been her death, in her scant nightgown and ruffled cap, a little shawl falling from her shoulders. She did not feel ill, only absolutely too weak and helpless to move. Her mind was just as active as ever, and her black eyes peered sharply out of her pinched face. She kept making efforts to rise, but she could not stir.

"Lor sakes !" she snapped out at length, " how long *hev* I got to lay here ? I'm mad !"

She saw some dust on the black paint of a chair which stood in the sun, and she eyed that distressfully.

"Jest look at that dust on the runs of that cheer!" she muttered. "What if anybody come in! I wonder if I can't reach it!"

The chair was near her, and she managed to stretch out her limp old hand and rub the dust off the rounds. Then she let it sink down, panting.

"I wonder ef I *ain't* goin' to die," she gasped. "I wonder ef I'm prepared. I never took nothin' that shouldn't belong to me that I knows on. Oh, dear me suz, I wish somebody would come!"

When her strained ears did catch the sound of footsteps outside, a sudden resolve sprang up in her heart.

"I won't let on to nobody how I've made them quilts over, an' how I hevn't had enough to eat—I won't."

When the door was tried she called out feebly, "Who is thar?"

The voice of Mrs. Peters, her next-door neighbor, came back in response: "It's me. What's the matter, Marthy?"

"I'm kinder used up; don't know how you'll git in; I can't git to the door to unlock it to save my life."

"Can't I get in at the window?"

"Mebbe you kin."

Mrs. Peters was a long-limbed, spare woman, and she got in through the window with considerable ease, it being quite low from the ground.

She turned pale when she saw Martha lying on the floor. "Why, Marthy, what is the matter? How long have you been laying there?"

"Ever since I got up. I was kinder dizzy, an' hed a

dreadful sinkin' feelin'. It ain't much, I reckon. Ef I could hev a cup of tea it would set me right up. Thar's a spoonful left in the pantry. Ef you jest put a few kindlin's in the stove, Mis' Peters, an' set in the kettle an' made me a cup, I could git up, I know. I've got to go an' kerry them quilts hum to Mis' Bliss an' Mis' Bennet."

" I don't believe but what you've got all tired out over the quilts. You've been working too hard."

" No, I 'ain't, Mis' Peters; it's nothin' but play piecin' quilts. All I mind is not havin' a front winder to set to while I'm doin' on't."

Mrs. Peters was a quiet, sensible woman of few words; she insisted upon carrying Martha into the bedroom and putting her comfortably to bed. It was easily done; she was muscular, and the old woman a very light weight. Then she went into the pantry. She was beginning to suspect the state of affairs, and her suspicions were strengthened when she saw the bare shelves. She started the fire, put on the tea-kettle, and then slipped across the yard to her own house for further reinforcements.

Pretty soon Martha was drinking her cup of tea and eating her toast and a dropped egg. She had taken the food with some reluctance, half starved as she was. Finally she gave in—the sight of it was too much for her. " Well, I will borry it, Mis' Peters," said she; "an' I'll pay you jest as soon as I kin git up."

After she had eaten she felt stronger. Mrs. Peters had hard work to keep her quiet until afternoon; then she would get up and carry the quilts home. The two ladies were profuse in praises. Martha, proud and smiling. Mrs. Bennet noticed the pink roses at once. " How pretty that calico did work in," she remarked.

"Yes," assented Martha, between an inclination to chuckle and to cry.

"Ef I ain't thankful I did them quilts over," thought she, creeping slowly homeward, her hard-earned two dollars knotted into a corner of her handkerchief for security.

About sunset Mrs. Peters came in again. "Marthy," she said, after a while, "Sam says he's out of work just now, and he'll cut through a front window for you. He's got some old sash and glass that's been laying round in the barn ever since I can remember. It'll be a real charity for you to take it off his hands, and he'll like to do it. Sam's as uneasy as a fish out of water when he hasn't got any work."

Martha eyed her suspiciously. "Thanky; but I don't want nothin' done that I can't pay for," said she, with a stiff toss of her head.

"It would be pay enough, just letting Sam do it, Marthy; but, if you really feel set about it, I've got some sheets that need turning. You can do them some time this summer, and that will pay us for all it's worth."

The black eyes looked at her sharply. "Air you sure?"

"Yes; it's fully as much as it's worth," said Mrs. Peters. "I'm most afraid it's more. There's four sheets, and putting in a window is nothing more than putting in a patch— the old stuff ain't worth anything."

When Martha fully realized that she was going to have a front window, and that her pride might suffer it to be given to her and yet receive no insult, she was as delighted as a child.

"Lor sakes!" said she, "jest to think that I shall have a front winder to set to! I wish mother could ha' lived to see it. Mebbe you kinder wonder at it, Mis' Peters—you've allers had front winders; but you haven't any idea what a great thing it seems to me. It kinder makes me feel younger. Thar's the Mosely children; they're 'bout all I've ever seen pass *this* winder, Mis' Peters. Jest see that green spot out thar; it's been greener than the rest of the yard all the spring, an' now thar's lots of dandelions blowed out on it, an' some clover. I b'lieve the sun shines more on it, somehow. Law me, to think I'm going to hev a front winder!"

"Sarah was in this afternoon," said Mrs. Peters, further (Sarah was her married daughter), "and she says she wants some braided rugs right away. She'll send the rags over by Willie to-morrow."

"You don't say so! Well I'll be glad to do it; an' thar's one thing 'bout it, Mis' Peters—mebbe you'll think it queer for me to say so, but I'm kinder thankful it's rugs she wants. I'm kinder sick of bed-quilts somehow."

ON THE WALPOLE ROAD.

WALPOLE was a lively little rural emporium of trade; thither the villagers from the small country hamlets thereabouts went to make the bulk of their modest purchases.

One summer afternoon two women were driving slowly along a road therefrom, in a dusty old-fashioned chaise, whose bottom was heaped up with brown-paper parcels.

One woman might have been seventy, but she looked younger, she was so hale and portly. She had a double, bristling chin, her gray eyes twinkled humorously over her spectacles, and she wore a wide-flaring black straw bonnet with purple bows on the inside of the rim. The afternoon was very warm, and she held in one black-mitted hand a palm-leaf fan, which she waved gently, now and then, over against her capacious bosom.

The other woman was younger—forty, perhaps; her face was plain-featured and energetic. She wore a gray serge dress and drab cotton gloves, and held tightly on to the reins as she drove. Now and then she would slap them briskly upon the horse's back. He was a heavy, hard-worked farm animal, and was disposed to jog along at an easy pace this warm afternoon.

There had not been any rain for a long time, and everything was very dusty. This road was not much travelled, and grass was growing between the wheel-ruts; but the soil flew up like smoke from the horse's hoofs and the wheels. The blackberry vines climbing over the stone walls on either side, and the meadow-sweet and hardhack bushes were powdered thickly with dust, and had gray leaves instead of green. The big-leaved things, such as burdock, growing close to the ground, had their veins all outlined in dust.

The two women rode in a peaceful sort of way; the old lady fanned herself mildly, and the younger one slapped the horse mechanically. Neither spoke, till they emerged into a more open space on a hill-crest. There they had an uninterrupted view of the northwest sky; the trees had hidden it before.

"I declare, Almiry," said the old lady, "we air goin' to hev a thunder-shower."

"It won't get up till we get home," replied the other, "an' ten chances to one it'll go round by the north anyway, and not touch us at all. That's the way they do half the time here. If I'd 'a seen a cloud as black as that down where I used to live, I'd 'a known for sure there was goin' to be a heavy tempest, but here there's no knowin' anything about it. I wouldn't worry anyway, Mis' Green, if it should come up before we get home: the horse ain't afraid of lightnin'."

The old lady looked comical. "He ain't afraid of anything, is he, Almiry?"

"No," answered her companion, giving the horse a spiteful slap; "he don't know enough to get scared even, that's a fact. I don't believe anything short of Gabriel's trumpet would start him up a bit."

"I don't think you ought to speak that way, Almiry,"

said the old lady ; "it's kinder makin' light o' sacred things, seems to me. But as long as you've spoke of it, I don't believe that would start him up either. Though I'll tell you one thing, Almiry: I don't believe thar's goin' to be anything very frightful 'bout Gabriel's trumpet. I think it's goin' to come kinder like the robins an' the flowers do in the spring, kinder meltin' right into everything else, sweet an' nateral like."

"That ain't accordin' to Scripture," said Almira, stoutly.

"It's accordin' to my Scripture. I tell you what 'tis, Almiry, I've found out one thing a-livin' so long, an' that is, thar ain't so much difference in things on this airth as thar is in the folks that see 'em. It's me a-seein' the Scripturs, an' it's you a-seein' the Scriptures, Almiry, an' you see one thing an' I another, an' I dare say we both see crooked mostly, with maybe a little straight mixed up with it, an' we'll never reely know how much is straight till we see to read it by the light of the New Jerusalem."

"You ought to ha' ben a minister, Mis' Green."

"Wa'al, so I would ha' ben ef I had been a man ; I allers thought I would. But I s'pose the Lord thought there was more need of an extra hand just then to raise up children, an' bake an' brew an' wash dishes. You'd better drive along a leetle faster ef you kin, Almiry."

Almira jerked the reins viciously and clucked, but the horse jogged along undisturbed. "It ain't no use," said she. "You might as well try to start up a stone post."

"Wa'al, mebbe the shower won't come up," said the old lady, and she leaned back and began peacefully fanning herself.

"That cloud makes me think of Aunt Rebecca's funeral,"

she broke out, suddenly. "Did I ever tell you about it, Almiry?"

"No; I don't think you ever did, Mis' Green."

"Wa'al, mebbe you'll like to hear it, as we're joggin' along. It'll keep us from getting aggervated at the horse, poor, dumb thing!"

"Wa'al, you see, Almiry, Aunt Rebecca was my aunt on my mother's side—my mother's oldest sister she was—an' I'd allers thought a sight of her. This happened twenty year ago or more, before Israel died. She was allers such an own-folks sort of a woman, an' jest the best hand when any one was sick I'll never forgit how she nussed me through the typhus fever, the year after mother died. Thar I was took sick all of a sudden, an' four leetle children cryin', an' Israel couldn't get anybody but that shiftless Lyons woman, far and near, to come an' help. When Aunt Rebecca heerd of it she jest left everything an' come. She packed off that Lyons woman, bag an' baggage, an' tuk right hold, as nobody but her could ha' known how to. I allers knew I should ha' died ef it hadn't been for her.

"She lived ten miles off, on this very road, too, but we allers used to visit back an' forth. I couldn't get along without goin' to see Aunt Rebecca once in so often; I'd get jest as lonesome an' homesick as could be.

"So, feelin' that way, it ain't surprisin' that it gave me an awful shock when I heerd she was dead that mornin'. They sent the word by a man that they hailed, drivin' by. He was comin' down here to see about sellin' a horse, an' he said he'd jest as soon stop an' tell us as not. A real nice sort of a man he was—a store-keeper from Comstock. Wa'al, I see Israel standin' out in the road an' talkin' with the man, an' I wondered what it could be about. But when he came in an' told me that Aunt Rebecca was dead, I jest sat right down, kinder stunned like. I couldn't ha' felt much worse ef it had been my mother. An' it was so awful sudden! Why, I'd seen her only the week before, an' she looked uncommon smart for her, I thought. Ef it had been Uncle Enos, her husband, I shouldn't ha' wondered. He'd had the heart-disease for years, an' we'd thought he might die any minute; but to think of her—

"I jest stared at Israel. I felt too bad to cry. I didn't, till I happened to look down at the apron I had on. It was like a dress she had; she had a piece left, an' she gave it to me for an apron. When I saw that, I bust right out sobbin'.

"'O Lord,' says I, 'this apron she give me! Oh dear! dear! dear!'

"'Sarah,' says Israel, 'it's the will of the Lord.'

"'I know it,' says I, 'but she's dead, an' she gave me this apron, dear blessed woman,' an' I went right on cryin', though he tried to stop me. Every time I looked at that apron, it seemed as if I should die.

"Thar wa'n't any particulars, Israel said. All the man that told him knew was that a woman hailed him from one of the front windows as he was drivin' by, and asked him to stop an' tell us. I s'posed most likely the woman that hailed him was Mis' Simmons, a widder woman that used to work for Aunt Rebecca busy times.

"Wa'al, Israel kinder hurried me to get ready. The funeral was app'inted at two o'clock, an' we had a horse that wa'n't much swifter on the road than the one you're drivin' now.

"So I got into my best black gown the quickest I could. I had a good black shawl, and a black bunnit too; so I looked quite decent. I felt reel glad I had em'. They were things I had when mother died. I don't see hardly how I had happened to keep the bunnit, but it was lucky I did. I got ready in such a flutter that I got on my black gown over the caliker one I'd been wearin', an' never knew it till I came to go to bed that night, but I don't think it was much wonder.

"We'd been havin' a terrible dry spell, jest as we've been havin' now, an' everything was like powder. I thought my dress would be spoilt before we got thar. The horse was dreadful lazy, an' it was nothin' but g'langin' an' slappin' an' whippin' all the way, an' it didn't amount to nothin' then.

"When we'd got half-way thar or so, thar come up an awful thunder-shower from the northwest, jest as it's doin' to-day. Wa'al, thar wa'n't nowhar to stop, an' we driv right along. The horse wa'n't afraid of lightnin', an' we got in under the shay top as far as we could, an' pulled the blanket up over us ; but we got drippin' wet. An' thar was Israel in his meetin' coat, an' me in my best gown. Take it with the dust an' everything, they never looked anyhow again.

"Wa'al, Israel g'langed to the horse, an' put the whip over her, but she jest jogged right along. What with feelin' so about Aunt Rebecca, an' worryin' about Israel's coat an' my best gown, I thought I should never live to git thar.

"When we driv by the meetin'-house at Four Corners, where Aunt Rebecca lived, it was five minutes after two, an' two was the time sot for the funeral. I did feel reel worked up to think we was late, an' we chief mourners. When we got to the house thar seemed to be consider'ble goin' on around it, folks goin' in an' out, an' standin' in the yard, an' Israel said he didn't believe we was late, after all. He hollered to a man standin' by the fence, an' asked him if they had had the funeral. The man said no; they was goin' to hev it at the meetin'-house at three o'clock. We was glad enough to hear that, an' Israel said he would drive round an' hitch the horse, an' I'd better go in an' get dried off a little, an' see the folks.

"It had slacked up then, an' was only drizzlin' a leetle, an' lightnin' a good ways off now an' then.

"Wa'al, I got out, an' went up to the house. Thar was quite a lot of men I knew standin' round the door an' in the entry, but they only bowed kinder stiff an' solemn, an' moved to let me pass. I noticed the entry floor was drippin' wet too. 'Been rainin' in,' thinks I. 'I wonder why they didn't shet the door.' I went right into the room on the left-hand side of the entry—that was the settin'-room— an' thar, a-settin' in a cheer by the winder, jest as straight an' smart as could be, in her new black bunnit an' gown, was—Aunt Rebecca.

"Wa'al, ef I was to tell you what I did, Almiry, I s'pose you'd think it was awful. But I s'pose the sudden change from feelin' so bad made me kinder highstericky. I jest sot right down in the first cheer I come to an' laughed; I laughed till the tears was runnin' down my cheeks, an' it was all I could do to breathe. There was quite a lot of Uncle Enos's folks settin' round the room—his brother's family an' some cousins—an' they looked at me as ef they thought I was crazy. But seein' them look only sot me off again. Some of the folks came in from the entry, an' stood starin' at me, but I jest laughed harder. Finally Aunt Rebecca comes up to me.

"'For mercy's sake, Sarah,' says she, 'what air you doin' so for?'

"'Oh, dear!' says I. 'I thought you was dead, an' thar you was a-settin'. Oh dear!'

"And then I begun to laugh again. I was awful 'shamed of myself, but I couldn't stop to save my life.

"'For the land's sake, Aunt Rebecca,' says I, 'is thar a funeral or a weddin'? An' ef thar is a funeral, who's dead?'

"'Come into the bedroom with me a minute, Sarah,' says she.

"Then we went into her bedroom, that opened out of the settin-room, an' sot down, an' she told me that it was Uncle Enos that was dead. It seems she was the one that hailed the man, an' he was a little hard of hearin', an' thar was a misunderstandin' between 'em some way.

"Uncle Enos had died very sudden, the day before, of heart-disease. He went into the settin'-room after breakfast, an' sot down by the winder, an' Aunt Rebecca found him thar dead in his cheer when she went in a few minutes afterwards.

"It was such awful hot weather they had to hurry about the funeral. But that wa'n't all. Then she went on to tell me the rest. They had had the awfulest time that ever was. The shower had come up about one o'clock, and the barn had been struck by lightnin'. It was a big new one that Uncle Enos had sot great store by. He had laid out consider'ble money on it, an' they'd jest got in twelve ton of hay. I s'pose that was how it happened to be struck. A barn is a good deal more likely to be when they've jest got hay in. Well, everybody sot to an' put the fire in the barn out. They handed buckets of water up to the men on the roof, an' put that out without much trouble by takin' it in time.

"But after they'd got that put out they found the house

was on fire. The same thunderbolt that struck the barn had struck that too, an' it was blazin' away at one end of the roof pretty lively.

" Wa'al, they went to work at that then, an' they'd jest got that fairly put out a few minutes before we come. Nothin' was hurt much, only thar was a good deal of water round : we had hard work next day cleanin' of it up.

" Aunt Rebecca allers was a calm sort of woman, an' she didn't seem near as much flustered by it all as most folks would have been.

" I couldn't help wonderin', an' lookin' at her pretty sharp to see how she took Uncle Enos's death, too. You see, thar was something kinder curious about their gittin' married. I'd heerd about it all from mother. I don't s'pose she ever wanted him, nor cared about him the best she could do, any more than she would have about any good, respectable man that was her neighbor. Uncle Enos was a pretty good sort of a man, though he was allers dreadful sot in his ways, an' I believe it would have been wuss than death, any time, for him to have given up anything he had determined to hev. But I must say I never thought so much of him after mother told me what she did. You see, the way of it was, my grandmother Wilson, Aunt Rebecca's mother, was awful sot on her hevin' him, an' she was dreadful nervous an' feeble, an' Aunt Rebecca jest give in to her. The wust of it was, thar was some one else she wanted too, an' he wanted her. Abner Lyons his name was ; he wa'n't any relation to the Lyons woman I had when I was sick. He was a real likely young feller, an' thar wa'n't a thing agin him that any one else could see ; but grandmother fairly hated him, an' mother said she did believe her mother would rather hev buried Rebecca than seen her married to him. Well, grandmother took on, an' acted so, that Aunt Rebecca give in an' said she'd marry Uncle Enos, an' the weddin'-day come.

"Mother said she looked handsome as a pictur', but thar was somethin' kinder awful about her when she stood up before the minister with Uncle Enos to be married.

"She was dressed in green silk, an' had some roses in her hair. I kin imagine jest how she must hev looked. She was a good-lookin' woman when I knew her, an' they said when she was young there wa'n't many to compare with her.

"Mother said Uncle Enos looked nice, but he had his mouth kinder hard sot, as ef now he'd got what he wanted, an' meant to hang on to it. He'd known all the time jest how matters was. Aunt Rebecca'd told him the whole story; she declared she wouldn't marry him, without she did.

"I s'pose, at the last minute, that Aunt Rebecca got kinder desp'rate, an' a realizin' sense of what she was doin' come over her, an' she thought she'd make one more effort to escape; for when the minister asked that question 'bout thar bein' any obstacles to their gettin' married, an' ef thar were, let' em speak up, or forever hold their peace, Aunt Rebecca did speak up. Mother said she looked straight at the parson, an' her eyes was shinin' an her cheeks white as lilies.

"'Yes,' says she, 'thar is an obstacle, an' I will speak, an' then I will forever hold my peace. I don't love this man I'm standin' beside of, an' I love another man. Now ef Enos Fairweather wants me after what I've said, I've promised to marry him, an' you kin go on; but I won't tell or act a lie before God an' man.'

"Mother said it was awful. You could hev heerd a pin drop anywheres in the room. The minister jest stopped short an' looked at Uncle Enos, an' Uncle Enos nodded his head for him to go on.

"But then the minister begun to hev doubts as to whether or no he ought to marry 'em after what Aunt Rebecca had said, an' it seemed for a minute as ef thar wouldn't be any weddin' at all.

"But grandmother begun to cry, an' take on, an' Aunt Rebecca jest turned round an' looked at her. 'Go on,' says she to the minister.

"Mother said ef thar was ever anybody looked fit to be a martyr, Aunt Rebecca did then. But it never seemed to me t'was right. Marryin' to please your relations an' dyin' to please the Lord is two things.

"Wa'al, I never thought much of Uncle Enos after I heerd that story, though, as I said before, I guess he was a pretty good sort of a man. The principal thing that was bad about him, I guess, was, he was bound to hev Aunt Rebecca, an' he didn't let anything, even proper self-respect stand in his way.

"Aunt Rebecca allers did her duty by him, an' was a good wife an' good housekeeper. They never had any children. But I don't s'pose she was ever really happy or contented, an' I don't see how she could hev respected Uncle Enos, scursly, for my part, but you'd never hev known but what she did.

"So I looked at her pretty sharp, as we sot thar in her little bedroom that opened out of the settin'-room; thar was jest room for one cheer beside the bed, an' I sot on the bed. It seemed rather awful, with *him* a-layin' dead in the best room, but I couldn't help wonderin' ef she wouldn't marry Abner Lyons now. He'd never got married, but lived, all by himself, jest at the rise of the hill from where Aunt Rebecca lived. He'd never had a housekeeper, but jest shifted for himself, an' folks said his house was as neat as wax, an' he could cook an' wash dishes as handy as a woman. He used to hev his washin' out on the line by seven o'clock of a Monday mornin', anyhow; that I know, for I've seen it myself; an' the clothes looked white as snow. I shouldn't hev been ashamed of 'em myself.

"Aunt Rebecca looked very calm, an' I don't think she'd ben cryin'. But then that wa'n't nothin' to go by; 'twa'n't her way. I don't believe she'd a cried ef it had been Abner Lyons. Though I don't know, maybe, ef she'd married the man she'd wanted, she'd cried easier. For all Aunt Rebecca was so kind an' sympathizin' to other folks, she'd always seemed like a stone 'bout her own troubles. I don't s'pose, ef the barn an' 'house had both burned down, an' left her without a roof over her head, she'd 'a seemed any different. I kin see her now, jest as she looked, settin' thar, tellin' me the story that would hev flustrated any other woman most to death. But her voice was jest as low an' even, an' never shook. Her hair was gray, but it was kinder crinkly, an' her forehead was as white an' smooth as a young girl's.

"Aunt Rebecca's troubles always stayed in her heart, I s'pose, an' never pricked through. Except for her gray hair, she never looked as ef she'd had one.

"She never took on any more when she went to the funeral, for they buried him at last, poor man. He had 'most as hard a time gittin' buried as he did gittin' married. I couldn't help peekin' round to see ef Abner Lyons was thar, an' he was, on the other side of the aisle from me. An' he was lookin' straight at Uncle Enos's coffin, that stood up in front under the pulpit, with the curiousest expression that I ever did see.

"He didn't look glad reely. I couldn't say he did, but all I could think of was a man who'd been runnin' an' runnin' to get to a place, an' at length had got in sight of it.

"Maybe 'twas dreadful for him to go to a man's funeral an' look that way, but natur' is natur', an' I always felt somehow that ef Uncle Enos chose to do as he did 'twa'n't anythin' more than he ought to hev expected when he was dead.

"But I did feel awful ashamed an' wicked, thinkin' of such things, with the poor man layin' dead before me. An' when I went up to look at him, layin' thar so helpless, I cried like a baby. Poor Uncle Enos! it ain't for us to be down on folks after everything's all over.

"Well, Aunt Rebecca married Abner Lyons 'bout two years after Uncle Enos died, an' they lived together jest five years an' seven months; then she was took sudden with cholera-morbus from eatin' currants, an' died. He lived a year an' a half or so longer, an' then he died in a kind of consumption.

"'Twa'n't long they had to be happy together, an' sometimes I used to think they wa'n't so happy after all; for thar's no mistake about it, Abner Lyons was awful fussy. I s'pose his livin' alone so long made him so; but I don't believe Aunt Rebecca ever made a loaf of bread, after she was married, without his havin' something to say about it; an' ef thar's anything that's aggervatin' to a woman, it's havin' a man fussin' around in her kitchen.

"But ef Aunt Rebecca didn't find anything just as she thought it was goin' to be, she never let on she was disapp'inted.

"I declare, Almiry, thar's the house in sight, an' the

shower has gone round to the northeast, an' we ain't had a speck of rain to lay the dust.

"Well, my story's gone round to the northeast too. Ain't you tired out hearin' me talk, Almiry?"

"No indeed, Mis' Green," replied Almira, slapping the reins; "I liked to hear you, only it's kind of come to me, as I've been listening, that I *had* heard it before. The last time I took you to Walpole, I guess, you told it."

"Wa'al, I declare, I shouldn't wonder ef I did."

Then the horse turned cautiously around the corner, and stopped willingly before the house.

A MISTAKEN CHARITY.

THERE were in a green field a little, low, weather-stained cottage, with a foot-path leading to it from the highway several rods distant, and two old women—one with a tin pan and old knife searching for dandelion greens among the short young grass, and the other sitting on the door-step watching her, or, rather, having the appearance of watching her.

"Air there enough for a mess, Harriét?" asked the old woman on the door-step. She accented oddly the last syllable of the Harriet, and there was a curious quality in her feeble, cracked old voice. Besides the question denoted by the arrangement of her words and the rising inflection, there was another, broader and subtler, the very essence of all questioning, in the tone of her voice itself; the cracked, quavering notes that she used reached out of themselves, and asked, and groped like fingers in the dark. One would have known by the voice that the old woman was blind.

The old woman on her knees in the grass searching for dandelions did not reply; she evidently had not heard the question. So the old woman on the door-step, after waiting a few minutes with her head turned expectantly, asked again, varying her question slightly, and speaking louder:

"Air there enough for a mess, do ye s'pose, Harriét?"

The old woman in the grass heard this time. She rose slowly and laboriously ; the effort of straightening out the rheumatic old muscles was evidently a painful one ; then she eyed the greens heaped up in the tin pan, and pressed them down with her hand.

"Wa'al, I don't know, Charlotte," she replied, hoarsely. "There's plenty on 'em here, but I 'ain't got near enough for a mess ; they do bile down so when you get 'em in the pot ; an' it's all I can do to bend my j'ints enough to dig 'em."

"I'd give consider'ble to help ye, Harriét," said the old woman on the door-step.

But the other did not hear her ; she was down on her knees in the grass again, anxiously spying out the dandelions.

So the old woman on the door-step crossed her little shrivelled hands over her calico knees, and sat quite still, with the soft spring wind blowing over her.

The old wooden door-step was sunk low down among the grasses, and the whole house to which it belonged had an air of settling down and mouldering into the grass as into its own grave.

When Harriet Shattuck grew deaf and rheumatic, and had to give up her work as tailoress, and Charlotte Shattuck lost her eyesight, and was unable to do any more sewing for her livelihood, it was a small and trifling charity for the rich man who held a mortgage on the little house in which they had been born and lived all their lives to give them the use of it, rent and interest free. He might as well have taken credit to himself for not charging a squirrel for his tenement in some old decaying tree in his woods.

So ancient was the little habitation, so wavering and

mouldering, the hands that had fashioned it had lain still so long in their graves, that it almost seemed to have fallen below its distinctive rank as a house. Rain and snow had filtered through its roof, mosses had grown over it, worms had eaten it, and birds built their nests under its eaves; nature had almost completely overrun and obliterated the work of man, and taken her own to herself again, till the house seemed as much a natural ruin as an old tree-stump.

The Shattucks had always been poor people and common people; no especial grace and refinement or fine ambition had ever characterized any of them; they had always been poor and coarse and common. The father and his father before him had simply lived in the poor little house, grubbed for their living, and then unquestioningly died. The mother had been of no rarer stamp, and the two daughters were cast in the same mould.

After their parents' death Harriet and Charlotte had lived along in the old place from youth to old age, with the one hope of ability to keep a roof over their heads, covering on their backs, and victuals in their mouths—an all-sufficient one with them.

Neither of them had ever had a lover; they had always seemed to repel rather than attract the opposite sex. It was not merely because they were poor, ordinary, and homely; there were plenty of men in the place who would have matched them well in that respect; the fault lay deeper—in their characters. Harriet, even in her girlhood, had a blunt, defiant manner that almost amounted to surliness, and was well calculated to alarm timid adorers, and Charlotte had always had the reputation of not being any too strong in her mind.

Harriet had gone about from house to house doing tailor-work after the primitive country fashion, and Charlotte had done plain sewing and mending for the neighbors. They had been, in the main, except when pressed by some temporary anxiety about their work or the payment thereof, happy and contented, with that negative kind of happiness and contentment which comes not from gratified ambition, but a lack of ambition itself. All that they cared for they had had in tolerable abundance, for Harriet at least had been swift and capable about her work. The patched, mossy old roof had been kept over their heads, the coarse, hearty food that they loved had been set on their table, and their cheap clothes had been warm and strong.

After Charlotte's eyes failed her, and Harriet had the rheumatic fever, and the little hoard of earnings went to the doctors, times were harder with them, though still it could not be said that they actually suffered.

When they could not pay the interest on the mortgage they were allowed to keep the place interest free; there was as much fitness in a mortgage on the little house, anyway, as there would have been on a rotten old apple-tree; and the people about, who were mostly farmers, and good friendly folk, helped them out with their living. One would donate a barrel of apples from his abundant harvest to the two poor old women, one a barrel of potatoes, another a load of wood for the winter fuel, and many a farmer's wife had bustled up the narrow foot-path with a pound of butter, or a dozen fresh eggs, or a nice bit of pork. Besides all this, there was a tiny garden patch behind the house, with a straggling row of currant bushes in it, and one of gooseberries, where Harriet contrived every year to raise a few pumpkins, which were the pride of her life. On the right of the garden were two old apple-trees, a Baldwin and a Porter, both yet in a tolerably good fruit-bearing state.

The delight which the two poor old souls took in their own pumpkins, their apples and currants, was indescribable. It was not merely that they contributed largely towards their living; they were their own, their private share of the great wealth of nature, the little taste set apart for them alone out of her bounty, and worth more to them on that account, though they were not conscious of it, than all the richer fruits which they received from their neighbors' gardens.

This morning the two apple-trees were brave with flowers, the currant bushes looked alive, and the pumpkin seeds were in the ground. Harriet cast complacent glances in their direction from time to time, as she painfully dug her dandelion greens. She was a short, stoutly built old woman, with a large face coarsely wrinkled, with a suspicion of a stubble of beard on the square chin.

When her tin pan was filled to her satisfaction with the sprawling, spidery greens, and she was hobbling stiffly towards her sister on the door-step, she saw another woman standing before her with a basket in her hand.

"Good-morning, Harriet," she said, in a loud, strident voice, as she drew near. "I've been fry'ng some doughnuts, and I brought you over some warm."

"I've been tellin' her it was real good in her," piped Charlotte from the door-step, with an anxious turn of her sightless face towards the sound of her sister's footstep.

Harriet said nothing but a hoarse "Good-mornin', Mis' Simonds." Then she took the basket in her hand, lifted the towel off the top, selected a doughnut, and deliberately tasted it.

"Tough," said she. "I s'posed so. If there is anything I 'spise on this airth it's a tough doughnut."

"Oh, Harriét!" said Charlotte, with a frightened look.

"They air tough," said Harriet, with hoarse defiance, "and if there is anything I 'spise on this airth it's a tough doughnut."

The woman whose benevolence and cookery were being thus ungratefully received only laughed. She was quite fleshy, and had a round, rosy, determined face.

"Well, Harriet," said she, "I am sorry they are tough, but perhaps you had better take them out on a plate, and give me my basket. You may be able to eat two or three of them if they are tough."

"They air tough—turrible tough," said Harriet, stubbornly; but she took the basket into the house and emptied it of its contents nevertheless.

"I suppose your roof leaked as bad as ever in that heavy rain day before yesterday?" said the visitor to Harriet, with an inquiring squint towards the mossy shingles, as she was about to leave with her empty basket.

"It was turrible," replied Harriet, with crusty acquiescence—"turrible. We had to set pails an' pans everywheres, an' move the bed out."

"Mr. Upton ought to fix it."

"There ain't any fix to it; the old ruff ain't fit to nail new shingles on to; the hammerin' would bring the whole thing down on our heads," said Harriet, grimly.

"Well, I don't know as it can be fixed, it's so old. I suppose the wind comes in bad around the windows and doors too?"

"It's like livin' with a piece of paper, or mebbe a sieve, 'twixt you an' the wind an' the rain," quoth Harriet, with a jerk of her head.

"You ought to have a more comfortable home in your old age," said the visitor, thoughtfully.

"Oh, it's well enough," cried Harriet, in quick alarm, and with a complete change of tone ; the woman's remark had brought an old dread over her. "The old house 'll last as long as Charlotte an' me do. The rain ain't so bad, nuther is the wind ; there's room enough for us in the dry places, an' out of the way of the doors an' windows. It's enough sight better than goin' on the town." Her square, defiant old face actually looked pale as she uttered the last words and stared apprehensively at the woman.

"Oh, I did not think of your doing that," she said, hastily and kindly. "We all know how you feel about that, Harriet, and not one of us neighbors will see you and Charlotte go to the poorhouse while we've got a crust of bread to share with you."

Harriet's face brightened. "Thank ye, Mis' Simonds," she said, with reluctant courtesy. "I'm much obleeged to you an' the neighbors. I think mebbe we'll be able to eat some of them doughnuts if they air tough," she added, mollifyingly, as her caller turned down the foot-path.

"My, Harriét," said Charlotte, lifting up a weakly, wondering, peaked old face, "what did you tell her them doughnuts was tough fur?"

"Charlotte, do you want everybody to look down on us, an' think we ain't no account at all, just like any beggars, 'cause they bring us in vittles?" said Harriet, with a grim glance at her sister's meek, unconscious face.

"No, Harriét," she whispered.

"Do you want *to go to the poor-house*?"

"No, Harriét." The poor little old woman on the door-step fairly cowered before her aggressive old sister.

"Then don't hender me agin when I tell folks their doughnuts is tough an' their pertaters is poor. If I don't kinder keep up an' show some sperrit, I sha'n't think nothing of myself, an' other folks won't nuther, and fust thing we know they'll kerry us to the poorhouse. You'd 'a been there before now if it hadn't been for me, Charlotte."

Charlotte looked meekly convinced, and her sister sat down on a chair in the doorway to scrape her dandelions.

"Did you git a good mess, Harriét?" asked Charlotte, in a humble tone.

"Toler'ble."

"They'll be proper relishin' with that piece of pork Mis' Mann brought in yesterday. O Lord, Harriet, it's a chink!"

Harriet sniffed.

Her sister caught with her sensitive ear the little contemptuous sound. "I guess," she said, querulously, and with more pertinacity than she had shown in the matter of the doughnuts, "that if you was in the dark, as I am, Harriet, you wouldn't make fun an' turn up your nose at chinks. If you had seen the light streamin' in all of a sudden through some little hole that you hadn't known of before when you set down on the door-step this mornin', and the wind with the smell of the apple blows in it came in your face, an' when Mis' Simonds brought them hot doughnuts, an' when I thought of the pork an' greens jest now— O Lord, how it did shine in! An' it does now. If you was me, Harriét, you would know there was chinks."

Tears began starting from the sightless eyes, and streaming pitifully down the pale old cheeks.

Harriet looked at her sister, and her grim face softened.

" Why, Charlotte, hev it that thar *is* chinks if you want to. Who cares ?"

" Thar *is* chinks, Harriét."

" Wa'al, thar *is* chinks, then. If I don't hurry, I sha'n't get these greens in in time for dinner."

When the two old women sat down complacently to their meal of pork and dandelion greens in their little kitchen they did not dream how destiny slowly and surely was introducing some new colors into their web of life, even when it was almost completed, and that this was one of the last meals they would eat in their old home for many a day. In about a week from that day they were established in the " Old Ladies' Home " in a neighboring city. It came about in this wise: Mrs. Simonds, the woman who had brought the gift of hot doughnuts, was a smart, energetic person, bent on doing good, and she did a great deal. To be sure, she always did it in her own way. If she chose to give hot doughnuts, she gave hot doughnuts ; it made not the slightest difference to her if the recipients of her charity would infinitely have preferred ginger cookies. Still, a great many would like hot doughnuts, and she did unquestionably a great deal of good.

She had a worthy coadjutor in the person of a rich and childless elderly widow in the place. They had fairly entered into a partnership in good works, with about an equal capital on both sides, the widow furnishing the money, and Mrs. Simonds, who had much the better head of the two, furnishing the active schemes of benevolence.

The afternoon after the doughnut episode she had gone to the widow with a new project, and the result was that entrance fees had been paid, and old Harriet and Charlotte made sure of a comfortable home for the rest of their lives.

The widow was hand in glove with officers of missionary boards and trustees of charitable institutions.   There
had been an unusual mortality among the inmates of the
" Home " this spring, there were several vacancies, and the
matter of the admission of Harriet and Charlotte was very
quickly and easily arranged.   But the matter which would
have seemed the least difficult—inducing the two old women
to accept the bounty which Providence, the widow, and Mrs.
Simonds were ready to bestow on them—proved the most
so.   The struggle to persuade them to abandon their tottering old home for a better was a terrible one.   The widow
had pleaded with mild surprise, and Mrs. Simonds with
benevolent determination ; the counsel and reverend eloquence of the minister had been called in ; and when they
yielded at last it was with a sad grace for the recipients of
a worthy charity.

It had been hard to convince them that the " Home "
was not an almshouse under another name, and their yield-
ing at length to anything short of actual force was only due
probably to the plea, which was advanced most eloquently to
Harriet, that Charlotte would be so much more comfortable.

The morning they came away, Charlotte cried pitifully,
and trembled all over her little shrivelled body.   Harriet
did not cry.   But when her sister had passed out the low,
sagging door she turned the key in the lock, then took it
out and thrust it slyly into her pocket, shaking her head to
herself with an air of fierce determination.

Mrs. Simonds's husband, who was to take them to the
depot, said to himself, with disloyal defiance of his wife's
active charity, that it was a shame, as he helped the two
distressed old souls into his light wagon, and put the poor
little box, with their homely clothes in it, in behind.

Mrs. Simonds, the widow, the minister, and the gentleman from the " Home " who was to take charge of them, were all at the depot, their faces beaming with the delight of successful benevolence. But the two poor old women looked like two forlorn prisoners in their midst. It was an impressive illustration of the truth of the saying "that it is more blessed to give than to receive."

Well, Harriet and Charlotte Shattuck went to the "Old Ladies' Home " with reluctance and distress. They stayed two months, and then—they ran away.

The " Home " was comfortable, and in some respects even luxurious ; but nothing suited those two unhappy, unreasonable old women.

The fare was of a finer, more delicately served variety than they had been accustomed to ; those finely flavored nourishing soups for which the " Home " took great credit to itself failed to please palates used to common, coarser food.

" O Lord, Harriét, when I set down to the table here there ain't no chinks," Charlotte used to say. " If we could hev some cabbage, or some pork an' greens, how the light would stream in !"

Then they had to be more particular about their dress. They had always been tidy enough, but now it had to be something more ; the widow, in the kindness of her heart, had made it possible, and the good folks in charge of the " Home," in the kindness of their hearts, tried to carry out the widow's designs.

But nothing could transform these two unpolished old women into two nice old ladies. They did not take kindly to white lace caps and delicate neckerchiefs. They liked their new black cashmere dresses well enough, but they felt as if they broke a commandment when they put them on every afternoon. They had always worn calico with long aprons at home, and they wanted to now; and they wanted to twist up their scanty gray locks into little knots at the back of their heads, and go without caps, just as they always had done.

Charlotte in a dainty white cap was pitiful, but Harriet was both pitiful and comical. They were totally at variance with their surroundings, and they felt it keenly, as people of their stamp always do. No amount of kindness and attention—and they had enough of both—sufficed to reconcile them to their new abode. Charlotte pleaded continually with her sister to go back to their old home.

"O Lord, Harriét, she would exclaim (by the way, Charlotte's "O Lord," which, as she used it, was innocent enough, had been heard with much disfavor in the " Home," and she, not knowing at all why, had been remonstrated with concerning it), "let us go home. I can't stay here no ways in this world. I don't like their vittles, an' I don't like to wear a cap; I want to go home and do different. The currants will be ripe, Harriét. O Lord, thar was almost a chink, thinking about 'em. I want some of 'em; an' the Porter apples will be gittin' ripe, an' we could have some apple-pie. This here ain't good; I want merlasses fur sweeting. Can't we get back no ways, Harriét? It ain't far, an' we could walk, an' they don't lock us in, nor nothin'. I don't want to die here; it ain't so straight up to heaven from here. O Lord, I've felt as if I was slantendicular from heaven ever since I've been here, an' it's been so awful dark. I ain't had any chinks. I want to go home, Harriét."

"We'll go to-morrow mornin'," said Harriet, finally;

"we'll pack up our things an' go ; we'll put on our old dresses, an' we'll do up the new ones in bundles, an' we'll jest shy out the back way to-morrow mornin' ; an' we'll go. I kin find the way, an' I reckon we kin git thar, if it is fourteen mile. Mebbe somebody will give us a lift."

And they went. With a grim humor Harriet hung the new white lace caps with which she and Charlotte had been so pestered, one on each post at the head of the bedstead, so they would meet the eyes of the first person who opened the door. Then they took their bundles, stole slyly out, and were soon on the high-road, hobbling along, holding each other's hands, as jubilant as two children, and chuckling to themselves over their escape, and the probable astonishment there would be in the " Home " over it.

" O Lord, Harriét, what do you s'pose they will say to them caps ?" cried Charlotte, with a gleeful cackle.

"I guess they'll see as folks ain't goin' to be made to wear caps agin their will in a free kentry," returned Harriet, with an echoing cackle, as they sped feebly and bravely along.

The " Home " stood on the very outskirts of the city, luckily for them. They would have found it a difficult undertaking to traverse the crowded streets. As it was, a short walk brought them into the free country road—free comparatively, for even here at ten o'clock in the morning there was considerable travelling to and from the city on business or pleasure.

People whom they met on the road did not stare at them as curiously as might have been expected. Harriet held her bristling chin high in air, and hobbled along with an appearance of being well aware of what she was about, that led folks to doubt their own first opinion that there was something unusual about the two old women.

Still their evident feebleness now and then occasioned from one and another more particular scrutiny. When they had been on the road a half-hour or so, a man in a covered wagon drove up behind them. After he had passed them, he poked his head around the front of the vehicle and looked back. Finally he stopped, and waited for them to come up to him.

"Like a ride, ma'am?" said he, looking at once bewildered and compassionate.

"Thankee," said Harriet, "we'd be much obleeged."

After the man had lifted the old women into the wagon, and established them on the back seat, he turned around, as he drove slowly along, and gazed at them curiously.

"Seems to me you look pretty feeble to be walking far," said he. "Where were you going?"

Harriet told him with an air of defiance.

"Why," he exclaimed, "it is fourteen miles out. You could never walk it in the world. Well, I am going within three miles of there, and I can go on a little farther as well as not. But I don't see— Have you been in the city?"

"I have been visitin' my married darter in the city," said Harriet, calmly.

Charlotte started, and swallowed convulsively.

Harriet had never told a deliberate falsehood before in her life, but this seemed to her one of the tremendous exigencies of life which justify a lie. She felt desperate. If she could not contrive to deceive him in some way, the man might turn directly around and carry Charlotte and her back to the "Home" and the white caps.

"I should not have thought your daughter would have

let you start for such a walk as that," said the man. "Is this lady your sister? She is blind, isn't she? She does not look fit to walk a mile."

"Yes, she's my sister," replied Harriet, stubbornly : "an' she's blind ; an' my darter didn't want us to walk. She felt reel bad about it. But she couldn't help it. She's poor, and her husband's dead, an' she's got four leetle children."

Harriet recounted the hardships of her imaginary daughter with a glibness that was astonishing. Charlotte swallowed again.

"Well," said the man, " I am glad I overtook you, for I don't think you would ever have reached home alive."

About six miles from the city an open buggy passed them swiftly. In it were seated the matron and one of the gentlemen in charge of the " Home." They never thought of looking into the covered wagon—and indeed one can travel in one of those vehicles, so popular in some parts of New England, with as much privacy as he could in his tomb. The two in the buggy were seriously alarmed, and anxious for the safety of the old women, who were chuckling maliciously in the wagon they soon left far behind. Harriet had watched them breathlessly until they disappeared on a curve of the road ; then she whispered to Charlotte.

A little after noon the two old women crept slowly up the foot-path across the field to their old home.

"The clover is up to our knees," said Harriet ; "an' the sorrel and the white-weed ; an' there's lots of yaller butterflies."

"O Lord, Harriét, thar's a chink, an' I do believe I saw one of them yaller butterflies go past it," cried Charlotte, trembling all over, and nodding her gray head violently.

Harriet stood on the old sunken door-step and fitted the

key, which she drew triumphantly from her pocket, in the lock, while Charlotte stood waiting and shaking behind her.

Then they went in. Everything was there just as they had left it. Charlotte sank down on a chair and began to cry. Harriet hurried across to the window that looked out on the garden.

"The currants air ripe," said she ; "*an'* them pumpkins hev run all over everything."

"O Lord, Harriét," sobbed Charlotte, "thar is so many chinks that they air all runnin' together !"

A GATHERER OF SIMPLES.

A DAMP air was blowing up, and the frogs were beginning to peep. The sun was setting in a low red sky. On both sides of the road were rich green meadows intersected by little canal-like brooks. Beyond the meadows on the west was a distant stretch of pine woods, that showed dark against the clear sky. Aurelia Flower was going along the road towards her home, with a great sheaf of leaves and flowers in her arms. There were the rosy spikes of hard-hack; the great white corymbs of thoroughwort, and the long blue racemes of lobelia. Then there were great bunches of the odorous tansy and pennyroyal in with the rest.

Aurelia was a tall, strongly-built woman; she was not much over thirty, but she looked older. Her complexion had a hard red tinge from exposure to sun and wind, and showed seams as unreservedly as granite. Her face was thin, and her cheek-bones high. She had a profusion of auburn hair, showing in a loose slipping coil beneath her limp black straw hat. Her dress, as a matter of fashion, was execrable; in point of harmony with her immediate surroundings, very well, though she had not thought of it in that way. There was a green under-skirt, and a brown over-skirt and basque of an obsolete cut. She had worn it

just so for a good many years, and never thought of alter-
ing it.   It did not seem to occur to her that though her
name was Flower, she was not really a flower in regard to
apparel, and had not its right of unchangeableness in the
spring.   When the trees hung out their catkins, she flaunted
her poor old greens and browns under them, rejoicing, and
never dreamed but they looked all right.   As far as dress
went, Aurelia was a happy woman.   She went over the road
to-night at a good pace, her armful of leaves and blossoms
nodding; her spare, muscular limbs bore her along easily.
She had been over a good many miles since noon, but she
never thought of being tired.

Presently she came in sight of her home, a square unpainted building, black with age.   It stood a little back
from the road on a gentle slope.   There were three great
maple-trees in front of the house; their branches rustled
against the roof.   On the left was a small garden; some
tall poles thickly twined with hops were prominent in it.

Aurelia went round to the side door of the house with
her armful of green things.   The door opened directly into
the great kitchen.   One on entering would have started
back as one would on seeing unexpected company in a
room.   The walls were as green as a lady's bower with
bunches and festoons of all sorts of New England herbs.
There they hung, their brave blossoms turning gray and
black, giving out strange, half-pleasant, half-disgusting
odors.   Aurelia took them in like her native air.   "It's
good to get home," murmured she to herself, for there was
no one else: she lived alone.

She took off her hat and disposed of her burden; then
she got herself some supper.   She did not build a fire in
the cooking-stove, for she never drank tea in warm weather.

Instead, she had a tumbler of root-beer which she had made herself. She set it out on one end of her kitchen-table with a slice of coarse bread and a saucer of cold beans. She sat down to them and ate with a good appetite. She looked better with her hat off. Her forehead was an important part of her face ; it was white and womanly, and her reddish hair lay round it in pretty curves ; then her brown eyes, under very strongly arched brows, showed to better advantage. Taken by herself, and not compared with other women, Aurelia was not so bad-looking ; but she never was taken by herself in that way, and nobody had ever given her any credit for comeliness. It would have been like looking at a jack-in-the-pulpit and losing all the impression that had ever been made on one by roses and hyacinths, and seeing absolutely nothing else but its green and brown lines : it is doubtful if it could be done.

She had finished her supper, and was sorting her fresh herbs, when the door opened and a woman walked in. She had no bonnet on her head : she was a neighbor, and this was an unceremonious little country place.

"Good-evenin', 'Relia," said she. There was an important look on her plain face, as if there were more to follow.

"Good-evenin', Mis' Atwood. Take a chair."

"Been herbin' again?"

"Yes ; I went out a little while this afternoon."

"Where'd you go?—up on Green Mountain?"

"No ; I went over to White's Woods. There were some kinds there I wanted."

"You don't say so! That's a matter of six miles, ain't it? Ain't you tired?"

"Lor', no," said Aurelia. "I reckon I'm pretty strong, or mebbe the smell of the herbs keeps me up;" and she laughed.

So did the other. "Sure enough—well, mebbe it does. I never thought of that. But it seems like a pretty long tramp to me, though my bein' so fleshy may make a difference. I could have walked it easier once."

"I shouldn't wonder if it did make a difference. I ain't got much flesh to carry round to tire me out."

"You're always pretty well, too, ain't you, 'Relia?"

"Lor', yes; I never knew what 'twas to be sick. How's your folks, Mis' Atwood? Is Viny any better than she was?"

"I don't know as she is, much. She feels pretty poorly most of the time. I guess I'll hev you fix some more of that root-beer for her. I thought that seemed to 'liven her up a little."

"I've got a jug of it all made, down cellar, and you can take it when you go home, if you want to."

"So I will, if you've got it. I was in hopes you might hev it."

The important look had not vanished from Mrs. Atwood's face, but she was not the woman to tell important news in a hurry, and have the gusto of it so soon over. She was one of the natures who always dispose of bread before pie. Now she came to it, however.

"I heard some news to-night, 'Relia," said she.

Aurelia picked out another spray of hardhack. "What was it?"

"Thomas Rankin's dead."

Aurelia clutched the hardhack mechanically. "You don't mean it, Mis' Atwood! When did he die? I hadn't heard he was sick."

"He wasn't, long. Had a kind of a fit this noon, and died right off. The doctor—they sent for Dr. Smith from

Alden — called it sunstroke. You know 'twas awful hot, and he'd been out in the field to work all the mornin'. *I* think 'twas heart trouble; it's in the Rankin family; his father died of it. Doctors don't know everything."

"Well, it's a dreadful thing," said Aurelia. "I can't realize it. There he's left four little children, and it ain't more'n a year since Mis' Rankin died. It *ain't* a year, is it?"

"It ain't a year into a month and sixteen days," said Mrs. Atwood, solemnly. "Viny and I was countin' of it up just before I come in here."

"Well, I guess 'tisn't, come to think of it. I couldn't have told exactly. The oldest of those children ain't more than eight, is she?"

"Ethelind is eight, coming next month : Viny and I was reckinin' it up. Then Edith is six, and Isadore is five, and Myrtie ain't but two, poor little thing."

"What do you s'pose will be done with 'em?"

"I don't know. Viny an' me was talking of it over, and got it settled that *her* sister, Mis' Loomis, over to Alden, would *hev* to hev 'em. It'll be considerable for her, too, for she's got two of her own, and I don't s'pose Sam Loomis has got much. But I don't see what else can be done. Of course strangers ain't goin' to take children when there is folks."

"Wouldn't *his* mother take 'em?"

"What, old-lady Sears? Lor', no. You know she was dreadful put out 'bout Thomas marryin' where he did, and declared he shouldn't hev a cent of her money. It was all her second husband's, anyway. John Rankin wasn't worth anything. She won't do anything for 'em. She's livin' in great style down near the city, they say. Got a nice house, and keeps help. She might hev 'em jest as well as not, but she won't. She's a hard woman to get along with, anyhow. She nagged both her husbands to death, an' Thomas never had no peace at home. Guess that was one reason why he was in such a hurry to get married. Mis' Rankin was a good-tempered soul, if she wasn't quite so drivin' as some."

"I do feel dreadfully to think of those children," said Aurelia.

"'Tis hard ; but we must try an' believe it will be ruled for the best. I s'pose I must go, for I left Viny all alone."

"Well, if you must, I'll get that root-beer for you, Mis' Atwood. I shall keep thinking 'bout those children all night."

A week or two after that, Mrs. Atwood had some more news ; but she didn't go to Aurelia with it, for Aurelia was the very sub-essence of it herself. She unfolded it gingerly to her daughter Lavinia—a pale, peaked young woman, who looked as if it would take more than Aurelia's root-beer to make her robust. Aurelia had taken the youngest Rankin child for her own, and Mrs. Atwood had just heard of it. "It's true," said she ; "I see her with it myself. Old-lady Sears never so much as sent a letter, let alone not coming to the funeral, and Mis' Loomis was glad enough to get rid of it."

Viny drank in the story as if it had been so much nourishing jelly. Her too narrow life was killing her as much as anything else.

Meanwhile Aurelia had the child, and was actively happy, for the first time in her life, to her own *naïve* astonishment, for she had never known that she was not so before. She had naturally strong affections, of an outward rather than an inward tendency. She was capable of much enjoyment

from pure living, but she had never had anything of which
to be so very fond. She could only remember her father as
a gloomy, hard-working man, who never noticed her much.
He had a melancholy temperament, which resulted in a
tragical end when Aurelia was a mere child. When she
thought of him, the same horror which she had when they
brought him home from the river crept over her now. They
had never known certainly just how Martin Flower had
come to die ; but folks never spoke of him to Aurelia and
her mother, and the two never talked of him together.
They knew that everybody said Martin Flower had drowned
himself ; they felt shame and a Puritan shrinking from the
sin.

Aurelia's mother had been a hard, silent woman before ;
she grew more hard and silent afterwards. She worked
hard, and taught Aurelia to. Their work was peculiar ;
they hardly knew themselves how they had happened to
drift into it ; it had seemed to creep in with other work, till
finally it usurped it altogether. At first, after her husband's
death, Mrs. Flower had tried millinery : she had learned the
trade in her youth. But she made no headway now in sewing rosebuds and dainty bows on to bonnets ; it did not
suit with tragedy. The bonnets seemed infected with her
own mood ; the bows lay flat with stern resolve, and the
rosebuds stood up fiercely ; she did not please her customers, even among those uncritical country folk, and they
dropped off. She had always made excellent root-beer, and
had had quite a reputation in the neighborhood for it. How
it happened she could not tell, but she found herself selling
it ; then she made hop yeast, and sold that. Then she was
a woman of fertile brain, and another project suggested
itself to her.

She and Aurelia ransacked the woods thereabouts for medicinal herbs, and disposed of them to druggists in a neighboring town. They had a garden also of some sorts— the different mints, thyme, lavender, coriander, rosemary, and others. It was an unusual business for two women to engage in, but it increased, and they prospered, according to their small ideas. But Mrs. Flower grew more and more bitter with success. What regrets and longing that her husband could have lived and shared it, and been spared his final agony, she had in her heart, nobody but the poor woman herself knew ; she never spoke of them. She died when Aurelia was twenty, and a woman far beyond her years. She mourned for her mother, but although she never knew it, her warmest love had not been called out. It had been hardly possible. Mrs. Flower had not been a lovable mother; she had rarely spoken to Aurelia but with cold censure for the last few years. People whispered that it was a happy release for the poor girl when her mother died ; they had begun to think she was growing like her husband, and perhaps was not " just right."

Aurelia went on with the business with calm equanimity, and made even profits every year. They were small, but more than enough for her to live on, and she paid the last dollar of the mortgage which had so fretted her father, and owned the whole house clear. She led a peaceful, innocent life, with her green herbs for companions ; she associated little with the people around, except in a business way. They came to see her, but she rarely entered their houses. Every room in her house was festooned with herbs ; she knew every kind that grew in the New England woods, and hunted them out in their season and brought them home ; she was a simple, sweet soul, with none of the morbid melancholy of her parents about her. She loved her woik, and the greenwood things were to her as friends, and the healing qualities of sarsaparilla and thoroughwort, and the sweetness of thyme and lavender, seemed to have entered into her nature, till she almost could talk with them in that way. She had never thought of being unhappy; but now she wondered at herself over this child. It was a darling of a child; as dainty and winsome a girl baby as ever was. Her poor young mother had had a fondness for romantic names, which she had bestowed, as the only heritage within her power, on all her children. This one was Myrtilla—Myrtie for short. The little thing clung to Aurelia from the first, and Aurelia found that she had another way of loving besides the way in which she loved lavender and thoroughwort. The comfort she took with the child through the next winter was unspeakable. The herbs were banished from the south room, which was turned into a nursery, and a warm carpet was put on the floor, that the baby might not take cold. She learned to cook for the baby—her own diet had been chiefly vegetarian. She became a charming nursing mother. People wondered. "It does beat all how handy 'Relia is with that baby," Mrs. Atwood told Viny.

Aurelia took even more comfort with the little thing when spring came, and she could take her out with her; then she bought a little straw carriage, and the two went after herbs together. Home they would come in the tender spring twilight, the baby asleep in her carriage, with a great sheaf of flowers beside her, and Aurelia with another over her shoulder.

She felt all through that summer as if she were too happy to have it last. Once she said so to one of the neighbors. "I feel as if it wa'n't right for me to be so perfectly happy," said she. "I feel some days as if I was walkin' an' walkin' an' walkin' through a garden of sweet-smellin' herbs, an' nothin' else ; an' as for Myrtie, she's a bundle of myrtle an' camphor out of King Solomon's garden. I'm so afraid it can't last."

Happiness had seemed to awake in Aurelia a taint of her father's foreboding melancholy. But she apparently had no reason for it until early fall. Then, returning with Myrtie one night from a trip to the woods, she found an old lady seated on her door-step, grimly waiting for her. She was an old woman and tremulous, but still undaunted and unshaken as to her spirit. Her tall, shrunken form was loaded with silk and jet. She stood up as Aurelia approached, wondering, and her dim old eyes peered at her aggressively through fine gold spectacles, which lent an additional glare to them.

"I suppose you are Miss Flower?" began the old lady, with no prefatory parley.

"Yes," said Aurelia, trembling.

"Well, my name's Mrs. Matthew Sears, an' I've come for my grandchild there."

Aurelia turned very white. She let her herbs slide to the ground. "I—hardly understand—I guess," faltered she. "Can't you let me keep her?"

"Well, I guess I won't have one of my grandchildren brought up by an old yarb-woman—not if I know it."

The old lady sniffed. Aurelia stood looking at her. She felt as if she had fallen down from heaven, and the hard reality of the earth had jarred the voice out of her. Then the old lady made a step towards the carriage, and caught up Myrtie in her trembling arms. The child screamed with fright. She had been asleep. She turned her little fright-

ened face towards Aurelia, and held out her arms, and cried,
"Mamma! mamma! mamma!" in a perfect frenzy of terror.
The old lady tried in vain to hush her. Aurelia found her
voice then. "You'd better let me take her and give her
her supper," she said, "and when she is asleep again I will
bring her over to you."

"Well," said the old lady, doubtfully. She was glad to
get the frantic little thing out of her arms, though.

Aurelia held her close and hushed her, and she subsi-
ded into occasional convulsive sobs, and furtive, frightened
glances at her grandmother.

"I s'pose you are stopping at the hotel?" said Aurelia.

"Yes, I am," said the old lady, stoutly. "You kin bring
her over as soon as she's asleep." Then she marched off
with uncertain majesty.

Some women would have argued the case longer, but Aurelia felt that there was simply no use in it. The old lady
was the child's grandmother: if she wanted her, she saw no
way but to give her up. She never thought of pleading, she
was so convinced of the old lady's determination.

She carried Myrtie into the house, gave her her supper, washed her, and dressed her in her little best dress.
Then she took her up in her lap and tried to explain to her
childish mind the change that was to be made in her life.
She told her she was going to live with her grandmother,
and she must be a good little girl, and love her, and do just
as she told her to. Myrtie sobbed with unreasoning grief,
and clung to Aurelia; but she wholly failed to take in the
full meaning of it all.

She was still fretful, and bewildered by her rude waken-
ing from her nap. Presently she fell asleep again, and
Aurelia laid her down while she got together her little ward-

robe.   There was a hop pillow in a little linen case, on which Myrtie had always slept; she packed that up with the other things.

Then she rolled up the little sleeping girl in a blanket, laid her in her carriage, and went over to the hotel.   It was not much of a hotel—merely an ordinary two-story house, where two or three spare rooms were ample accommodation for the few straggling guests who came to this little rural place.   It was only a few steps from Aurelia's house. The old lady had the chamber of honor—a large square room on the first floor, opening directly on to the piazza. In spite of all Aurelia's care, Myrtie woke up and began to cry when she was carried in.   She had to go off and leave her screaming piteously after her.   Out on the piazza she uttered the first complaint, almost, of her life to the hostess, Mrs. Simonds, who had followed her there.

"Don't feel bad, 'Relia," said the woman, who was almost crying herself.   "I know it's awful hard, when you was taking so much comfort.   We all feel for you."

Aurelia looked straight ahead.   She had the bundle of little clothes and the hop pillow in her arms; the old lady had said, in a way that would have been funny if it had not been for the poor heart that listened, that she didn't want any yarb pillows, nor any clothes scented with yarbs nuther.

"I don't mean to be wicked," said Aurelia, "but I can't help thinking that Providence ought to provide for women. I wish Myrtie was *mine.*"

The other woman wiped her eyes at the hungry way in which she said "mine."

"Well, I can't do anything; but I'm sorry for you, if that's all.   You'd make enough sight better mother for

Myrtie than that cross old woman. I don't b'lieve she more'n half wants her, only she's *sot*. She doesn't care anything about having the other children; she's going to leave them with Mis' Loomis; but she says her grandchildren ain't going to be living with strangers, an' she ought to hev been consulted. After all you've done for the child, to treat you as she has to-night, she's the most ungrateful— I know one thing; I'd charge her for Myrtie's board—a good price, too."

"Oh, I don't want anything of that sort," said poor Aurelia, dejectedly, listening to her darling's sobs. "You go in an' try to hush her, Mis' Simonds. Oh!"

"So I will. Her grandmother can't do anything with her, poor little thing! I've got some peppermints. I do believe she's spankin' her—the—"

Aurelia did not run in with Mrs. Simonds; she listened outside till the pitiful cries hushed a little; then she went desolately home.

She sat down in the kitchen, with the little clothes in her lap. She did not think of going to bed; she did not cry nor moan to herself; she just sat there still. It was not very late when she came home—between eight and nine. In about half an hour, perhaps, she heard a sound outside that made her heart leap—a little voice crying pitifully, and saying, between the sobs, "Mamma! mamma!"

Aurelia made one spring to the door. There was the tiny creature in her little nightgown, shaking all over with cold and sobs.

Aurelia caught her up, and all her calm was over. "Oh, you darling! you darling! you darling!" she cried, covering her little cold body all over with kisses. "You sha'n't leave me—you sha'n't! you sha'n't! Little sweetheart—all I've got in the world. I guess they sha'n't take you away when you don't want to go. Did you cry, and mamma go off and leave you? Did they whip you? They never shall again — never! never! There, there, blessed, don't cry; mamma'll get you all warm, and you shall go to sleep on your own little pillow. Oh, you darling! darling! darling!"

Aurelia busied herself about the child, rubbing the little numb limbs, and getting some milk heated. She never asked how she came to get away; she never thought of anything except that she had her. She stopped every other minute to kiss her and croon to her; she laughed and cried. Now she gave way to her feelings; she was almost beside herself. She had the child all warm and fed and comforted by the kitchen fire when she heard steps outside, and she knew at once what was coming, and a fierce resolve sprang up in her heart: they should not have that child again to-night. She cast a hurried glance around; there was hardly a second's time. In the corner of the kitchen was a great heap of herbs which she had taken down from the walls where they had been drying; the next day she had intended to pack them and send them off. She caught up Myrtie and covered her with them. "Lie still, darling!" she whispered. "Don't make a bit of noise, or your grandmother will get you again." Myrtie crouched under them, trembling.

Then the door opened; Mr. Simonds stood there with a lantern. "That little girl's run away," he began—"slipped out while the old lady was out of the room a minute. Beats all how such a little thing knew enough. She's here, ain't she?"

"No," said Aurelia, "she ain't."

"You don't mean it?"

"Yes."

"Ain't you seen her, though?"

"No."

Mr. Simonds, who was fat and placid, began to look grave. "Then, all there is about it, we've got to have a hunt," said he. "'Twon't do to have that little tot out in her nightgown long. We hadn't a thought but that she was here. Must have lost her way."

Aurelia watched him stride down the yard. Then she ran after him. "Mr. Simonds!" He turned. "I told you a lie. Myrtie's in the corner of the kitchen under a heap of herbs."

"Why, what on earth—"

"I wanted to keep her so to-night." Aurelia burst right out in loud sobs.

"There, 'Relia! It's a confounded shame. You shall keep her. I'll make it all right with the old lady some-how. I reckon, as long as the child's safe, she'll be glad to get rid of her to-night. She wouldn't have slept much. Go right into the house, 'Relia, and don't worry."

Aurelia obeyed. She hung over the little creature, asleep in her crib, all night. She watched her every breath. She never thought of sleeping herself — her last night with Myrtie. The seconds were so many grains of gold-dust. Her heart failed her when day broke. She washed and dressed Myrtie at the usual time, and gave her her breakfast. Then she sat down with her and waited. The child's sorrow was soon forgotten, and she played about as usual. Aurelia watched her despairingly. She began to wonder at length why they did not come for her. It grew later and later. She would not carry her back her-self, she was resolved on that.

It was ten o'clock before any one came; then it was Mrs. Simonds. She had a strange look on her face.

"Relia," she said, standing in the door and looking at her and Myrtie, "you ain't heard what has happened to our house this mornin', hev you?"

"No," said Aurelia, awed.

"Old Mis' Sears is dead. Had her third shock: she's had two in the last three years. She was took soon after Mr. Simonds got home. We got a doctor right off, but she died 'bout an hour ago."

"Oh," said Aurelia, "I've been a wicked woman."

"No you ain't, Aurelia; don't you go to feeling so. There's no call for the living to be unjust to themselves because folks are dead. You did the best you could. An' now you're glad you can keep the child; you can't help it. I thought of it myself the first thing."

"Oh, I was such a wicked woman to think of it myself," said Aurelia. "If I could only have done something for the poor old soul! Why didn't you call me?"

"I told Mr. Simonds I wouldn't; you'd had enough."

There was one thing, however, which Aurelia found to do —a simple and touching thing, though it probably meant more to her than to most of those who knew of it.

On the day of the funeral the poor old woman's grave was found lined with fragrant herbs from Aurelia's garden —thyme and lavender and rosemary. She had cried when she picked them, because she could not help being glad, and they were all she could give for atonement.

A CONFLICT ENDED.

In Acton there were two churches, a Congregational and a Baptist. They stood on opposite sides of the road, and the Baptist edifice was a little farther down than the other. On Sunday morning both bells were ringing. The Baptist bell was much larger, and followed quickly on the soft peal of the Congregational with a heavy brazen clang which vibrated a good while. The people went flocking through the street to the irregular jangle of the bells. It was a very hot day, and the sun beat down heavily; parasols were bobbing over all the ladies' heads.

More people went into the Baptist church, whose society was much the larger of the two. It had been for the last ten years—ever since the Congregational had settled a new minister. His advent had divided the church, and a good third of the congregation had gone over to the Baptist brethren, with whom they still remained.

It is probable that many of them passed their old sanctuary to-day with the original stubborn animosity as active as ever in their hearts, and led their families up the Baptist steps with the same strong spiritual pull of indignation.

One old lady, who had made herself prominent on the opposition, trotted by this morning with the identical wiry vehemence which she had manifested ten years ago. She wore a full black silk skirt, which she held up inanely in front, and allowed to trail in the dust in the rear.

Some of the stanch Congregational people glanced at her amusedly. One fleshy, fair-faced girl in blue muslin said to her companion, with a laugh: " See that old lady trailing her best black silk by to the Baptist. Ain't it ridiculous how she keeps on showing out? I heard some one talking about it yesterday."

" Yes."

The girl colored up confusedly. " Oh dear !" she thought to herself. The lady with her had an unpleasant history connected with this old church quarrel. She was a small, bony woman in a shiny purple silk, which was strained very tightly across her sharp shoulder-blades. Her bonnet was quite elaborate with flowers and plumes, as was also her companion's. In fact, she was the village milliner, and the girl was her apprentice.

When the two went up the church steps, they passed a man of about fifty, who was sitting thereon well to one side. He had a singular face—a mild forehead, a gently curving mouth, and a terrible chin, with a look of strength in it that might have abashed mountains. He held his straw hat in his hand, and the sun was shining full on his bald head.

The milliner half stopped, and gave an anxious glance at him ; then passed on. In the vestibule she stopped again.

" You go right in, Margy," she said to the girl. " I'll be along in a minute."

" Where be you going, Miss Barney ?"

" You go right in. I'll be there in a minute."

Margy entered the audience-room then, as if fairly brushed in by the imperious wave of a little knotty hand, and Esther Barney stood waiting until the rush of entering people was over. Then she stepped swiftly back to the side of the man seated on the steps. She spread her large black parasol deliberately, and extended the handle towards him.

" No, no, Esther ; I don't want it—I don't want it."

" If you're determined on setting out in this broiling sun, Marcus Woodman, you jest take this parasol of mine an' use it."

" I don't want your parasol, Esther. I—"

" Don't you say it over again. Take it."

" I won't—not if I don't want to."

" You'll get a sun-stroke."

" That's my own lookout."

" Marcus Woodman, you take it."

She threw all the force there was in her intense, nervous nature into her tone and look ; but she failed in her attempt, because of the utter difference in quality between her own will and that with which she had to deal. They were on such different planes that hers slid by his with its own momentum ; there could be no contact even of antagonism between them. He sat there rigid, every line of his face stiffened into an icy obstinacy. She held out the parasol towards him like a weapon.

Finally she let it drop at her side, her whole expression changed.

" Marcus," said she, " how's your mother ?"

He started. " Pretty well, thank you, Esther."

" She's out to meeting, then ?"

" Yes."

" I've been a-thinking—I ain't drove jest now—that maybe I'd come over an' see her some day this week."

He rose politely then. " Wish you would, Esther. Mother'd be real pleased, I know."

"Well, I'll see—Wednesday, p'rhaps, if I ain't too busy. I must go in now; they're 'most through singing."

"Esther—"

"I don't believe I can stop any longer, Marcus."

"About the parasol—thank you jest the same if I don't take it. Of course you know I can't set out here holding a parasol; folks would laugh. But I'm obliged to you all the same. Hope I didn't say anything to hurt your feelings?"

"Oh no; why, no, Marcus. Of course I don't want to make you take it if you don't want it. I don't know but it would look kinder queer, come to think of it. Oh dear! they are through singing."

"Say, Esther, I don't know but I might as well take that parasol, if you'd jest as soon. The sun is pretty hot, an' I might get a headache. I forgot my umbrella, to tell the truth."

"I might have known better than to have gone at him the way I did," thought Esther to herself, when she was seated at last in the cool church beside Margy. "Seems as if I might have got used to Marcus Woodman by this time."

She did not see him when she came out of church; but a little boy in the vestibule handed her the parasol, with the remark, "Mr. Woodman said for me to give this to you."

She and Margy passed down the street towards home. Going by the Baptist church, they noticed a young man standing by the entrance. He stared hard at Margy.

She began to laugh after they had passed him. "Did you see that fellow stare?" said she. "Hope he'll know me next time."

"That's George Elliot ; he's that old lady's son you was speaking about this morning."

"Well, that's enough for me."

"He's a real good, steady young man."

Margy sniffed.

"P'rhaps you'll change your mind some day."

She did, and speedily, too. That glimpse of Margy Wilson's pretty, new face—for she was a stranger in the town—had been too much for George Elliot. He obtained an introduction, and soon was a steady visitor at Esther Barney's house. Margy fell in love with him easily. She had never had much attention from the young men, and he was an engaging young fellow, small and bright-eyed, though with a nervous persistency like his mother's in his manner.

"I'm going to have it an understood thing," Margy told Esther, after her lover had become constant in his attentions, "that I'm going with George, and I ain't going with his mother. I can't bear that old woman."

But poor Margy found that it was not so easy to thrust determined old age off the stage, even when young Love was flying about so fast on his butterfly wings that he seemed to multiply himself, and there was no room for anything else, because the air was so full of Loves. That old mother, with her trailing black skirt and her wiry obstinacy, trotted as unwaveringly through the sweet stir as a ghost through a door.

One Monday morning Margy could not eat any breakfast, and there were tear stains around her blue eyes.

"Why, what's the matter, Margy?" asked Esther, eying her across the little kitchen-table.

"Nothing's the matter. I ain't hungry any to speak of,

that's all. I guess I'll go right to work on Mis' Fuller's bonnet."

" I'd try an' eat something if I was you. Be sure you cut that velvet straight, if you go to work on it."

When the two were sitting together at their work in the little room back of the shop, Margy suddenly threw her scissors down. " There !" said she, " I've done it ; I knew I should. I've cut this velvet bias. I knew I should cut everything bias I touched to-day."

There was a droll pucker on her mouth ; then it began to quiver. She hid her face in her hands and sobbed. " Oh, dear, dear, dear !"

" Margy Wilson, what is the matter ?"

" George and I—had a talk last night. We've broke the engagement, an' it's killing me. An' now I've cut this velvet bias. Oh, dear, dear, *dear*, dear !"

" For the land's sake, don't mind anything about the velvet. What's come betwixt you an' George ?"

" His mother—horrid old thing ! He said she'd got to live with us, and I said she shouldn't. Then he said he wouldn't marry any girl that wasn't willing to live with his mother, and I said he wouldn't ever marry me, then. If George Elliot thinks more of his mother than he does of me, he can have her. I don't care. I'll show him I can get along without him."

" Well, I don't know, Margy. I'm real sorry about it. George Elliot's a good, likely young man ; but if you didn't want to live with his mother, it was better to say so right in the beginning. And I don't know as I blame you much : she's pretty set in her ways."

" I guess she is. I never could bear her. I guess he'll find out—"

Margy dried her eyes defiantly, and took up the velvet again. " I've spoilt this velvet. I don't see why being disappointed in love should affect a girl so's to make her cut bias."

There was a whimsical element in Margy which seemed to roll uppermost along with her grief.

Esther looked a little puzzled. " Never mind the velvet, child : it ain't much, anyway." She began tossing over some ribbons to cover her departure from her usual reticence. " I'm real sorry about it, Margy. Such things are hard to bear, but they can be lived through. I know something about it myself. You knew I'd had some of this kind of trouble, didn't you ?"

" About Mr. Woodman, you mean ?"

" Yes, about Marcus Woodman. I'll tell you what 'tis, Margy Wilson, you've got one thing to be thankful for, and that is that there ain't anything ridickerlous about this affair of yourn. That makes it the hardest of anything, according to my mind—when you know that everybody's laughing, and you can hardly help laughing yourself, though you feel 'most ready to die."

" Ain't that Mr. Woodman crazy ?"

" No, he ain't crazy ; he's got too much will for his common-sense, that's all, and the will teeters the sense a little too far into the air. I see all through it from the beginning. I could read Marcus Woodman jest like a book."

" I don't see how in the world you ever come to like such a man."

"Well, I s'pose love's the strongest when there ain't any good reason for it. They say it is. I can't say as I ever really admired Marcus Woodman much. I always see right through him ; but that didn't hinder my thinking so much of him that I never felt as if I could marry any other man. And I've had chances, though I shouldn't want you to say so."

"You turned him off because he went to sitting on the church steps?"

"Course I did. Do you s'pose I was going to marry a man who made a laughing-stock of himself that way?"

"I don't see how he ever come to do it. It's the funniest thing I ever heard of."

"I know it. It seems so silly nobody 'd believe it. Well, all there is about it, Marcus Woodman's got so much mulishness in him it makes him almost miraculous. You see, he got up an' spoke in that church meeting when they had such a row about Mr. Morton's being settled here— Marcus was awful set again' him. I never could see any reason why, and I don't think he could. He said Mr. Morton wa'n't doctrinal; that was what they all said; but I don't believe half of 'em knew what doctrinal was. I never could see why Mr. Morton wa'n't as good as most ministers —enough sight better than them that treated him so, anyway. I always felt that they was really setting him in a pulpit high over their heads by using him the way they did, though they didn't know it.

"Well, Marcus spoke in that church meeting, an' he kept getting more and more set every word he said. He always had a way of saying things over and over, as if he was making steps out of 'em, an' raising of himself up on 'em, till there was no moving him at all. And he did that night. Finally, when he was up real high, he said, as for him, if Mr. Morton was settled over that church, he'd never go inside the door himself as long as he lived. Somebody spoke out then—I never quite knew who 'twas, though I suspected—an' says, 'You'll have to set on the steps, then, Brother Woodman.'

" Everybody laughed at that but Marcus. He didn't see nothing to laugh at. He spoke out awful set, kinder gritting his teeth, ' I will set on the steps fifty years before I'll go into this house if that man's settled here.'

" I couldn't believe he'd really do it. We were going to be married that spring, an' it did seem as if he might listen to me ; but he wouldn't. The Sunday Mr. Morton begun to preach, he begun to set on them steps, an' he's set there ever since, in all kinds of weather. It's a wonder it 'ain't killed him ; but I guess it's made him tough."

" Why, didn't he feel bad when you wouldn't marry him ?"

" Feel bad ? Of course he did. He took on terribly. But it didn't make any difference ; he wouldn't give in a hair's breadth. I declare it did seem as if I should die. His mother felt awfully too—she's a real good woman. I don't know what Marcus would have done without her. He wants a sight of tending and waiting on ; he's dreadful babyish in some ways, though you wouldn't think it.

" Well, it's all over now, as far as I'm concerned. I've got over it a good deal, though sometimes it makes me jest as mad as ever to see him setting there. But I try to be reconciled, and I get along jest as well, mebbe, as if I'd had him—I don't know. I fretted more at first than there was any sense in, and I hope you won't."

" I ain't going to fret at all, Miss Barney. I may cut bias for a while, but I sha'n't do anything worse."

" How you do talk, child !"

A good deal of it was talk with Margy ; she had not as much courage as her words proclaimed. She was capable of a strong temporary resolution, but of no enduring one. She gradually weakened as the days without her lover went on, and one Saturday night she succumbed entirely. There was quite a rush of business, but through it all she caught a conversation between some customers—two pretty young girls.

"Who was that with you last night at the concert?"

"That—oh, that was George Elliot. Didn't you know him?"

"He's got another girl," thought Margy, with a great throb.

The next Sunday night, coming out of meeting with Miss Barney, she left her suddenly. George Elliot was one of a waiting line of young men in the vestibule. She went straight up to him. He looked at her in bewilderment, his dark face turning red.

"Good-evening, Miss Wilson," he stammered out, finally.

"Good-evening," she whispered, and stood looking up at him piteously. She was white and trembling.

At last he stepped forward suddenly and offered her his arm. In spite of his resentment, he could not put her to open shame before all his mates, who were staring curiously.

When they were out in the dark, cool street, he bent over her. "Why, Margy, what does all this mean?"

"Oh, George, let her live with us, please. I want her to. I know I can get along with her if I try. I'll do everything I can. Please let her live with us."

"Who's *her?*"

"Your mother."

"And I suppose *us* is you and I? I thought that was all over, Margy; ain't it?"

"Oh, George, I am sorry I treated you so."

"And you are willing to let mother live with us now?"

"I'll do anything. Oh, George!"

" Don't cry, Margy. There—nobody's looking—give us a kiss. It's been a long time ; ain't it, dear? So you've made up your mind that you're willing to let mother live with us ?"

"Yes."

" Well, I don't believe she ever will, Margy. She's about made up her mind to go and live with my brother Edward, whether or no. So you won't be troubled with her. I dare say she might have been a little of a trial as she grew older."

"You didn't tell me."

" I thought it was your place to give in, dear."

"Yes, it was, George."

" I'm mighty glad you did. I tell you what it is, dear, I don't know how you've felt, but I've been pretty miserable lately."

" Poor George !"

They passed Esther Barney's house, and strolled along half a mile farther. When they returned, and Margy stole softly into the house and up-stairs, it was quite late, and Esther had gone to bed. Margy saw the light was not out in her room, so she peeped in. She could not wait till morning to tell her.

"Where have you been ?" said Esther, looking up at her out of her pillows.

"Oh, I went to walk a little way with George."

"Then you've made up ?"

"Yes."

" Is his mother going to live with you ?"

" No ; I guess not. She's going to live with Edward. But I told him I was willing she should. I've about made up my mind it's a woman's place to give in mostly. I s'pose you think I'm an awful fool."

"No, I don't; no, I don't, Margy. I'm real glad it's all right betwixt you and George. I've seen you weren't very happy lately."

They talked a little longer; then Margy said "Good-night," going over to Esther and kissing her. Being so rich in love made her generous with it. She looked down sweetly into the older woman's thin, red-cheeked face. "I wish you were as happy as I," said she. "I wish you and Mr. Woodman could make up too."

'That's an entirely different matter. I couldn't give in in such a thing as that."

Margy looked at her; she was not subtle, but she had just come out triumphant through innocent love and sub-mission, and used the wisdom she had gained thereby.

"Don't you believe," said she, "if you was to give in the way I did, that he would?"

Esther started up with an astonished air. That had nev-er occurred to her before. "Oh, I don't believe he would. You don't know him; he's awful set. Besides, I don't know but I'm better off the way it is."

In spite of herself, however, she could not help thinking of Margy's suggestion. Would he give in? She was hard-ly disposed to run the risk. With her peculiar cast of mind, her feeling for the ludicrous so keen that it almost amount-ed to a special sense, and her sensitiveness to ridicule, it would have been easier for her to have married a man un-der the shadow of a crime than one who was the deserving target of gibes and jests. Besides, she told herself, it was possible that he had changed his mind, that he no longer cared for her. How could she make the first overtures? She had not Margy's impulsiveness and innocence of youth to excuse her.

Also, she was partly influenced by the reason which she had given Margy : she was not so very sure that it would be best for her to take any such step. She was more fixed in the peace and pride of her old maidenhood than she had realized, and was more shy of disturbing it. Her comfortable meals, her tidy housekeeping, and her prosperous work had become such sources of satisfaction to her that she was almost wedded to them, and jealous of any interference.

So it is doubtful if there would have been any change in the state of affairs if Marcus Woodman's mother had not died towards spring. Esther was greatly distressed about it.

" I don't see what Marcus is going to do," she told Margy. " He ain't any fitter to take care of himself than a baby, and he won't have any housekeeper, they say."

One evening, after Marcus's mother had been dead about three weeks, Esther went over there. Margy had gone out to walk with George, so nobody knew. When she reached the house—a white cottage on a hill—she saw a light in the kitchen window.

" He's there," said she. She knocked on the door softly. Marcus shuffled over to it—he was in his stocking feet— and opened it.

" Good-evening, Marcus," said she, speaking first.

" Good-evening."

" I hadn't anything special to do this evening, so I thought I'd look in a minute and see how you was getting along."

" I ain't getting along very well ; but I'm glad to see you. Come right in."

When she was seated opposite him by the kitchen fire, she surveyed him and his surroundings pityingly. Everything had an abject air of forlornness ; there was neither

tidiness nor comfort.   After a few words she rose energet-
ically.   " See here, Marcus," said she, "you jest fill up
that tea-kettle, and I'm going to slick up here a little for
you while I stay."

" Now, Esther, I don't feel as if—"

" Don't you say nothing.   Here's the tea-kettle.   I might
jest as well be doing that as setting still."

He watched her, in a way that made her nervous, as she
flew about putting things to rights ; but she said to herself
that this was easier than sitting still, and gradually leading
up to the object for which she had come.   She kept wondering if she could ever accomplish it.   When the room was
in order, finally, she sat down again, with a strained-up look
in her face.

" Marcus," said she, " I might as well begin.   There was
something I wanted to say to you to-night."

He looked at her, and she went on :

" I've been thinking some lately about how matters used
to be betwixt you an' me, and it's jest possible—I don't
know—but I might have been a little more patient than I
was.   I don't know as I'd feel the same way now if—"

" Oh, Esther, what do you mean ?"

" I ain't going to tell you, Marcus Woodman, if you can't
find out.   I've said full enough ; more'n I ever thought I
should."

He was an awkward man, but he rose and threw himself
on his knees at her feet with all the grace of complete
unconsciousness of action.   " Oh, Esther, you don't mean,
do you ?—you don't mean that you'd be willing to—marry
me ?"

" No ; not if you don't get up.   You look ridickerlous."

" Esther, do you mean it ?"

"Yes. Now get up."

"You ain't thinking—I can't give up what we had the trouble about, any more now than I could then."

"Ain't I said once that wouldn't make any difference?"

At that he put his head down on her knees and sobbed.

"Do, for mercy sake, stop. Somebody 'll be coming in. 'Tain't as if we was a young couple."

"I ain't going to till I've told you about it, Esther. You ain't never really understood. In the first of it, we was both mad ; but we ain't now, and we can talk it over. Oh, Esther, I've had such an awful life ! I've looked at you, and— Oh, dear, dear, dear !"

"Marcus, you scare me to death crying so."

"I won't. Esther, look here—it's the gospel truth : I ain't a thing again' Mr. Morton now."

"Then why on earth don't you go into the meeting-house and behave yourself?"

"Don't you suppose I would if I could? I can't, Esther —I can't."

"I don't know what you mean by can't."

"Do you s'pose I've took any comfort sitting there on them steps in the winter snows an' the summer suns? Do you s'pose I've took any comfort not marrying you? Don't you s'pose I'd given all I was worth any time the last ten year to have got up an' walked into the church with the rest of the folks?"

"Well, I'll own, Marcus, I don't see why you couldn't if you wanted to."

"I ain't sure as I see myself, Esther. All I know is I can't make myself give it up. I can't. I ain't made strong enough to."

"As near as I can make out, you've taken to sitting on

the church steps the way other men take to smoking and drinking."

"I don't know but you're right, Esther, though I hadn't thought of it in that way before."

"Well, you must try to overcome it."

"I never can, Esther. It ain't right for me to let you think I can."

"Well, we won't talk about it any more to-night. It's time I was going home."

"Esther—did you mean it?"

"Mean what?"

"That you'd marry me any way?"

"Yes, I did. Now do get up. I do hate to see you looking so silly."

Esther had a new pearl-colored silk gown, and a little mantle like it, and a bonnet trimmed with roses and plumes, and she and Marcus were married in June.

The Sunday on which she came out a bride they were late at church; but late as it was, curious people were lingering by the steps to watch them. What would they do? Would Marcus Woodman enter that church door which his awful will had guarded for him so long?

They walked slowly up the steps between the watching people. When they came to the place where he was accustomed to sit, Marcus stopped short and looked down at his wife with an agonized face.

"Oh, Esther, I've—got—to stop."

"Well, we'll both sit down here, then."

"*You?*"

"Yes; I'm willing."

"No; you go in."

"No, Marcus; I sit with you on our wedding Sunday."

Her sharp, middle-aged face as she looked up at him was fairly heroic. This was all that she could do : her last weapon was used. If this failed, she would accept the chances with which she had married, and before the eyes of all these tittering people she would sit down at his side on these church steps. She was determined, and she would not weaken.

He stood for a moment staring into her face. He trembled so that the bystanders noticed it. He actually leaned over towards his old seat as if wire ropes were pulling him down upon it. Then he stood up straight, like a man, and walked through the church door with his wife.

The people followed. Not one of them even smiled. They had felt the pathos in the comedy.

The sitters in the pews watched Marcus wonderingly as he went up the aisle with Esther. He looked strange to them ; he had almost the grand mien of a conqueror.

A PATIENT WAITER.

"Be sure you sweep it clean, Lily."

"Yes, 'm. I ain't leavin' a single stone on it."

"I'm 'most afraid to trust you. I think likely as not he may come to-day, an' not wait to write. It's so pleasant, I feel jest as if somebody was comin'."

"I'm a-sweepin' it real clean, Aunt Fidelia."

"Well, be pertickler. An' you'd better sweep the sidewalk a little ways in front of the yard. I saw a lot of loose stones on it yesterday."

"Yes, 'm."

The broom was taller than the child, but she was sturdy, and she wielded it with joyful vigor. Down the narrow path between the rows of dahlias she went. Her smooth yellow head shone in the sun. Her long blue gingham apron whisked about her legs as she swept.

The dahlias were in full bloom, and they nodded their golden and red balls gently when the child jostled them. Beyond the dahlias on either side were zinnias and candy-tuft and marigolds. The house was very small. There was only one window at the side of the front door. A curved green trellis stood against the little space of house wall on the other side, and a yellow honeysuckle climbed on it.

Fidelia Almy stood in the door with a cloth in her hand.

She had been dusting the outside of the door and the threshold, rubbing off every speck punctiliously.

Fidelia stood there in the morning light with her head nodding like a flower in a wind. It nodded so all the time. She had a disease of the nerves. Her yellow-gray hair was crimped, and put up carefully in a little coil, with two long curls on either side. Her long, delicate face, which always had a downward droop as it nodded, had a soft polish like ivory.

When Lily Almy, who was Fidelia's orphan niece, whom she was bringing up, had reached the gate with her broom, she peered down the road ; then she ran back eagerly.

"Oh, Aunt Fidelia," she said, in a precise, slow voice, which was copied from her aunt's, "there's a man comin'. Do you s'pose it's him ?"

"What kind of a lookin' man ?" Fidelia's head nodded faster ; a bright red spot gleamed out on either cheek.

"A real handsome man. He's tall, and he's got reddish whiskers. And he's got a carpet bag."

"That's the way he looks."

"Oh, Aunt Fidelia, do you s'pose it's him."

"'Tain't very likely to be."

"Here he is."

Fidelia ran into the house, and knelt down by the parlor window, just peering over the sill. Her whole body seemed wavering like her head ; her breath came in great gasps. The man, who was young and handsome, walked past.

Lily ran in. "'Twa'n't him, was it ?" said she.

"I didn't much expect it was. I've always thought he'd come on a Tuesday. I've dreamed 'bout his comin' Tuesday more times than I can tell. Now I'm goin' to fix the flowers in the vases, and then I'm goin' down to the post-office. I feel jest as if I might git a letter to-day. There was one in the candle last night."

Fidelia moved, nodding, among her flowers in her front yard. She gathered up her purple calico apron, and cut the flowers into it.

"You run out into the garden an' git some sparrow-grass for green," she told Lily, "an' pick some of that striped grass under the parlor window, an' some of them spider-lilies by the fence."

The little white-painted mantel-shelf in Fidelia's parlor was like an altar, upon which she daily heaped floral offerings. And who knows what fair deity in bright clouds she saw when she made her sacrifice?

Fidelia had only two vases, tall gilt and white china ones, with scrolling tops; these stood finely in the centre, holding their drooping nosegays. Beside these were broken china bowls, cream jugs without handles, tumblers, wine-glasses, saucers, and one smart china mug with "Friendship's Offering" in gold letters. Slightly withered flowers were in all of them. Fidelia threw them out, and filled all the vessels with fresh ones. The green asparagus sprays brushed the shelf, the striped grass overtopped the gay flowers.

"There," said Fidelia, "now I'm goin' to the post-office."

"If anybody comes, I'll ask him in here, an' tell him you'll be right back, sha'n't I?" said Lily.

"Tell him I'll be back in jest a few minutes, an' give him the big rockin'-chair."

The post-office was a mile away, in the corner of a country store. Twice a day, year out and year in, Fidelia journeyed thither.

"It's only Fidelia Almy," people said, looking out of the

windows, as the poor solitary figure with its nodding head went by through summer suns and winter winds.

Once in a while they hailed her. " See if there's any thing for me, won't you, Fidelia ?"

At last it was an understood thing that Fidelia should carry the mail to the dozen families between her house and the post-office. She often had her black worked bag filled up with letters, but there was never one of her own. Fidelia Almy never had a letter.

" That woman's been comin' here the last thirty years," the postmaster told a stranger one day, " an' she ain't never had a letter sence I've been here, an' I don't believe she ever did before."

Fidelia used to come in a little before the mail was distributed, and sit on an old settee near the door, waiting. Her face at those times had a wild, strained look ; but after the letters were all in the boxes it settled back into its old expression, and she travelled away with her bag of other people's letters, nodding patiently.

On her route was one young girl who had a lover in a neighboring town. Her letters came regularly. She used to watch for Fidelia, and run to meet her, her pretty face all blushes. Fidelia always had the letter separated from the others, and ready for her. She always smiled when she held it out. "They keep a-comin'," she said one day, " an' there don't seem to be no end to it. But if I was you, Louisa, I'd try an' git him to settle over here, if you ain't married before long. There's slips, an' it ain't always safe trustin' to letters."

The girl told her lover what Fidelia had said, with tender laughter and happy pity. " Poor thing," she said. " She had a beau, you know, Willy, and he went away thirty years ago, and ever since then she's been looking for a letter from him, and she's kind of cracked over it. And she's afraid it'll turn out the same way with me."

Then she and her sweetheart laughed together at the idea of this sad, foolish destiny for this pretty, courageous young thing.

To-day Fidelia, with her black broadcloth bag, worked on one side with a wreath and on the other with a bunch of flowers, walked slowly to the office and back. As the years went on she walked slower. This double journey of hers seemed to tire her more. Once in a while she would sit down and rest on the stone wall. The clumps of dusty way-side flowers, meadow-sweet and tansy, stood around her; over her head was the blue sky. But she clutched her black letter-bag, and nodded her drooping head, and never looked up. Her sky was elsewhere.

When she came in sight of her own house Lily, who was watching at the gate, came running to meet her.

"Oh, Aunt Fidelia," said she, "Aunt Sally's in there."

"Did she take off her shoes an' let you brush 'em before she went in?"

"She wouldn't. She went right straight in. She jest laughed when I asked her to take her shoes off. An', Aunt Fidelia, she's done somethin' else. I couldn't help it."

"What?"

"She's been eatin' some of Mr. Lennox's plum-cake up. I couldn't stop her, Aunt Fidelia. I told her she mus'n't."

"You didn't say nothin' 'bout Mr. Lennox, did you?"

"No, I didn't, Aunt Fidelia. Oh, did you get a letter!"

"No; I didn't much think I would to-day. Oh dear! there's Sally eatin' cake right in the front entry."

A stout old woman, with a piece of cake in her hand,

stood in the front door as Fidelia and Lily came up between the dahlias.

" How d'ye do, Fidelia ?" cried she, warmly.

" Pretty well, thank you. How do you do, Sally ?" Fidelia answered. She shook hands, and looked at the other with a sort of meek uneasiness. " Hadn't you jest as soon step out here whilst you're eatin' that cake ?" asked she, timidly. " I've jest swept the entry."

"No ; I ain't goin' to step out there an inch," said the other, mumbling the cake vigorously between her old jaws. " If you ain't the worst old maid, Fidelia ! Ain't seen all the sister you've got in the world for a year, an' wantin' her to go out-doors to eat a piece of cake. Hard work to git the cake, too."

" It don't make any difference," said Fidelia. " I'm real kind o' used up every time I sweep nowadays, that's all."

" Better stop sweepin', then ; there ain't no need of so much fussin'. It's more'n half that's got your nerves out of kilter—sweepin' an' scrubbin' from mornin' till night, an' wantin' folks to take off their shoes before they come in, as if they was goin' into a heathen temple. Well, I ain't goin' to waste all my breath scoldin' when I've come over to see you. How air you now, Fidelia ?"

" I'm 'bout the same as ever." Fidelia, following her sister into the parlor, stooped slyly to pick up some crumbs which had fallen on the entry floor.

" Just as shaky, ain't you ? Why, Fidelia Almy, what in creation have you got this room rigged up so fur ?"

" Rigged up how ?"

" Why, everything covered up this way. What hev you got this old sheet over the carpet fur ?"

" It was fadin' dreadfully."

"Fadin'! Good land! If you ain't got every chair sewed up in caliker, an' the pictures in old piller-cases, an'— Fidelia Almy, if you ain't got the solar lamp a-settin' in a little bag!"

"The gilt was gittin' real kind o' tarnished."

"Tarnished! An' every single thing on the table—the chiner card-basket an' Mrs. Hemans's Poems pinned up in a white rag! Good land! Well, I've always heard tell that there was two kinds of old maids—old maids an' consarned old maids—an' I guess you're one of the last sort. Why, what air you cuttin' on so fur?"

Fidelia gathered up all her trembling meekness and weakness into a show of dignity. "Things are all fadin' and wearin' out, an' I want to keep 'em decent as long as I last. I ain't got no money to buy any more. I ain't got no husband nor sons to do for me, like you, an' I've got to take care of things if I hev anything. An'—I'm goin to."

Her sister laughed. "Well, good land! I don't care. Cover up your things if you want to. There ain't no need of your gittin' riled. But this room does look enough to make a cat laugh. All them flowers on the mantel, an' all those white things. I declare, Fidelia Almy, it does look jest as if 'twas laid out. Well, we won't talk no more about it. I'm goin' out to hev a cup of tea. I put the teapot on, an' started the fire."

Poor Fidelia had a distressing day with her visiting sister. All her prim household arrangements were examined and commented on. Not a closet nor bureau drawer escaped inspection. When the guest departed, at length, the woman and the child looked at each other with relief.

"Ain't you glad she's gone?" asked Lily. She had been pink with indignation all day.

" Hush, child ; you mustn't. She's my sister, an' I'm always glad to see her, if she is a little tryin' sometimes."

" She wanted you to take the covers off an' let the things git spoiled before Mr. Lennox comes, didn't she ?"

" She don't know nothin' about that."

" Are you goin' to make another plum-cake to-night, Aunt Fidelia ?"

" I don' know. I guess we'd better sweep first."

The two worked hard and late that night. They swept every inch of floor which that profane dusty foot had trod. The child helped eagerly. She was Fidelia's confidante, and she repaid her confidence with the sweetest faith and sympathy. Nothing could exceed her innocent trust in Fidelia's pathetic story and pathetic hopes. This sad human experience was her fairy tale of childhood. That recreant lover, Ansel Lennox, who had left his sweetheart for California thirty years ago, and promised falsely to write and return, was her fairy prince. Her bright imagination pictured him beautiful as a god.

" He was about as handsome a young man as you ever see," said poor Fidelia. And a young Apollo towered up before Lily's credulous eyes. The lapse of thirty years affected the imagination of neither ; but Lily used to look at her aunt reflectively sometimes.

" I wish you could have some medicine to make you stop shakin' before that handsome Mr. Lennox comes," she said once.

" I'm in hopes that medicine I'm takin' will stop it," said Fidelia. " I think, mebbe, it's a little better now. I'm glad I thought to put that catnip in ; it makes it a good deal more quietin'."

On the narrow ledge of shelf behind Fidelia's kitchen

sink stood always a blue quart bottle of medicine. She prepared it herself from roots and herbs. She experimented and added new ingredients, and swallowed it with a touching faith that it would cure her. Beside this bottle stood another of sage tea ; that was for her hair. She used it plentifully every day in the hope that it would stop the gray hairs coming, and bring back the fine color. Fidelia used to have pretty golden hair.

Lily teased her to make the sage tea stronger. "You've been usin' it a dreadful long time, Aunt Fidelia," said she, "an' your hair's jest as gray as 'twas before."

"Takes quite a long time before you can see any difference," said Fidelia.

Many a summer morning, when the dew was heavy, she and Lily used to steal out early and bathe their faces in it. Fidelia said it would make people rosy and keep away the wrinkles.

"It works better on me than it does on you, don't it ?" asked pink-and-white Lily, innocently, once. The two were out in the shining white field together. The morning lit up Lily as it did the flowers. Her eyes had lovely blue sparkles in them ; her yellow hair, ruffled by the wind, glittered as radiantly between one and the light as the cobweb lines across the grasses. She looked wonderingly at her aunt, with her nodding gray head, plunging her little yellow hands into the dewy green things. Those dull tints and white hairs and wrinkles showed forth so plainly in the clear light that even the child's charming faith was disturbed a little. Would the dew ever make this old creature pretty again ?

But—"You can't expect it to work in a minute," replied Fidelia, cheerfully. And Lily was satisfied.

" I guess it'll work by the time Mr. Lennox comes," she said.

Fidelia was always neat and trim in her appearance, her hair was always carefully arranged, and her shoes tidy ; but summer and winter she wore one sort of gown—a purple calico. She had a fine black silk hung away in the closet up-stairs. She had one or two good woollens, and some delicate cambrics. There was even one white muslin, with some lace in neck and sleeves, hanging there. But she never wore one of them. Her sister scolded her for it, and other people wondered. Fidelia's child-confidante alone knew the reason why. This poor, nodding, enchanted princess was saving her gay attire till the prince returned and the enchantment ceased, and she was beautiful again.

" You mustn't say nothin' about it," Fidelia had said ; " but I ain't goin' to put on them good dresses an' tag 'em right out. Mebbe the time 'll come when I'll want 'em more."

" Mr. Lennox 'll think that black silk is beautiful," said Lily, " an' that white muslin."

" I had that jest after he went away, an' I ain't never put it on. I thought I wouldn't ; muslin don't look half so nice after the new look gits off it."

So Lily waited all through her childhood. She watched her aunt start forth on her daily pilgrimages to the post-office, with the confident expectation that one of these days she would return with a letter from Mr. Lennox. She regarded that sacred loaf of plum-cake which was always kepc on hand, and believed that he might appear to dispose of it at any moment. She had the sincerest faith that the time was coming when the herb medicine would quiet poor Fidelia's tremulous head, when the sage tea would turn all the gray hairs gold, and the dew would make her yellow, seamy cheeks smooth and rosy, when she would put on that magnificent black silk or that dainty girlish muslin, and sit in the parlor with Mr. Lennox, and have the covers off the chairs, and the mantel-piece blooming with flowers.

So the child and the woman lived happily with their beautiful chimera, until gradually he vanished into thin air for one of them.

Lily could not have told when the conviction first seized her that Mr. Lennox would never write, would never come; that Aunt Fidelia's gray hair would never turn gold, nor her faded cheeks be rosy; that her nodding head would nod until she was dead.

It was hardly until she was a woman herself, and had a lover of her own. It is possible that he gave the final overthrow to her faith, that it had not entirely vanished before. She told him all about Mr. Lennox. She scarcely looked upon it as a secret to be kept now. She had ascertained that many people were acquainted with Fidelia Almy's poor romance, except in its minor details.

So Lily told her lover. "Good Lord!" he said. "How long is it since he went?"

"Forty years now," said Lily. They were walking home from meeting one Sunday night.

"Forty years! Why, there ain't any more chance of hearing anything from him— Did he have any folks here?"

"No. He was a clerk in a store here. He fell in love with Aunt Fidelia, and went off to California to get some more money before he got married."

"Didn't anybody ever hear anything from him?"

"Aunt Fidelia always said not; but Aunt Sally told me

once that she knew well enough that he got married out there right after he went away ; she said she heard it pretty straight. She never had any patience with Aunt Fidelia. If she'd known half the things— Poor Aunt Fidelia ! She's getting worse lately. She goes to the post-office Sundays. I can't stop her. Every single Sunday, before meeting, down she goes."

"Why, she can't get in."

" I know it. She just tries the door, and comes back again."

" Why, dear, she's crazy, ain't she ?"

" No, she ain't crazy ; she's rational enough about every-thing else. All the way I can put it is, she's just been point-ed one way all her life, and going one way, and now she's getting nearer the end of the road, she's pointed sharper and she's going faster. She's had a hard time. I'm going to do all I can for her, anyhow. I'll help her get ready for Mr. Lennox as long as she lives."

Fidelia took great delight in Lily's love affair. All that seemed to trouble her was the suspicion that the young man might leave town, and the pair be brought to letter-writing.

" You mind, Lily," she would say ; " don't you let Valen-tine settle anywhere else before you're married. If you do, you'll have to come to writin' letters, an' letters ain't to be depended on. There's slips. You'd get sick of waitin' the way I have. I ain't minded it much ; but you're young, an' it would be different."

When Valentine Rowe did find employment in a town fifty miles away, poor Fidelia seemed to have taken upon herself a double burden of suspense.

In those days she was much too early for the mails, and waited, breathless, in the office for hours. When she got a letter for Lily she went home radiant; she seemed to forget her own disappointment.

Lily's letters came regularly for a long time. Valentine came to see her occasionally too. Then, one day, when Lily expected a letter, it did not come. Her aunt dragged herself home feebly.

"It ain't come, Lily," said she. "The trouble's begun. You poor child, how air you goin' to go through with it?"

Lily laughed. "Why, Aunt Fidelia!" said she, "what are you worrying for? I haven't missed a letter before. Something happened so Valentine couldn't write Sunday, that's all. It don't trouble me a mite."

However, even Lily was troubled at length. Weeks went by, and no letter came from Valentine Rowe. Fidelia tottered home despondent day after day. The girl had a brave heart, but she began to shudder, watching her. She felt as if she were looking into her own destiny.

"I'm going to write to Valentine," she said, suddenly, one day, after Fidelia had returned from her bootless journey.

Fidelia looked at her fiercely. "Lily Almy," said she, "whatever else you do, don't you do that. Don't you force yourself on any feller, when there's a chance you ain't wanted. Don't you do anything that ain't modest. You'd better live the way I've done."

"He may be sick," said Lily, pitifully.

"The folks he's with would write. Don't you write a word. I didn't write. An' mebbe you'll hear to-morrow. I guess we'd better sweep the parlor to-day."

This new anxiety seemed to wear on Fidelia more than her own had done. She now talked more about Valentine Rowe than Mr. Lennox. Her faith in Lily's case did not seem as active as in her own.

"I wouldn't go down to the post-office, seems to me," Lily said one morning—Fidelia tottered going out the door; "you don't look fit to. I'll go by an' by."

"I can go well enough," said Fidelia, in her feeble, shrill voice. "You ain't goin' to begin as long as I can help it." And she crawled slowly out of the yard between the rows of dahlias, and down the road, her head nodding, her flabby black bag hanging at her side.

That was the last time she ever went to the post-office. That day she returned with her patient, disappointed heart for the last time.

When poor Fidelia Almy left her little house again she went riding, lying quietly, her nodding head still forever. She had passed out of that strong wind of Providence which had tossed her so hard, into the eternal calm. She rode past the post-office on her way to the little green grave-yard, and never knew nor cared whether there was a letter for her or not. But the bell tolled, and the summer air was soft and sweet, and the little funeral train passed by; and maybe there was one among the fair, wide possibilities of heaven.

The first day on which Fidelia gave up going to the post-office, Lily began going in her stead. In the morning Fidelia looked up at her pitifully from her pillow, when she found that she could not rise.

"You'll have to go to the office, Lily," she whispered; "an' you'd better hurry, cr you'll be late for the mail."

That was the constant cry to which the poor girl had to listen. It was always, "Hurry, hurry, or you'll be late for the mail."

Lily was a sweet, healthy young thing, but the contagion of this strained faith and expectation seemed to seize upon her in her daily tramps to the post-office. Sometimes, going along the road, she could hardly believe herself not to be the veritable Fidelia Almy, living life over again, beginning a new watch for her lost lover's letter. She put her hand to her head to see if it nodded. She kept whispering to herself, "Hurry, hurry, or you'll be late for the mail."

Fidelia lay ill a week before she died, and the week had nearly gone, when Lily flew home from the office one night, jubilant. She ran in to the sick woman. "Oh, Aunt Fidelia!" she cried, "the letter's come!"

Fidelia had not raised herself for days, but she sat up now erect. All her failing forces seemed to gather themselves up and flash and beat, now the lifeward wind for them blew. The color came into her cheeks, her eyes shone triumphant. "Ansel's—letter!"

Lily sobbed right out in the midst of her joy: "Oh, poor Aunt Fidelia! poor Aunt Fidelia! I didn't think—I forgot. I was awful cruel. It's a letter from Valentine. He's been sick. The folks wrote, but they put on the wrong state—Massachusetts instead of Vermont. He's comin' right home, an' he's goin' to stay. He's goin' to settle here. Poor Aunt Fidelia! I didn't think."

Fidelia lay back on her pillow. "You dear child," she whispered, "you won't have to."

Valentine Rowe came the morning of the day on which she died. She eagerly demanded to see him.

"You're a-goin' to settle here, ain't you?" she asked him. "Don't you go away again before you're married; don't you do it. It ain't safe trustin' to letters; there's slips."

The young man looked down at her with tears in his honest eyes. "I'll settle here sure," said he. "Don't you worry. I'll promise you."

Fidelia looked up at him, and shut her eyes peacefully. "The dear child!" she murmured.

Along the middle of the afternoon she called Lily. She wanted her to put her head down, so she could tell her something.

"Them dresses," she whispered, "up-stairs. You'd better take em' an' use 'em. You can make that white one over for a weddin' dress. An' you'd better take the covers off the things in the parlor when you're married, an'—eat the plum-cake."

Near sunset she called Lily again. "The evenin' mail," she whispered. "It's time for it. You'd better hurry, or you'll be late. I shouldn't be—a bit—surprised if the letter came to night."

Lily broke down and cried. "Oh, dear, poor aunty!" she sobbed. The awful pitifulness of it all seemed to overwhelm her suddenly. She could keep up no longer.

But Fidelia did not seem to notice it. She went on talking. "Ansel Lennox—promised he'd write when he went away, an' he said he'd come again. It's time for the evenin' mail. You'd better hurry, or you'll be late. He—promised he'd write, an'"—she looked up at Lily suddenly; a look of triumphant resolution came into her poor face—"*I ain't goin' to give it up yet.*"

From *A New England Nun* (1891)

A NEW ENGLAND NUN.

IT was late in the afternoon, and the light was waning. There was a difference in the look of the tree shadows out in the yard. Somewhere in the distance cows were lowing and a little bell was tinkling ; now and then a farm-wagon tilted by, and the dust flew ; some blue-shirted laborers with shovels over their shoulders plodded past ; little swarms of flies were dancing up and down before the peoples' faces in the soft air. There seemed to be a gentle stir arising over everything for the mere sake of subsidence—a very premonition of rest and hush and night.

This soft diurnal commotion was over Louisa Ellis also. She had been peacefully sewing at her sitting-room window all the afternoon. Now she quilted her needle carefully into her work, which she folded precisely, and laid in a basket with her thimble and thread and scissors. Louisa Ellis could not remember that ever in her life she had mislaid one of these little feminine appurtenances, which had become, from long use and constant association, a very part of her personality.

Louisa tied a green apron round her waist, and got out a flat straw hat with a green ribbon. Then she went into the garden with a little blue crockery bowl, to pick some currants for her tea. After the currants were picked she sat on the back door-step and stemmed them, collecting the stems carefully in her apron, and afterwards throwing them into the hen-coop. She looked sharply at the grass beside the step to see if any had fallen there.

Louisa was slow and still in her movements ; it took her a long time to prepare her tea ; but when ready it was set forth with as much grace as if she had been a veritable guest to her own self. The little square table stood exactly in the centre of the kitchen, and was covered with a starched linen cloth whose border pattern of flowers glistened. Louisa had a damask napkin on her tea-tray, where were arranged a cut-glass tumbler full of teaspoons, a silver cream-pitcher, a china sugar-bowl, and one pink china cup and saucer. Louisa used china every day — something which none of her neighbors did. They whispered about it among themselves. Their daily tables were laid with common crockery, their sets of best china stayed in the parlor closet, and Louisa Ellis was no richer nor better bred than they. Still she would use the china. She had for her supper a glass dish full of sugared currants, a plate of little cakes, and one of light white biscuits. Also a leaf or two of lettuce, which she cut up daintily. Louisa was very fond of lettuce, which she raised to perfection in her little garden. She ate quite heartily, though in a delicate, pecking way ; it seemed almost surprising that any considerable bulk of the food should vanish.

After tea she filled a plate with nicely baked thin corn-cakes, and carried them out into the back-yard.

" Cæsar !" she called. " Cæsar ! Cæsar !"

There was a little rush, and the clank of a chain, and a large yellow-and-white dog appeared at the door of his tiny hut, which was half hidden among the tall grasses and flowers.

Louisa patted him and gave him the corn-cakes. Then she returned to the house and washed the tea-things, polishing the china carefully. The twilight had deepened ; the chorus of the frogs floated in at the open window wonderfully loud and shrill, and once in a while a long sharp drone from a tree-toad pierced it. Louisa took off her green gingham apron, disclosing a shorter one of pink and white print. She lighted her lamp, and sat down again with her sewing.

In about half an hour Joe Dagget came. She heard his heavy step on the walk, and rose and took off her pink-and-white apron. Under that was still another—white linen with a little cambric edging on the bottom ; that was Louisa's company apron. She never wore it without her calico sewing apron over it unless she had a guest. She had barely folded the pink and white one with methodical haste and laid it in a table-drawer when the door opened and Joe Dagget entered.

He seemed to fill up the whole room. A little yellow canary that had been asleep in his green cage at the south window woke up and fluttered wildly, beating his little yellow wings against the wires. He always did so when Joe Dagget came into the room.

" Good-evening," said Louisa. She extended her hand with a kind of solemn cordiality.

" Good - evening, Louisa," returned the man, in a loud voice.

She placed a chair for him, and they sat facing each other, with the table between them. He sat bolt-upright, toeing out his heavy feet squarely, glancing with a good-humored uneasiness around the room. She sat gently erect, folding her slender hands in her white-linen lap.

"Been a pleasant day," remarked Dagget.

"Real pleasant," Louisa assented, softly. "Have you been haying?" she asked, after a little while.

"Yes, I've been haying all day, down in the ten-acre lot. Pretty hot work."

"It must be."

"Yes, it's pretty hot work in the sun."

"Is your mother well to-day?"

"Yes, mother's pretty well."

"I suppose Lily Dyer's with her now?"

Dagget colored. "Yes, she's with her," he answered, slowly.

He was not very young, but there was a boyish look about his large face. Louisa was not quite as old as he, her face was fairer and smoother, but she gave people the impression of being older.

"I suppose she's a good deal of help to your mother," she said, further.

"I guess she is; I don't know how mother'd get along without her," said Dagget, with a sort of embarrassed warmth.

"She looks like a real capable girl. She's pretty-looking too," remarked Louisa.

"Yes, she is pretty fair looking."

Presently Dagget began fingering the books on the table. There was a square red autograph album, and a Young Lady's Gift-Book which had belonged to Louisa's mother. He took them up one after the other and opened them; then laid them down again, the album on the Gift-Book.

Louisa kept eying them with mild uneasiness. Finally she rose and changed the position of the books, putting the album underneath. That was the way they had been arranged in the first place.

Dagget gave an awkward little laugh. " Now what difference did it make which book was on top ?" said he.

Louisa looked at him with a deprecating smile. " I always keep them that way," murmured she.

"You do beat everything," said Dagget, trying to laugh
again. His large face was flushed.

He remained about an hour longer, then rose to take
leave. Going out, he stumbled over a rug, and trying to
recover himself, hit Louisa's work-basket on the table, and
knocked it on the floor.

He looked at Louisa, then at the rolling spools ; he
ducked himself awkwardly toward them, but she stopped
him. " Never mind," said she ; " I'll pick them up after
you're gone."

She spoke with a mild stiffness. Either she was a little
disturbed, or his nervousness affected her, and made her
seem constrained in her effort to reassure him.

When Joe Dagget was outside he drew in the sweet evening
air with a sigh, and felt much as an innocent and perfectly
well-intentioned bear might after his exit from a china shop.

Louisa, on her part, felt much as the kind-hearted, long-
suffering owner of the china shop might have done after
the exit of the bear.

She tied on the pink, then the green apron, picked up all
the scattered treasures and replaced them in her work-
basket, and straightened the rug. Then she set the lamp
on the floor, and began sharply examining the carpet. She
even rubbed her fingers over it, and looked at them.

" He's tracked in a good deal of dust," she murmured.
" I thought he must have."

Louisa got a dust-pan and brush, and swept Joe Dagget's
track carefully.

If he could have known it, it would have increased his perplexity and uneasiness, although it would not have disturbed his loyalty in the least. He came twice a week to see Louisa Ellis, and every time, sitting there in her delicately sweet room, he felt as if surrounded by a hedge of lace. He was afraid to stir lest he should put a clumsy foot or hand through the fairy web, and he had always the consciousness that Louisa was watching fearfully lest he should.

Still the lace and Louisa commanded perforce his perfect respect and patience and loyalty. They were to be married in a month, after a singular courtship which had lasted for a matter of fifteen years. For fourteen out of the fifteen years the two had not once seen each other, and they had seldom exchanged letters. Joe had been all those years in Australia, where he had gone to make his fortune, and where he had stayed until he made it. He would have stayed fifty years if it had taken so long, and come home feeble and tottering, or never come home at all, to marry Louisa.

But the fortune had been made in the fourteen years, and he had come home now to marry the woman who had been patiently and unquestioningly waiting for him all that time.

Shortly after they were engaged he had announced to Louisa his determination to strike out into new fields, and secure a competency before they should be married. She had listened and assented with the sweet serenity which never failed her, not even when her lover set forth on that long and uncertain journey. Joe, buoyed up as he was by his sturdy determination, broke down a little at the last, but Louisa kissed him with a mild blush, and said good-by.

" It won't be for long," poor Joe had said, huskily ; but it was for fourteen years.

In that length of time much had happened. Louisa's mother and brother had died, and she was all alone in the world. But greatest happening of all—a subtle happening which both were too simple to understand—Louisa's feet had turned into a path, smooth maybe under a calm, serene sky, but so straight and unswerving that it could only meet a check at her grave, and so narrow that there was no room for any one at her side.

Louisa's first emotion when Joe Dagget came home (he had not apprised her of his coming) was consternation, although she would not admit it to herself, and he never dreamed of it. Fifteen years ago she had been in love with him—at least she considered herself to be. Just at that time, gently acquiescing with and falling into the natural drift of girlhood, she had seen marriage ahead as a reasonable feature and a probable desirability of life. She had listened with calm docility to her mother's views upon the subject. Her mother was remarkable for her cool sense and sweet, even temperament. She talked wisely to her daughter when Joe Dagget presented himself, and Louisa accepted him with no hesitation. He was the first lover she had ever had.

She had been faithful to him all these years. She had never dreamed of the possibility of marrying any one else. Her life, especially for the last seven years, had been full of a pleasant peace, she had never felt discontented nor impatient over her lover's absence ; still she had always looked forward to his return and their marriage as the inevitable conclusion of things. However, she had fallen into a way of placing it so far in the future that it was almost equal to placing it over the boundaries of another life.

When Joe came she had been expecting him, and expecting to be married for fourteen years, but she was as much surprised and taken aback as if she had never thought of it.

Joe's consternation came later. He eyed Louisa with an instant confirmation of his old admiration. She had changed but little. She still kept her pretty manner and soft grace, and was, he considered, every whit as attractive as ever. As for himself, his stent was done ; he had turned his face away from fortune-seeking, and the old winds of romance whistled as loud and sweet as ever through his ears. All the song which he had been wont to hear in them was Louisa ; he had for a long time a loyal belief that he heard it still, but finally it seemed to him that although the winds sang always that one song, it had another name. But for Louisa the wind had never more than murmured ; now it had gone down, and everything was still. She listened for a little while with half-wistful attention ; then she turned quietly away and went to work on her wedding clothes.

Joe had made some extensive and quite magnificent alterations in his house. It was the old homestead ; the newly-married couple would live there, for Joe could not desert his mother, who refused to leave her old home. So Louisa must leave hers. Every morning, rising and going about among her neat maidenly possessions, she felt as one looking her last upon the faces of dear friends. It was true that in a measure she could take them with her, but, robbed of their old environments, they would appear in such new guises that they would almost cease to be themselves.

Then there were some peculiar features of her happy solitary life which she would probably be obliged to relinquish
altogether. Sterner tasks than these graceful but half-
needless ones would probably devolve upon her. There
would be a large house to care for ; there would be company to entertain ; there would be Joe's rigorous and feeble
old mother to wait upon ; and it would be contrary to all
thrifty village traditions for her to keep more than one ser-
vant. Louisa had a little still, and she used to occupy herself pleasantly in summer weather with distilling the sweet
and aromatic essences from roses and peppermint and spear-
mint. By-and-by her still must be laid away. Her store of
essences was already considerable, and there would be no
time for her to distil for the mere pleasure of it. Then
Joe's mother would think it foolishness ; she had already
hinted her opinion in the matter. Louisa dearly loved to
sew a linen seam, not always for use, but for the simple,
mild pleasure which she took in it. She would have been
loath to confess how more than once she had ripped a seam
for the mere delight of sewing it together again. Sitting
at her window during long sweet afternoons, drawing her
needle gently through the dainty fabric, she was peace itself.
But there was small chance of such foolish comfort in the
future. Joe's mother, domineering, shrewd old matron that
she was even in her old age, and very likely even Joe himself, with his honest masculine rudeness, would laugh and
frown down all these pretty but senseless old maiden ways.

Louisa had almost the enthusiasm of an artist over the
mere order and cleanliness of her solitary home. She had
throbs of genuine triumph at the sight of the window-panes
which she had polished until they shone like jewels. She
gloated gently over her orderly bureau-drawers, with their

exquisitely folded contents redolent with lavender and sweet clover and very purity. Could she be sure of the endurance of even this ? She had visions, so startling that she half repudiated them as indelicate, of coarse masculine belongings strewn about in endless litter ; of dust and disorder arising necessarily from a coarse masculine presence in the midst of all this delicate harmony.

Among her forebodings of disturbance, not the least was with regard to Cæsar. Cæsar was a veritable hermit of a dog. For the greater part of his life he had dwelt in his secluded hut, shut out from the society of his kind and all innocent canine joys. Never had Cæsar since his early youth watched at a woodchuck's hole ; never had he known the delights of a stray bone at a neighbor's kitchen door. And it was all on account of a sin committed when hardly out of his puppyhood. No one knew the possible depth of remorse of which this mild-visaged, altogether innocent-looking old dog might be capable ; but whether or not he had encountered remorse, he had encountered a full measure of righteous retribution. Old Cæsar seldom lifted up his voice in a growl or a bark ; he was fat and sleepy ; there were yellow rings which looked like spectacles around his dim old eyes ; but there was a neighbor who bore on his hand the imprint of several of Cæsar's sharp white youthful teeth, and for that he had lived at the end of a chain, all alone in a little hut, for fourteen years. The neighbor, who was choleric and smarting with the pain of his wound, had demanded either Cæsar's death or complete ostracism. So Louisa's brother, to whom the dog had belonged, had built him his little kennel and tied him up. It was now fourteen years since, in a flood of youthful spirits, he had inflicted that memorable bite, and with the exception of short excursions, always at the end of the chain, under the strict guardianship of his master or Louisa, the old dog had remained a close prisoner. It is doubtful if, with his limited ambition, he took much pride in the fact, but it is certain that he was possessed of considerable cheap fame. He was regarded by all the children in the village and by many adults as a very monster of ferocity. St. George's dragon could hardly have surpassed in evil repute Louisa Ellis's old yellow dog. Mothers charged their children with solemn emphasis not to go too near to him, and the children listened and believed greedily, with a fascinated appetite for terror, and ran by Louisa's house stealthily, with many sidelong and backward glances at the terrible dog. If perchance he sounded a hoarse bark, there was a panic. Wayfarers chancing into Louisa's yard eyed him with respect, and inquired if the chain were stout. Cæsar at large might have seemed a very ordinary dog, and excited no comment whatever ; chained, his reputation overshadowed him, so that he lost his own proper outlines and looked darkly vague and enormous. Joe Dagget, however, with his good-humored sense and shrewdness, saw him as he was. He strode valiantly up to him and patted him on the head, in spite of Louisa's soft clamor of warning, and even attempted to set him loose. Louisa grew so alarmed that he desisted, but kept announcing his opinion in the matter quite forcibly at intervals. " There ain't a better-natured dog in town," he would say, " and it's downright cruel to keep him tied up there. Some day I'm going to take him out."

Louisa had very little hope that he would not, one of these days, when their interests and possessions should be more completely fused in one. She pictured to herself

Cæsar on the rampage through the quiet and unguarded village. She saw innocent children bleeding in his path. She was herself very fond of the old dog, because he had belonged to her dead brother, and he was always very gentle with her ; still she had great faith in his ferocity. She always warned people not to go too near him. She fed him on ascetic fare of corn-mush and cakes, and never fired his dangerous temper with heating and sanguinary diet of flesh and bones. Louisa looked at the old dog munching his simple fare, and thought of her approaching marriage and trembled. Still no anticipation of disorder and confusion in lieu of sweet peace and harmony, no forebodings of Cæsar on the rampage, no wild fluttering of her little yellow canary, were sufficient to turn her a hair's-breadth. Joe Dagget had been fond of her and working for her all these years. It was not for her, whatever came to pass, to prove untrue and break his heart. She put the exquisite little stitches into her wedding-garments, and the time went on until it was only a week before her wedding-day. It was a Tuesday evening, and the wedding was to be a week from Wednesday.

There was a full moon that night. About nine o'clock Louisa strolled down the road a little way. There were harvest-fields on either hand, bordered by low stone walls. Luxuriant clumps of bushes grew beside the wall, and trees —wild cherry and old apple-trees—at intervals. Presently Louisa sat down on the wall and looked about her with mildly sorrowful reflectiveness. Tall shrubs of blueberry and meadow-sweet, all woven together and tangled with blackberry vines and horsebriers, shut her in on either side. She had a little clear space between them. Opposite her, on the other side of the road, was a spreading tree ;

the moon shone between its boughs, and the leaves twinkled like silver. The road was bespread with a beautiful shifting dapple of silver and shadow ; the air was full of a mysterious sweetness. " I wonder if it's wild grapes?" murmured Louisa. She sat there some time. She was just thinking of rising, when she heard footsteps and low voices, and remained quiet. It was a lonely place, and she felt a little timid. She thought she would keep still in the shadow and let the persons, whoever they might be, pass her.

But just before they reached her the voices ceased, and the footsteps. She understood that their owners had also found seats upon the stone wall. She was wondering if she could not steal away unobserved, when the voice broke the stillness. It was Joe Dagget's. She sat still and listened.

The voice was announced by a loud sigh, which was as familiar as itself. "Well," said Dagget, " you've made up your mind, then, I suppose ?"

" Yes," returned another voice ; " I'm going day after to-morrow."

" That's Lily Dyer," thought Louisa to herself. The voice embodied itself in her mind. She saw a girl tall and full-figured, with a firm, fair face, looking fairer and firmer in the moonlight, her strong yellow hair braided in a close knot. A girl full of a calm rustic strength and bloom, with a masterful way which might have beseemed a princess. Lily Dyer was a favorite with the village folk ; she had just the qualities to arouse the admiration. She was good and handsome and smart. Louisa had often heard·her praises sounded.

" Well," said Joe Dagget, " I ain't got a word to say."

" I don't know what you could say," returned Lily Dyer.

"Not a word to say," repeated Joe, drawing out the words heavily. Then there was a silence. "I ain't sorry," he began at last, "that that happened yesterday—that we kind of let on how we felt to each other. I guess it's just as well we knew. Of course I can't do anything any different. I'm going right on an' get married next week. I ain't going back on a woman that's waited for me fourteen years, an' break her heart."

"If you should jilt her to-morrow, I wouldn't have you," spoke up the girl, with sudden vehemence.

"Well, I ain't going to give you the chance," said he; "but I don't believe you would, either."

"You'd see I wouldn't. Honor's honor, an' right's right. An' I'd never think anything of any man that went against 'em for me or any other girl; you'd find that out, Joe Dagget."

"Well, you'll find out fast enough that I ain't going against 'em for you or any other girl," returned he. Their voices sounded almost as if they were angry with each other. Louisa was listening eagerly.

"I'm sorry you feel as if you must go away," said Joe, "but I don't know but it's best."

"Of course it's best. I hope you and I have got common-sense."

"Well, I suppose you're right." Suddenly Joe's voice got an undertone of tenderness. "Say, Lily," said he, "I'll get along well enough myself, but I can't bear to think— You don't suppose you're going to fret much over it?"

"I guess you'll find out I sha'n't fret much over a married man."

"Well, I hope you won't—I hope you won't, Lily. God knows I do. And — I hope — one of these days — you'll —come across somebody else—"

"I don't see any reason why I shouldn't." Suddenly her tone changed. She spoke in a sweet, clear voice, so loud that she could have been heard across the street. "No, Joe Dagget," said she, "I'll never marry any other man as long as I live. I've got good sense, an' I ain't going to break my heart nor make a fool of myself; but I'm never going to be married, you can be sure of that. I ain't that sort of a girl to feel this way twice."

Louisa heard an exclamation and a soft commotion behind the bushes; then Lily spoke again—the voice sounded as if she had risen. "This must be put a stop to," said she. "We've stayed here long enough. I'm going home."

Louisa sat there in a daze, listening to their retreating steps. After a while she got up and slunk softly home herself. The next day she did her housework methodically; that was as much a matter of course as breathing; but she did not sew on her wedding-clothes. She sat at her window and meditated. In the evening Joe came. Louisa Ellis had never known that she had any diplomacy in her, but when she came to look for it that night she found it, although meek of its kind, among her little feminine weapons. Even now she could hardly believe that she had heard aright, and that she would not do Joe a terrible injury should she break her troth-plight. She wanted to sound him without betraying too soon her own inclinations in the matter. She did it successfully, and they finally came to an understanding; but it was a difficult thing, for he was as afraid of betraying himself as she.

She never mentioned Lily Dyer. She simply said that while she had no cause of complaint against him, she had lived so long in one way that she shrank from making a change.

"Well, I never shrank, Louisa," said Dagget.   "I'm going to be honest enough to say that I think maybe it's better this way ; but if you'd wanted to keep on, I'd have stuck to you till my dying day.   I hope you know that."

"Yes, I do," said she.

That night she and Joe parted more tenderly than they had done for a long time.   Standing in the door, holding each other's hands, a last great wave of regretful memory swept over them.

"Well, this ain't the way we've thought it was all going to end, is it, Louisa ?" said Joe.

She shook her head.   There was a little quiver on her placid face.

"You let me know if there's ever anything I can do for you," said he.   "I ain't ever going to forget you, Louisa." Then he kissed her, and went down the path.

Louisa, all alone by herself that night, wept a little, she hardly knew why ; but the next morning, on waking, she felt like a queen who, after fearing lest her domain be wrested away from her, sees it firmly insured in her possession.

Now the tall weeds and grasses might cluster around Cæsar's little hermit hut, the snow might fall on its roof year in and year out, but he never would go on a rampage through the unguarded village.   Now the little canary might turn itself into a peaceful yellow ball night after night, and have no need to wake and flutter with wild terror against its bars.   Louisa could sew linen seams, and distil roses, and dust and polish and fold away in lavender, as long as she listed.   That afternoon she sat with her needle-work at the window, and felt fairly steeped in peace.   Lily Dyer, tall and erect and blooming, went past ; but she felt no qualm. If Louisa Ellis had sold her birthright she did not know it, the taste of the pottage was so delicious, and had been her sole satisfaction for so long. Serenity and placid narrowness had become to her as the birthright itself. She gazed ahead through a long reach of future days strung together like pearls in a rosary, every one like the others, and all smooth and flawless and innocent, and her heart went up in thankfulness. Outside was the fervid summer afternoon ; the air was filled with the sounds of the busy harvest of men and birds and bees ; there were halloos, metallic clatterings, sweet calls, and long hummings. Louisa sat, prayerfully numbering her days, like an uncloistered nun.

A VILLAGE SINGER.

THE trees were in full leaf, a heavy south wind was blowing, and there was a loud murmur among the new leaves.
The people noticed it, for it was the first time that year that
the trees had so murmured in the wind. The spring had
come with a rush during the last few days.

The murmur of the trees sounded loud in the village
church, where the people sat waiting for the service to begin. The windows were open ; it was a very warm Sunday
for May.

The church was already filled with this soft sylvan music
—the tender harmony of the leaves and the south wind, and
the sweet, desultory whistles of birds—when the choir arose
and began to sing.

In the centre of the row of women singers stood Alma
Way. All the people stared at her, and turned their ears
critically. She was the new leading soprano. Candace
Whitcomb, the old one, who had sung in the choir for forty
years, had lately been given her dismissal. The audience
considered that her voice had grown too cracked and uncertain on the upper notes. There had been much complaint, and after long deliberation the church-officers had
made known their decision as mildly as possible to the old
singer. She had sung for the last time the Sunday before,

and Alma Way had been engaged to take her place. With the exception of the organist, the leading soprano was the only paid musician in the large choir. The salary was very modest, still the village people considered it large for a young woman. Alma was from the adjoining village of East Derby ; she had quite a local reputation as a singer.

Now she fixed her large solemn blue eyes ; her long, delicate face, which had been pretty, turned paler ; the blue flowers on her bonnet trembled ; her little thin gloved hands, clutching the singing-book, shook perceptibly ; but she sang out bravely. That most formidable mountain-height of the world, self-distrust and timidity, arose before her, but her nerves were braced for its ascent. In the midst of the hymn she had a solo ; her voice rang out piercingly sweet ; the people nodded admiringly at each other ; but suddenly there was a stir ; all the faces turned toward the windows on the south side of the church. Above the din of the wind and the birds, above Alma Way's sweetly strain-ing tones, arose another female voice, singing another hymn to another tune.

" It's her," the women whispered to each other ; they were half aghast, half smiling.

Candace Whitcomb's cottage stood close to the south side of the church. She was playing on her parlor organ, and singing, to drown out the voice of her rival.

Alma caught her breath ; she almost stopped ; the hymn-book waved like a fan ; then she went on. But the long husky drone of the parlor organ and the shrill clamor of the other voice seemed louder than anything else.

When the hymn was finished, Alma sat down. She felt faint ; the woman next her slipped a peppermint into her hand. " It ain't worth minding," she whispered, vigorously.

Alma tried to smile ; down in the audience a young man was watching her with a kind of fierce pity.

In the last hymn Alma had another solo. Again the parlor organ droned above the carefully delicate accompaniment of the church organ, and again Candace Whitcomb's voice clamored forth in another tune.

After the benediction, the other singers pressed around Alma. She did not say much in return for their expressions of indignation and sympathy. She wiped her eyes furtively once or twice, and tried to smile. William Emmons, the choir leader, elderly, stout, and smooth-faced, stood over her, and raised his voice. He was the old musical dignitary of the village, the leader of the choral club and the singing-schools. "A most outrageous proceeding," he said. People had coupled his name with Candace Whitcomb's. The old bachelor tenor and old maiden soprano had been wont to walk together to her home next door after the Saturday night rehearsals, and they had sung duets to the parlor organ. People had watched sharply her old face, on which the blushes of youth sat pitifully, when William Emmons entered the singing-seats. They wondered if he would ever ask her to marry him.

And now he said further to Alma Way that Candace Whitcomb's voice had failed utterly of late, that she sang shockingly, and ought to have had sense enough to know it.

When Alma went down into the audience-room, in the midst of the chattering singers, who seemed to have descended, like birds, from song flights to chirps, the minister approached her. He had been waiting to speak to her. He was a steady-faced, fleshy old man, who had preached from that one pulpit over forty years. He told Alma, in his slow way, how much he regretted the annoyance to which she had been subjected, and intimated that he would endeavor to prevent a recurrence of it. "Miss Whitcomb—must be—reasoned with," said he; he had a slight hesitation of speech, not an impediment. It was as if his thoughts did not slide readily into his words, although both were present. He walked down the aisle with Alma, and bade her good-morning when he saw Wilson Ford waiting for her in the door-way. Everybody knew that Wilson Ford and Alma were lovers; they had been for the last ten years.

Alma colored softly, and made a little imperceptible motion with her head; her silk dress and the lace on her mantle fluttered, but she did not speak. Neither did Wilson, although they had not met before that day. They did not look at each other's faces—they seemed to see each other without that—and they walked along side by side.

They reached the gate before Candace Whitcomb's little house. Wilson looked past the front yard, full of pink and white spikes on flowering bushes, at the lace-curtained windows; a thin white profile, stiffly inclined, apparently over a book, was visible at one of them. Wilson gave his head a shake. He was a stout man, with features so strong that they overcame his flesh. "I'm going up home with you, Alma," said he; "and then—I'm just coming back, to give Aunt Candace one blowing up."

"Oh, don't, Wilson."

"Yes, I shall. If you want to stand this kind of a thing you may; I sha'n't."

"There's no need of your talking to her. Mr. Pollard's going to."

"Did he say he was?"

"Yes. I think he's going in before the afternoon meeting, from what he said."

"Well, there's one thing about it, if she does that thing again this afternoon, I'll go in there and break that old organ up into kindling-wood." Wilson set his mouth hard, and shook his head again.

Alma gave little side glances up at him, her tone was deprecatory, but her face was full of soft smiles. "I suppose she does feel dreadfully about it," said she. "I can't help feeling kind of guilty, taking her place."

"I don't see how you're to blame. It's outrageous, her acting so."

"The choir gave her a photograph album last week, didn't they?"

"Yes. They went there last Thursday night, and gave her an album and a surprise-party. She ought to behave herself."

"Well, she's sung there so long, I suppose it must be dreadful hard for her to give it up."

Other people going home from church were very near Wilson and Alma. She spoke softly that they might not hear; he did not lower his voice in the least. Presently Alma stopped before a gate.

"What are you stopping here for?" asked Wilson.

"Minnie Lansing wanted me to come and stay with her this noon."

"You're going home with me."

"I'm afraid I'll put your mother out."

"Put mother out! I told her you were coming, this morning. She's got all ready for you. Come along; don't stand here."

He did not tell Alma of the pugnacious spirit with which his mother had received the announcement of her coming, and how she had stayed at home to prepare the dinner, and make a parade of her hard work and her injury.

Wilson's mother was the reason why he did not marry Alma. He would not take his wife home to live with her, and was unable to support separate establishments. Alma was willing enough to be married and put up with Wilson's mother, but she did not complain of his decision. Her delicate blond features grew sharper, and her blue eyes more hollow. She had had a certain fine prettiness, but now she was losing it, and beginning to look old, and there was a prim, angular, old maiden carriage about her narrow shoulders.

Wilson never noticed it, and never thought of Alma as not possessed of eternal youth, or capable of losing or regretting it.

"Come along, Alma," said he ; and she followed meekly after him down the street.

Soon after they passed Candace Whitcomb's house, the minister went up the front walk and rang the bell. The pale profile at the window had never stirred as he opened the gate and came up the walk. However, the door was promptly opened, in response to his ring. "Good-morning, Miss Whitcomb," said the minister.

"*Good*-morning." Candace gave a sweeping toss of her head as she spoke. There was a fierce upward curl to her thin nostrils and her lips, as if she scented an adversary. Her black eyes had two tiny cold sparks of fury in them, like an enraged bird's. She did not ask the minister to enter, but he stepped lumberingly into the entry, and she retreated rather than led the way into her little parlor. He settled into the great rocking-chair and wiped his face. Candace sat down again in her old place by the window. She was a tall woman, but very slender and full of pliable motions, like a blade of grass.

" It's a—very pleasant day," said the minister.

Candace made no reply. She sat still, with her head drooping. The wind stirred the looped lace-curtains ; a tall rose-tree outside the window waved ; soft shadows floated through the room. Candace's parlor organ stood in front of an open window that faced the church ; on the corner was a pitcher with a bunch of white lilacs. The whole room was scented with them. Presently the minister looked over at them and sniffed pleasantly.

" You have—some beautiful—lilacs there."

Candace did not speak. Every line of her slender figure looked flexible, but it was a flexibility more resistant than rigor.

The minister looked at her. He filled up the great rocking-chair ; his arms in his shiny black coat-sleeves rested squarely and comfortably upon the hair-cloth arms of the chair.

" Well, Miss Whitcomb, I suppose I—may as well come to — the point. There was — a little — matter I wished to speak to you about. I don't suppose you were—at least I can't suppose you were—aware of it, but—this morning, during the singing by the choir, you played and—sung a little too—loud. That is, with—the windows open. It—disturbed us—a little. I hope you won't feel hurt—my dear Miss Candace, but I knew you would rather I would speak of it, for I knew—you would be more disturbed than anybody else at the idea of such a thing."

Candace did not raise her eyes ; she looked as if his words might sway her through the window. " I ain't disturbed at it," said she. " I did it on purpose ; I meant to."

The minister looked at her.

" You needn't look at me. I know jest what I'm about.

I sung the way I did on purpose, an' I'm goin' to do it again, an' I'd like to see you stop me. I guess I've got a right to set down to my own organ, an' sing a psalm tune on a Sabbath day, 'f I want to; an' there ain't no amount of talkin' an' palaverin' a-goin' to stop me. See there!" Candace swung aside her skirts a little. "Look at that!"

The minister looked. Candace's feet were resting on a large red-plush photograph album.

"Makes a nice footstool, don't it?" said she.

The minister looked at the album, then at her; there was a slowly gathering alarm in his face; he began to think she was losing her reason.

Candace had her eyes full upon him now, and her head up. She laughed, and her laugh was almost a snarl. "Yes; I thought it would make a beautiful footstool," said she. "I've been wantin' one for some time." Her tone was full of vicious irony.

"Why, miss—" began the minister; but she interrupted him:

"I know what you're a-goin' to say, Mr. Pollard, an' now I'm goin' to have my say; I'm a-goin' to speak. I want to know what you think of folks that pretend to be Christians treatin' anybody the way they've treated me? Here I've sung in those singin'-seats forty year. I 'ain't never missed a Sunday, except when I've been sick, an' I've gone an' sung a good many times when I'd better been in bed, an' now I'm turned out without a word of warnin'. My voice is jest as good as ever 'twas; there can't anybody say it ain't. It wa'n't ever quite so high-pitched as that Way girl's, mebbe; but she flats the whole durin' time. My voice is as good an' high to-day as it was twenty year ago; an' if it wa'n't, I'd like to know where the Christianity comes in. I'd like to know if it wouldn't be more to the credit of folks in a church to keep an old singer an' an old minister, if they didn't sing an' hold forth quite so smart as they used to, ruther than turn 'em off an' hurt their feelin's. I guess it would be full as much to the glory of God. S'pose the singin' an' the preachin' wa'n't quite so good, what difference would it make? Salvation don't hang on anybody's hittin' a high note, that I ever heard of. Folks are gettin' as high-steppin' an' fussy in a meetin'-house as they are in a tavern, nowadays. S'pose they should turn you off, Mr. Pollard, come an' give you a photograph album, an' tell you to clear out, how'd you like it? I ain't findin' any fault with your preachin'; it was always good enough to suit me; but it don't stand to reason folks 'll be as took up with your sermons as when you was a young man. You can't expect it. S'pose they should turn you out in your old age, an' call in some young bob squirt, how'd you feel? There's William Emmons, too; he's three years older'n I am, if he does lead the choir an' run all the singin' in town. If my voice has gi'en out, it stan's to reason his has. It ain't, though. William Emmons sings jest as well as he ever did. Why don't they turn him out the way they have me, an' give him a photograph album? I dun know but it would be a good idea to send everybody, as soon as they get a little old an' gone by, an' young folks begin to push, onto some desert island, an' give 'em each a photograph album. Then they can sit down an' look at pictures the rest of their days. Mebbe government 'll take it up.

"There they come here last week Thursday, all the choir, jest about eight o'clock in the evenin', an' pretended they'd come to give me a nice little surprise. Surprise! h'm! Brought cake an' oranges, an' was jest as nice as they could

be, an' I was real tickled. I never had a surprise-party before in my life. Jenny Carr she played, an' they wanted me
to sing alone, an' I never suspected a thing. I've been mad
ever since to think what a fool I was, an' how they must
have laughed in their sleeves.

" When they'd gone I found this photograph album on the
table, all done up as nice as you please, an' directed to Miss
Candace Whitcomb from her many friends, an' I opened it,
an' there was the letter inside givin' me notice to quit.

" If they'd gone about it any decent way, told me right
out honest that they'd got tired of me, an' wanted Alma
Way to sing instead of me, I wouldn't minded so much ; I
should have been hurt 'nough, for I'd felt as if some that
had pretended to be my friends wa'n't ; but it wouldn't have
been as bad as this. They said in the letter that they'd always set great value on my services, an' it wa'n't from any
lack of appreciation that they turned me off, but they thought
the duty was gettin' a little too arduous for me. H'm ! I
hadn't complained. If they'd turned me right out fair an'
square, showed me the door, an' said, ' Here, you get out,'
but to go an' spill molasses, as it were, all over the threshold, tryin' to make me think it's all nice an' sweet—

" I'd sent that photograph album back quick's I could
pack it, but I didn't know who started it, so I've used it
for a footstool. It's all it's good for, 'cordin' to my way
of thinkin'. An' I ain't been particular to get the dust off
my shoes before I used it neither."

Mr. Pollard, the minister, sat staring. He did not look
at Candace ; his eyes were fastened upon a point straight
ahead. He had a look of helpless solidity, like a block of
granite. This country minister, with his steady, even temperament, treading with heavy precision his one track for

over forty years, having nothing new in his life except the new sameness of the seasons, and desiring nothing new, was incapable of understanding a woman like this, who had lived as quietly as he, and all the time held within herself the elements of revolution. He could not account for such violence, such extremes, except in a loss of reason. He had a conviction that Candace was getting beyond herself. He himself was not a typical New-Englander ; the national elements of character were not pronounced in him. He was aghast and bewildered at this outbreak, which was tropical, and more than tropical, for a New England nature has a floodgate, and the power which it releases is an accumulation. Candace Whitcomb had been a quiet woman, so delicately resolute that the quality had been scarcely noticed in her, and her ambition had been unsuspected. Now the resolution and the ambition appeared raging over her whole self.

She began to talk again. " I've made up my mind that I'm goin' to sing Sundays the way I did this mornin', an' I don't care what folks say," said she. " I've made up my mind that I'm goin' to take matters into my own hands. I'm goin' to let folks see that I ain't trod down quite flat, that there's a little rise left in me. I ain't goin' to give up beat yet a while ; an' I'd like to see anybody stop me. If I ain't got a right to play a psalm tune on my organ an' sing, I'd like to know. If you don't like it, you can move the meetin'-house."

Candace had had an inborn reverence for clergymen. She had always treated Mr. Pollard with the utmost deference. Indeed, her manner toward all men had been marked by a certain delicate stiffness and dignity. Now she was talking to the old minister with the homely freedom with which she might have addressed a female gossip over the back fence. He could not say much in return. He did not feel competent to make headway against any such tide of passion ; all he could do was to let it beat against him. He made a few expostulations, which increased Candace's vehemence ; he expressed his regret over the whole affair, and suggested that they should kneel and ask the guidance of the Lord in the matter, that she might be led to see it all in a different light.

Candace refused flatly. " I don't see any use prayin' about it," said she. " I don't think the Lord's got much to do with it, anyhow."

It was almost time for the afternoon service when the minister left. He had missed his comfortable noontide rest, through this encounter with his revolutionary parishioner. After the minister had gone, Candace sat by the window and waited. The bell rang, and she watched the people file past. When her nephew Wilson Ford with Alma appeared, she grunted to herself. " She's thin as a rail," said she ; "guess there won't be much left of her by the time Wilson gets her. Little soft-spoken nippin' thing, she wouldn't make him no kind of a wife, anyway. Guess it's jest as well."

When the bell had stopped tolling, and all the people entered the church, Candace went over to her organ and seated herself. She arranged a singing-book before her, and sat still, waiting. Her thin, colorless neck and temples were full of beating pulses ; her black eyes were bright and eager ; she leaned stiffly over toward the music-rack, to hear better. When the church organ sounded out she straightened herself ; her long skinny fingers pressed her own organ-keys with nervous energy. She worked the pedals with all her strength ; all her slender body was in motion. When the first notes of Alma's solo began, Candace sang. She had really possessed a fine voice, and it was wonderful how little she had lost it. Straining her throat with jealous fury, her notes were still for the main part true. Her voice filled the whole room ; she sang with wonderful fire and expression. That, at least, mild little Alma Way could never emulate. She was full of steadfastness and unquestioning constancy, but there were in her no smouldering fires of ambition and resolution. Music was not to her what it had been to her older rival. To this obscure woman, kept relentlessly by circumstances in a narrow track, singing in the village choir had been as much as Italy was to Napoleon —and now on her island of exile she was still showing fight.

After the church service was done, Candace left the organ and went over to her old chair by the window. Her knees felt weak, and shook under her. She sat down, and leaned back her head. There were red spots on her cheeks. Pretty soon she heard a quick slam of her gate, and an impetuous tread on the gravel-walk. She looked up, and there was her nephew Wilson Ford hurrying up to the door. She cringed a little, then she settled herself more firmly in her chair.

Wilson came into the room with a rush. He left the door open, and the wind slammed it to after him.

"Aunt Candace, where are you ?" he called out, in a loud voice.

She made no reply. He looked around fiercely, and his eyes seemed to pounce upon her.

"Look here, Aunt Candace," said he, "are you crazy ?" Candace said nothing. "Aunt Candace !" She did not seem to see him. " If you don't answer me," said Wilson, " I'll just go over there and pitch that old organ out of the window !"

" Wilson Ford !" said Candace, in a voice that was almost a scream.

" Well, what say ! What have you got to say for yourself, acting the way you have ? I tell you what 'tis, Aunt Candace, I won't stand it."

" I'd like to see you help yourself."

" I will help myself. I'll pitch that old organ out of the window, and then I'll board up the window on that side of your house. Then we'll see."

" It ain't your house, and it won't never be."

" Who said it was my house ? You're my aunt, and I've got a little lookout for the credit of the family. Aunt Candace, what are you doing this way for ?"

" It don't make no odds what I'm doin' so for. I ain't bound to give my reasons to a young fellar like you, if you do act so mighty toppin'. But I'll tell you one thing, Wilson Ford, after the way you've spoke to-day, you sha'n't never have one cent of my money, an' you can't never marry that Way girl if you don't have it. You can't never take her home to live with your mother, an' this house would have been mighty nice an' convenient for you some day. Now you won't get it. I'm goin' to make another will. I'd made one, if you did but know it. Now you won't get a cent of my money, you nor your mother neither. An' I ain't goin' to live a dreadful while longer, neither. Now I wish you'd go home ; I want to lay down. I'm 'bout sick."

Wilson could not get another word from his aunt. His indignation had not in the least cooled. Her threat of disinheriting him did not cow him at all ; he had too much rough independence, and indeed his aunt Candace's house had always been too much of an air-castle for him to contemplate seriously. Wilson, with his burly frame and his headlong common-sense, could have little to do with air-castles, had he been hard enough to build them over graves. Still, he had not admitted that he never could marry Alma. All his hopes were based upon a rise in his own fortunes, not by some sudden convulsion, but by his own long and steady labor. Some time, he thought, he should have saved enough for the two homes.

He went out of his aunt's house still storming. She arose after the door had shut behind him, and got out into the kitchen. She thought that she would start a fire and make a cup of tea. She had not eaten anything all day. She put some kindling-wood into the stove and touched a match to it; then she went back to the sitting-room, and settled down again into the chair by the window. The fire in the kitchen-stove roared, and the light wood was soon burned out. She thought no more about it. She had not put on the teakettle. Her head ached, and once in a while she shivered. She sat at the window while the afternoon waned and the dusk came on. At seven o'clock the meeting bell rang again, and the people flocked by. This time she did not stir. She had shut her parlor organ. She did not need to out-sing her rival this evening; there was only congregational singing at the Sunday-night prayer-meeting.

She sat still until it was nearly time for meeting to be done; her head ached harder and harder, and she shivered more. Finally she arose. "Guess I'll go to bed," she muttered. She went about the house, bent over and shaking, to lock the doors. She stood a minute in the back door, looking over the fields to the woods. There was a red light over there. "The woods are on fire," said Candace. She watched with a dull interest the flames roll up, withering and destroying the tender green spring foliage. The air was full of smoke, although the fire was half a mile away.

Candace locked the door and went in. The trees with their delicate garlands of new leaves, with the new nests of song birds, might fall, she was in the roar of an intenser fire ; the growths of all her springs and the delicate wontedness of her whole life were going down in it. Candace went to bed in her little room off the parlor, but she could not sleep. She lay awake all night. In the morning she crawled to the door and hailed a little boy who was passing. She bade him go for the doctor as quickly as he could, then to Mrs. Ford's, and ask her to come over. She held on to the door while she was talking. The boy stood staring wonderingly at her. The spring wind fanned her face. She had drawn on a dress skirt and put her shawl over her shoulders, and her gray hair was blowing over her red cheeks.

She shut the door and went back to her bed. She never arose from it again. The doctor and Mrs. Ford came and looked after her, and she lived a week. Nobody but herself thought until the very last that she would die ; the doctor called her illness merely a light run of fever ; she had her senses fully.

But Candace gave up at the first. " It's my last sickness," she said to Mrs. Ford that morning when she first entered ; and Mrs. Ford had laughed at the notion ; but the sick woman held to it. She did not seem to suffer much physical pain ; she only grew weaker and weaker, but she was distressed mentally. She did not talk much, but her eyes followed everybody with an agonized expression.

On Wednesday William Emmons came to inquire for her.

Candace heard him out in the parlor. She tried to raise herself on one elbow that she might listen better to his voice.

"William Emmons come in to ask how you was," Mrs. Ford said, after he was gone.

"I—heard him," replied Candace. Presently she spoke again. "Nancy," said she, "where's that photograph album?"

"On the table," replied her sister, hesitatingly.

"Mebbe—you'd better—brush it up a little."

"Well."

Sunday morning Candace wished that the minister should be asked to come in at the noon intermission. She had refused to see him before. He came and prayed with her, and she asked his forgiveness for the way she had spoken the Sunday before. "I—hadn't ought to—spoke so," said she. "I was—dreadful wrought up."

"Perhaps it was your sickness coming on," said the minister, soothingly.

Candace shook her head. "No—it wa'n't. I hope the Lord will—forgive me."

After the minister had gone, Candace still appeared unhappy. Her pitiful eyes followed her sister everywhere with the mechanical persistency of a portrait.

"What is it you want, Candance?" Mrs. Ford said at last. She had nursed her sister faithfully, but once in a while her impatience showed itself.

"Nancy!"

"What say?"

"I wish—you'd go out when—meetin's done, an'—head off Alma an' Wilson, an'—ask 'em to come in. I feel as if—I'd like to—hear her sing."

Mrs. Ford stared. "Well," said she.

The meeting was now in session. The windows were all open, for it was another warm Sunday. Candace lay listening to the music when it began, and a look of peace came over her face. Her sister had smoothed her hair back, and put on a clean cap. The white curtain in the bedroom window waved in the wind like a white sail. Candace almost felt as if she were better, but the thought of death seemed easy.

Mrs. Ford at the parlor window watched for the meeting to be out. When the people appeared, she ran down the walk and waited for Alma and Wilson. When they came she told them what Candace wanted, and they all went in together.

"Here's Alma an' Wilson, Candace," said Mrs. Ford, leading them to the bedroom door.

Candace smiled. "Come in," she said, feebly. And Alma and Wilson entered and stood beside the bed. Candace continued to look at them, the smile straining her lips.

"Wilson!"

"What is it, Aunt Candace?"

"I ain't altered that—will. You an' Alma can—come here an'—live—when I'm—gone. Your mother won't mind livin' alone. Alma can have—all—my things."

"Don't, Aunt Candace." Tears were running over Wilson's cheeks, and Alma's delicate face was all of a quiver.

"I thought—maybe—Alma 'd be willin' to—sing for me," said Candace.

"What do you want me to sing?" Alma asked, in a trembling voice.

"'Jesus, lover of my soul.'"

Alma, standing there beside Wilson, began to sing. At first she could hardly control her voice, then she sang sweetly and clearly.

Candace lay and listened.   Her face had a holy and radiant expression.   When Alma stopped singing it did not disappear, but she looked up and spoke, and it was like a secondary glimpse of the old shape of a forest tree through the smoke and flame of the transfiguring fire the instant before it falls.   "You flatted a little on—soul," said Candace.

A GALA DRESS.

"I DON'T care anything about goin' to that Fourth of July picnic, 'Liz'beth."

"I wouldn't say anything more about it, if I was you, Em'ly. I'd get ready an' go."

"I don't really feel able to go, 'Liz'beth."

"I'd like to know why you ain't able."

"It seems to me as if the fire-crackers an' the tootin' on those horns would drive me crazy; an' Matilda Jennings says they're goin' to have a cannon down there, an' fire it off every half-hour. I don't feel as if I could stan' it. You know my nerves ain't very strong, 'Liz'beth."

Elizabeth Babcock uplifted her long, delicate nose with its transparent nostrils, and sniffed. Apparently her sister's perverseness had an unacceptable odor to her. "I wouldn't talk so if I was you, Em'ly. Of course you're goin'. It's your turn to, an' you know it. I went to meetin' last Sabbath. You just put on that dress an' go."

Emily eyed her sister. She tried not to look pleased. "I know you went to meetin' last," said she, hesitatingly; "but—a Fourth of July picnic is—a little more of—a rarity." She fairly jumped, her sister confronted her with such sudden vigor.

"Rarity! Well, I hope a Fourth of July picnic ain't

quite such a treat to me that I'd ruther go to it than meet-in'! I should think you'd be ashamed of yourself speakin' so, Em'ly Babcock."

Emily, a moment before delicately alert and nervous like her sister, shrank limply in her limp black muslin. "I—didn't think how it sounded, 'Liz'beth."

"Well, I should say you'd better think. It don't sound very becomin' for a woman of your age, an' professin' what you do. Now you'd better go an' get out that dress, an' rip the velvet off, an' sew the lace on. There won't be any too much time. They'll start early in the mornin'. I'll stir up a cake for you to carry, when I get tea."

"Don't you s'pose I could get along without a cake?" Emily ventured, tremulously.

"Well, I shouldn't think you'd want to go, an' be be-holden to other folks for your eatin'; I shouldn't."

"I shouldn't want anything to eat."

"I guess if you go, you're goin' like other folks. I ain't goin' to have Matilda Jennings peekin' an' pryin' an' tellin' things, if I know it. You'd better get out that dress."

"Well," said Emily, with a long sigh of remorseful satis-faction. She arose, showing a height that would have ap-proached the majestic had it not been so wavering. The sisters were about the same height, but Elizabeth usually impressed people as being the taller. She carried herself with so much decision that she seemed to keep every inch of her stature firm and taut, old woman although she was.

"Let's see that dress a minute," she said, when Emily returned. She wiped her spectacles, set them firmly, and began examining the hem of the dress, holding it close to her eyes. "You're gettin' of it all tagged out," she de-clared, presently. "I thought you was. I thought I see some ravellin's hangin' the other day when I had it on. It's jest because you don't stan' up straight. It ain't any longer for you than it is for me, if you didn't go all bent over so. There ain't any need of it."

Emily oscillated wearily over her sister and the dress. " I ain't very strong in my back, an' you know I've got a weakness in my stomach that henders me from standin' up as straight as you do," she rejoined, rallying herself for a feeble defence.

"You can stan' up jest as well as I can, if you're a mind to."

" I'll rip that velvet off now, if you'll let me have the dress, 'Liz'beth."

Elizabeth passed over the dress, handling it gingerly. " Mind you don't cut it rippin' of it off," said she.

Emily sat down, and the dress lay in shiny black billows over her lap. The dress was black silk, and had been in its day very soft and heavy ; even now there was considerable wear left in it. The waist and over-skirt were trimmed with black velvet ribbon. Emily ripped off the velvet ; then she sewed on some old-fashioned, straight-edged black lace full of little embroidered sprigs. The sisters sat in their parlor at the right of the front door. The room was very warm, for there were two west windows, and a hot afternoon sun was beating upon them. Out in front of the house was a piazza, with a cool uneven brick floor, and a thick lilac growth across the western end. The sisters might have sat there and been comfortable, but they would not.

" Set right out in the face an' eyes of all the neighbors !" they would have exclaimed with dismay had the idea been suggested. There was about these old women and all their belongings a certain gentle and deprecatory reticence. One felt it immediately upon entering their house, or indeed upon coming in sight of it. There were never any heads at the windows; the blinds were usually closed. Once in a while a passer-by might see an old woman, well shielded by shawl and scooping sun-bonnet, start up like a timid spirit in the yard, and softly disappear through a crack in the front door. Out in the front yard Emily had a little bed of flowers—of balsams and nasturtiums and portulacas; she tended them with furtive glances toward the road. Elizabeth came out in the early morning to sweep the brick floor of the piazza, and the front door was left ajar for a hurried flitting should any one appear.

This excessive shyness and secrecy had almost the aspect of guilt, but no more guileless and upright persons could have been imagined than these two old women. They had over their parlor windows full, softly-falling, old muslin curtains, and they looped them back to leave bare the smallest possible space of glass. The parlor chairs retreated close to the walls, the polish of the parlor table lit up a dim corner. There were very few ornaments in sight ; the walls were full of closets and little cupboards, and in them all superfluities were tucked away to protect them from dust and prying eyes. Never a door in the house stood open, every bureau drawer was squarely shut. A whole family of skeletons might have been well hidden in these guarded recesses ; but skeletons there were none, except, perhaps, a little innocent bone or two of old-womanly pride and sensitiveness.

The Babcock sisters guarded nothing more jealously than the privacy of their meals. The neighbors considered that there was a decided reason for this. "The Babcock girls have so little to eat that they're ashamed to let folks see it," people said. It was certain that the old women regarded intrusion at their meals as an insult, but it was doubtful if they would not have done so had their table been set out with all the luxuries of the season instead of scanty bread and butter and no sauce. No sauce for tea was regarded as very poor living by the village women.

To-night the Babcocks had tea very soon after the lace was sewed on the dress. They always had tea early. They were in the midst of it when the front-door opened, and a voice was heard calling out in the hall.

The sisters cast a dismayed and indignant look at each other ; they both arose ; but the door flew open, and their little square tea-table, with its green-and-white china pot of weak tea, its plate of bread and little glass dish of butter, its two china cups, and thin silver teaspoons, was displayed to view.

" My !" cried the visitor, with a little backward shuffle. " I do hope you'll scuse me ! I didn't know you was eatin' supper. I wouldn't ha' come in for the world if I'd known. I'll go right out ; it wa'n't anything pertickler, anyhow." All the time her sharp and comprehensive gaze was on the tea-table. She counted the slices of bread, she measured the butter, as she talked. The sisters stepped forward with dignity.

"Come into the other room," said Elizabeth ; and the visitor, still protesting, with her backward eyes upon the tea-table, gave way before her.

But her eyes lighted upon something in the parlor more eagerly than they had upon that frugal and exclusive table. The sisters glanced at each other in dismay. The black silk dress lay over a chair. The caller, who was their

neighbor Matilda Jennings, edged toward it as she talked.
" I thought I'd jest run over an' see if you wa'n't goin' to
the picnic to-morrow," she was saying. Then she clutched
the dress and diverged. "Oh, you've been fixin' your
dress !" she said to Emily, with innocent insinuation. Insinuation did not sit well upon Matilda Jennings, none of
her bodily lines were adapted to it, and the pretence was
quite evident. She was short and stout, with a hard, sallow rotundity of cheek, her small black eyes were bright-
pointed under fleshy brows.

" Yes, I have," replied Emily, with a scared glance at
Elizabeth.

" Yes," said Elizabeth, stepping firmly into the subject,
and confronting Matilda with prim and resolute blue eyes.
" She has been fixin' of it. The lace was ripped off, an'
she had to mend it."

" It's pretty lace, ain't it ? I had some of the same kind
on a mantilla once when I was a girl. This makes me
think of it. The sprigs in mine was set a little closer. Let
me see, 'Liz'beth, your black silk dress is trimmed with velvet, ain't it ?"

Elizabeth surveyed her calmly. " Yes ; I've always worn
black velvet on it," said she.

Emily sighed faintly. She had feared that Elizabeth
could not answer desirably and be truthful.

" Let me see," continued Matilda, " how was that velvet
put on your waist ?"

" It was put on peaked."

" In one peak or two ?"

" One."

" Now I wonder if it would be too much trouble for you
jest to let me see it a minute. I've been thinkin' of fixin'

over my old alpaca a little, an' I've got a piece of black velvet ribbon I've steamed over, an' it looks pretty good. I thought mebbe I could put it on like yours."

Matilda Jennings, in her chocolate calico, stood as relentlessly as any executioner before the Babcock sisters. They, slim and delicate and pale in their flabby black muslins, leaned toward each other, then Elizabeth straightened herself. " Some time when it's convenient I'd jest as soon show it as not," said she.

" Well, I'd be much obleeged to you if you would," returned Matilda. Her manner was a trifle overawed, but there was a sharper gleam in her eyes. Pretty soon she went home, and ate her solitary and substantial supper of bread and butter, cold potatoes, and pork and beans. Matilda Jennings was as poor as the Babcocks. She had never, like them, known better days. She had never possessed any fine old muslins nor black silks in her life, but she had always eaten more.

The Babcocks had always delicately and unobtrusively felt themselves above her. There had been in their lives a faint savor of gentility and aristocracy. Their father had been college-educated and a doctor. Matilda's antecedents had been humble, even in this humble community. She had come of wood-sawyers and garden-laborers. In their youth, when they had gone to school and played together, they had always realized their height above Matilda, and even old age and poverty and a certain friendliness could not do away with it.

The Babcocks owned their house and a tiny sum in the bank, upon the interest of which they lived. Nobody knew how much it was, nobody would ever know while they lived. They might have had more if they would have sold or mortgaged their house, but they would have died first. They starved daintily and patiently on their little income. They mended their old muslins and Thibets, and wore one dress between them for best, taking turns in going out.

It seemed inconsistent, but the sisters were very fond of society, and their reserve did not interfere with their pleasure in the simple village outings. They were more at ease abroad than at home, perhaps because there were not present so many doors which could be opened into their secrecy. But they had an arbitrary conviction that their claims to respect and consideration would be forever forfeited should they appear on state occasions in anything but black silk. To their notions of etiquette, black silk was as sacred a necessity as feathers at the English court. They could not go abroad and feel any self-respect in those flimsy muslins and rusty woollens, which were very flimsy and rusty. The old persons in the village could hardly remember when the Babcocks had a new dress. The dainty care with which they had made those tender old fabrics endure so long was wonderful. They held up their skirts primly when they walked ; they kept their pointed elbows clear of chairs and tables. The black silk in particular was taken off the minute its wearer entered her own house. It was shaken softly, folded, and laid away in a linen sheet.

Emily was dressed in it on the Fourth of July morning when Matilda Jennings called for her. Matilda came in her voluminous old alpaca, with her tin lunch-pail on her arm. She looked at Emily in the black silk, and her countenance changed. "My! you ain't goin' to wear that black silk trailin' round in the woods, are you?" said she.

"I guess she won't trail around much," spoke up Elizabeth. "She's got to go lookin' decent."

Matilda's poor old alpaca had many a threadbare streak and mended slit in its rusty folds, the elbows were patched, it was hardly respectable. But she gave the skirt a defiant switch, and jerked the patched elbows. "Well, I allers believed in goin' dressed suitable for the occasion," said she, sturdily, and as if that was her especial picnic costume out of a large wardrobe. However, her bravado was not deeply seated, all day long she manœuvred to keep her patches and darns out of sight, she arranged the skirt nervously every time she changed her position, she held her elbows close to her sides, and she made many little flings at Emily's black silk.

The festivities were nearly over, the dinner had been eaten, Matilda had devoured with relish her brown-bread and cheese and cold pork, and Emily had nibbled daintily at her sweet-cake, and glanced with inward loathing at her neighbor's grosser fare. The speeches by the local celebrities were delivered, the cannon had been fired every half-hour, the sun was getting low in the west, and a golden mist was rising among the ferny undergrowth in the grove. "It's gettin' damp ; I can see it risin'," said Emily, who was rheumatic; "I guess we'd better walk 'round a little, an' then go home."

"Well," replied Matilda, "I'd jest as soon. You'd better hold up your dress."

The two old women adjusted themselves stiffly upon their feet, and began ranging the grove, stepping warily over the slippery pine-needles. The woods were full of merry calls ; the green distances fluttered with light draperies. Every little while came the sharp bang of a fire-cracker, the crash of cannon, or the melancholy hoot of a fish-horn. Now and then blue gunpowder smoke curled up with the golden steam from the dewy ground. Emily was near-sighted; she moved on with innocently peering eyes, her long neck craned forward. Matilda had been taking the lead, but she suddenly stepped aside. Emily walked on unsuspectingly, holding up her precious black silk. There was a quick puff of smoke, a leap of flame, a volley of vicious little reports, and poor Emily Babcock danced as a martyr at her fiery trial might have done; her gentle dignity completely deserted her. "Oh, oh, oh!" she shrieked.

Matilda Jennings pushed forward; by that time Emily was standing, pale and quivering, on a little heap of ashes. "You stepped into a nest of fire-crackers," said Matilda; "a boy jest run; I saw him. What made you stan' there in 'em? Why didn't you get out?"

"I—couldn't," gasped Emily; she could hardly speak.

"Well, I guess it ain't done much harm; them boys ought to be prosecuted. You don't feel as if you was burned anywhere, do you, Em'ly?"

"No—I guess not."

"Seems to me your dress— Jest let me look at your dress, Em'ly. My! ain't that a wicked shame! Jest look at all them holes, right in the flouncin', where it 'll show!"

It was too true. The flounce that garnished the bottom of the black silk was scorched in a number of places. Emily looked at it and felt faint. "I must go right home," she moaned. "Oh, dear!"

"Mebbe you can darn it, if you're real pertickler about it," said Matilda, with an uneasy air.

Emily said nothing; she went home. Her dress switched the dust off the wayside weeds, but she paid no attention to it; she walked so fast that Matilda could hardly keep up with her. When she reached her own gate she swung it swiftly to before Matilda's face, then she fled into the house.

Elizabeth came to the parlor door with a letter in her hand. She cried out, when she saw her sister's face, "What *is* the matter, Em'ly, for pity sakes?"

"You can't never go out again, 'Liz'beth; you can't! you can't!"

"Why can't I go out, I'd like to know? What do you mean, Em'ly Babcock?"

"You can't, you never can again. I stepped into some fire-crackers, an' I've burned some great holes right in the flouncin'. You can't never wear it without folks knowin'. Matilda Jennings will tell. Oh, 'Liz'beth, what will you do?"

"Do?" said Elizabeth. "Well, I hope I ain't so set on goin' out at my time of life as all that comes to. Let's see it. H'm, I can mend that."

"No, you can't. Matilda would see it if you did. Oh, dear! oh, dear!" Emily dropped into a corner and put her slim hands over her face.

"Do stop actin' so," said her sister. "I've jest had a letter, an' Aunt 'Liz'beth is dead."

After a little Emily looked up. "When did she die?" she asked, in a despairing voice.

"Last week."

"Did they ask us to the funeral?"

"Of course they did; it was last Friday, at two o'clock in the afternoon. They knew the letter couldn't get to us till after the funeral; but of course they'd ask us."

"What did they say the matter was?"

"Old age, I guess, as much as anything. Aunt 'Liz'beth was a good deal over eighty."

Emily sat reflectively ; she seemed to be listening while her sister related more at length the contents of the letter. Suddenly she interrupted.   " 'Liz'beth."

" Well ?"

" I was thinkin', 'Liz'beth—you know those crape veils we wore when mother died ?"

" Well, what of 'em ?"

" I—don't see why—you couldn't—make a flounce of those veils, an' put on this dress when you wore it ; then she wouldn't know."

" I'd like to know what I'd wear a crape flounce for ?"

" Why, mournin' for Aunt 'Liz'beth."

" Em'ly Babcock, what sense would there be in my wearin' mournin' when you didn't ?"

" You was named for her, an' it's a very diff'rent thing. You can jest tell folks that you was named for your aunt that jest died, an' you felt as if you ought to wear a little crape on your best dress."

" It 'll be an awful job to put on a different flounce every time we wear it."

" I'll do it ; I'm perfectly willin' to do it.   Oh, 'Liz'beth, I shall die if you ever go out again an' wear that dress."

" For pity sakes, don't, Em'ly !   I'll get out those veils after supper an' look at 'em."

The next Sunday Elizabeth wore the black silk garnished with a crape flounce to church.   Matilda Jennings walked home with her, and eyed the new trimming sharply.   " Got a new flounce, ain't you ?" said she, finally.

" I had word last week that my aunt 'Liz'beth Taylor was dead, an' I thought it wa'n't anything more'n fittin' that I should put on a little crape," replied Elizabeth, with dignity.

" Has Em'ly put on mournin' too?"

" Em'ly ain't any call to. She wa'n't named after her, as I was, an' she never saw her but once, when she was a little girl. It ain't more'n ten year since I saw her. She lived out West. I didn't feel as if Em'ly had any call to wear crape."

Matilda said no more, but there was unquelled suspicion in her eye as they parted at the Babcock gate.

The next week a trunk full of Aunt Elizabeth Taylor's clothes arrived from the West. Her daughter had sent them. There was in the trunk a goodly store of old woman's finery, two black silks among the other gowns. Aunt Elizabeth had been a dressy old lady, although she died in her eighties. It was a great surprise to the sisters. They had never dreamed of such a thing. They palpitated with awe and delight as they took out the treasures. Emily clutched Elizabeth, the thin hand closing around the thin arm.

" 'Liz'beth !"

" What is it?"

" We—won't say—anything about this to anybody. We'll jest go together to meetin' next Sabbath, an' wear these black silks, *an' let Matilda Jennings see.*"

Elizabeth looked at Emily. A gleam came into her dim blue eyes ; she tightened her thin lips. " *Well, we will,*" said she.

The following Sunday the sisters wore the black silks to church. During the week they appeared together at a sewing meeting, then at church again. The wonder and curiosity were certainly not confined to Matilda Jennings. The eccentricity which the Babcock sisters displayed in not going into society together had long been a favorite topic in the town. There had been a great deal of speculation over it. Now that they had appeared together three consecutive times, there was much talk.

On the Monday following the second Sunday Matilda Jennings went down to the Babcock house. Her cape-bonnet was on one-sided, but it was firmly tied. She opened the door softly, when her old muscles were strain-ing forward to jerk the latch. She sat gently down in the proffered chair, and displayed quite openly a worn place over the knees in her calico gown.

" We had a pleasant Sabbath yesterday, didn't we ?" said she.

" Real pleasant," assented the sisters.

" I thought we had a good discourse."

The Babcocks assented again.

" I heerd a good many say they thought it was a good discourse," repeated Matilda, like an emphatic chorus. Then she suddenly leaned forward, and her face, in the depths of her awry bonnet, twisted into a benevolent smile. " I was real glad to see you out together," she whispered, with meaning emphasis.

The sisters smiled stiffly.

Matilda paused for a moment ; she drew herself back, as if to gather strength for a thrust ; she stopped smiling. " I was glad to see you out together, for I thought it was too bad the way folks was talkin'," she said.

Elizabeth looked at her. " How were they talkin' ?"

"Well, I don' know as there's any harm in my tellin' you. I've been thinkin' mebbe I ought to for some time. It's been round consider'ble lately that you an' Em'ly didn't get along well, an' that was the reason you didn't go out more together. I told 'em I hadn't no idea 'twas so,

though, of course, I couldn't really tell. I was real glad to
see you out together, 'cause there's never any knowin' how
folks do get along, an' I was real glad to see you'd settled
it if there had been any trouble."

"There ain't been any trouble."

"Well, I'm glad if there ain't been any, an' if there has,
I'm glad to see it settled, an' I know other folks will be
too."

Elizabeth stood up. "If you want to know the reason
why we haven't been out together, I'll tell you," said she.
"You've been tryin' to find out things every way you could,
an' now I'll tell you. You've drove me to it. We had just
one decent dress between us, an' Em'ly an' me took turns
wearin' it, an' Em'ly used to wear lace on it, an' I used to
rip off the lace an' sew on black velvet when I wore it, so
folks shouldn't know it was the same dress. Em'ly an' me
never had a word in our lives, an' it's a wicked lie for folks
to say we have."

Emily was softly weeping in her handkerchief; there was
not a tear in Elizabeth's eyes ; there were bright spots on
her cheeks, and her slim height overhung Matilda Jennings
imposingly.

"My aunt 'Liz'beth, that I was named for, died two or
three weeks ago," she continued, "an' they sent us a trunk
full of her clothes, an' there was two decent dresses among
'em, an' that's the reason why Em'ly an' me have been out
together sence. Now, Matilda Jennings, you have found
out the whole story, an' I hope you're satisfied."

Now that the detective instinct and the craving inquisi-
tiveness which were so strong in this old woman were satisfied, she should have been more jubilant than she was. She
had suspected what nobody else in town had suspected ;

she had verified her suspicion, and discovered what the secrecy and pride of the sisters had concealed from the whole village, still she looked uneasy and subdued. " I sha'n't tell anybody," said she.

" You can tell nobody you're a mind to."

" I sha'n't tell nobody." Matilda Jennings arose; she had passed the parlor door, when she faced about. " I s'pose I kinder begretched you that black silk," said she, " or I shouldn't have cared so much about findin' out. I never had a black silk myself, nor any of my folks that I ever heard of. I ain't got nothin' decent to wear any-way."

There was a moment's silence. " We sha'n't lay up any-thing," said Elizabeth then, and Emily sobbed responsively. Matilda passed on, and opened the outer door. Elizabeth whispered to her sister, and Emily nodded, eagerly. " You tell her," said she.

" Matilda," called Elizabeth. Matilda looked back. " I was jest goin' to say that, if you wouldn't resent it, it got burned some, but we mended it nice, that you was perfectly welcome to that—black silk. Em'ly an' me don't really need it, and we'd be glad to have you have it."

There were tears in Matilda Jennings's black eyes, but she held them unwinkingly. " Thank ye," she said, in a gruff voice, and stepped along over the piazza, down the steps. She reached Emily's flower garden. The peppery sweetness of the nasturtiums came up in her face; it was quite early in the day, and the portulacas were still out in a splendid field of crimson and yellow. Matilda turned about, her broad foot just cleared a yellow portulaca which had straggled into the path, but she did not notice it. The homely old figure pushed past the flowers and into the house again. She stood before Elizabeth and Emily. " Look here," said she, with a fine light struggling out of her coarse old face, " I want to tell you—*I see them fire-crackers a-siz-zlin' before Em'ly stepped in 'em.*"

SISTER LIDDY.

THERE were no trees near the almshouse ; it stood in its bare, sandy lot, and there were no leaves or branches to cast shadows on its walls. It seemed like the folks whom it sheltered, out in the full glare of day, without any little kindly shade between itself and the dull, unfeeling stare of curiosity. The almshouse stood upon rising ground, so one could see it for a long distance. It was a new building, Mansard-roofed and well painted. The village took pride in it : no town far or near had such a house for the poor. It was so fine and costly that the village did not feel able to give its insane paupers separate support in a regular asylum ; so they lived in the almshouse with the sane paupers, and there was a padded cell in case they waxed too violent.

Around the almshouse lay the town fields. In summer they were green with corn and potatoes, now they showed ugly plough ridges sloping over the uneven ground, and yellow corn stubble. Beyond the field at the west of the almshouse was a little wood of elms and oaks and wild apple-trees. The yellow leaves had all fallen from the elms and the apple-trees, but most of the brown ones stayed on the oaks.

Polly Moss stood at the west window in the women's

sitting-room and gazed over at the trees. "It's cur'us how them oak leaves hang on arter the others have all fell off," she remarked.

A tall old woman sitting beside the stove looked around suddenly. She had singular bright eyes, and a sardonic smile around her mouth. "It's a way they allers have," she returned, scornfully. "Guess there ain't nothin' very cur'us about it. When the oak leaves fall off an' the others hang on, then you can be lookin' for the end of the world ; that's goin' to be one of the signs."

"Allers a-harpin' on the end of the world," growled another old woman, in a deep bass voice. "I've got jest about sick on't. Seems as if I should go crazy myself, hearin' on't the whole time." She was sewing a seam in coarse cloth, and she sat on a stool on the other side of the stove. She was short and stout, and she sat with a heavy settle as if she were stuffed with lead.

The tall old woman took no further notice. She sat rigidly straight, and fixed her bright eyes upon the top of the door, and her sardonic smile deepened.

The stout old woman gave an ugly look at her ; then she sewed with more impetus. Now and then she muttered something in her deep voice.

There were, besides herself, three old women in the room —Polly Moss, the tall one, and a pretty one in a white cap and black dress. There was also a young woman ; she sat in a rocking-chair and leaned her head back. She was handsome, but she kept her mouth parted miserably, and there were ghastly white streaks around it and her nostrils. She never spoke. Her pretty black hair was rough, and her dress sagged at the neck. She had been living out at a large farm, and had overworked. She had no friends or

relatives to take her in ; so she had come to the almshouse
to rest and try to recover.   She had no refuge but the almshouse or the hospital, and she had a terrible horror of a
hospital.   Dreadful visions arose in her ignorant childish
mind whenever she thought of one.   She had a lover, but
he had not been to see her since she came to the almshouse, six weeks before ; she wept most of the time over
that and her physical misery.

Polly Moss stood at the window until a little boy trudged
into the room, bringing his small feet down with a clapping
noise.   He went up to Polly and twitched her dress.   She
looked around at him.   " Well, now, Tommy, what do ye
want ?"

" Come out-doors an' play hide an' coot wis me, Polly."

Tommy was a stout little boy.   He wore a calico tier
that sagged to his heels in the back, and showed in front
his little calico trousers.   His round face was pleasant and
innocent and charming.

Polly put her arms around the boy and hugged him.
" Tommy's a darlin'," she said ; " can't he give poor Polly
a kiss ?"

Tommy put up his lips.   " Come out-doors an' play hide
an' coot wis me," he said again, breathing the words out
with the kiss.

" Now, Tommy, jest look out of the winder.   Don't he
see that it's rainin', hey ?"

The child shook his head stubbornly, although he was
looking straight at the window, which revealed plainly
enough that long sheets of rain were driving over the fields.
" Come out-doors and play hide an' coot wis me, Polly."

" Now, Tommy, jest listen to Polly.   Don't he know he
can't go out-doors when it's rainin' this way ?   He'd get all

wet, an' Polly too. But I'll tell you what Polly an' Tommy can do. We'll jest go out in the hall an' we'll roll the
ball. Tommy go run quick an' get his ball."

Tommy raised a shout, and clapped out of the room ;
his sweet nature was easily diverted. Polly followed him.
She had a twisting limp, and was so bent that she was not
much taller than Tommy, her little pale triangular face
seemed to look from the middle of her flat chest.

"The wust-lookin' objeck," growled the stout old woman
when Polly was out of the room : "looks more like an old
cat that's had to airn it's own livin' than a human bein'.
It 'bout makes me sick to look at her." Her deep tones
travelled far ; Polly, out in the corridor waiting for Tommy,
heard every word.

"She is a dretful-lookin' cretur," assented the pretty old
woman. As she spoke she puckered her little red mouth
daintily, and drew herself up with a genteel air.

The stout old woman surveyed her contemptuously.
"Well, good looks don't amount to much, nohow," said
she, "if folks ain't got common-sense to balance 'em. I'd
enough sight ruther know a leetle somethin' than have a
dolly-face myself."

"Seems to me she is about the dretfulest-lookin' cretur
that I ever did see," repeated the pretty old woman, quite
unmoved. Aspersions on her intellect never aroused her
in the least.

The stout old woman looked baffled. "Jest turn your
head a leetle that way, will you, Mis' Handy?" she said,
presently.

The pretty old woman turned her head obediently.
"What is it?" she inquired, with a conscious simper.

"Jest turn your head a leetle more. Yes, it's funny I

ain't never noticed it afore. Your nose is a leetle grain crooked—ain't it, Mis' Handy?"

Mrs. Handy's face turned a deep pink—even her little ears and her delicate old neck were suffused ; her blue eyes looked like an enraged bird's. "Crooked! H'm! I shouldn't think that folks that's got a nose like some folks had better say much about other folks' noses. There can't nobody tell me nothin' about my nose ; I know all about it. Folks that wouldn't wipe their feet on some folks, nor look twice at 'em, has praised it. My nose ain't crooked an' never was, an' if anybody says so it's 'cause they're so spity, 'cause they're so mortal homely themselves. Guess I know." She drew breath, and paused for a return shot, but she got none. The stout old woman sewed and chuckled to herself, the tall one still fixed her eyes upon the top of the door, and the young woman leaned back with her lips parted, and her black eyes rolled.

The pretty old woman began again in defence of her nose ; she talked fiercely, and kept feeling of it. Finally she arose and went out of the room with a flirt.

Then the stout old woman laughed. "She's gone to look at her nose in the lookin'-glass, an' make sure it ain't crooked : if it ain't a good joke !" she exclaimed, delightedly.

But she got no response. The young woman never stirred, and the tall old one only lowered her gaze from the door to the stove, which she regarded disapprovingly. "I call it the devil's stove," she remarked, after a while.

The stout old woman gave a grunt and sewed her seam ; she was done with talking to such an audience. The shouts of children out in the corridor could be heard. "Pesky young ones !" she muttered.

In the corridor Polly Moss played ball with the children. She never caught the ball, and she threw it with weak, aimless jerks; her back ached, but she was patient, and her face was full of simple childish smiles. There were two children besides Tommy—his sister and a little boy.

The corridor was long; doors in both sides led into the paupers' bedrooms. Suddenly one of the doors flew open, and a little figure shot out. She went down the corridor with a swift trot like a child. She had on nothing but a woollen petticoat and a calico waist; she held her head down, and her narrow shoulders worked as she ran; her mop of soft white hair flew out. The children looked around at her; she was a horrible caricature of themselves.

The stout old woman came pressing out of the sitting-room. She went directly to the room that the running figure had left, and peered in; then she looked around significantly. "I knowed it," she said; "it's tore all to pieces agin. I'd jest been thinkin' to myself that Sally was dretful still, an' I'd bet she was pullin' her bed to pieces. There 'tis, an' made up jest as nice a few minutes ago! I'm goin' to see Mis' Arms."

Mrs. Arms was the matron. The old woman went off with an important air, and presently she returned with her. The matron was a large woman with a calm, benignant, and weary face.

Polly Moss continued to play ball, but several other old women had assembled, and they all talked volubly. They demonstrated that Sally had torn her bed to pieces, that it had been very nicely made, and that she should be punished.

The matron listened; she did not say much. Then she returned to the kitchen, where she was preparing dinner.

Some of the paupers assisted her. An old man, with his baggy trousers hitched high, chopped something in a tray, an old woman peeled potatoes, and a young one washed pans at the sink. The young woman, as she washed, kept looking over her shoulder and rolling her dark eyes at the other people in the room. She was mindful of every motion behind her back.

Mrs. Arms herself worked and directed the others. When dinner was ready the old man clanged a bell in the corridor, and everybody flocked to the dining-room except the young woman at the kitchen sink ; she still stood there washing dishes. The dinner was coarse and abundant. The paupers, with the exception of the sick young woman, ate with gusto. The children were all hearty, and although the world had lost all its savor for the hearts and minds of the old ones, it was still somewhat salt to their palates. Now that their thoughts had ceased reaching and grasping, they could still put out their tongues, for that primitive instinct of life with which they had been born still survived and gave them pleasure. In this world it is the child only that is immortal.

The old people and the children ate after the same manner. There was a loud smacking of lips and gurgling noises. The rain drove against the windows of the dining-room, with its bare floor, its board tables and benches, and rows of feeding paupers. The smooth yellow heads of the children seemed to catch all the light in the room. Once in a while they raised imperious clamors. The overseer sat at one end of the table and served the beef. He was stout, and had a handsome, heavy face.

The meal was nearly finished when there was a crash of breaking crockery, a door slammed, and there was a wild shriek out in the corridor. The overseer and one of the old men who was quite able-bodied sprang and rushed out of the room. The matron followed, and the children tagged at her heels. The others continued feeding as if nothing had happened. "That Agnes is wuss agin," remarked the stout old woman. "I've seed it a-comin' on fer a couple of days. They'd orter have put her in the cell yesterday; I told Mis' Arms so, but they're allers puttin' off, an' puttin' off."

"They air a-takin' on her up to the cell now," said the pretty old woman; and she brought around her knifeful of cabbage with a sidewise motion, and stretched her little red mouth to receive it.

Out in the corridor shriek followed shriek; there were loud voices and scuffling. The children were huddled in the doorway, peeping, but the old paupers continued to eat. The sick young woman laid down her knife and fork and wept.

Presently the shrieks and the scuffling grew faint in the distance; the children had followed on. Then, after a little, they all returned and the dinner was finished.

After dinner, when the women paupers had done their share of the clearing away, they were again assembled in their sitting-room. The windows were cloudy with fine mist; the rain continued to drive past them from over the yellow stubbly fields. There was a good fire in the stove, and the room was hot and close. The stout old woman sewed again on her coarse seam, the others were idle. There were now six old women present; one of them was the little creature whom they called Sally. She sat close to the stove, bent over and motionless. Her clothing hardly covered her. The sick young woman was absent; she was lying down on the lounge in the matron's room, and the children too were in there.

Polly Moss sat by the window. The old women began talking among themselves. The pretty old one had taken off her cap and had it in her lap, perking up the lace and straightening it. It was a flimsy rag, like a soiled cobweb. The stout old woman cast a contemptuous glance at it. She raised her nose and her upper lip scornfully. "I don't see how you can wear that nasty thing nohow, Mis' Handy," said she.

Mrs. Handy flushed pink again. She bridled and began to speak, then she looked at the little soft soiled mass in her lap, and paused. She had not the force of character to proclaim black white while she was looking at it. Had the old cap been in the bureau drawer, or even on her head, she might have defended it to the death, but here before her eyes it silenced her.

But after her momentary subsidence she aroused herself; her blue eyes gleamed dimly at the stout old woman. "It was a handsome cap when it was new, anyhow!" said she; "better'n some folks ever had, I'll warrant. Folks that ain't got no caps at all can't afford to be flingin' at them that has, if they ain't quite so nice as they was. You'd orter have seen the cap I had when my daughter was married! All white wrought lace, an' bows of pink ribbon, an' long streamers, an' some artificial roses on't. I don't s'pose you ever see anythin' like it, Mis' Paine."

The stout woman was Mrs. Paine. "Mebbe I ain't," said she, sarcastically.

The tall old woman chimed in suddenly; her thin, nervous voice clanged after the others like a sharply struck bell. "I ain't never had any caps to speak of," she proclaimed; "never thought much of 'em, anyhow; heatin' things ; an' I never heard that folks in heaven wore caps. But I have had some good clothes. I've got a piece of silk in my bureau drawer. That silk would stand alone. An' I had a good thibet ; there was rows an' rows of velvet ribbon on it. I always had good clothes ; my husband, he wanted I should, an' he got 'em fer me. I airned some myself, too. I 'ain't got any now, an' I dunno as I care if I ain't, fer the signs are increasin'."

"Allers a-harpin' on that," muttered the stout old woman.

"I had a handsome blue silk when I was marri'd," vouchsafed Mrs. Handy.

"I've seen the piece of it," returned the tall one; "it ain't near so thick as mine is."

The old woman who had not been present in the morning now spoke. She had been listening with a superior air. She was the only one in the company who had possessed considerable property, and had fallen from a widely differing estate. She was tall and dark and gaunt; she towered up next the pretty old woman like a scraggy old pine beside a faded lily. She was a single woman, and she had lost all her property through an injudicious male relative. "Well," she proclaimed, "everybody knows I've had things if I ain't got 'em now. There I had a whole house, with Brussels carpets on all the rooms except the kitchen, an' stuffed furniture, an' beddin' packed away in chists, an' bureau drawers full of things. An' I ruther think I've had silk dresses an' bunnits an' caps."

"I remember you had a real handsome blue bunnit once, but it warn't so becomin' as some you'd had, you was so dark-complected," remarked the pretty old woman, in a soft, spiteful voice. "I had a white one, drawn silk, an' white feathers on't, when I was married, and they all said it was real becomin'. I was allers real white myself. I had a white muslin dress with a flounce on it, once, too, an' a black silk spencer cape."

"I had a fitch tippet an' muff that cost twenty-five dollars," remarked the stout old woman, emphatically, "*an'* a cashmire shawl."

"I had two cashmire shawls, an' *my* tippet cost fifty dollars," retorted the dark old woman, with dignity.

"My fust baby had an elegant blue cashmire cloak, all worked with silk as deep as that," said Mrs. Handy. She now had the old cap on her head, and looked more assertive.

"Mine had a little wagon with a velvet cushion to ride in; an' I had a tea-set, real chiny, with a green sprig on't," said the stout old woman.

"I had a Brittany teapot," returned Mrs. Handy.

"I had gilt vases as tall as that on my parlor mantel-shelf," said the dark old woman.

"I had a chiny figger, a girl with a basket of flowers on her arm, once," rejoined the tall one ; "it used to set side of the clock. An' when I was fust married I used to live in a white house, with a flower-garden to one side. I can smell them pinks an' roses now, an' I s'pose I allers shall, jest as far as I go."

"I had a pump in my kitchen sink, an' things real handy," said the stout old one ; "an' I used to look as well as anybody, an' my husband too, when we went to meetin'. I remember one winter I had a new brown alpaca with velvet buttons, an' he had a new great-coat with a velvet collar."

Suddenly the little cowering Sally raised herself and gave

testimony to her own little crumb of past comfort. Her wits were few and scattering, and had been all her days, but the conversation of the other women seemed to set some vibrating into momentary concord. She laughed, and her bleared blue eyes twinkled. "I had a pink caliker gownd once," she quavered out. "Mis' Thompson, she gin it me when I lived there."

"Do hear the poor cretur," said the pretty old woman, with an indulgent air.

Now everybody had spoken but Polly Moss. She sat by the misty window, and her little pale triangular face looked from her sunken chest at the others. This conversation was a usual one. Many and many an afternoon the almshouse old women sat together and bore witness to their past glories. Now they had nothing, but at one time or another they had had something over which to plume themselves and feel that precious pride of possession. Their present was to them a state of simple existence, they regarded their future with a vague resignation ; they were none of them thinkers, and there was no case of rapturous piety among them. In their pasts alone they took real comfort, and they kept, as it were, feeling of them to see if they were not still warm with life.

The old women delighted in these inventories and comparing of notes. Polly Moss alone had never spoken. She alone had never had anything in which to take pride. She had been always deformed and poor and friendless. She had worked for scanty pay as long as she was able, and had then drifted and struck on the almshouse, where she had grown old. She had not even a right to the charity of this particular village : this was merely the place where her working powers had failed her ; but no one could trace her back to her birthplace, or the town which was responsible for her support. Polly Moss herself did not know— she went humbly where she was told. All her life the world had seemed to her simply standing-ground; she had gotten little more out of it.

Every day, when the others talked, she listened admiringly, and searched her memory for some little past treasure of her own, but she could not remember any. The dim image of a certain delaine dress, with bright flowers scattered over it, which she had once owned, away back in her girlhood, sometimes floated before her eyes when they were talking, and she had a half-mind to mention that, but her heart would fail her. She feared that it was not worthy to be compared with the others' fine departed gowns; it paled before even Sally's pink calico. Polly's poor clothes, covering her pitiful crookedness, had never given her any firm stimulus to gratulation. So she was always silent, and the other old women had come to talk at her. Their conversation acquired a gusto from this listener who could not join in. When a new item of past property was given, there was always a side-glance in Polly's direction.

None of the old women expected to ever hear a word from Polly, but this afternoon, when they had all, down to Sally, testified, she spoke up:

"You'd orter have seen my sister Liddy," said she; her voice was very small, it sounded like the piping of a feeble bird in a bush.

There was a dead silence. The other old women looked at each other. "Didn't know you ever had a sister Liddy," the stout old woman blurted out, finally, with an amazed air.

"My sister Liddy was jest as handsome as a pictur'," Polly returned.

The pretty old woman flushed jealously. "Was she fair-complected?" she inquired.

"She was jest as fair as a lily—a good deal fairer than you ever was, Mis' Handy, an' she had long yaller curls a-hangin' clean down to her waist, an' her cheeks were jest as pink, an' she had the biggest blue eyes I ever see, an' the beautifulest leetle red mouth."

"Lor'!" ejaculated the stout old woman, and the pretty old woman sniffed.

But Polly went on; she was not to be daunted; she had been silent all this time; and now her category poured forth, not piecemeal, but in a flood, upon her astonished hearers.

"Liddy, she could sing the best of anybody anywheres around," she continued; "nobody ever heerd sech singin'. It was so dretful loud an' sweet that you could hear it 'way down the road when the winders was shut. She used to sing in the meetin'-house, she did, an' all the folks used to sit up an' look at her when she begun. She used to wear a black silk dress to meetin', an' a white cashmire shawl, an' a bunnit with a pink wreath around the face, an' she had white kid gloves. Folks used to go to that meetin'-house jest to hear Liddy sing an' see her. They thought 'nough sight more of that than they did of the preachin'.

"Liddy had a feather fan, an' she used to sit an' fan her when she wa'n't singin', an' she allers had scent on her hand-kercher. An' when meetin' was done in the evenin' all the young fellars used to be crowdin' 'round, an' pushin' and bowin' an' scrapin', a-tryin' to get a chance to see her home. But Liddy she wouldn't look at none of them; she married a real rich fellar from Bostown. He was jest as straight as an arrer, an' he had black eyes an' hair, an' he wore a beautiful coat an' a satin vest, an' he spoke jest as perlite.

"When Liddy was married she had a whole chistful of clothes, real fine cotton cloth, all tucks an' laid-work, an' she had a pair of silk stockin's, an' some white shoes. An' her weddin' dress was white satin, with a great long trail to it, an' she had a lace veil, an' she wore great long ear-drops that shone like everythin'. *An'* she come out bride in a blue silk dress, an' a black lace mantilly, an' a white bunnit trimmed with lutestring ribbon."

"Where did your sister Liddy live arter she was married?" inquired the pretty old woman, with a subdued air.

"She lived in Bostown, an' she had a great big house with a parlor an' settin'-room, an' a room to eat in besides the kitchen. An' she had real velvet carpets on all the floors down to the kitchen, an' great pictur's in gilt frames a-hangin' on all the walls. An' her furnitur' was all stuffed, an' kivered with red velvet, an' she had a pianner, an' great big marble images a-settin' on her mantel-shelf. An' she had a coach with lamps on the sides, an' blue satin cushings, to ride in, an' four horses to draw it, an' a man to drive. An' she allers had a hired girl in the kitchen. I never knowed Liddy to be without a hired girl.

"Liddy's husband, he thought everythin' of her; he never used to come home from his work without he brought her somethin', an' she used to run out to meet him. She was allers dretful lovin', an' had a good disposition. Liddy, she had the beautifulest baby you ever see, an' she had a cradle lined with blue silk to rock him in, an' he had a white silk cloak, an' a leetle lace cap—"

"I shouldn't think your beautiful sister Liddy an' her husband would let you come to the poor-house," interrupted the dark old woman.

"Liddy's dead, or she wouldn't."

" Are her husband an' the baby dead, too ?"

" They're all dead," responded Polly Moss. She looked out of the window again, her face was a burning red, and there were tears in her eyes.

There was silence among the other old women. They were at once overawed and incredulous. Polly left the room before long, then they began to discuss the matter. " I dun know whether to believe it or not," said the dark old woman.

" Well, I dun know, neither; I never knowed her to tell anythin' that wa'n't so," responded the stout old one, doubtfully.

The old women could not make up their minds whether to believe or disbelieve. The pretty one was the most incredulous of any. She said openly that she did not believe it possible that such a " homely cretur " as Polly Moss could have had such a handsome sister.

But, credulous or not, their interest and curiosity were lively. Every day Polly Moss was questioned and cross-examined concerning her sister Liddy. She rose to the occasion ; she did not often contradict herself, and the glories of her sister were increased daily. Old Polly Moss, her little withered face gleaming with reckless enthusiasm, sang the praises of her sister Liddy as wildly and faithfully as any minnesinger his angel mistress, and the old women listened with ever-increasing bewilderment and awe.

It was two weeks before Polly Moss died with pneumonia that she first mentioned her sister Liddy, and there was not one afternoon until the day when she was taken ill that she did not relate the story, with new and startling additions, to the old women.

Polly was not ill long, she settled meekly down under the

disease : her little distorted frame had no resistance in it. She died at three o'clock in the morning. The afternoon before, she seemed better ; she was quite rational, and she told the matron that she wanted to see her comrades, the old women. " I've got somethin' to tell 'em, Mis' Arms," Polly whispered, and her eyes were piteous. .

So the other old women came into the room. They stood around Polly's little iron bed and looked at her. " I—want to—tell you—somethin'," she began. But there was a soft rush, and the sick young woman entered. She pressed straight to the matron; she disregarded the others. Her wan face seemed a very lamp of life—to throw a light over and above all present darkness, even of the grave. She moved nimbly; she was so full of joy that her sickly body seemed permeated by it, and almost a spiritual one. She did not appear in the least feeble. She caught the matron's arm. " Charley has come, Mis' Arms !" she cried out. " Charley has come ! He's got a house ready. He's goin' to marry me, an' take me home, an' take care of me till I get well. I'm goin' right away !"

The old women all turned away from Polly and stared at the radiant girl. The matron sent her away, with a promise to see her in a few minutes. " Polly's dyin'," she whispered, and the girl stole out with a hushed air, but the light in her face was not dimmed. What was death to her, when she had just stepped on a height of life where one can see beyond it?

"Tell them what you wanted to, now, Polly," said the matron.

" I—want to tell you — somethin'," Polly repeated. " I s'pose I've been dretful wicked, but I ain't never had nothin' in my whole life. I—s'pose the Lord orter have been enough, but it's dretful hard sometimes to keep holt of him, an' not look anywheres else, when you see other folks a-clawin' an' gettin' other things, an' actin' as if they was wuth havin'. I ain't never had nothin' as fur as them other things go; I don't want nothin' else now. I've—got past 'em. I see I don't want nothin' but the Lord. But I used to feel dretful bad an' wicked when I heerd you all talkin' 'bout things you'd had, an' I hadn't never had nothin', so—" Polly Moss stopped talking, and coughed. The matron supported her. The old women nudged each other; their awed, sympathetic, yet sharply inquiring eyes never left her face. The children were peeping in at the open door; old Sally trotted past—she had just torn her bed to pieces. As soon as she got breath enough, Polly Moss finished what she had to say. "I—s'pose I—was dretful wicked," she whispered; "but—I never had any sister Liddy."

A POETESS.

THE garden-patch at the right of the house was all a gay spangle with sweet-peas and red-flowering beans, and flanked with feathery asparagus. A woman in blue was moving about there. Another woman, in a black bonnet, stood at the front door of the house. She knocked and waited. She could not see from where she stood the blue-clad woman in the garden. The house was very close to the road, from which a tall evergreen hedge separated it, and the view to the side was in a measure cut off.

The front door was open; the woman had to reach to knock on it, as it swung into the entry. She was a small woman and quite young, with a bright alertness about her which had almost the effect of prettiness. It was to her what greenness and crispness are to a plant. She poked her little face forward, and her sharp pretty eyes took in the entry and a room at the left, of which the door stood open. The entry was small and square and unfurnished, except for a well-rubbed old card-table against the back wall. The room was full of green light from the tall hedge, and bristling with grasses and flowers and asparagus stalks.

"Betsey, you there?" called the woman. When she spoke, a yellow canary, whose cage hung beside the front door, began to chirp and twitter.

"Betsey, you there?" the woman called again. The bird's chirps came in a quick volley; then he began to trill and sing.

"She ain't there," said the woman. She turned and went out of the yard through the gap in the hedge; then she looked around. She caught sight of the blue figure in the garden. "There she is," said she.

She went around the house to the garden. She wore a gay cashmere-patterned calico dress with her mourning bonnet, and she held it carefully away from the dewy grass and vines.

The other woman did not notice her until she was close to her and said, "Good-mornin', Betsey." Then she started and turned around.

"Why, Mis' Caxton! That you?" said she.

"Yes. I've been standin' at your door for the last half-hour. I was jest goin' away when I caught sight of you out here."

In spite of her brisk speech her manner was subdued. She drew down the corners of her mouth sadly.

"I declare I'm dreadful sorry you had to stan' there so long!" said the other woman.

She set a pan partly filled with beans on the ground, wiped her hands, which were damp and green from the wet vines, on her apron, then extended her right one with a solemn and sympathetic air.

"It don't make much odds, Betsey," replied Mrs. Caxton. "I ain't got much to take up my time nowadays." She sighed heavily as she shook hands, and the other echoed her.

"We'll go right in now. I'm dreadful sorry you stood there so long," said Betsey.

"You'd better finish pickin' your beans."

"No; I wa'n't goin' to pick any more. I was jest goin' in."

"I declare, Betsey Dole, I shouldn't think you'd got enough for a cat!" said Mrs. Caxton, eying the pan.

"I've got pretty near all there is. I guess I've got more flowerin' beans than eatin' ones, anyway."

"I should think you had," said Mrs. Caxton, surveying the row of bean-poles topped with swarms of delicate red flowers. "I should think they were pretty near all flowerin' ones. Had any peas?"

"I didn't have more'n three or four messes. I guess I planted sweet-peas mostly. I don't know hardly how I happened to."

"Had any summer squash?"

"Two or three. There's some more set, if they ever get ripe. I planted some gourds. I think they look real pretty on the kitchen shelf in the winter."

"I should think you'd got a sage bed big enough for the whole town."

"Well, I have got a pretty good-sized one. I always liked them blue sage-blows. You'd better hold up your dress real careful goin' through here, Mis' Caxton, or you'll get it wet."

The two women picked their way through the dewy grass, around a corner of the hedge, and Betsey ushered her visitor into the house.

"Set right down in the rockin-chair," said she. "I'll jest carry these beans out into the kitchen."

"I should think you'd better get another pan and string 'em, or you won't get 'em done for dinner."

"Well, mebbe I will, if you'll excuse it, Mis' Caxton. The beans had ought to boil quite a while; they're pretty old."

Betsey went into the kitchen and returned with a pan and an old knife. She seated herself opposite Mrs. Caxton, and began to string and cut the beans.

"If I was in your place I shouldn't feel as if I'd got enough to boil a kettle for," said Mrs. Caxton, eying the beans. "I should 'most have thought when you didn't have any more room for a garden than you've got that you'd planted more real beans and peas instead of so many flowerin' ones. I'd rather have a good mess of green peas boiled with a piece of salt pork than all the sweet-peas you could give me. I like flowers well enough, but I never set up for a butterfly, an' I want something else to live on." She looked at Betsey with pensive superiority.

Betsey was near-sighted ; she had to bend low over the beans in order to string them. She was fifty years old, but she wore her streaky light hair in curls like a young girl. The curls hung over her faded cheeks and almost concealed them. Once in a while she flung them back with a childish gesture which sat strangely upon her.

"I dare say you're in the right of it," she said, meekly.

"I know I am. You folks that write poetry wouldn't have a single thing to eat growin' if they were left alone. And that brings to mind what I come for. I've been thinkin' about it ever since—our—little Willie—left us." Mrs. Caxton's manner was suddenly full of shamefaced dramatic fervor, her eyes reddened with tears.

Betsey looked up inquiringly, throwing back her curls. Her face took on unconsciously lines of grief so like the other woman's that she looked like her for the minute.

"I thought maybe," Mrs. Caxton went on, tremulously, "you'd be willin' to—write a few lines."

"Of course I will, Mis' Caxton. I'll be glad to, if I can do 'em to suit you," Betsey said, tearfully.

"I thought jest a few—lines. You could mention how —handsome he was, and good, and I never had to punish him but once in his life, and how pleased he was with his little new suit, and what a sufferer he was, and—how we hope he is at rest—in a better land."

"I'll try, Mis' Caxton, I'll try," sobbed Betsey. The two women wept together for a few minutes.

"It seems as if—I couldn't have it so sometimes," Mrs. Caxton said, brokenly. "I keep thinkin' he's in the other —room. Every time I go back home when I've been away it's like—losin' him again. Oh, it don't seem as if I could go home and not find him there—it don't, it don't! Oh, you don't know anything about it, Betsey. You never had any children!"

"I don't s'pose I do, Mis' Caxton; I don't s'pose I do."

Presently Mrs. Caxton wiped her eyes. "I've been thinkin'," said she, keeping her mouth steady with an effort, "that it would be real pretty to have—some lines printed on some sheets of white paper with a neat black border. I'd like to send some to my folks, and one to the Perkinses in Brigham, and there's a good many others I thought would value 'em."

"I'll do jest the best I can, Mis' Caxton, an' be glad to. It's little enough anybody can do at such times."

Mrs. Caxton broke out weeping again. "Oh, it's true, it's true, Betsey!" she sobbed. "Nobody can do anything, and nothin' amounts to anything—poetry or anything else —when he's *gone*. Nothin' can bring him back. Oh, what shall I do, what shall I do?"

Mrs. Caxton dried her tears again, and arose to take

leave. "Well, I must be goin', or Wilson won't have any dinner," she said, with an effort at self-control.

"Well, I'll do jest the best I can with the poetry," said Betsey. "I'll write it this afternoon." She had set down her pan of beans and was standing beside Mrs. Caxton. She reached up and straightened her black bonnet, which had slipped backward.

"I've got to get a pin," said Mrs. Caxton, tearfully. "I can't keep it anywheres. It drags right off my head, the veil is so heavy."

Betsey went to the door with her visitor. "It's dreadful dusty, ain't it?" she remarked, in that sad, contemptuous tone with which one speaks of discomforts in the presence of affliction.

"Terrible," replied Mrs. Caxton. "I wouldn't wear my black dress in it nohow; a black bonnet is bad enough. This dress is 'most too good. It's enough to spoil everything. Well, I'm much obliged to you, Betsey, for bein' willin' to do that."

"I'll do jest the best I can, Mis' Caxton."

After Betsey had watched her visitor out of the yard she returned to the sitting-room and took up the pan of beans. She looked doubtfully at the handful of beans all nicely strung and cut up. "I declare I don't know what to do," said she. "Seems as if I should kind of relish these, but it's goin' to take some time to cook 'em, tendin' the fire an' everything, an' I'd ought to go to work on that poetry. Then, there's another thing, if I have 'em to-day, I can't to-morrow. Mebbe I shall take more comfort thinkin' about 'em. I guess I'll leave 'em over till to-morrow."

Betsey carried the pan of beans out into the kitchen and set them away in the pantry. She stood scrutinizing the shelves like a veritable Mother Hubbard. There was a plate containing three or four potatoes and a slice of cold boiled pork, and a spoonful of red jelly in a tumbler; that was all the food in sight. Betsey stooped and lifted the lid from an earthen jar on the floor. She took out two slices of bread. "There!" said she. "I'll have this bread and that jelly this noon, an' to-night I'll have a kind of dinner-supper with them potatoes warmed up with the pork. An' then I can sit right down an' go to work on that poetry."

It was scarcely eleven o'clock, and not time for dinner. Betsey returned to the sitting-room, got an old black portfolio and pen and ink out of the chimney cupboard, and seated herself to work. She meditated, and wrote one line, then another. Now and then she read aloud what she had written with a solemn intonation. She sat there thinking and writing, and the time went on. The twelve-o'clock bell rang, but she never noticed it; she had quite forgotten the bread and jelly. The long curls drooped over her cheeks; her thin yellow hand, cramped around the pen, moved slowly and fitfully over the paper. The light in the room was dim and green, like the light in an arbor, from the tall hedge before the windows. Great plumy bunches of asparagus waved over the tops of the looking-glass; a framed sampler, a steel engraving of a female head taken from some old magazine, and sheaves of dried grasses hung on or were fastened to the walls; vases and tumblers of flowers stood on the shelf and table. The air was heavy and sweet.

Betsey in this room, bending over her portfolio, looked like the very genius of gentle, old-fashioned, sentimental poetry. It seemed as if one, given the premises of herself and the room, could easily deduce what she would write, and read without seeing those lines wherein flowers rhymed sweetly with vernal bowers, home with beyond the tomb, and heaven with even.

The summer afternoon wore on. It grew warmer and closer; the air was full of the rasping babble of insects, with the cicadas shrilling over them; now and then a team passed, and a dust cloud floated over the top of the hedge; the canary at the door chirped and trilled, and Betsey wrote poor little Willie Caxton's obituary poetry.

Tears stood in her pale blue eyes; occasionally they rolled down her cheeks, and she wiped them away. She kept her handkerchief in her lap with her portfolio. When she looked away from the paper she seemed to see two childish forms in the room—one purely human, a boy clad in his little girl petticoats, with a fair chubby face; the other in a little straight white night-gown, with long, shining wings, and the same face. Betsey had not enough imagination to change the face. Little Willie Caxton's angel was still himself to her, although decked in the paraphernalia of the resurrection.

" I s'pose I can't feel about it nor write about it anything the way I could if I'd had any children of my own an' lost 'em. I s'pose it *would* have come home to me different," Betsey murmured once, sniffing. A soft color flamed up under her curls at the thought. For a second the room seemed all aslant with white wings, and smiling with the faces of children that had never been. Betsey straightened herself as if she were trying to be dignified to her inner consciousness. "That's one trouble I've been clear of, anyhow," said she; "an' I guess I can enter into her feelin's considerable."

She glanced at a great pink shell on the shelf, and remembered how she had often given it to the dead child to play with when he had been in with his mother, and how he had put it to his ear to hear the sea.

"Dear little fellow!" she sobbed, and sat awhile with her handkerchief at her face.

Betsey wrote her poem upon backs of old letters and odd scraps of paper. She found it difficult to procure enough paper for fair copies of her poems when composed; she was forced to be very economical with the first draft. Her portfolio was piled with a loose litter of written papers when she at length arose and stretched her stiff limbs. It was near sunset; men with dinner-pails were tramping past the gate, going home from their work.

Betsey laid the portfolio on the table. "There! I've wrote sixteen verses," said she, "an' I guess I've got everything in. I guess she'll think that's enough. I can copy it off nice to-morrow. I can't see to-night to do it, anyhow."

There were red spots on Betsey's cheeks; her knees were unsteady when she walked. She went into the kitchen and made a fire, and set on the tea-kettle. "I guess I won't warm up them potatoes to-night," said she; "I'll have the bread an' jelly, an' save 'em for breakfast. Somehow I don't seem to feel so much like 'em as I did, an' fried potatoes is apt to lay heavy at night."

When the kettle boiled, Betsey drank her cup of tea and soaked her slice of bread in it; then she put away her cup and saucer and plate, and went out to water her garden. The weather was so dry and hot it had to be watered every night. Betsey had to carry the water from a neighbor's well; her own was dry. Back and forth she went in the deepening twilight, her slender body strained to one side with the heavy water-pail, until the garden-mould looked dark and wet. Then she took in the canary-bird, locked up her house, and soon her light went out. Often on these summer nights Betsey went to bed without lighting a lamp at all. There was no moon, but it was a beautiful starlight night. She lay awake nearly all night, thinking of her poem. She altered several lines in her mind.

She arose early, made herself a cup of tea, and warmed over the potatoes, then sat down to copy the poem. She wrote it out on both sides of note-paper, in a neat, cramped hand. It was the middle of the afternoon before it was finished. She had been obliged to stop work and cook the beans for dinner, although she begrudged the time. When the poem was fairly copied, she rolled it neatly and tied it with a bit of black ribbon ; then she made herself ready to carry it to Mrs. Caxton's.

It was a hot afternoon. Betsey went down the street in her thinnest dress—an old delaine, with delicate bunches of faded flowers on a faded green ground. There was a narrow green belt ribbon around her long waist. She wore a green barège bonnet, stiffened with rattans, scooping over her face, with her curls pushed forward over her thin cheeks in two bunches, and she carried a small green parasol with a jointed handle. Her costume was obsolete, even in the little country village where she lived. She had worn it every summer for the last twenty years. She made no more change in her attire than the old perennials in her garden. She had no money with which to buy new clothes, and the old satisfied her. She had come to regard them as being as unalterably a part of herself as her body.

Betsey went on, setting her slim, cloth-gaitered feet daintily in the hot sand of the road. She carried her roll of poetry in a black-mitted hand. She walked rather slowly. She was not very strong; there was a limp feeling in her knees; her face, under the green shade of her bonnet, was pale and moist with the heat.

She was glad to reach Mrs. Caxton's and sit down in her parlor, damp and cool and dark as twilight, for the blinds and curtains had been drawn all day. Not a breath of the fervid out-door air had penetrated it.

"Come right in this way; it's cooler than the sittin'-room," Mrs. Caxton said; and Betsey sank into the hair-cloth rocker and waved a palm-leaf fan.

Mrs. Caxton sat close to the window in the dim light, and read the poem. She took out her handkerchief and wiped her eyes as she read. "It's beautiful, beautiful," she said, tearfully, when she had finished. "It's jest as comfortin' as it can be, and you worked that in about his new suit so nice. I feel real obliged to you, Betsey, and you shall have one of the printed ones when they're done. I'm goin' to see to it right off."

Betsey flushed and smiled. It was to her as if her poem had been approved and accepted by one of the great magazines. She had the pride and self-wonderment of recognized genius. She went home buoyantly, under the wilting sun, after her call was done. When she reached home there was no one to whom she could tell her triumph, but the hot spicy breath of the evergreen hedge and the fervent sweetness of the sweet-peas seemed to greet her like the voices of friends.

She could scarcely wait for the printed poem. Mrs. Caxton brought it, and she inspected it, neatly printed in its black border. She was quite overcome with innocent pride.

"Well, I don't know but it does read pretty well," said she.

"It's beautiful," said Mrs. Caxton, fervently. "Mr. White said he never read anything any more touchin', when I carried it to him to print. I think folks are goin' to think a good deal of havin' it. I've had two dozen printed."

It was to Betsey like a large edition of a book. She had written obituary poems before, but never one had been printed in this sumptuous fashion. "I declare I think it would look pretty framed!" said she.

"Well, I don't know but it would," said Mrs. Caxton. "Anybody might have a neat little black frame, and it would look real appropriate."

"I wonder how much it would cost?" said Betsey.

After Mrs. Caxton had gone, she sat long, staring admiringly at the poem, and speculating as to the cost of a frame. "There ain't no use; I can't have it nohow, not if it don't cost more'n a quarter of a dollar," said she.

Then she put the poem away and got her supper. Nobody knew how frugal Betsey Dole's suppers and breakfasts and dinners were. Nearly all her food in the summer came from the scanty vegetables which flourished between the flowers in her garden. She ate scarcely more than her canary-bird, and sang as assiduously. Her income was almost infinitesimal: the interest at a low per cent. of a tiny sum in the village savings-bank, the remnant of her father's little hoard after his funeral expenses had been paid. Betsey had lived upon it for twenty years, and considered herself well-to-do. She had never received a cent for her poems; she had not thought of such a thing as possible. The appearance of this last in such shape was worth more to her than its words represented in as many dollars.

Betsey kept the poem pinned on the wall under the look-ing-glass ; if any one came in, she tried with delicate hints to call attention to it. It was two weeks after she received it that the downfall of her innocent pride came.

One afternoon Mrs. Caxton called. It was raining hard. Betsey could scarcely believe it was she when she went to the door and found her standing there.

"Why, Mis' Caxton !" said she. "Ain't you wet to your skin ?"

"Yes, I guess I be, pretty near. I s'pose I hadn't ought to come 'way down here in such a soak ; but I went into Sarah Rogers's a minute after dinner, and something she said made me so mad, I made up my mind I'd come down here and tell you about it if I got drowned." Mrs. Caxton was out of breath ; rain-drops trickled from her hair over her face ; she stood in the door and shut her umbrella with a vicious shake to scatter the water from it. "I don't know what you're goin' to do with this," said she ; "it's drippin'."

"I'll take it out an' put it in the kitchen sink."

"Well, I'll take off my shawl here too, and you can hang it out in the kitchen. I spread this shawl out. I thought it would keep the rain off me some. I know one thing, I'm goin' to have a waterproof if I live."

When the two women were seated in the sitting-room, Mrs. Caxton was quiet for a moment. There was a hesi-tating look on her face, fresh with the moist wind, with strands of wet hair clinging to the temples.

"I don't know as I had ought to tell you," she said, doubtfully.

"Why hadn't you ought to ?"

"Well, I don't care ; I'm goin' to, anyhow. I think you'd

ought to know, an' it ain't so bad for you as it is for me.
It don't begin to be. I put considerable money into 'em.
I think Mr. White was pretty high, myself."

Betsey looked scared. "What is it?" she asked, in a
weak voice.

"*Sarah Rogers says that the minister told her Ida that that
poetry you wrote was jest as poor as it could be, an' it was in
dreadful bad taste to have it printed an' sent round that way.*
What do you think of that?"

Betsey did not reply. She sat looking at Mrs. Caxton
as a victim whom the first blow had not killed might look
at her executioner. Her face was like a pale wedge of ice
between her curls.

Mrs. Caxton went on. "Yes, she said that right to my
face, word for word. An' there was something else. She
said the minister said that you had never wrote anything
that could be called poetry, an' it was a dreadful waste of
time. I don't s'pose he thought 'twas comin' back to you.
You know he goes with Ida Rogers, an' I s'pose he said it
to her kind of confidential when she showed him the poetry.
There! I gave Sarah Rogers one of them nice printed
ones, an' she acted glad enough to have it. Bad taste!
H'm! If anybody wants to say anything against that
beautiful poetry, printed with that nice black border, they
can. I don't care if it's the minister, or who it is. I don't
care if he does write poetry himself, an' has had some
printed in a magazine. Maybe his ain't quite so fine as he
thinks 'tis. Maybe them magazine folks jest took his for
lack of something better. I'd like to have you send that
poetry there. Bad taste! I jest got right up. 'Sarah
Rogers,' says I, 'I hope you won't never do anything yourself in any worse taste.' I trembled so I could hardly

speak, and I made up my mind I'd come right straight over here."

Mrs. Caxton went on and on. Betsey sat listening, and saying nothing. She looked ghastly. Just before Mrs. Caxton went home she noticed it. "Why, Betsey Dole," she cried, "you look as white as a sheet. You ain't takin' it to heart as much as all that comes to, I hope. Goodness, I wish I hadn't told you!"

"I'd a good deal ruther you told me," replied Betsey, with a certain dignity. She looked at Mrs. Caxton. Her back was as stiff as if she were bound to a stake.

"Well, I thought you would," said Mrs. Caxton, uneasily; "and you're dreadful silly if you take it to heart, Betsey, that's all I've got to say. Goodness, I guess I don't, and it's full as hard on me as 'tis on you!"

Mrs. Caxton arose to go. Betsey brought her shawl and umbrella from the kitchen, and helped her off. Mrs. Caxton turned on the door-step and looked back at Betsey's white face. "Now don't go to thinkin' about it any more," said she. "I ain't goin' to. It ain't worth mindin'. Everybody knows what Sarah Rogers is. Good-by."

"Good-by, Mis' Caxton," said Betsey. She went back into the sitting-room. It was a cold rain, and the room was gloomy and chilly. She stood looking out of the window, watching the rain pelt on the hedge. The bird-cage hung at the other window. The bird watched her with his head on one side; then he begun to chirp.

Suddenly Betsey faced about and began talking. It was not as if she were talking to herself; it seemed as if she recognized some other presence in the room. "I'd like to know if it's fair," said she. "I'd like to know if you think it's fair. Had I ought to have been born with the wantin'

to write poetry if I couldn't write it—had I? Had I ought
to have been let to write all my life, an' not know before
there wa'n't any use in it? Would it be fair if that canary-
bird there, that ain't never done anything but sing, should
turn out not to be singin'? Would it, I'd like to know?
S'pose them sweet-peas shouldn't be smellin' the right
way? I ain't been dealt with as fair as they have, I'd like
to know if I have."

The bird trilled and trilled. It was as if the golden
down on his throat bubbled. Betsey went across the room
to a cupboard beside the chimney. On the shelves were
neatly stacked newspapers and little white rolls of writing-
paper. Betsey began clearing the shelves. She took out
the newspapers first, got the scissors, and cut a poem neatly out of the corner of each. Then she took up the clipped
poems and the white rolls in her apron, and carried them
into the kitchen. She cleaned out the stove carefully, re-
moving every trace of ashes; then she put in the papers,
and set them on fire. She stood watching them as their
edges curled and blackened, then leaped into flame. Her
face twisted as if the fire were curling over it also. Other
women might have burned their lovers' letters in agony of
heart. Betsey had never had any lover, but she was burning all the love-letters ,that had passed between her and
life. When the flames died out she got a blue china sugar-
bowl from the pantry and dipped the ashes into it with one
of her thin silver teaspoons; then she put on the cover and
set it away in the sitting-room cupboard.

The bird, who had been silent while she was out, began
chirping again. Betsey went back to the pantry and got a
lump of sugar, which she stuck between the cage wires.
She looked at the clock on the kitchen shelf as she went

by. It was after six. " I guess I don't want any supper to-night," she muttered.

She sat down by the window again. The bird pecked at his sugar. Betsey shivered and coughed. She had coughed more or less for years. People said she had the old-fashioned consumption. She sat at the window until it was quite dark ; then she went to bed in her little bedroom out of the sitting-room. She shivered so she could not hold herself upright crossing the room. She coughed a great deal in the night.

Betsey was always an early riser. She was up at five the next morning. The sun shone, but it was very cold for the season. The leaves showed white in a north wind, and the flowers looked brighter than usual, though they were bent with the rain of the day before. Betsey went out in the garden to straighten her sweet-peas.

Coming back, a neighbor passing in the street eyed her curiously. " Why, Betsey, you sick ?" said she.

"No ; I'm kinder chilly, that's all," replied Betsey.

But the woman went home and reported that Betsey Dole looked dreadfully, and she didn't believe she'd ever see another summer.

It was now late August. Before October it was quite generally recognized that Betsey Dole's life was nearly over. She had no relatives, and hired nurses were rare in this little village. Mrs. Caxton came voluntarily and took care of her, only going home to prepare her husband's meals. Betsey's bed was moved into the sitting-room, and the neighbors came every day to see her, and brought little delicacies. Betsey had talked very little all her life ; she talked less now, and there was a reticence about her which somewhat intimidated the other women. They would look pityingly and solemnly at her, and whisper in the entry when they went out.

Betsey never complained ; but she kept asking if the minister had got home. He had been called away by his mother's illness, and returned only a week before Betsey died.

He came over at once to see her. Mrs. Caxton ushered him in one afternoon.

"Here's Mr. Lang come to see you, Betsey," said she, in the tone she would have used towards a little child. She placed the rocking-chair for the minister, and was about to seat herself, when Betsey spoke:

"Would you mind goin' out in the kitchen jest a few minutes, Mis' Caxton?" said she.

Mrs. Caxton arose, and went out with an embarrassed trot. Then there was silence. The minister was a young man—a country boy who had worked his way through a country college. He was gaunt and awkward, but sturdy in his loose clothes. He had a homely, impetuous face, with a good forehead.

He looked at Betsey's gentle, wasted face, sunken in the pillow, framed by its clusters of curls ; finally he began to speak in the stilted fashion, yet with a certain force by reason of his unpolished honesty, about her spiritual welfare. Betsey listened quietly ; now and then she assented. She had been a church member for years. It seemed now to the young man that this elderly maiden, drawing near the end of her simple, innocent life, had indeed her lamp, which no strong winds of temptation had ever met, well trimmed and burning.

When he paused, Betsey spoke. "Will you go to the cupboard side of the chimney and bring me the blue sugar-bowl on the top shelf?" said she, feebly.

The young man stared at her a minute ; then he went to the cupboard, and brought the sugar-bowl to her. He held it, and Betsey took off the lid with her weak hand. "Do you see what's in there?" said she.

"It looks like ashes."

"It's—the ashes of all—the poetry I—ever wrote."

"Why, what made you burn it, Miss Dole?"

"I found out it wa'n't worth nothin'."

The minister looked at her in a bewildered way. He began to question if she were not wandering in her mind. He did not once suspect his own connection with the matter.

Betsey fastened her eager, sunken eyes upon his face. "What I want to know is—if you'll 'tend to—havin' this—buried with me."

The minister recoiled. He thought to himself that she certainly was wandering.

"No, I ain't out of my head," said Betsey. "I know what I'm sayin'. Maybe it's queer soundin', but it's a notion I've took. If you'll—'tend to it, I shall be—much obliged. I don't know anybody else I can ask."

"Well, I'll attend to it, if you wish me to, Miss Dole," said the minister, in a serious, perplexed manner. She replaced the lid on the sugar-bowl, and left it in his hands.

"Well, I shall be much obliged if you will 'tend to it ; an' now there's something else," said she.

"What is it, Miss Dole?"

She hesitated a moment. "You write poetry, don't you?"

The minister colored. "Why, yes ; a little sometimes."

"It's good poetry, ain't it? They printed some in a magazine."

The minister laughed confusedly. "Well, Miss Dole, I

don't know how good poetry it may be, but they did print some in a magazine."

Betsey lay looking at him. "I never wrote none that was—good," she whispered, presently ; "but I've been thinkin'—if you would jest write a few—lines about me— afterward— I've been thinkin' that—mebbe my—dyin' was goin' to make me—a good subject for—poetry, if I never wrote none. If you would jest write a few lines."

The minister stood holding the sugar-bowl ; he was quite pale with bewilderment and sympathy. "I'll—do the best I can, Miss Dole," he stammered.

"I'll be much obliged," said Betsey, as if the sense of grateful obligation was immortal like herself. She smiled, and the sweetness of the smile was as evident through the drawn lines of her mouth as the old red in the leaves of a withered rose. The sun was setting ; a red beam flashed softly over the top of the hedge and lay along the opposite wall ; then the bird in his cage began to chirp. He chirped faster and faster until he trilled into a triumphant song.

CHRISTMAS JENNY.

The day before there had been a rain and a thaw, then in the night the wind had suddenly blown from the north, and it had grown cold. In the morning it was very clear and cold, and there was the hard glitter of ice over everything. The snow-crust had a thin coat of ice, and all the open fields shone and flashed. The tree boughs and trunks, and all the little twigs, were enamelled with ice. The roads were glare and slippery with it, and so were the door-yards. In old Jonas Carey's yard the path that sloped from the door to the well was like a frozen brook.

Quite early in the morning old Jonas Carey came out with a pail, and went down the path to the well. He went slowly and laboriously, shuffling his feet, so he should not fall. He was tall and gaunt, and one side of his body seemed to slant towards the other, he settled so much more heavily upon one foot. He was somewhat stiff and lame from rheumatism.

He reached the well in safety, hung the pail, and began pumping. He pumped with extreme slowness and steadiness; a certain expression of stolid solemnity, which his face wore, never changed.

When he had filled his pail he took it carefully from the pump spout, and started back to the house, shuffling as be-

fore. He was two thirds of the way to the door, when he
came to an extremely slippery place. Just there some roots
from a little cherry-tree crossed the path, and the ice made
a dangerous little pitch over them.

Old Jonas lost his footing, and sat down suddenly ; the
water was all spilled. The house door flew open, and an
old woman appeared.

" Oh, Jonas, air you hurt ?" she cried, blinking wildly and
terrifiedly in the brilliant light.

The old man never said a word. He sat still and looked
straight before him, solemnly.

" Oh, Jonas, you ain't broke any bones, hev you ?" The
old woman gathered up her skirts and began to edge off
the door-step, with trembling knees.

Then the old man raised his voice. " Stay where you
be," he said, imperatively.   " Go back into the house !"

He began to raise himself, one joint at a time, and the
old woman went back into the house, and looked out of the
window at him.

When old Jonas finally stood upon his feet it seemed as
if he had actually constructed himself, so piecemeal his rising had been.   He went back to the pump, hung the pail
under the spout, and filled it.   Then he started on the return with more caution than before.   When he reached the
dangerous place his feet flew up again, he sat down, and the
water was spilled.

The old woman appeared in the door ; her dim blue
eyes were quite round, her delicate chin was dropped.
" Oh, Jonas !"

" Go back !" cried the old man, with an imperative jerk of
his head towards her, and she retreated.   This time he arose
more quickly, and made quite a lively shuffle back to the pump.

But when his pail was filled and he again started on the return, his caution was redoubled. He seemed to scarcely move at all. When he approached the dangerous spot his progress was hardly more perceptible than a scaly leaf-slug's. Repose almost lapped over motion. The old woman in the window watched breathlessly.

The slippery place was almost passed, the shuffle quickened a little—the old man sat down again, and the tin pail struck the ice with a clatter.

The old woman appeared. "Oh, Jonas!"

Jonas did not look at her; he sat perfectly motionless.

"Jonas, air you hurt? Do speak to me for massy sake!" Jonas did not stir.

Then the old woman let herself carefully off the step. She squatted down upon the icy path, and hitched along to Jonas. She caught hold of his arm—"Jonas, you don't feel as if any of your bones were broke, do you?" Her voice was almost sobbing, her small frame was all of a tremble.

"Go back!" said Jonas. That was all he would say. The old woman's tearful entreaties did not move him in the least. Finally she hitched herself back to the house, and took up her station in the window. Once in a while she rapped on the pane, and beckoned piteously.

But old Jonas Carey sat still. His solemn face was inscrutable. Over his head stretched the icy cherry-branches, full of the flicker and dazzle of diamonds. A woodpecker flew into the tree and began tapping at the trunk, but the ice-enamel was so hard that he could not get any food. Old Jonas sat so still that he did not mind him. A jay flew on the fence within a few feet of him ; a sparrow pecked at some weeds piercing the snow-crust beside the door.

Over in the east arose the mountain, covered with frosty foliage full of silver and blue and diamond lights. The air was stinging. Old Jonas paid no attention to anything. He sat there.

The old woman ran to the door again. "Oh, Jonas, you'll freeze, settin' there!" she pleaded. "Can't you git up? Your bones ain't broke, air they?" Jonas was silent.

"Oh, Jonas, there's Christmas Jenny comin' down the road—what do you s'pose she'll think?"

Old Jonas Carey was unmoved, but his old wife eagerly watched the woman coming down the road. The woman looked oddly at a distance: like a broad green moving bush; she was dragging something green after her, too. When she came nearer one could see that she was laden with evergreen wreaths—her arms were strung with them; long sprays of ground-pine were wound around her shoulders, she carried a basket trailing with them, and holding also many little bouquets of bright-colored everlasting flowers. She dragged a sled, with a small hemlock-tree bound upon it. She came along sturdily over the slippery road. When she reached the Carey gate she stopped and looked over at Jonas. "Is he hurt?" she sang out to the old woman.

"I dunno—he's fell down three times."

Jenny came through the gate, and proceeded straight to Jonas. She left her sled in the road. She stooped, brought her basket on a level with Jonas's head, and gave him a little push with it. "What's the matter with ye?" Jonas did not wink. "Your bones ain't broke, are they?"

Jenny stood looking at him for a moment. She wore a black hood, her large face was weather-beaten, deeply tanned, and reddened. Her features were strong, but heavily cut. She made one think of those sylvan faces with features composed of bark-wrinkles and knot-holes, that one can fancy looking out of the trunks of trees. She was not an aged woman, but her hair was iron-gray, and crinkled as closely as gray moss.

Finally she turned towards the house. "I'm comin' in a minute," she said to Jonas's wife, and trod confidently up the icy steps.

"Don't you slip," said the old woman, tremulously.

"I ain't afraid of slippin'." When they were in the house she turned around on Mrs. Carey, "Don't you fuss, he ain't hurt."

"No, I don't s'pose he is. It's jest one of his tantrums. But I dunno what I am goin' to do. Oh, dear me suz, I dunno what I am goin' to do with him sometimes!"

"Leave him alone—let him set there."

"Oh, he's tipped all that water over, an' I'm afeard he'll —freeze down. Oh, dear!"

"Let him freeze! Don't you fuss, Betsey."

"I was jest goin' to git breakfast. Mis' Gill she sent us in two sassage-cakes. I was goin' to fry 'em, an' I jest asked him to go out an' draw a pail of water, so's to fill up the tea-kittle. Oh, dear!"

Jenny sat her basket in a chair, strode peremptorily out of the house, picked up the tin pail which lay on its side near Jonas, filled it at the well, and returned. She wholly ignored the old man. When she entered the door his eyes relaxed their solemn stare at vacancy, and darted a swift glance after her.

"Now fill up the kittle, an' fry the sassages," she said to Mrs. Carey.

"Oh, I'm afeard he won't git up, an' they'll be cold!

Sometimes his tantrums last a consider'ble while. You see he sot down three times, an' he's awful mad."

" I don't see who he thinks he's spitin'."

" I dunno, 'less it's Providence."

" I reckon Providence don't care much where he sets."

" Oh, Jenny, I'm dreadful afeard he'll freeze down."

" No, he won't. Put on the sassages."

Jonas's wife went about getting out the frying-pan, crooning over her complaint all the time. " He's dreadful fond of sassages," she said, when the odor of the frying sausages became apparent in the room.

" He'll smell 'em an' come in," remarked Jenny, dryly. " He knows there ain't but two cakes, an' he'll be afeard you'll give me one of 'em."

She was right. Before long the two women, taking sly peeps from the window, saw old Jonas lumberingly getting up. " Don't say nothin' to him about it when he comes in," whispered Jenny.

When the old man clumped into the kitchen, neither of the women paid any attention to him. His wife turned the sausages, and Jenny was gathering up her wreaths. Jonas let himself down into a chair, and looked at them uneasily. Jenny laid down her wreaths. " Goin' to stay to breakfast ?" said the old man.

" Well, I dunno," replied Jenny. " Them sassages do smell temptin'."

All Jonas's solemnity had vanished, he looked foolish and distressed.

" Do take off your hood, Jenny," urged Betsey. " I ain't very fond of sassages myself, an' I'd jest as liv's you'd have my cake as not."

Jenny laughed broadly and good-naturedly, and began

gathering up her wreaths again. "Lor', I don't want your sassage-cake," said she. "I've had my breakfast I'm goin' down to the village to sell my wreaths."

Jonas's face lit up. "Pleasant day, ain't it?" he remarked, affably.

Jenny grew sober. "I don't think it's a very pleasant day; guess you wouldn't if you was a woodpecker or a blue-jay," she replied.

Jonas looked at her with stupid inquiry.

"They can't git no breakfast," said Jenny. "They can't git through the ice on the trees. They'll starve if there ain't a thaw pretty soon. I've got to buy 'em somethin' down to the store. I'm goin' to feed a few of 'em. I ain't goin' to see 'em dyin' in my door-yard if I can help it. I've given 'em all I could spare from my own birds this mornin'."

"It's too bad, ain't it?"

"I think it's too bad. I was goin' to buy me a new caliker dress if this freeze hadn't come, but I can't now. What it would cost will save a good many lives. Well, I've got to hurry along if I'm goin' to git back to-day."

Jenny, surrounded with her trailing masses of green, had to edge herself through the narrow doorway. She went straight to the village and peddled her wares from house to house. She had her regular customers. Every year, the week before Christmas, she came down from the mountain with her evergreens. She was popularly supposed to earn quite a sum of money in that way. In the summer she sold vegetables, but the green Christmas traffic was regarded as her legitimate business—it had given her her name among the villagers. However, the fantastic name may have arisen from the popular conception of Jenny's character. She also was considered somewhat fantastic, although there was no doubt of her sanity. In her early youth she had had an unfortunate love affair, that was supposed to have tinctured her whole life with an alien element. " Love-cracked," people called her.

"Christmas Jenny's kind of love-cracked," they said. She was Christmas Jenny in midsummer, when she came down the mountain laden with green peas and string-beans and summer squashes.

She owned a little house and a few acres of cleared land on the mountain, and in one way or another she picked up a living from it.

It was noon to-day before she had sold all her evergreens and started up the mountain road for home. She had laid in a small stock of provisions, and she carried them in the basket which had held the little bunches of life-everlasting and amaranth flowers and dried grasses.

The road wound along the base of the mountain. She had to follow it about a mile ; then she struck into a cart-path which led up to the clearing where her house was.

After she passed Jonas Carey's there were no houses and no people, but she met many living things that she knew. A little field-mouse, scratching warily from cover to cover, lest his enemies should spy him, had appreciative notice from Jenny Wrayne. She turned her head at the call of a jay, and she caught a glimmer of blue through the dazzling white boughs. She saw with sympathetic eyes a woodpecker drumming on the ice-bound trunk of a tree. Now and then she scattered, with regretful sparseness, some seeds and crumbs from her parcels.

At the point where she left the road for the cart-path there was a gap in the woods, and a clear view of the village below. She stopped and looked back at it. It was quite a large village ; over it hung a spraying net-work of frosty branches ; the smoke arose straight up from the chimneys. Down in the village street a girl and a young man were walking, talking about her, but she did not know that.

The girl was the minister's daughter. She had just become engaged to the young man, and was walking with him in broad daylight with a kind of shamefaced pride. Whenever they met anybody she blushed, and at the same time held up her head proudly, and swung one arm with an airy motion. She chattered glibly and quite loudly, to cover her embarrassment.

"Yes," she said, in a sweet, crisp voice, "Christmas Jenny has just been to the house, and we've bought some wreaths. We're going to hang them in all the front windows. Mother didn't know as we ought to buy them of her, there's so much talk, but I don't believe a word of it, for my part."

"What talk ?" asked the young man. He held himself very stiff and straight, and never turned his head when he shot swift, smiling glances at the girl's pink face.

"Why, don't you know ? It's town-talk. They say she's got a lot of birds and rabbits and things shut up in cages, and half starves them ; and then that little deaf-and-dumb boy, you know—they say she treats him dreadfully. They're going to look into it. Father and Deacon Little are going up there this week."

"Are they ?" said the young man. He was listening to the girl's voice with a sort of rapturous attention, but he had little idea as to what she was saying. As they walked, they faced the mountain.

It was only the next day when the minister and Deacon Little made the visit. They started up a flock of sparrows that were feeding by Jenny's door; but the birds did not fly very far—they settled into a tree and watched. Jenny's house was hardly more than a weather-beaten hut, but there was a grape-vine trained over one end, and the front yard was tidy. Just before the house stood a tall pine-tree. At the rear, and on the right, stretched the remains of Jenny's last summer's garden, full of plough-ridges and glistening corn-stubble.

Jenny was not at home. The minister knocked and got no response. Finally he lifted the latch, and the two men walked in. The room seemed gloomy after the brilliant light outside ; they could not see anything at first, but they could hear a loud and demonstrative squeaking and chirping and twittering that their entrance appeared to excite.

At length a small pink-and-white face cleared out of the gloom in the chimney-corner. It surveyed the visitors with no fear nor surprise, but seemingly with an innocent amiability.

" That's the little deaf-and-dumb boy," said the minister, in a subdued voice. The minister was an old man, narrow-shouldered, and clad in long-waisted and wrinkly black. Deacon Little reared himself in his sinewy leanness until his head nearly touched the low ceiling. His face was sallow and severely corrugated, but the features were handsome.

Both stood staring remorselessly at the little deaf-and-dumb boy, who looked up in their faces with an expression of delicate wonder and amusement. The little boy was dressed like a girl, in a long blue gingham pinafore. He sat in the midst of a heap of evergreens, which he had been twining into wreaths ; his pretty, soft, fair hair was damp, and lay in a very flat and smooth scallop over his full white forehead.

"He looks as if he was well cared for," said Deacon Little. Both men spoke in hushed tones—it was hard for them to realize that the boy could not hear, the more so because every time their lips moved his smile deepened. He was not in the least afraid.

They moved around the room half guiltily, and surveyed everything. It was unlike any apartment that they had ever entered. It had a curious sylvan air; there were heaps of evergreens here and there, and some small green trees leaned in one corner. All around the room—hung on the walls, standing on rude shelves—were little rough cages and hutches, from which the twittering and chirping sounded. They contained forlorn little birds and rabbits and field-mice. The birds had rough feathers and small, dejected heads, one rabbit had an injured leg, one field-mouse seemed nearly dead. The men eyed them sharply. The minister drew a sigh; the deacon's handsome face looked harder. But they did not say what they thought, on account of the little deaf-and-dumb boy, whose pleasant blue eyes never left their faces. When they had made the circuit of the room, and stood again by the fireplace, he suddenly set up a cry. It was wild and inarticulate, still not wholly dissonant, and it seemed to have a meaning of its own. It united with the cries of the little caged wild creatures, and it was all like a soft clamor of eloquent appeal to the two visitors, but they could not understand it.

They stood solemn and perplexed by the fireplace. "Had we better wait till she comes?" asked the minister.

"I don't know," said Deacon Little.

Back of them arose the tall mantel-shelf. On it were a

clock and a candlestick, and regularly laid bunches of brilliant dried flowers, all ready for Jenny to put in her basket and sell.

Suddenly there was a quick scrape on the crusty snow outside, the door flew open, and Jonas Carey's wife came in. She had her shawl over her head, and she was panting for breath.

She stood before the two men, and a sudden crust of shy formality seemed to form over her. "Good-arternoon," she said, in response to their salutations.

She looked at them for a moment, and tightened her shawl-pin; then the restraint left her. "I knowed you was here," she cried, in her weak, vehement voice; "I knowed it. I've heerd the talk. I knowed somebody was goin' to come up here an' spy her out. I was in Mis' Gregg's the other day, an' her husband came home; he'd been down to the store, an' he said they were talkin' 'bout Jenny, an' sayin' she didn't treat Willy and the birds well, an' the town was goin' to look into it. I knowed you was comin' up here when I seed you go by. I told Jonas so. An' I knowed she wa'n't to home, an' there wa'n't nothin' here that could speak, an' I told Jonas I was comin'. I couldn't stan' it nohow. It's dreadful slippery. I had to go on my hands an' knees in some places, an' I've sot down twice, but I don't care. I ain't goin' to have you comin' up here to spy on Jenny, an' nobody to home that's got any tongue to speak for her."

Mrs. Carey stood before them like a ruffled and defiant bird that was frighting herself as well as them with her temerity. She palpitated all over, but there was a fierce look in her dim blue eyes.

The minister began a deprecating murmur, which the

deacon drowned. "You can speak for her all you want to, Mrs. Carey," said he. "We ain't got any objections to hearin' it. An' we didn't know but what she was home. Do you know what she does with these birds and things?"

"Does with 'em? Well, I'll tell you what she does with 'em. She picks 'em up in the woods when they're starvin' an' freezin' an' half dead, an' she brings 'em in here, an' takes care of 'em an' feeds 'em till they git well, an' then she lets 'em go again. That's what she does. You see that rabbit there? Well, he's been in a trap. Somebody wanted to kill the poor little cretur. You see that robin? Somebody fired a gun at him an' broke his wing.

"That's what she does. I dunno but it 'mounts to jest about as much as sendin' money to missionaries. I dunno but what bein' a missionary to robins an' starvin' chippies an' little deaf-an'-dumb children is jest as good as some other kinds, an' that's what she is.

"I ain't afeard to speak; I'm goin' to tell the whole story. I dunno what folks mean by talkin' about her the way they do. There, she took that little dumbie out of the poor-house. Nobody else wanted him. He don't look as if he was abused very bad, far's I can see. She keeps him jest as nice an' neat as she can, an' he an' the birds has enough to eat, if she don't herself.

"I guess I know 'bout it. Here she is goin' without a new caliker dress, so's to git somethin' for them birds that can't git at the trees, 'cause there's so much ice on 'em.

"You can't tell me nothin'. When Jonas has one of his tantrums she can git him out of it quicker'n anybody I ever see. She ain't goin' to be talked about and spied upon if I can help it. They tell about her bein' love-cracked. H'm. I dunno what they call love-cracked. I know that Anderson fellar went off an' married another girl, when Jenny jest as much expected to have him as could be. He ought to ha' been strung up. But I know one thing—if she did git kind of twisted out of the reg'lar road of lovin', she's in another one, that's full of little dumbies an' starvin' chippies an' lame rabbits, an' she ain't love-cracked no more'n other folks."

Mrs. Carey, carried away by affection and indignation, almost spoke in poetry. Her small face glowed pink, her blue eyes were full of fire, she waved her arms under her shawl. The little meek old woman was a veritable enthusiast.

The two men looked at each other. The deacon's handsome face was as severe and grave as ever, but he waited for the minister to speak. When the minister did speak it was apologetically. He was a gentle old man, and the deacon was his mouthpiece in matters of parish discipline. If he failed him he betrayed how feeble and kindly a pipe was his own. He told Mrs. Carey that he did not doubt everything was as it should be; he apologized for their presence; he praised Christmas Jenny. Then he and the deacon retreated. They were thankful to leave that small, vociferous old woman, who seemed to be pulling herself up by her enthusiasm until she reached the air over their heads, and became so abnormal that she was frightful. Indeed, everything out of the broad, common track was a horror to these men and to many of their village fellows. Strange shadows, that their eyes could not pierce, lay upon such, and they were suspicious. The popular sentiment against Jenny Wrayne was originally the outcome of this characteristic, which was a remnant of the old New England witchcraft superstition. More than anything else, Jenny's eccentricity, her possibly uncanny deviation from the ordinary ways of life, had brought this inquiry upon her. In actual meaning, although not even in self-acknowledgment, it was a witch-hunt that went up the mountain road that December afternoon.

They hardly spoke on the way. Once the minister turned to the deacon. "I rather think there's no occasion for interference," he said, hesitatingly.

"I guess there ain't any need of it," answered the deacon.

The deacon spoke again when they had nearly reached his own house. "I guess I'll send her up a little somethin' Christmas," said he. Deacon Little was a rich man.

"Maybe it would be a good idea," returned the minister. "I'll see what I can do."

Christmas was one week from that day. On Christmas morning old Jonas Carey and his wife, dressed in their best clothes, started up the mountain road to Jenny Wrayne's. Old Jonas wore his great-coat, and had his wife's cashmere scarf wound twice around his neck. Mrs. Carey wore her long shawl and her best bonnet. They walked along quite easily. The ice was all gone now; there had been a light fall of snow the day before, but it was not shoe-deep. The snow was covered with the little tracks of Jenny's friends, the birds and the field-mice and the rabbits, in pretty zigzag lines.

Jonas Carey and his wife walked along comfortably until they reached the cart-path, then the old man's shoestring became loose, and he tripped over it. He stooped and tied it laboriously; then he went on. Pretty soon he stopped again. His wife looked back. "What's the matter?" said she.

"Shoestring untied," replied old Jonas, in a half inarticulate grunt.

"Don't you want me to tie it, Jonas?"

Jonas said nothing more ; he tied viciously.

They were in sight of Jenny's house when he stopped again, and sat down on the stone wall beside the path. "Oh, Jonas, what is the matter?"

Jonas made no reply. His wife went up to him, and saw that the shoestring was loose again. "Oh, Jonas, do let me tie it ; I'd just as soon as not. Sha'n't I, Jonas?"

Jonas sat there in the midst of the snowy blackberry vines, and looked straight ahead with a stony stare.

His wife began to cry. "Oh, Jonas," she pleaded, "don't you have a tantrum to-day. Sha'n't I tie it? I'll tie it real strong. Oh, Jonas!"

The old woman fluttered around the old man in his great-coat on the wall, like a distressed bird around her mate. Jenny Wrayne opened her door and looked out ; then she came down the path. "What's the matter?" she asked.

"Oh, Jenny, I dunno what *to* do. He's got another— tantrum!"

"Has he fell down?"

"No ; that ain't it. His shoestring's come untied three times, an' he don't like it, an' he's sot down on the wall. I dunno but he'll set there all day. Oh, dear me suz, when we'd got most to your house, an' I was jest thinkin' we'd come 'long real comfort'ble! I want to tie it for him, but he won't let me, an' I don't darse to when he sets there like that. Oh, Jonas, jest let me tie it, won't you? I'll tie it real nice an' strong, so it won't undo again."

Jenny caught hold of her arm. "Come right into the house," said she, in a hearty voice. She quite turned her back upon the figure on the wall.

"Oh, Jenny, I can't go in an' leave him a-settin' there.

I shouldn't wonder if he sot there all day. You don't know nothin' about it. Sometimes I have to stan' an' argue with him for hours afore he'll stir."

"Come right in. The turkey's most done, an' we'll set right down as soon as 'tis. It's 'bout the fattest turkey I ever see. I dunno where Deacon Little could ha' got it. The plum-puddin's all done, an' the vegetables is 'most ready to take up. Come right in, an' we'll have dinner in less than half an hour."

After the two women had entered the house the figure on the wall cast an uneasy glance at it without turning his head. He sniffed a little.

It was quite true that he could smell the roasting turkey, and the turnip and onions, out there.

In the house, Mrs. Carey laid aside her bonnet and shawl, and put them on the bed in Jenny's little bedroom. A Christmas present, a new calico dress, which Jenny had received the night before, lay on the bed also. Jenny showed it with pride. "It's that chocolate color I've always liked," said she. "I don't see what put it into their heads."

"It's real handsome," said Mrs. Carey. She had not told Jenny about her visitors; but she was not used to keeping a secret, and her possession of one gave a curious expression to her face. However, Jenny did not notice it. She hurried about preparing dinner. The stove was covered with steaming pots; the turkey in the oven could be heard sizzling. The little deaf-and-dumb boy sat in his chimney-corner, and took long sniffs. He watched Jenny, and regarded the stove in a rapture, or he examined some treasures that he held in his lap. There were picture-books and cards, and boxes of candy, and oranges. He held them all tightly gathered into his pinafore. The little caged wild things twittered sweetly and pecked at their food. Jenny laid the table with the best table-cloth and her mother's flowered china. The mountain farmers, of whom Jenny sprang, had had their little decencies and comforts, and there were china and a linen table-cloth for a Christmas dinner, poor as the house was.

Mrs. Carey kept peering uneasily out of the window at her husband on the stone wall.

"If you want him to come in you'll keep away from the window," said Jenny; and the old woman settled into a chair near the stove.

Very soon the door opened, and Jonas came in. Jenny was bending over the potato kettle, and she did not look around. "You can put his great-coat on the bed, if you've a mind to, Mrs. Carey," said she.

Jonas got out of his coat, and sat down with sober dignity; he had tied his shoestring very neatly and firmly. After a while he looked over at the little deaf-and-dumb boy, who was smiling at him, and he smiled back again.

The Careys stayed until evening. Jenny set her candle in the window to light them down the cart-path. Down in the village the minister's daughter and her betrothed were out walking to the church, where there was a Christmas-tree. It was quite dark. She clung closely to his arm, and once in a while her pink cheek brushed his sleeve. The stars were out, many of them, and more were coming. One seemed suddenly to flash out on the dark side of the mountain.

"There's Christmas Jenny's candle," said the girl. And it was Christmas Jenny's candle, but it was also something more. Like all common things, it had, and was, its own poem, and that was—a Christmas star.

A SOLITARY.

IT was snowing hard, as it had been for twenty-four hours. The evergreen-trees hung low with the snow. Nicholas Gunn's little house was almost hidden beneath it. The snow shelved out over the eaves, and clung in damp masses to the walls. Nicholas sat on his door-step, and the snow fell upon him. His old cap had become a tall white crown; there was a ridge of snow upon his bent shoulders. He sat perfectly still; his eyes were fixed upon the weighted evergreens across the road, but he did not seem to see them. He looked as calmly passive beneath the storm as a Buddhist monk.

There were no birds stirring, and there was no wind. All the sound came from the muffled rustle of the snow on the trees, and that was so slight as to seem scarcely more than a thought of sound. The road stretched to the north and south through the forest of pine and cedar and hemlock. Nicholas Gunn's was the only house in sight.

Stephen Forster came up the road from the southward. He bent his head and struggled along; the snow was above his knees, and at every step he lifted his feet painfully, as from a quicksand. He advanced quite noiselessly until he began to cough. The cough was deep and rattling, and he had to stand still in the snow while it was upon him.

Nicholas Gunn never looked up. Stephen bent himself almost double, the cough became a strangle, but Nicholas kept his calm eyes fixed upon the evergreens.

At last Stephen righted himself and kept on. He was very small; his clothes were quite covered with snow, and patches of it clung to his face. He looked like some little winter-starved, white-furred animal, creeping painfully to cover. When he came opposite the house he half halted, but Nicholas never stirred nor looked his way, and he kept on. It was all that he could do to move, the cough had exhausted him; he carried a heavy basket, too.

He had proceeded only a few paces beyond the house when his knees bent under him, he fairly sank down into the snow. He groaned a little, but Nicholas did not turn his head.

After a little, Stephen raised himself, lifted his basket, and went staggering back. "Mr. Gunn," said he.

Nicholas turned his eyes slowly and looked at him, but he did not speak.

"Can't I go into your house an' set down an' rest a few minutes? I'm 'most beat out."

"No, you can't," replied Nicholas Gunn.

"I dun' know as I can git home."

Nicholas made no rejoinder. He turned his eyes away. Stephen stood looking piteously at him. His sharply cut delicate face gleamed white through the white fall of the snow.

"If you'd jest let me set there a few minutes," he said.

Nicholas sat immovable.

Stephen tried to walk on, but suddenly another coughing-fit seized him. He stumbled across the road, and propped himself against a pine-tree, setting the basket down in the snow. He twisted himself about the snowy tree trunk, and the coughs came in a rattling volley.

Nicholas Gunn looked across at him, and waited until Stephen got his breath. Then he spoke. "Look a-here!" said he.

"What say?"

"If you want to set in the house a few minutes, you **can**. There ain't no fire there."

"Thank ye."

It was some time before Stephen Forster gathered strength enough to return across the road to the house. He leaned against the tree, panting, the tears running down his cheeks. Nicholas did not offer to help him. When at last Stephen got across the road, he arose to let him pass through the door ; then he sat down again on the door-step.

Stephen Forster set his basket on the floor, and staggered across the room to a chair. He leaned his head back against the wall and panted. The room was bitterly cold ; the snow drifted in through the open door where Nicholas sat. There was no furniture except a cooking-stove, a cot bed, one chair, and a table ; but there were ornaments. Upon the walls hung various little worsted and cardboard decorations. There was a lamp-mat on the table, and in one corner was a rude bracket holding a bouquet of wax flowers under a tall glass shade. There was also a shelf full of books beside the window.

Stephen Forster did not notice anything. He sat with his eyes closed. Once or twice he tried feebly to brush the snow off his clothes, that was all. Nicholas never turned his head. He looked like a stone image there in the door-way. In about twenty minutes Stephen arose, took his basket up, and went timidly to the door.

"I'm much obleeged to ye, Mr. Gunn," said he. "I guess I can git along now."

Nicholas got up, and the snow fell from his shoulders in great cakes. He stood aside to let Stephen pass. Stephen, outside the door, paused, and looked up at him.

"I'm much obleeged to ye," he said again. "I guess I can git home now. I had them three coughin'-spells after I left the store, and I got 'most beat out."

Nicholas grunted, and sat down again. Stephen looked at him a minute, then he smiled abashedly and went away, urging his feeble little body through the storm. Nicholas watched him, then he turned his head with a stiff jerk.

"If he wants to go out in such weather, he can. I don't care," he muttered.

It was nearly four o'clock in the afternoon, the snow was gradually ceasing. Presently a yellow light could be seen through the woods in the west. Some birds flew into one of the snowy trees, a wood-sled creaked down the road, the driver stared at Nicholas in the doorway, he turned his head and stared again. It was evident that he was not one of the village people. They had witnessed the peculiarities of Nicholas Gunn for the last six years. They still stared, but not as assiduously.

The driver of the wood-sled, as soon as he went down the slope in the road, and could no longer see Nicholas, began to whistle. The whistle floated back like a wake of merry sound.

Presently Nicholas arose, took off his cap, and beat it against the door-post to rid it of its dome of snow; then he shook himself like a dog, and stamped; then he went into the house, and stood looking irresolutely at the cold stove.

"Should like a fire to heat up my hasty-puddin' mighty well, so—I won't have it," said he.

He took a wooden bucket, and went with it out of doors, around the house, over a snow-covered path, to a spring. The water trickled into its little basin from under a hood of snow. Nicholas plunged in his bucket, withdrew it filled with water, and carried it back to the house. The path led through the woods ; all the trees and bushes were white arcs. Some of the low branches bowed over the path, and Nicholas, passing under them, had to stoop.

Nicholas, back in his house, got a bowl out of a rude closet ; it was nearly full of cold hasty-pudding. He stood there and swallowed it in great gulps.

The light was waning fast, although it lasted longer than usual on account of the snow, which, now the clouds were gone, was almost like a sheet of white light.

Nicholas, when he had finished his supper, plunged out again into this pale dusk. He tramped, knee-deep, down the road for a long way. He reached the little village centre, left it behind, and went on between white meadow-lands and stretches of woods. Once in a while he met a man plodding down to the store, but there were few people abroad, the road would not be cleared until morning.

Finally Nicholas turned about, and went back until he reached the village store. Its windows and glass door were full of yellow light, in which one could see many heads moving. When Nicholas opened the clanging door and went in, all the heads turned towards him. There was hardly a man there as tall as he. He went across the store with a kind of muscular shamble ; his head, with its wild light beard, had a lofty lift to it. The lounging men watched him furtively as he bought some Indian meal and matches at the counter. When he had gone out with his purchases there was a burst of laughter. The store-keeper thrust a small sharp face over the counter.

"If a man is such a darned fool as to live on meal and matches, I ain't got nothin' to say, so long as he pays me the money down," said he. He had a hoarse cold, and his voice was a facetious whisper.

There was another shout of laughter; Nicholas could hear it as he went down the street. The stranger who had driven the wood-sled past Nicholas's house was among the men. He was snow-bound overnight in the village. He was a young fellow, with innocent eyes and a hanging jaw. He nudged the man next him.

"What in creation ails the fellar, anyhow?" said he. "I seed him a-settin' on his door-step this afternoon, and the snow a-drivin' right on him."

"He ain't right in his upper story," replied the man. "Somethin' went again him ; his wife run off with another fellar, or somethin', an' he's cracked."

"Why don't they shet him up ?"

"He ain't dangerous. Reckon he won't hurt nobody but himself. If he wants to set out in a drivin' snow-storm, and tramp till he's tuckered out, it ain't nothin' to nobody else but himself. There ain't no use bringin' that kind of crazy on the town."

"'Twouldn't cost the town much," chimed in another man. "He's worth property. Shouldn't be surprised if he was worth three thousand dollars. And there he is a-livin' on corn meal and water."

An old man, in a leather-cushioned arm-chair beside the stove, turned his grizzly quizzical face toward the others, and cleared his throat. They all bent forward attentively. He had a reputation for wit.

"Makes me think of old Eph Huntly, and the story Squire Morse used to tell about him," said he. He paused impressively, and they waited. Then he went on. "Seems old Eph got terrible hard up one time. One thing after another went again him. He'd been laid up with the rheumatiz all winter; then his wife she'd been sick, an' they was 'most eat up with medicine an' doctors' bills. Then his hay crop had failed, an' his pertaters had rotted, an' finally, to cap the climax, his best cow died, an' the int'rest money was due on the mortgage, an' he didn't have a cent to pay it with. Well, he couldn't raise the money nohow, an' the day come when he s'posed the farm would have to go. Lawyer Holmes he held the mortgage, an' he expected to see him drive into the yard any time. Well, old Eph he jest goes out in the yard, an' he ketches a nice fat crower, an' he kills him, an' picks him. Then he takes him in to his wife. She was takin' on terrible 'cause she thought the farm had got to go, an' sez he, 'Sukey Ann, I want you to go an' cook this crower jest as good as you know how.' 'Oh, Lor'!' sez she, 'I don't want no crower,' an' she boohooed right out. But old Eph he made her go an' stuff that crower, an' cook him, an' bile onions, turnips, an' squash, an' all the fixin's. He said he never felt so bad in his life, an' he never got to sech a desprit pitch, an' he was goin' to have a good dinner anyhow. Well, it so happened that Lawyer Holmes he driv into the yard jest as old Eph an' his wife were settin' down to dinner, an' he see that nice baked crower an' the fixin's all set out, an' he didn't know what to make on't. It seemed to him Eph couldn't be so dreadful bad off, or he wouldn't have any heart for extra dinners, an' mebbe he had some way of raisin' the money in prospect. Then Lawyer Holmes he was mighty fond of his victuals himself, an' the upshot of it was, he sot down to the table, an' eat a good meal of the crower an' fixin's, an' there wa'n't no mortgage foreclosed that day, an' before long Eph he managed to raise the money somehow. Now if Nicholas Gunn jest had a leetle grain of old Eph's sense, he'd jest git better victuals the wuss he felt, an' let one kinder make up for t'other, instead of livin' on Injun meal an' matches. I ruther guess I wouldn't take to no meal an' matches if my Ann Lizy left me. I'd live jest as high as I could to keep my spirits up."

There was a burst of applause. The old man sat winking and grinning complacently.

"Nicholas Gunn is a darned fool, or else he's cracked," said the storekeeper in his hoarse whisper.

Meanwhile Nicholas Gunn went home. He put his meal away in the closet; he lighted a candle with one of his matches; he read awhile in the Bible; then he went to bed. He did not sleep in the cot bed; that was too luxurious for him. He slept, rolled in a blanket, on the bare floor.

Nicholas Gunn, whether his eccentricities arose from mystical religious fervor or from his own personal sorrows, would have been revered and worshipped as a saintly ascetic among some nations; among New-Englanders he met with the coarse ridicule of the loafers in a country store. Idle meditation and mortification of the flesh, except for gain, were among them irreconcilable with sanity. Nicholas would have had more prestige had he fled to the Himalayas and built himself a cell in some wild pass; however, prestige was not what he sought.

The next morning a wind had arisen; it blew stiff and

cold from the north. The snow was drifted into long waves, and looked like a frozen sea. A flock of sparrows had collected before Nicholas Gunn's door, and he stood watching them. They were searching for crumbs; this deep snow had shortened their resources wofully; all their larders were buried. There were no crumbs before this door; but they searched assiduously, with their feathers ruffled in the wind. Stephen Forster came up the road with his market-basket; it was all he could do to face the wind. His thin coat was buttoned tight across his narrow shoulders; his old tippet blew out. He advanced with a kind of sidewise motion, presenting his body like a wedge to the wind; he could not walk fairly against it.

When he was opposite Nicholas, the sparrows flew up at his feet; he paused, and shifted his basket. "Good-mornin', Mr. Gunn," said he, in a weak voice.

Nicholas nodded. Stephen's face was mottled with purple; his nose and mouth looked shrunken; his shoes were heavy with snow.

"If you want to go in an' set down a few minutes, you can," said Nicholas.

Stephen moved forward eagerly. "Thank ye, Mr. Gunn, I am kinder beat out, an' I'd like to set a few minutes," he said.

He went in and sat down. The wind rushed in great gusts past the open door. Stephen began to cough. Nicholas hesitated, his face was surly, then he shut the door with a bang.

While Stephen rested himself in the house, Nicholas marched up and down before it like a sentinel. He did not seem to see Stephen when he came out, but he stood before him in his track.

"I'm much obleeged, Mr. Gunn," said he.

Nicholas nodded. Stephen hesitated a minute, then he went on up the road. The snow blew up around him in a dazzling cloud, and almost hid him from sight.

"It's the last time I do it," muttered Nicholas.

But it was not. Every morning, storm or shine, Stephen Forster toiled painfully over the road with his market-basket, and every morning Nicholas Gunn invited him into his fireless hermitage to rest. A freezing hospitality, but he offered it, and Stephen accepted it with a fervent gratitude.

It grew apparently more and more necessary. Stephen crept more and more feebly over the road ; he had to keep setting his basket down. Nicholas never asked him if he were ill, he never questioned him at all, although he knew nothing about him but his name. Nicholas did not know the names even of many of the village people ; he had never offered nor invited confidences. Stephen also did not volunteer any information as to his circumstances during his morning calls upon Nicholas ; indeed, he was too exhausted ; he merely gave his gentle and timid thanks for the hospitality.

There came a night in January when the cold reached the greatest intensity of the season. The snow creaked underfoot, the air was full of sparkles, there were noises like guns in the woods, for the trees were almost freezing The moon was full, and seemed like a very fire of death, radiating cold instead of heat.

Nicholas Gunn, stern anchorite that he was, could not sleep for the cold. He got up and paced his room. He would not kindle a fire in the stove. He swung his arms and stamped. Suddenly he heard a voice outside. It sounded almost like a child's. "Mr. Gunn !" it cried.

Nicholas stopped and listened. It came again—" Mr. —Gunn !"

" Who's there ?" Nicholas sung out, gruffly.

" It's—me."

Then Nicholas knew it was Stephen Forster. He opened the door, and Stephen stood there in the moonlight.

" What are ye out for this time of night ?" asked Nicholas.

Stephen chattered so that he could hardly speak. He cowered before Nicholas ; the moonlight seemed to strike his little, shivering form like a broadside of icy spears. " I'm 'fraid I'm freezin'," he gasped. " Can't ye take me in ?"

" What are ye out for this time of night ?" repeated Nicholas, in a rough, loud tone.

" I had to. I'll tell you when I git a leetle warmer. I dun' know but—I'm freezin'."

Stephen's voice, indeed, sounded as if ice were forming over it, muffling it. Nicholas suddenly grasped him by one arm.

" Come in, then, if ye've got to," he growled.

He pulled so suddenly and strongly that Stephen made a run into the house, and his heels flew up weakly. Nicholas whirled him about and seated him on his cot bed.

" Now lay down here," he ordered, " and I'll cover ye up."

Stephen obeyed. Nicholas pulled off his boots, gave his feet a fierce rub, and fixed the coverings over him with rough energy. Then he began pacing the room again.

Presently he went up to the bed. " Warmer ?"

" I guess—so." Stephen's shivering seemed to shake the room.

Nicholas hustled a coat off of a peg, and put it over Stephen. Then he paced again. Stephen began to cough. Nicholas made an exclamation, and stamped angrily out of the house. There was a little lean-to at the back, and there was some fuel stored in it. Nicholas came back quickly with his arms full of wood. He piled it into the stove, set a match to it, and put on a kettle of water. Then he dragged the cot bed, with Stephen on it, close to the stove, and began to rub him under the bedclothes. His face was knit savagely, but he rubbed with a tender strength.

"Warmer?" said he.

"Yes, I—be," returned Stephen, gratefully.

The fire burned briskly ; the sharp air began to soften. Soon the kettle steamed. Nicholas got a measure of meal out of his cupboard, and prepared some porridge in a little stewpan. When it began to boil, he bent over the stove and stirred carefully, lest it should lump. When it was thick enough, he dished it, salted it, and carried it to Stephen.

"There, eat it," said he. "It's the best I've got ; it 'll warm ye some. I ain't got no spirits ; never keep any in the house."

"I guess I ain't—very hungry, Mr. Gunn," said Stephen, feebly.

"Eat it."

Stephen raised himself, and drained the bowl with convulsive gulps. Tears stood in his eyes, and he gasped when he lay back again. However, the warm porridge revived him. Presently he looked at Nicholas, who was putting more wood on the fire.

"I s'pose you think it's terrible queer that I come here this way," said he; "but there wa'n't no other way. I dun' know whether you know how I've been livin' or not."

"No, I don't."

"Well, I've been livin' with my half-sister, Mis' Morrison. Mebbe you've heard of her?"

"No, I ain't."

"She keeps boarders. We ain't lived in this town more'n three years; we moved here from Jackson. Mis' Morrison's husband's dead, so she keeps boarders. She's consider'ble older'n me. I ain't never been very stout, but I used to tend in a store till I got worse. I coughed so, it used to plague the customers. Then I had to give it up, and when Mis' Morrison's husband died, and she come here, I come with her; she thought there'd be some chores I could do for my board. An' I've worked jest as hard as I could, an' I ain't complained. I've been down to the store to get meat for the boarders' dinner when I couldn't scarcely get along over the ground. But I cough so bad nights that the boarders they complain, an' Mis' Morrison says I must go to—the poor-house. I heard her talkin' with the hired girl about it. She's goin' to get the selectmen to the house to-morrow mornin'. An'—I ain't a-goin' to the poor-house! None of my folks have ever been there, an' I ain't goin'! I'll risk it but what I can get some work to do. I ain't quite so fur gone yet. I waited till the house was still, an' then I cut. I thought if you'd take me in till mornin', I could git down to the depot, an' go to Jackson before the selectmen come. I've got a little money— enough to take me to Jackson—I've been savin' of it up these three years, in case anything happened. It's some I earned tendin' store. I'm willin' to pay you for my night's lodgin'."

Nicholas nodded grimly. He had stood still, listening to the weak, high-pitched voice from the bed.

"It's in my vest pocket, in my pocketbook," said Stephen. "If you'll come here, I'll give it to you, and you can take what you think it's worth. I pinned the pocket up, so's to be sure I didn't lose it."

Stephen began fumbling at his vest. Nicholas lifted a cover from the stove.

"I don't want none of your money," said he. "Keep your money."

"I've got enough to pay you, an' take me to Jackson."

"I tell ye, stop talkin' about your money."

Stephen said no more; he looked terrified. The air grew warmer. Everything was quiet, except for the detonations of the frost in the forest outside, and its sharp cracks in the house walls. Soon Stephen fell asleep, and lay breathing short and hard. Nicholas sat beside him.

It was broad daylight when Stephen aroused himself. He awoke suddenly and completely, and began to get out of bed. "I guess it's time I was goin'," said he. "I'm much obleeged to you, Mr. Gunn."

"You lay still."

Stephen looked at him.

"You lay still," repeated Nicholas.

Stephen sank back irresolutely; his timid, bewildered eyes followed Nicholas, who was smoothing his hair and beard before a little looking-glass near the window. There was a good fire in the cooking-stove, and the room was quite warm, although it was evidently a very cold day. The two windows were thickly coated with frost, and the room was full of dim white light. One of the windows faced towards the east, but the sun was still hidden by the trees across the road.

Nicholas smoothed his hair and his wild beard slowly and punctiliously.

Stephen watched him. " Mr. Gunn," he said, at length. " What say ?"

" I'm afraid—I sha'n't get to the depot before the train goes if I don't start pretty soon."

Nicholas went on smoothing his beard. At length he laid his comb down and turned around. " Look a-here !" said he ; " you might jest as well understand it. You ain't a-goin' to any depot to-day, an' you ain't a-goin' to any train, an' you ain't a-goin' to any depot to-morrow nor any train, an' you ain't a-goin' the next day, nor the next, nor the next, nor the next after that."

" What be I a-goin' to do ?"

" You are a-goin' to stay jest where you are. I've fought against your comin' as long as I could, an' now you've come, an' I've turned the corner, you are a-goin' to stay. When I've been walkin' in the teeth of my own will on one road, an' havin' all I could do to breast it, I ain't a-goin' to do it on another. I've give up, an' I'm a-goin to stay give up. You lay still."

Stephen's small anxious face on the pillow looked almost childish. His helplessness of illness seemed to produce the same expression as the helplessness of infancy. His hollow, innocent blue eyes were fixed upon Nicholas with blank inquiry. " Won't Mis' Morrison be after me ?" he asked, finally.

" No, she won't. Don't you worry. I'm a-goin' over to see her. You lay still." Nicholas shook his coat before he put it on ; he beat his cap against the wall, then adjusted it carefully. " Now," said he, " I'm a-goin'. I've left enough wood in the stove, an' I guess it 'll keep warm

till I get back. I sha'n't be gone any longer than I can
help."

"Mr. Gunn !"

"What say ?"

"I ruther guess I'd better be a-goin'."

Nicholas looked sternly at Stephen. "You lay still," he
repeated. "Don't you try to get up whilst I'm gone ; you
ain't fit to. Don't you worry. I'm goin' to fix it all right.
I'm goin' to bring you something nice for breakfast. You
lay still."

Stephen stared at him, his thin shoulders hitched uneasily under the coverlid.

"You're goin' to lay still, ain't you ?" repeated Nicholas.

"Yes ; I will, if you say so," replied Stephen. He
sighed and smiled feebly.

The truth was that this poor cot in the warm room
seemed to him like a couch under the balsam-dropping
cedars of Lebanon, and all at once he felt that divine rest
which comes from leaning upon the will of another.

"Well, I do say so," returned Nicholas. He looked at
the fire again, then he went out. He turned in the door-
way, and nodded admonishingly at Stephen. "Mind you
don't try to get up," he said again.

Nicholas went out of sight down the road, taking long
strides over the creaking snow. He was gone about a
half-hour. When he returned, his arms were full of packages. He opened the door, and looked anxiously at the
bed. Stephen twisted his face towards him and smiled.
Nicholas piled the packages up on the table, and lifted a
stove-cover.

"I've seen Mis' Morrison, and it's all right," said he.

"What did she say ?" asked Stephen, in an awed voice.

"Well, she didn't say much of anything. She was fryin' griddle-cakes for the boarders' breakfasts. She said she felt real bad about lettin' you go, but she didn't see no other way, an' she'd be glad to have you visit me jest as long as you wanted to. She's goin' to pack up your clothes."

"I ain't got many clothes. There's my old coat an' vest an' my other pants, but they're 'most worn out. I ain't got but one real good shirt besides this one I've got on. That was in the wash, or I'd brought it."

"Clothes enough," said Nicholas.

He crammed the stove with wood, and began undoing the packages. There were coffee, bread, and butter, some little delicate sugar cookies, some slices of ham, and eggs. There were also a pail of milk and a new tin coffee-pot.

Nicholas worked busily. He made coffee, fried the ham and eggs, and toasted slices of bread. When everything was ready, he carried a bowl of water to Stephen for him to wash his hands and face before breakfast. He even got his comb, and smoothed his hair.

Then he set the breakfast out on the table, and brought it up to the bedside. He had placed a chair for himself, and was just sitting down, when he stopped suddenly. "I don't know as it's just fair for me not to tell you a little something about myself before we really begin livin' together," said he. "It won't take but a minute. I don't know but you've heard stories about me that I wa'n't quite right. Well, I am ; that is, I s'pose I am. All is, I've had lots of trouble, an' it come mainly through folks I set by ; an' I figured out a way to get the better of it. I figured out that if I didn't care anything for anybody, I shouldn't have no trouble from 'em ; an' if I didn't care anything for myself, I shouldn't have any from myself. I 'bout made up my mind that all the trouble an' wickedness in this world come from carin' about yourself or somebody else, so I thought I'd quit it.   I let folks alone, an' I wouldn't do anything for 'em ; an' I let myself alone as near as I could, an' didn't do anything for myself.   I kept cold when I wanted to be warm, an' warm when I wanted to be cold. I didn't eat anything I liked, an' I left things around that hurt me to see.   My wife she made them wax flowers an' them gimcracks.   Then I used to read the Bible, 'cause I used to believe in it an' didn't now, an' it made me feel worse.   I did about everything I could to spite myself, an' get all the feelin' out of me, so I could be a little easier in my mind."

Nicholas paused a moment.   Stephen was looking at him with bewildered intensity.

"Well, I was all wrong," Nicholas went on.   "I've give it all up.   I've got to go through with the whole of it like other folks, an' I guess I've got grit enough.   I've made up my mind that men's tracks cover the whole world, and there ain't standin'-room outside of 'em.   I've got to go with the rest.   Now we'll have breakfast."

Nicholas ate heartily ; it was long since he had tasted such food ; even Stephen had quite an appetite.   Nicholas pressed the food upon him ; his face was radiant with kindness and delight.   Stephen Forster, innocent, honest, and simple-hearted, did not in the least understand him, but that did not matter.   There is a higher congeniality than that of mutual understanding; there is that of need and supply.

After breakfast Nicholas cleared away the dishes and washed them.   The sun was so high then that it struck the windows, and the frost-work sparkled like diamonds.

Nicholas opened the door; he was going down to the spring

for more water ; he saw a flock of sparrows in the bushes across the road, and stopped ; then he set his pail down noiselessly and went back for a piece of bread. He broke it and scattered the crumbs before the door, then went off a little way and stood watching. When the sparrows settled down upon the crumbs he laughed softly, and went on towards the spring over the shining crust of snow.

A VILLAGE LEAR.

"JEST wait a minute, Sary." The old man made a sly backward motion of his hand; his voice was a cautious whisper.

Sarah Arnold stood back and waited. She was a large, fair young woman in a brown calico dress. She held a plate of tapioca pudding that she had brought for the old man's dinner, and she was impatient to give it to him and be off; but she said nothing. The old man stood in the shop door; he had in one hand a stick of red-and-white peppermint candy, and he held it out enticingly towards a little boy in a white frock. The little boy had a sweet, rosy face, and his glossy, fair hair was carefully curled. He stood out in the green yard, and there were dandelions blooming around his feet. It was May, and the air was sweet and warm; over on one side of the yard there was some linen laid out to bleach in the sun.

The little boy looked at the old man and frowned, yet he seemed fascinated.

The old man held out the stick of candy, and coaxed, in his soft, cracked voice. "Jest look a-here, Willy!" said he; "jest look a-here! See what gran'pa's got: a whole stick of candy! He bought it down to the store on purpose for Willy, an' he can have it if he'll jest come here an' give

gran'pa a kiss. Does Willy want it, hey?—Willy want it?"
The old man took a step forward.

But the child drew back, and shook his head violently,
while the frown deepened. "No, no," said he, with baby
vehemence.

The old man stepped back and began again. It was as
if he were enticing a bird. "Now, Willy," said he, "jest
look a-here! Don't Willy like candy?"

The child did not nod, but his blue, solemn eyes were
riveted on the candy.

"Well," the grandfather went on, "here's a whole stick
of candy come from the store, real nice pep'mint candy,
an' Willy shall have it if he'll jest come here an' give gran'-
pa a kiss."

The child reached out a desperate hand. "Gimme!" he
cried, imperatively.

"Yes, Willy shall have it jest as soon as he gives gran'pa
a kiss." The old man waved the stick of candy ; his sunken
mouth was curved in a sly smile. "Jest look at it! Willy,
see it! Red-an'-white candy, real sweet an' nice, with pep'-
mint in it. An' it's all twisted! Willy want it?"

The child began to take almost imperceptible steps forward, his eyes still fixed on the candy. His grandfather
stood motionless, while his smile deepened. Once he rolled
his eyes delightedly around at Sarah. The child advanced
with frequent halts.

Suddenly the old man made a spring forward. "Now
I've got ye!" he cried. He threw his arms around the boy
and hugged him tight.

The child struggled. "Lemme go!—lemme go!" he half
sobbed.

"Yes, Willy shall go jest as soon as he gives gran'pa the

kiss," said the old man. "Give gran'pa the kiss, and then he shall have the candy an' go."

The child put up his pretty rosy face and pursed his lips sulkily. The grandfather bent down and gave him an ecstatic kiss.

"There! Now Willy shall have the candy, 'cause he's kissed gran'pa. He's a good boy, an' gran'pa 'll let him have the candy right off. He sha'n't wait no longer."

The child snatched the candy and fled across the yard.

The old man laughed, and his laugh was a shrill, rapturous cackle, like the high notes of an old parrot. He turned to the young woman. "I knowed I could toll him in," he said; "I knowed I could. The little fellar likes candy, I tell ye."

Sarah smiled sympathetically and extended the plate of pudding. "I brought you over a little of our pudding," said she. "Mother thought you might relish it."

The old man took it quite eagerly. "Brought a spoon in't, didn't ye?"

"Yes; I thought maybe you'd like to eat it out here."

"Well, I guess I may jest as well eat it out here, an' not carry it into the house. Viny might kinder git the notion that it would clutter up some. I'll jest set down here an' eat this, an' then I won't want no dinner in the house. I guess they're goin' to have beef, an' I don't relish beef much lately. I'd ruther have soft victuals; but Viny she don't cook much soft victuals; the folks in the house don't care much about 'em."

The old man held the plate of pudding, but did not at once begin to eat; his eyes still followed the little boy, who stood aloof under a blooming apple-tree and sucked his candy.

"Jest look at him," he said, admiringly. "I tell ye what 'tis, Sary, that little fellar does like candy. I can allers toll him in with a stick of candy. He's dreadful kind o' bashful. I s'pose Ellen she don't jest like to have him round in the shop here much. She dresses him up real nice an' clean in them little white frocks, an' she's afeard he'll get somethin' on 'em ; so I guess she tells him he must keep away, an' it makes him kind of afeard. I s'pose she thinks I ain't none too clean nuther to be a-handlin' of him, an' I dun know as I be, but I allers wash my hands real pertickler afore I tech him. I've got my tin wash-dish there on the bench, an' I'm real pertickler 'bout it."

The old man waved his hand towards a rusty tin wash-basin on the old shoemaker's bench under the window. There was a smoky curtain over the window ; the plastered walls and the ceiling were dark with smoke; the place was full of brown lights. Sarah, in her brown dress, with her fair rosy face, stood waiting until the old man should finish talking.

"Well, I must go now," said she. "I haven't been to dinner myself."

"You jest wait a minute," whispered the old man, with a mysterious air. In the little shop, beside the old shoemaker's bench, was a table that was brown and dark with age and dirt, and it was heaped with litter. There was a drawer in it, and this the old man opened with an effort ; it stuck a little. "Look a-here," he whispered—"look a-here, Sary."

Sarah came close, and peered around his elbow.

The old man took a little parcel from the midst of the leather chips and waxed threads and pegs that half filled the drawer. He unrolled it carefully. "Look a-here," he said again, with a chuckle. He held up a stick of pink candy. "There," he went on, winking an old blue eye at Sarah, "I ain't goin' to give that to him till to-morrer. To-morrer I'll jest toll him in with that, don't ye see? Hey?"

"That's checkerberry, ain't it?"

"Yes, that's checkerberry, an' the tother was pep'mint. I got two sticks of candy down to the store this mornin', one checkerberry an' the tother pep'mint. Ye see, I put a patch on a shoe for the Briggs boy last week, an' he give me ten cents for't. I'd kinder calkilated to lay it out in terbacker—I ain't had none lately—but the more I thought 'bout it the more I thought I'd git a leetle candy. Ye never see sech a chap fer candy as he is; he'll hang off, an' hang off, but he can't stan' it to lose the candy nohow. I dun know but the Old Nick could toll him in with a stick of candy, he's in such a takin' for't; never see sech a fellar fer candy." The old man raised his cackling laugh again, and Sarah laughed too, going out the back door of the shop. "I'm real obleeged to your mother, Sary; you tell her," he called after her.

He replaced the candy in the drawer, still chuckling to himself; then he sat down to his pudding. He sat on his shoemaker's bench, well back from the door, and ate. He smacked his lips loudly; he liked this soft, sweet food.

Barney Swan was a small, frail old man; he stooped weakly, and did not look much larger than a child, sitting there on his bench. His face, too, was like a child's; his sunken mouth had an innocent, infantile expression, and his eyes had that blank, fixed gaze, with an occasional twinkle of shrewdness, that babies' eyes have. His thin white hair hung to his shoulders, and he had no beard. He owned only one decent coat, and that he kept for Sundays: he always went to meeting. On week-days he wore his brown calico shirt sleeves and his old sagging vest. His bagging, brownish black trousers were hauled high around his waist, and his ankles showed like a little boy's.

Old Barney Swan had sat upon that shoemaker's bench the greater part of his time for sixty years. His father before him had been a shoemaker and cobbler; he had learned the trade when a child, and been faithful to it all his life. Now not only his own powers had failed, but hand shoemaking and cobbling were at a discount. There were two thriving boot and shoe factories in the town, and the new boots and shoes were finer to see than the old coarsely cobbled ones. Old Barney was too old to go to work in the shoe factory, but it is doubtful if he would have done so in any case. He had always had a vein of childish obstinacy in spite of his mildness, and it had not decreased with age. "If folks want to wear them manufactured shoes, they can," he would say, with a sudden stiffening of his bent back; "old shackly things! You'd orter seen them shoes the Briggs boy brought in here t'other day; they wa'n't wuth treein' up, an' they never had been."

Although now old Barney's revenue was derived from the Briggs boy and sundry other sturdy, stubbed urchins, whose shoe-leather demanded the cheapest and most thorough repairs to be had, he had accumulated quite a little property through his faithful toil on that leathern seat on the end of that old bench. But it had seemed easier for him to accumulate property than to care for it. His greatest talent was for patient, unremitting labor and economy; his financial conceptions were limited to them. Ten years before, he had made a misadventure and lost a few hundred dollars, and was so humbled and dejected over it that

he had made his property over to his daughters on consideration of a life support. They had long been urging him
to make such an arrangement. He had two daughters,
Malvina and Ellen. His wife had died when they were
about twenty. The wife had been a delicate, feeble woman,
yet with a certain spirit of her own. In her day the daughters had struggled hard for the mastery of the little household, but with only partial success; after her death they
were entirely victorious. Barney had always thought his
daughters perfect; they had their own way in everything,
with the exception of the money. He clung to that for a
while. He was childishly fond of the few dollars he had
earned all by himself and stowed away in his house and
acres of green meadow-land and the village savings-bank.
He was fond of the dollars for themselves; the sense of
treasure pleased him. He did not care to spend for himself; there were few things that he wished for except a
decent meeting-coat and a little tobacco. The tobacco
was one point upon which he displayed his obstinacy; his
daughters had never been able entirely to do away with
that, although they waged constant war upon it. He would
still occasionally have his little comforting pipe, and chew
in spite of all berating and disgust. But the tobacco was
sadly curtailed since the property had changed hands; he
had only his little earnings with which to purchase it. The
daughters gave him no money to spend. They argued that
"father ain't fit to spend money." So his most urgent ne-
cessities were doled out to him.

When the property was divided, Malvina, the elder
daughter, had for her share the homestead and a part of
the money in the bank; Ellen, the younger, had the larger
portion of the bank money and some wooded property.

Malvina stipulated to furnish a home and care for the old man as long as he lived, and Ellen was to pay her sister a certain sum towards his support. Both daughters were married at the time; Malvina had one daughter of her own. Malvina had remained at her old home after her marriage, but Ellen had removed to a town some twenty miles away. Her father had visited there several times, but he never liked to remain long. He would never have gone had not Malvina insisted upon it. She considered that her sister ought to share her burden, and sometimes give her a relief. So Barney would go, although with reluctance; in fact, his little shoe-shop was to him his beloved home, his small solitary nest, where he could fold his old wings in peace. Nobody knew how regretfully he thought of it during his visits at Ellen's. While there he sat mostly in her kitchen, by the cooking-stove, and miserably pored over the almanac or the religious paper. Occasionally he would steal out behind the barn and smoke a pipe, but there was always a hard reckoning with Ellen afterwards, and it was a dearly purchased pleasure. Ellen was a small, fair woman; she was delicate, much as her mother had been, and her weakness and nervousness made her imperious will less evident but more potent. Old Barney stood more in awe of her than of Malvina. He was anxiously respectful towards her husband, who was a stout, silent man, covering his own projects and his own defeats with taciturnity. He was a steady grubber on a farm, and very close with old Barney's money, of which, however, his wife understood that she had full control. She had had out of it a set of red-plush parlor furniture and a new silk dress. Once in a while old Barney, while on a visit, would stand on the parlor threshold and gaze admiringly in at the furniture; but did he venture to step over, his daughter would check him. "Now don't go in there, father," she would cry out; "you'll track in somethin'."

"No, I ain't a-goin' in, Ellen," Barney would reply, and meekly shuffle back.

Old Barney was intensely loyal towards both of his daughters; not even to himself would he admit anything to their disadvantage. He always spoke admiringly of them, and would acknowledge no preference for one above the other. Still he undoubtedly preferred Malvina. She was a large, stout woman, but some people thought that she looked like her father. When the property was divided, Malvina had had every room in the house newly painted and papered; then she stood before them like a vigilant watch-dog. She had been neat before, but with her new paint and paper and a few new carpets her neatness became almost a monomania. She was fairly fierce, and her voice sounded like a bark sometimes when old Barney, with shoes heavy with loam and clothes stained with tobacco juice, shuffled into her spotless house. However, in a certain harsh way she did her duty by her simple old father. She saw to it that his clothes were comfortably warm and mended, and he had enough to eat, although his own individual tastes were never consulted. Still, he was scrupulously bidden to meals, and his plate was well filled. She did not like to have him in the house, and showed that she did not, but she had no compunctions upon that point, for he preferred the shop. She never gave him spending-money, for she did not consider that he was capable of spending money judiciously. She bought all that he had herself. She was a good financier, and made a little go a long way.

Malvina's husband was dead, and her daughter was now

eighteen years old. Her name was Annie. She was a
pretty girl, and had a lover. She was to be married soon.
They had not told old Barney about it, but he found it out
two weeks before the wedding. He stood in his shop door
one morning and called cautiously to Sarah Arnold. (The
Arnolds lived in the next house, and Sarah was out in the
yard picking some roses.) "Sary, come here a minute,'
he called. And Sarah came, with her roses in her hand.
The old man beckoned her mysteriously into the shop.
He drew well back from the door, after having peered
sharply at the house windows. Then he began : " Ye
heard on't, Sary," whispered he—"what's goin' on in
there ? Hey ?" He gave his hand a backward jerk towards the house.

Sarah laughed. " I suppose so," said she.

" How long ye known it ? Hey ?"

" Well, I've heard 'twas coming off before long."

" The weddin's goin' to be in two weeks. Did ye know
that ? Hey ?"

" I heard so."

" Well, it's the first I've heard on't. I knew that young
fellar'd been shinin' round there consider'ble, an' I spos'd
'twas comin' off some time or other, but I didn't have no idee
'twas goin' to be so soon. Look a-here, Sary "— Sarah,
placid and fair and pleasant, holding her roses, gazed attentively at him—" *I'm—a-goin' to—give her somethin' !*"

" What are you going to give her ?"

" Ye'll see. I've got some money laid up, an' I know a
way to raise a leetle more. Ye'll see when the time comes
—ye'll see." The old man raised his pleasant cackle, then
he hushed it suddenly, with a wary glance towards the house.
" You mind you don't say nothin' about it, Sary," said he.

"No, I won't say a word about it," returned Sarah. Then she went home with her roses and her own thoughts. She herself was to be married soon, but there would be no such commotion over her wedding as over Annie's. The Arnolds were very humble folk, according to the social status of the village, and were not on very intimate terms with their neighbors! Old Mr. Arnold took care of people's gardens and sawed wood for a living, and Mrs. Arnold and Sarah sewed, and even went out for extra work when some of the more prosperous village people had company. However, Sarah was going to marry a young man who had saved quite a sum of money. He was building a new house on a cross street at the foot of a meadow that lay behind Barney Swan's shop. Sarah had told Barney all about it, and he often strolled down the meadow and watched the workmen on the new house with a wise and interested air. He was very fond of Sarah. Sarah had her own opinion about Annie and the old man's daughters, but she was calm about expressing it even to her mother. She was a womanly young girl. However, once in a while her indignation grew warm.

"I think it's a shame," she told her mother, when she carried her roses into the house, "that they haven't told Grandpa Swan about Annie's going to be married, and the poor old man's planning to give her a present." The tears stood in Sarah's blue eyes. She crowded the roses into a tumbler.

It was only the next day that old Barney called her into the shop to display the present. He had been so eager about it that he was not able to wait. However, the idea that the gift must not be presented to his granddaughter until her wedding-day was firmly fixed in his mind. He had obtained in some way this notion of etiquette, and he was resolved to abide by it, no matter how impatient he might be. "I've got it here all ready, but I ain't a-goin' to give it to her till the day she's married, ye know," he told Sarah while he was fumbling in the table-drawer (that was his poor little treasure-box). There he kept his surreptitious quids of tobacco and his pipe and his small hoards of pennies. His hands trembled as he drew out a little square parcel. He undid it with slow pains. "Look a-here!" In a little jeweller's box, on a bed of pink cotton, lay a gold-plated brooch with a red stone in the centre. The old man stood holding it, and looking at Sarah with a speechless appeal for admiration.

"Why, ain't it handsome!" said she; "it's just as pretty as it can be!"

Old Barney still did not speak; he stood holding the box, as silent as a statue whose sole purpose is to pose for admiration.

"Where did you get it?" asked Sarah.

The old man ushered in his words with an exultant chuckle. "Down to Bixby's; an' 'twas jest about the pertiest thing he had in his hull store. It cost consider'ble; I ain't a-goin' to tell ye how much, but I didn't pay no ninepence for't, I can tell ye. But I had a leetle somethin' laid up, an' there was some truck I traded off. I was bound I'd git somethin' wuth somethin' whilst I was about it."

As Barney spoke, Sarah noticed that his old silver watch-chain was gone, and a suspicion as to the "truck" seized her, but she did not speak of it. She admired the brooch to Barney's full content, and he stowed it away in the drawer with pride and triumph. He was true to his resolution not to mention the present to his granddaughter, but he could not help throwing out sundry sly hints to the effect that one was forthcoming. However, no one paid any attention to them ; they knew too well the state of Barney's exchequer to have any great expectations, and all the family were in the habit of disregarding the old man's chatter. He always talked a great deal, and asked many questions ; and they seemed to look upon him much in the light of a venerable cricket, constantly chirping upon their hearth, which for some obscure religious reasons they were bound to harbor.

The question of old Barney's appearance at the marriage was quite a serious one. The wedding was to be a brilliant affair for the village, and the old man was not to be considered in the light of an ornament. Still the idea of not allowing him to be present could not decently be entertained, and Malvina began training him to make the best appearance possible. She instructed him as to his deportment, and had even made a new black silk stock for him to wear at the wedding. He was so delighted that he wanted to take possession at once, and hide it away in his table-drawer, but she would not allow it. She had planned how he should be well shaven and thoroughly brushed, and his pockets searched for tobacco, on the wedding morning. "I should feel like goin' through the floor if your grandfather should come in lookin' the way he does sometimes," she told her daughter Annie.

Annie concerned herself very little about it. She was a young girl of a sweet, docile temperament. She was somewhat delicate physically, and was indolent, partly from that, partly from her nature. Now her mother was making her work so hard over her wedding clothes that she was half ill ; her little forefinger was all covered with needle-pricks, and there were hollows under her eyes.   Malvina had always been a veritable queen mother to Annie.

Ellen and her little boy visited Malvina for several weeks before the wedding.   Ellen assisted about the sewing ; she was a fine sewer.

Old Barney did not dare stay much in the house, but he wandered about the yard, and absurdly peeped in at the doors and windows.   Back in his second childhood, he had all the delighted excitement of a child over a great occasion. It was perhaps a poor and pitiful happiness, but he was as happy in his own way as Annie was over her coming marriage, and, after all, happiness is only one's own heartful.

But three days before the wedding old Barney was attacked with a severe cold, and all his anticipations came to naught.   The cold grew worse, and his daughters promptly decided that he could not be present at the wedding. "There ain't no use talkin' 'bout it, father," said Malvina ; "you can't go.   You'd jest cough an' sneeze right through it, an' we can't have such work."

The old man pleaded, even with tears, but with no avail ; on the wedding day he was almost forcibly exiled to his little shop in the yard.   The excitement in the house reached a wild height, and he was not allowed to enter after breakfast ; his dinner of bread and butter and tea was brought down to the shop.   He sat in the door and watched the house and the hurrying people.   He called Sarah Arnold over many times ; he was in a panic over his present. " How am I goin' to give her that breastpin, if they don't let me go to the weddin' ?" he queried, with sharp anxiety. "There sha'n't nobody else give her that pin nohow."

" I guess you'll have a chance," Sarah said, comfortingly.

When it was time for the people to come to the wedding,

Ellen, in her silk dress, with her hair finely crimped, came rustling out to the shop, and ordered old Barney away from the door.

"Do keep away from the door, father," said she, "for mercy sakes. Such a spectacle as you are, an' the folks beginnin' to come ! I should think you'd know better." Ellen's forehead was all corrugated with anxious lines ; she was nervous and fretful. She even pushed her father away from the door with one long, veiny hand ; then she shut the door with a clash.

Then Barney stood at the window and watched. He held the little jewelry-box tightly clutched in his hand. The window-panes were all clouded and cobwebbed ; it was hard for his dim old eyes to see through them, but he held back the stained curtain and peered as sharply as he could.

He saw the neighbors come to the wedding. Several covered wagons were hitched out in the yard. When the minister came into the yard he could scarcely keep himself from rushing to the door.

"There he is !" he said out loud to himself. "There he is ! He's come to marry 'em !"

The hubbub of voices in the house reached old Barney's ears. A little after the minister arrived there was a hush. "He's marryin' of 'em !" ejaculated Barney. He danced up and down before the window.

After the hush the voices swelled out louder than before. Barney kept his eyes riveted upon the house. It was some two hours before people began to issue from the doors.

"The weddin's over !" shouted Barney. He looked quite wild ; he gave himself a little shake, and opened the shop door and took up his stand there. Everybody could see him in his brown calico shirt-sleeves, and his slouching, untidy vest and trousers.　His white locks straggled over his shoulders; his face was not very clean.　Suddenly Ellen, standing and smirking in the house door, spied him. Presently she came across the yard, swaying her rattling skirts with a genteel air.　She smiled all the way, and old Barney innocently smiled back at her when she reached him.　But he jumped, her voice was so fierce.

"You go right in there this minute, father, an' keep that door *shut*," she said between her smiling lips.

She shut the door upon Barney, but she had no sooner reached the house than he opened it again and stood there. He still held the box.

The bridal pair were to set up housekeeping in a village ten miles away.　They were to drive over that night.　When at last the bridegroom and the bride appeared in the door, old Barney leaned forward, breathless.　The bridegroom's glossy buggy and bay horse stood in the yard; the horse was restive, and a young man was holding him by the bridle.

Old Barney did not venture to step outside his shop door. Malvina and Ellen were both in the yard, but it was as if his soul were feeling for ways to approach the young couple. He leaned forward, his eyes were intent and prominent, the hand that held the jewelry-box shook with long, rigid motions.

The bride, at her husband's side, stepped across the green yard to the buggy.　This was a simple country wedding, and Annie rode in her wedding dress to her new home. The wedding dress was white muslin, full of delicate frills and loops of ribbons that the wind caught.　Annie, coming across the yard, was blown to one side like a white flower. Her slender neck and arms showed pink through the muslin, and she wore her wedding bonnet, which was all white, with bows of ribbon and plumes.　Her cheeks were very red.

Old Barney opened his mouth wide. "Good Lord!" said he, with one great gasp of admiration. He laughed in a kind of rapture ; he forgot for a minute his wedding present. "Look at 'em!—jest look at 'em!" he repeated. Suddenly he called out, "Annie! Annie! jest look a-here! See what gran'pa's got for ye."

Annie stopped and looked. She hesitated, and seemed about to approach Barney, when the horse started ; the young man had hard work to hold him. The bridegroom lifted the bride into the carriage as soon as the horse was quiet enough, sprang in after her, and they flew out of the yard, with everybody shouting merrily after them. Old Barney's piteous cry of "Annie! Annie! jest come here a minute!" was quite lost.

The old man went into the shop and closed the door of his own accord. Then he replaced the little box in the table-drawer. Then he settled down on his old shoe-bench, and dropped his head on his hands. Soon he had a severe coughing-spell. Nobody came near him until it was quite dark ; then Malvina came and asked him, in a hard, absent way, if he were not coming into the house to have any supper that night.

Old Barney arose and shuffled after her into the house ; he ate the supper that she gave him ; then he went to bed. He never took Annie's gold brooch out of the drawer again. He never spoke of it to Sarah Arnold nor any one else. He had the grieved dignity that pertains to the donor of a scorned gift. As the weeks went on, his cold grew no better ; he coughed harder and harder. Once Malvina bought some cough medicine for him, but it did no good. The old man grew thinner and weaker, but she did not realize that ; the cough arrested her attention ; it tired her to hear it so constantly. She told him that there was no need of his coughing so much.

Sarah Arnold was married in August. She and her husband went to live in their new house across the meadow from old Barney's shop.

Sarah had been married a few weeks when one night old Barney came toddling down the meadow to her house. He was so weak that he tottered, but he almost ran. The short growth of golden-rod brushing his ankles seemed enough to throw him over. He waded through it as through a golden sea that would soon throw him from his footing and roll over him, but he never slackened his pace until he reached Sarah's door. She had seen him coming, and ran to meet him.

"Why, what is the matter?" she cried. Old Barney's face was pale and wild. He looked at her and gasped. She caught him by the arm and dragged him into the house, and set him in a chair. "What *is* the matter?" she asked again. She looked white and frightened herself.

Old Barney did not reply for a minute ; he seemed to be collecting breath. Then he burst out in a great sobbing cry : "My shop ! my shop ! She's goin' to have my shop tore down ! They're goin' to begin to-morrer. They're movin' my bench. Oh ! oh !"

Sarah stood close to him and patted his head. "Who's goin' to have it torn down?"

"Mal—viny."

"When did she say so?"

"Jest—now—come out an' told me. Says the—old—thing looks dreadful bad out—in the yard, an' she wants it —tore down. She's goin' to have me—go to Ellen's an' stay—all winter. Puttin' my bench up—in the garret. I ain't—a-goin' to have the—bench to set on—no longer, I ain't. Oh, hum !"

Sarah's pleasant mouth was set hard. She made old Barney lie down on her sitting-room lounge, and got him a cup of tea. It was evident that the old man was completely exhausted ; he could not have walked home had he tried. Sarah sat down beside him and heard his complaint, and tried to comfort him. When her husband came home to tea she told him the story, and he went up across the meadow to the shop before he took off his coat.

" It's so," he growled, when he returned. " They're lugging the things out. It's a blasted shame. Poor old man !"

Sarah's husband had a brown boyish face and a set chin ; he took off his coat and began washing his hands at the kitchen sink with such energy that the leather stains might have been the ingratitude of the world.

" Did you say anything about his being down here ?" asked Sarah.

" No, I didn't. Let 'em hunt."

About nine o'clock that evening Malvina, holding her skirts up well, came striding over the meadow. She had missed her father, and traced him to Sarah's. Sarah and her husband had put him to bed in their pretty little spare chamber when Malvina came in. It was evident that the old man was very ill ; he was wandering a little, and he had terrible paroxysms of coughing ; his breath was labored. Malvina stood looking at him ; Sarah's husband kept opening his mouth to speak, and his wife kept nudging him to be silent. Finally he spoke—

" He's all upset because his shop's going to be torn down," said he ; but his voice was not as bold as his intentions.

" 'Tain't that," replied Malvina. " He's dretful careless ;

he's been goin' round in his stockin'-feet, an' he's got more cold. I dun know what's goin' to be done. I don't see how I can get him home to-night."

"He can stay here just as well as not," said Sarah, nudging her husband again.

"Well, I'll come over an' git him home in the mornin'," Malvina said.

But she could not get him home when she came over in the morning. Old Barney never went home again. He died the second day after he came to Sarah's. Both of his daughters came to see him, and did what they could, but he did not seem to notice them much. An hour before he died he called Sarah. She ran into the room. Just then there was nobody else in the house. Old Barney sat up in bed, and he was pointing out of the window over the meadow. His pointing forefinger shook, his face was ghastly, but there was a strange, childish delight in it.

"Look a-there, Sary—jest look a-there," said old Barney "Over in the meader—look. There's Ellen a-comin', an' Viny, an' they look jest as they did when they was young; an' Ellen she's a-bringin' me some tea, an' Viny she's a-bringin' me some custard puddin'. An' there's Willy a-dancin' along. Jest see the leetle fellar a-comin' to see gran'pa all of his own accord. An' there's Annie all in her white dress, jest as pretty as a pictur', a-comin' arter her breastpin. Jest see 'em, Sary." The old man laughed. Out of his ghastly, death-stricken features shone the expression of a happy child. "Jest look at 'em, Sary," he repeated.

Sarah looked, and she saw only the meadow covered with a short waving crop of golden-rod, and over it the September sky.

UP PRIMROSE HILL.

"We can, Mis' Rowe; this winder ain't fastened. I can slide it up easy 'nough."

"Where does it go to?"

"Into the kitchen. I declare, there's the tea-kittle on the stove; an' I should think the door was open into the butt'ry. Yes, 'tis. Mis' Rowe, the dishes are settin' on the shelves jest the way they were left."

"Can you see 'em?"

"Yes, I can. I don't b'lieve there's one speck of harm in our gettin' in an' lookin' round a little."

"Oh, Mis' Daggett, do you think we'd ought to?"

"I'd like to know what harm 'twould do."

"S'pose they should find it out?"

"I don't see who *they* is. There ain't one of the Primroses left but Maria, an' it ain't likely she'll be round here to find it out very soon."

"It's awful 'bout her, ain't it?"

"I dun know as I think it's very awful; it ain't any more than she deserves for treatin' Abel Rice the way she did."

"I've heard her husband had spent 'most all her money."

"Guess it's true 'nough. They said once she was goin' to leave him."

"I never really believed he struck her the way they said he did; did you?"

"Guess it's true 'nough. I tell you what it is, Mis' Rowe, I b'lieve folks get their desarts in this world sometimes.— We can get in here jest as easy as not, if we are a mind to."

"Oh, Mis' Daggett, I dun know 'bout it."

"There ain't a bit of harm in't," said Mrs. Daggett, who was long and vigorous and sinewy. Then with no more ado she pushed up the grating old window.

Mrs. Rowe, who was a delicate little body, stood timorously aloof in a bed of mint that had grown up around the kitchen door of the old Primrose house. There was a small wilderness of mint and sweetbrier and low pink-flowering mallow around the door. All the old foot-tracks were concealed by them.

The window was not very high; Mrs. Daggett put one knee on the sill and climbed in easily enough. Mrs. Rowe watched her with dilated eyes; occasionally she peered behind her; she had a sideway poise like a deer. It was perfectly evident that if she were to see any one approaching she would fly and leave her companion to her fate.

"Come, you get in now," said Mrs. Daggett. Her harsh, yellow old face peered out of the window; back of it was a dark green gloom. All the windows but that were closed and blinded.

"Oh, Mis' Daggett, I dun know as I darse to!"

"Come along!"

"I don't b'lieve I can get in."

"Yes, you can; it ain't high."

Mrs. Rowe approached slowly; she lifted one feeble knee. "It's no use, I can't noway," said she.

Mrs. Daggett caught hold of her arms and pulled. "Now you climb while I pull!" she cried.

"Oh, I can't noway, Mis' Daggett! You'll pull my arms out by the roots. I guess you'd better stop."

"I'll get out an' boost you in," Mrs. Daggett said, briskly, and strode over the window-sill.

But the "boosting" was not successful; finally little Mrs. Rowe recoiled in terror. "I'm afraid you'll make me go in there head-first," said she. "I guess you'd better stop, Mis' Daggett. You go in an' look round, an' I'll wait here for you."

"I'll tell you what we can do: I'll set out a chair; you can climb in jest as easy as not, then."

Mrs. Daggett again climbed in, set out one of the dusty kitchen chairs, and Mrs. Rowe with many quavers made her entry. For a moment the two women stood close together, looking about them; Mrs. Rowe was quite pale, Mrs. Daggett shrewdly observant. "I'm goin' to open them other blinds an' have a little more light," she declared at length.

"Oh, do you s'pose you'd better?"

"I'd like to know what harm it can do." Mrs. Daggett forced up the old windows, and defiantly threw open the blinds.

The kitchen was a large one, with an old billowy floor and the usual furnishings. Mrs. Daggett lifted the tea-kettle and examined it. "It's all one bed of rust," said she; "set up with water in't, most likely; that Mis' Loomis that was here when old Mr. Primrose died wa'n't no kind of a housekeeper. I'm a-goin' into the butt'ry."

"Oh, do you think we'd better?"

"I'd like to know what harm it can do."

Mrs. Daggett advanced with virtuous steadfastness, and the other woman, casting fearful backward glances, followed hesitatingly in her wake. They entered the pantry, which was as large as a small room, and stood with their chins tipped, scanning the shelves. "There's a whole set of white ware," said Mrs. Daggett, "an' there's some blue packed away on the top shelf. I s'pose there's a chiny closet in the parlor, where the chiny is : they must have had some chiny dishes. Ain't that a nice platter? That's jest what I want, a platter that size. What's in here?"

"Oh, don't, Mis' Daggett; seems to me I wouldn't !"·

"What's the harm, I'd like to know?"

Mrs. Daggett lifted the cover from a small jar. "It's quince sauce, sure's you live," said she, sniffing cautiously. "It don't look to me as if it was hurt one mite. I'm goin' to taste of it."

"Oh, Mis' Daggett !"

"I am." Mrs. Daggett found a knife, and plunged it defiantly into the quince sauce. "It's jest as good as ever 'twas; it ain't worked one mite. You taste of it, Mis' Rowe."

"Oh, I don't b'lieve I'd better, Mis' Daggett." Mrs. Rowe looked with tremulous longing at the sauce which her friend held towards her on the tip of the knife.

"Land sakes! take it! What harm can it do?" Mrs. Daggett gave the knife a shove nearer, and Mrs. Rowe opened her mouth.

"It is good, ain't it?" she said, after tasting reflectively.

"I don't see why it ain't. Have some more."

"I guess I hadn't better."

"I'm goin' to. Might just as well ; it's only spoilin' here." Mrs. Daggett helped herself to some generous dips of the sauce, and Mrs. Rowe also took sundry tastes between her remonstrances. They found nothing else that was edible, except some spices. Mrs. Daggett took a pinch of the cinnamon. "Ain't lost its strength one mite," she remarked; "thought I'd like to see if it had."

The Primrose house was a large, old-fashioned edifice. It had been the mansion-house of this tiny village, and its owners had been the grandees. The town was named for them; they had been almost like feudal lords of the little settlement. Now they all were dead with the exception of one daughter, and she had not been near her old home for twenty years. The house had been shut up since her father's death, five years ago. The great square rooms were damp and musty, and even the furniture seemed to have acquired an air of distance and reserve.

When the two curious women penetrated the statelier and more withdrawn recesses of the house, Mrs. Rowe eyed every chair as if it were alive and drawing up itself haughtily before interlopers. But Mrs. Daggett had no such feelings. She investigated everything unsparingly. She began opening a bureau drawer in one of the front chambers. Mrs. Rowe, watching her, fairly danced with weak and fascinated terror. "Oh, don't, Mis' Daggett—don't you open them drawers! You scare me dreadfully!" she cried.

"I'd like to know what harm it can do." Mrs. Daggett pulled out the drawer with a jerk. "Oh, my!" she exclaimed; "ain't this elegant!"

Mrs. Rowe tremblingly slid towards her and peeped around her shoulder, and just then came a loud peal of the doorbell. Mrs. Rowe clutched Mrs. Daggett: "Oh, Mis' Daggett, come—come quick, for mercy sake! That's the doorbell! Oh, Mis' Daggett, they'll ketch us here—they will! they will!"

"Keep still!" returned Mrs. Daggett. "No, they won't ketch us, neither. I dun know as we're doin' any harm if they did." She gave the bureau drawer a shove to, and led the retreat. "Come on down the back stairs," she said. "Don't break your neck ; there's time 'nough."

When they were half-way down the stairs the bell rang again. "Oh !" gasped Mrs. Rowe—"oh, Mis' Daggett, they'll ketch us !"

"No, they won't, neither; come along." Mrs. Daggett climbed first out of the kitchen window. She thought that she could assist her friend better in that way. "I'll stand outside here and lift you down," she said. "Don't hurry so ; you'll fall an' break your bones."

Mrs. Rowe mounted a chair with frantic haste, and got into the window. Mrs. Daggett extended both arms, and she jumped. "Mercy sakes ! I'm ketched onto somethin' !" she screamed. "Oh, Mis' Daggett !" In fact, Mrs. Rowe's skirt had caught on something inside, and she pitched helplessly against her friend. "I hear 'em a-comin'," she groaned. "Oh, what shall I do ! what shall I do !"

"Can't you hang here a minute, till I reach in an' un-hitch it ?"

"Oh, I can't !—I can't ! Don't you let go of me, Mis' Daggett—don't you ! I shall fall and break my bones if you do. Oh, I hear 'em a-comin' ! Oh, Mis' Daggett, you pull as hard as you can ! It's my alpacky dress. I ain't had it but three years, but I don't care nothin' 'bout that. Oh, Mis' Daggett !"

Mrs. Rowe struggled wildly, and Mrs. Daggett pulled ; finally the alpaca skirt gave way. Mrs. Rowe as she turned and fled cast one despairing glance at it. "It's spoilt !" she groaned ; " a great three-cornered piece gouged out of it. Oh, Mis' Daggett, do hurry !"

Mrs. Daggett paused to shut the window ; then she overtook her friend with long, vigorous strides. "I wa'n't goin' to leave that window up," she remarked, "not if I knew it."

The women skirted the house well to the right, and passed into the road.

"Now I'm goin' to walk by an' see who 'tis," said Mrs. Daggett.

"Oh, don't, Mis' Daggett; let's go right home."

"I'm jest goin' to walk up by the path where I can see in. Come along; they won't know we've been in the house."

Mrs. Daggett fairly pushed her timid friend in the direction that she wished.

The Primrose house was thickly surrounded by trees, and stood far back from the road; one could only get an uninterrupted view of the front door by looking directly up the walk.

Mrs. Daggett took a cautious glance as she passed the gate; then she stopped short. "Good land!" she exclaimed, "it ain't anybody but Abel Rice. If we ain't a passel of fools!" She could see between the trees a tall man with a yellow beard leaning against the front door of the Primrose house.

"Are you sure it's him?" quavered Mrs. Rowe.

"Course I'm sure. Don't you s'pose I know Abel Rice? If it ain't the greatest piece of work! There, I knew all about his goin' there an' ringin' the bell."

"I never knew as he did really."

"Well, I knew he did. Mrs. Adoniram White said she'd seen him time an' time again. To think of our runnin' away for a luny like Abel Rice!"

"It's awful 'bout his goin' there, ain't it?"

"Yes, 'tis awful. They say they've talked an' talked to

him, but they can't make him b'lieve Maria Primrose don't live there; an' every once in a while, no matter what he's doin', hoein' potatoes or what, he'll steal off an' go up there an' ring the door-bell. I wish Maria could see him sometimes, an' realize what she did when she jilted him for that rich feller she married."

"It would serve her jest right; don't you think 'twould?"

"Yes, I do think it would serve her jest right."

The two were now walking along the sidewalk, leaving the Primrose house out of sight. Presently they came to the house where Mrs. Rowe lived, and she turned in at the gate. "Good-afternoon, Mis' Daggett," said she.

"Good-afternoon. Say, Mis' Rowe, look here a minute."

Mrs. Rowe stepped back obediently. Mrs. Daggett approached her lips to her ear and dropped her voice to a whisper: "If—I was you, I wouldn't say nothin' about our goin' in there to Marthy."

"I ain't goin' to," rejoined Mrs. Rowe, with a wise air; "you needn't be afraid of that, Mis' Daggett."

"I ain't done nothin' I'm ashamed of, but it's jest as well not to tell everything you know. I'm dreadful sorry you tore your dress so, Mis' Rowe."

The rent in Mrs. Rowe's black alpaca dress attracted immediate attention when she entered the house; she turned herself cautiously, but her sister, Mrs. Joy, noticed it at once. "Why, Hannah, how did you tear your dress so?" said she.

"I ketched it," replied Mrs. Rowe, with a meek sigh, turning her head to look at the three-cornered rent.

"Why, I should think you did! I guess you'll have one job mendin' it. What did you ketch it onto?"

"On a nail. I see Abel Rice a-standin' ringin' the front-

door bell at the Primrose house when I come by." Mrs.
Rowe had very little diplomacy in her nature, but she could
fly as skittishly as any other woman from a distasteful subject.

"I want to know!" said Mrs. Joy, with ready interest.
"I never really knew whether to b'lieve them stories about
his ringin' that bell or not."

"I see him with my own eyes." Mrs. Rowe was laying
aside her bonnet and shawl, uncovering her small gray head
and her narrow alpaca shoulders, which had a deprecating
slope to them. One could judge more correctly of her
character from her shoulders than from her face, which was
shifty, reflecting lights and shadows from others; her shoulders were the immovable sign of herself.

Mrs. Joy did not resemble her in the least ; she was
larger and stouter, with a rosy face whose lines were all
drawn with decision. When she was talking she surveyed
one steadily with her full bright eyes that seldom winked.
People called her a handsome woman. Her daughter Annie, who sat at the window with her crochet-work, resem-
bled her, only she was young and girlishly slim, her bright,
clear eyes were blue instead of black, and her hair was
light. There was a brilliant color on her rather thin
cheeks. She crocheted some scarlet worsted very rapidly.
making her slender fingers fly. Her mother had a significant side tone for her in her voice when she spoke again.

"Well, there's no use talkin', Abel Rice couldn't have had
any brains to speak of, or he wouldn't have lost 'em so
easy," said she. "This goin' crazy for love is something I
don't put much stock in, for my part. Folks must have a
weak spot somewhere, or it would take something more
than love to tip 'em over. I guess none of the Rices are

any too smart, when it comes right down to it. It ain't a family I should want to get into."

Annie never said a word ; she crocheted faster.

Mrs. Rowe had dropped her shawl-pin, and had been hunting for it. Just then she found it, and rose up. " I should be kind of afraid if Frank Rice had any—such kind of trouble, it might affect him the same way. Shouldn't you ?" said she.

She fairly jumped when her sister replied : " Afraid of it ? No, I guess I shouldn't be afraid of it. I guess there don't many folks get crazy for — love." Mrs. Joy pronounced " love " with an affectedly sweet drawl.

Mrs. Rowe colored shamefacedly. " I s'pose Abel did ; don't you ?"

" No, I don't, neither. Most likely he'd got crazy anyway ; it was in him."

" Well, I dun know." Mrs. Rowe always departed from an argument with a mild profession of ignorance. She stood in awe of her sister.

When she left the room to put away her bonnet, Mrs. Joy turned to Annie : " Ain't you goin' to see him to-night ?" she asked.

" I—haven't made up my mind."

" I should think it was about time you did. There's the picnic comin' off to-morrow."

" No, it isn't, either."

" When is it, I'd like to know ?"

" The day after to-morrow."

" Well, you ain't got any too much time ; you'd ought to let him know a little beforehand, so he can get somebody else. I should think you'd better see him when he goes home to-night ; it will do jest as well as any way."

Annie kept her eyes upon her crocheting; her cheeks grew redder. "I've—about made up my mind that I shall go with him, anyway," she muttered.

"What?"

"I've about made up my mind to go with Frank the way I said I would."

Mrs. Joy's eyes snapped. "Well, if you do, you'll have to give up all thoughts of Henry Simpson, that's all," said she. "If he sees you at that picnic with Frank Rice, he'll think it's all decided, an' he'll let you alone."

"Sometimes I think I'd rather wish he would."

"I'd like to know what you mean."

"I've made up my mind that I don't want him, anyway."

"H'm! I'd like to know why."

Annie crocheted silently for a minute. "Well, I suppose that I like Frank the best," she murmured, with a shame-faced air.

"Oh! Well, I s'pose that's all that's necessary, then. I s'pose if you—*love* him, there ain't anything more to be said."

The manner with which her mother's voice lingered upon *love* made it seem at once shameful and ridiculous to the girl; but she raised a plea in her own defence.

"I don't care," said she; "I don't think it's right to get married unless you do love the one you marry."

"I guess you'll find out that there's something besides *love* if you do get married to Frank Rice, or I'll miss my guess. When you get settled down there in that little cooped-up house with his father and mother and crazy uncle, an' don't have enough money to buy you a calico dress, you'll find out it ain't all—*love*."

"He'd build a piece on to the house."

"An' run in debt for it ; you know he ain't got a cent. Well, Annie Joy, I've said all I'm goin' to. You know how things are jest as well as I can tell you. You know how I've dug an' scrimped all my life, an' you know how we're situated now ; it's jest all we can do to get along, an' your father's an old man. If you marry Frank Rice you'll have to live jest as I've done, only you won't be so well off, if anything ; your father had a good house, all paid for, when we started. You'll have to work an' slave, an' never go anywhere nor have anything ; you'll have to make up your mind to it. An' if you have Henry Simpson, you'll live over in Lennox, an' have everything nice, an' people will look up to you. You'll have to take your choice, that's all I've got to say."

Mrs. Joy got up and went out of the room with a heavy flourish. On the threshold she turned : "Ain't it most time for him to go by ?"

Annie nodded. Soon after her mother left the room she saw at a swift glance the young man of whom they had been speaking coming down the sidewalk. She looked quickly away, and never raised her eyes from her crocheting when he went by.

"Has he been past ?" asked her mother when she came in.

"Yes."

Mrs. Joy compressed her lips. "Well, you can do jest as you are a mind to," said she.

Yet she continued to talk and advance arguments. If Annie did not go to the picnic with Frank, she had little doubt that matters would be brought to a favorable climax with regard to the other young man, who had lately paid her much attention. She was making a new dress for

Annie to wear, and she sewed and reasoned with her all that evening and during the next day.

In the afternoon a young girl, an acquaintance of Annie's, came in. She had just returned from Lennox, where she had been shopping. Lennox was a large village—the city for this little hamlet of Primrose Hill.

"I saw somebody there," said the girl, with a significant smile at Annie, "and he looked real handsome. He was driving a beautiful horse, and he's got one of those new-style carriages. If I was some folks I should feel pretty fine."

"Alice would give all her old shoes to get a chance like you," remarked Mrs. Joy after the visitor had gone.

"I don't believe she'd treat another fellow mean to get it," said Annie. She had looked doubtfully pleased at the girl's joking.

"I don't see as your treatin' him mean if you let him know beforehand. I guess you ain't the only girl that changes her mind. Mebbe he'll take up with Alice. I should think she'd make him a real good wife."

"He won't : I can tell you that much. He can't bear her."

"Well, he'll find somebody. It's 'most time for him to go by, ain't it?"

"I suppose so," replied Annie, coldly.

It was late in the afternoon. An hour ago Mrs. Daggett had called for Mrs. Rowe, and the two old women had sauntered up the street together. "I didn't tell you what I see in that bureau drawer," Mrs. Daggett had whispered when they started forth; "it was the handsomest black satin I ever laid my eyes on. I—*mean to see it again.*"

"Oh, Mis' Daggett!"

"I'd like to know what harm it can do."

The two, in their homely black gowns, had moved on towards the Primrose house. Frank Rice would have to pass it on his way home from his work: he lived a half-mile beyond.

Mrs. Joy, as she talked to Annie, kept her face turned towards the road, watching for him. "There he is," she said, presently. Annie bent over her work. "Do you hear?" her mother repeated, sharply.

"Yes, I hear." Suddenly Annie sat up straight and looked in her mother's eyes. "I can't do it," said she.

"I'd like to know why not. Hurry, or he'll be gone by."

Annie sat quite still for a minute; her eyes were staring and her mouth set hard. Then she arose and went out of the front door and down the walk. The man reached the gate just as she did. She started, and turned a white face back towards the window; it was Frank Rice's uncle Abel, who, people said, had lost his wits because Maria Primrose had jilted him. He passed, and Annie clung to the gate. An awful voice of prophetic denunciation seemed to cry through all her weakness and ignoble ambition. Her mother appeared in the door, and drew back hastily; she had seen Frank Rice coming, following in the track of his uncle. She remarked for the first time a strong resemblance between the two men, and it thrilled her with a strange horror. She went back into the sitting-room, and peered around a corner of a window. When Frank reached the gate, she saw Annie step forward. She saw them stand and talk for a few minutes; then they walked slowly up the street together.

"What's she doin' that for?" muttered her mother with a bewildered air; she felt singularly shocked and subdued.

Annie and Frank went out of sight in the direction of the Primrose house.

It might have been an hour later when a woman came slowly up the hill which gave its name to the little settlement. She had walked from Lennox; she had not money enough to pay her fare in the coach which ran between the two villages. It rattled past her on the road; the passengers thrust out their heads and stared at her. "I declare, I believe that's Maria Primrose," said one woman to another. Maria Primrose, to call her as her old neighbors did by her maiden name, toiled slowly up Primrose Hill. She was a middle-aged woman, with a slender figure like a girl's; but her face, which had been handsome, had not kept its youth so well; one on passing her saw it with a certain disappointment. Her black clothes had an elegant and almost foreign air; some of the rich silk pleatings were frayed, but that did not hurt the general effect.

When she had come within half a mile of the Primrose house she saw a man at work in a potato field on the left of the road. She stopped and looked at him. Everything was very dusty, and the wind blew; great clouds of dust rolled up from the road, and passed like smoke over the fields; now the setting sun shone through it and gave it a gold color. Maria saw the man through a cloud of golden dust.

He threw down his hoe and came towards her, and she stood waiting. When he was near enough, on the other side of the stone wall, she looked in his face. His large blue eyes looked straight at her with a gentle and indifferent stare, his yellow-bearded mouth smiled pleasantly and vacantly.

Maria went on. Presently she heard a quick shuffle behind her, and Abel Rice passed, never turning his head ; he was soon out of sight. When Maria Primrose went up the path to her old home, he stood straight and gaunt before the door ; he had pulled the bell, and he was listening. When he saw Maria he shuffled off the end of the piazza, and disappeared among the trees. She looked after him for a second, then she unlocked the door.

There was a scream and a patter of feet up in the second story, then a scramble over the back stairs ; Mrs. Daggett and Mrs. Rowe were making their escape from the house. Annie Joy and Frank Rice were also fleeing from the precincts of the Primrose house. Its front piazza had looked quiet and isolated, and they had strolled up there and seated themselves. They arose and went away when Abel Rice came and rang the bell to summon his lost sweetheart ; they held each other's hands, and sped along between the trees. They saw Maria, and quickened their pace ; but before they had passed out into the road, Frank cast a hasty glance around, and the two kissed each other.

Maria Primrose entered her old home to pass the remainder of her life in lonely and unavailing regret and a dulness which was not peace ; the two curious old women hustled guiltily out of the kitchen window ; Abel Rice went his solemn and miserable way ; and the young lovers passed happily forth, starting up before her like doves. There had been a wreck, and the sight of it had prevented another.

A CHURCH MOUSE.

"I never heard of a woman's bein' saxton."

"I dun' know what difference that makes; I don't see why they shouldn't have women saxtons as well as men saxtons, for my part, nor nobody else neither. They'd keep dusted 'nough sight cleaner. I've seen the dust layin' on my pew thick enough to write my name in a good many times, an' ain't said nothin' about it. An' I ain't goin' to say nothin' now again Joe Sowen, now he's dead an' gone. He did jest as well as most men do. Men git in a good many places where they don't belong, an' where they set as awkward as a cow on a hen-roost, jest because they push in ahead of women. I ain't blamin' 'em; I s'pose if I could push in I should, jest the same way. But there ain't no reason that I can see, nor nobody else neither, why a woman shouldn't be saxton."

Hetty Fifield stood in the rowen hay-field before Caleb Gale. He was a deacon, the chairman of the selectmen, and the rich and influential man of the village. One look-ing at him would not have guessed it. There was nothing imposing about his lumbering figure in his calico shirt and baggy trousers. However, his large face, red and moist with perspiration, scanned the distant horizon with a stiff and reserved air; he did not look at Hetty.

" How'd you go to work to ring the bell?" said he.   " It would have to be tolled, too, if anybody died."

" I'd jest as lief ring that little meetin'-house bell as to stan' out here an' jingle a cow-bell," said Hetty ; " an' as for tollin', I'd jest as soon toll the bell for Methusaleh, if he was livin' here !   I'd laugh if I ain't got strength 'nough for that."

" It takes a kind of a knack."

" If I ain't got as much knack as old Joe Sowen ever had, I'll give up the ship."

" You couldn't tend the fires."

" Couldn't tend the fires—when I've cut an' carried in all the wood I've burned for forty year !   Couldn't keep the fires a-goin' in them two little wood-stoves !"

" It's consider'ble work to sweep the meetin'-house." .

" I guess I've done 'bout as much work as to sweep that little meetin'-house, I ruther guess I have."

" There's one thing you ain't thought of."

" What's that ?"

" Where'd you live ?   All old Sowen got for bein' saxton was twenty dollar a year, an' we couldn't pay a woman so much as that.   You wouldn't have enough to pay for your livin' anywheres."

" Where am I goin' to live whether I'm saxton or not ?" Caleb Gale was silent.

There was a wind blowing, the rowen hay drifted round Hetty like a brown-green sea touched with ripples of blue and gold by the asters and golden-rod.   She stood in the midst of it like a May-weed that had gathered a slender toughness through the long summer ; her brown cotton gown clung about her like a wilting leaf, outlining her harsh little form.   She was as sallow as a squaw, and she had pretty black eyes ; they were bright, although she was old. She kept them fixed upon Caleb. Suddenly she raised herself upon her toes ; the wind caught her dress and made it blow out ; her eyes flashed. " I'll tell you where I'm goin' to live," said she. *"I'm goin' to live in the meetin'-house."*

Caleb looked at her. *" Goin' to live in the meetin'-house !"*

" Yes, I be."

" Live in the meetin'-house !"

" I'd like to know why not."

" Why—you couldn't—live in the meetin'-house. You're crazy."

Caleb flung out the rake which he was holding, and drew it in full of rowen. Hetty moved around in front of him, he raked imperturbably ; she moved again right in the path of the rake, then he stopped. " There ain't no sense in such talk."

" All I want is jest the east corner of the back gall'ry, where the chimbly goes up. I'll set up my cookin'-stove there, an' my bed, an' I'll curtain it off with my sunflower quilt, to keep off the wind."

" A cookin'-stove an' a bed in the meetin'-house !"

" Mis' Grout she give me that cookin'-stove, an' that bed I've allers slept on, before she died. She give 'em to me before Mary Anne Thomas, an' I moved 'em out. They air settin' out in the yard now, an' if it rains that stove an' that bed will be spoilt. It looks some like rain now. I guess you'd better give me the meetin'-house key right off."

" You don't think you can move that cookin'-stove an' that bed into the meetin'-house — I ain't goin' to stop to hear such talk."

" My worsted-work, all my mottoes I've done, an' my wool flowers, air out there in the yard."

Caleb raked. Hetty kept standing herself about until he was forced to stop, or gather her in with the rowen hay. He looked straight at her, and scowled ; the perspiration trickled down his cheeks. " If I go up to the house can Mis' Gale git me the key to the meetin'-house ?" said Hetty.

" No, she can't."

" Be you goin' up before long ?"

" No, I ain't." Suddenly Caleb's voice changed : it had been full of stubborn vexation, now it was blandly argumentative. " Don't you see it ain't no use talkin' such nonsense, Hetty ? You'd better go right along, an' make up your mind it ain't to be thought of."

" Where be I goin' to-night, then ?"

" To-night ?"

" Yes ; where be I a-goin' ?"

" Ain't you got any place to go to ?"

" Where do you s'pose I've got any place ? Them folks air movin' into Mis' Grout's house, an' they as good as told me to clear out. I ain't got no folks to take me in. I dun' know where I'm goin' ; mebbe I can go to your house ?"

Caleb gave a start. " We've got company to home," said he, hastily. " I'm 'fraid Mis' Gale wouldn't think it was convenient."

Hetty laughed. " Most everybody in the town has got company," said she.

Caleb dug his rake into the ground as if it were a hoe, then he leaned on it, and stared at the horizon. There was a fringe of yellow birches on the edge of the hay-field ; beyond them was a low range of misty blue hills. " You ain't got no place to go to, then ?"

" I dun' know of any. There ain't no poor-house here, an' I ain't got no folks."

Caleb stood like a statue. Some crows flew cawing over the field. Hetty waited. "I s'pose that key is where Mis' Gale can find it?" she said, finally.

Caleb turned and threw out his rake with a jerk. "She knows where 'tis; it's hangin' up behind the settin'-room door. I s'pose you can stay there to-night, as long as you ain't got no other place. We shall have to see what can be done."

Hetty scuttled off across the field. "You mustn't take no stove nor bed into the meetin'-house," Caleb called after her; "we can't have that, nohow."

Hetty went on as if she did not hear.

The golden-rod at the sides of the road was turning brown; the asters were in their prime, blue and white ones; here and there were rows of thistles with white tops. The dust was thick; Hetty, when she emerged from Caleb's house, trotted along in a cloud of it. She did not look to the right or left, she kept her small eager face fixed straight ahead, and moved forward like some little animal with the purpose to which it was born strong within it.

Presently she came to a large cottage-house on the right of the road; there she stopped. The front yard was full of furniture, tables and chairs standing among the dahlias and clumps of marigolds. Hetty leaned over the fence at one corner of the yard, and inspected a little knot of household goods set aside from the others. There were a small cooking-stove, a hair trunk, a yellow bedstead stacked up against the fence, and a pile of bedding. Some children in the yard stood in a group and eyed Hetty. A woman appeared in the door—she was small, there was a black smutch on her face, which was haggard with fatigue, and she scowled in the sun as she looked over at Hetty. "Well, got a place to stay in?" said she, in an unexpectedly deep voice.

"Yes, I guess so," replied Hetty.

"I dun' know how in the world I can have you. All the beds will be full — I expect his mother some to-night, an' I'm dreadful stirred up anyhow."

"Everybody's havin' company; I never see anything like it." Hetty's voice was inscrutable. The other woman looked sharply at her.

"You've got a place, ain't you?" she asked, doubtfully.

"Yes, I have."

At the left of this house, quite back from the road, was a little unpainted cottage, hardly more than a hut. There was smoke coming out of the chimney, and a tall youth lounged in the door. Hetty, with the woman and children staring after her, struck out across the field in the little footpath towards the cottage. "I wonder if she's goin' to stay there?" the woman muttered, meditating.

The youth did not see Hetty until she was quite near him, then he aroused suddenly as if from sleep, and tried to slink off around the cottage. But Hetty called after him. "Sammy," she cried, "Sammy, come back here, I want you!"

"What d'ye want?"

"Come back here!"

The youth lounged back sulkily, and a tall woman came to the door. She bent out of it anxiously to hear Hetty.

"I want you to come an' help me move my stove an' things," said Hetty.

"Where to?"

"Into the meetin'-house."

"The meetin'-house?"

"Yes, the meetin'-house."

The woman in the door had sodden hands; behind her arose the steam of a wash-tub. She and the youth stared at Hetty, but surprise was too strong an emotion for them to grasp firmly.

"I want Sammy to come right over an' help me," said Hetty.

"He ain't strong enough to move a stove," said the woman.

"Ain't strong enough!"

"He's apt to git lame."

"Most folks are. Guess I've got lame. Come right along, Sammy!"

"He ain't able to lift much."

"I s'pose he's able to be lifted, ain't he?"

"I dun' know what you mean."

"The stove don't weigh nothin'," said Hetty; "I could carry it myself if I could git hold of it. Come, Sammy!"

Hetty turned down the path, and the youth moved a little way after her, as if perforce. Then he stopped, and cast an appealing glance back at his mother. Her face was distressed. "Oh, Sammy, I'm afraid you'll git sick," said she.

"No, he ain't goin' to git sick," said Hetty. "Come, Sammy." And Sammy followed her down the path.

It was four o'clock then. At dusk Hetty had her gay sunflower quilt curtaining off the chimney-corner of the church gallery; her stove and little bedstead were set up, and she had entered upon a life which endured successfully for three months. All that time a storm brewed; then it broke; but Hetty sailed in her own course for the three months.

It was on a Saturday that she took up her habitation in the meeting-house. The next morning, when the boy who had been supplying the dead sexton's place came and shook the door, Hetty was prompt on the other side. "Deacon Gale said for you to let me in so I could ring the bell," called the boy.

"Go away," responded Hetty. "I'm goin' to ring the bell; I'm saxton."

Hetty rang the bell with vigor, but she made a wild, irregular jangle at first; at the last it was better. The village people said to each other that a new hand was ringing. Only a few knew that Hetty was in the meeting-house. When the congregation had assembled, and saw that gaudy tent pitched in the house of the Lord, and the resolute little pilgrim at the door of it, there was a commotion. The farmers and their wives were stirred out of their Sabbath decorum. After the service was over, Hetty, sitting in a pew corner of the gallery, her little face dark and watchful against the flaming background of her quilt, saw the people below gathering in groups, whispering, and looking at her.

Presently the minister, Caleb Gale, and the other deacon came up the gallery stairs. Hetty sat stiffly erect. Caleb Gale went up to the sunflower quilt, slipped it aside, and looked in. He turned to Hetty with a frown. To-day his dignity was supported by important witnesses. "Did you bring that stove an' bedstead here?"

Hetty nodded.

"What made you do such a thing?"

"What was I goin' to do if I didn't? How's a woman as old as me goin' to sleep in a pew, an' go without a cup of tea?"

The men looked at each other. They withdrew to another corner of the gallery and conferred in low tones;

then they went down-stairs and out of the church.   Hetty
smiled when she heard the door shut.   When one is hard
pressed, one, however simple, gets wisdom as to vantage-
points.   Hetty comprehended hers perfectly.   She was the
propounder of a problem ; as long as it was unguessed, she
was sure of her foothold as propounder.   This little village
in which she had lived all her life had removed the shelter
from her head ; she being penniless, it was beholden to
provide her another ; she asked it what.   When the old
woman with whom she had lived died, the town promptly
seized the estate for taxes—none had been paid for years.
Hetty had not laid up a cent ; indeed, for the most of the
time she had received no wages.   There had been no money
in the house ; all she had gotten for her labor for a sickly,
impecunious old woman was a frugal board.   When the
old woman died, Hetty gathered in the few household articles for which she had stipulated, and made no complaint.
She walked out of the house when the new tenants came
in ; all she asked was, "What are you going to do with
me?"   This little settlement of narrow-minded, prosperous
farmers, however hard a task charity might be to them,
could not turn an old woman out into the fields and high-
ways to seek for food as they would a Jersey cow.   They
had their Puritan consciences, and her note of distress
would sound louder in their ears than the Jersey's bell
echoing down the valley in the stillest night.   But the
question as to Hetty Fifield's disposal was a hard one to
answer.   There was no almshouse in the village, and no
private family was willing to take her in.   Hetty was strong
and capable ; although she was old, she could well have
paid for her food and shelter by her labor ; but this could
not secure her an entrance even among this hard-working

and thrifty people, who would ordinarily grasp quickly enough at service without wage in dollars and cents. Hetty had somehow gotten for herself an unfortunate name in the village. She was held in the light of a long-thorned brier among the beanpoles, or a fierce little animal with claws and teeth bared. People were afraid to take her into their families ; she had the reputation of always taking her own way, and never heeding the voice of authority. "I'd take her in an' have her give me a lift with the work," said one sickly farmer's wife ; "but, near's I can find out, I couldn't never be sure that I'd get molasses in the beans, nor saleratus in my sour-milk cakes, if she took a notion not to put it in. I don't dare to risk it."

Stories were about concerning Hetty's authority over the old woman with whom she had lived. "Old Mis' Grout never dared to say her soul was her own," people said. Then Hetty's sharp, sarcastic sayings were repeated ; the justice of them made them sting. People did not want a tongue like that in their homes.

Hetty as a church sexton was directly opposed to all their ideas of church decorum and propriety in general ; her pitching her tent in the Lord's house was almost sacrilege ; but what could they do? Hetty jangled the Sabbath bells for the three months ; once she tolled the bell for an old man, and it seemed by the sound of the bell as if his long, calm years had swung by in a weak delirium ; but people bore it. She swept and dusted the little meeting-house, and she garnished the walls with her treasures of worsted-work. The neatness and the garniture went far to quiet the dissatisfaction of the people. They had a crude taste. Hetty's skill in fancy-work was quite celebrated. Her wool flowers were much talked of, and young girls tried to copy them. So these wreaths and clusters of red and blue and yellow wool roses and lilies hung as acceptably between the meeting-house windows as pictures of saints in a cathedral.

Hetty hung a worsted motto over the pulpit; on it she set her chiefest treasure of art, a white wax cross with an ivy vine trailing over it, all covered with silver frost-work. Hetty always surveyed this cross with a species of awe ; she felt the irresponsibility and amazement of a genius at his own work.

When she set it on the pulpit, no queen casting her rich robes and her jewels upon a shrine could have surpassed her in generous enthusiasm. " I guess when they see that they won't say no more," she said.

But the people, although they shared Hetty's admiration for the cross, were doubtful. They, looking at it, had a double vision of a little wax Virgin upon an altar. They wondered if it savored of popery. But the cross remained, and the minister was mindful not to jostle it in his gestures.

It was three months from the time Hetty took up her abode in the church, and a week before Christmas, when the problem was solved. Hetty herself precipitated the solution. She prepared a boiled dish in the meeting-house, upon a Saturday, and the next day the odors of turnip and cabbage were strong in the senses of the worshippers. They sniffed and looked at one another. This superseding the legitimate savor of the sanctuary, the fragrance of peppermint lozenges and wintergreen, the breath of Sunday clothes, by the homely week-day odors of kitchen vegetables, was too much for the sensibilities of the people. They looked indignantly around at Hetty, sitting before her sunflower hanging, comfortable from her good dinner of the day be-

27

fore, radiant with the consciousness of a great plateful of cold vegetables in her tent for her Sabbath dinner.

Poor Hetty had not many comfortable dinners. The selectmen doled out a small weekly sum to her, which she took with dignity as being her hire ; then she had a mild forage in the neighbors' cellars and kitchens, of poor apples and stale bread and pie, paying for it in teaching her art of worsted-work to the daughters. Her Saturday's dinner had been a banquet to her: she had actually bought a piece of pork to boil with the vegetables ; somebody had given her a nice little cabbage and some turnips, without a thought of the limitations of her housekeeping. Hetty herself had not a thought. She made the fires as usual that Sunday morning ; the meeting-house was very clean, there was not a speck of dust anywhere, the wax cross on the pulpit glistened in a sunbeam slanting through the house. Hetty, sitting in the gallery, thought innocently how nice it looked.

After the meeting, Caleb Gale approached the other deacon. " Somethin's got to be done," said he. And the other deacon nodded. He had not smelt the cabbage until his wife nudged him and mentioned it ; neither had Caleb Gale.

In the afternoon of the next Thursday, Caleb and the other two selectmen waited upon Hetty in her tabernacle. They stumped up the gallery stairs, and Hetty emerged from behind the quilt and stood looking at them scared and defiant. The three men nodded stiffly ; there was a pause ; Caleb Gale motioned meaningly to one of the others, who shook his head ; finally he himself had to speak. " I'm 'fraid you find it pretty cold here, don't you, Hetty ?" said he.

" No, thank ye ; it's very comfortable," replied Hetty, polite and wary.

"It ain't very convenient for you to do your cookin' here, I guess."

"It's jest as convenient as I want. I don't find no fault."

"I guess it's rayther lonesome here nights, ain't it?"

"I'd 'nough sight ruther be alone than have comp'ny, any day."

"It ain't fit for an old woman like you to be livin' alone here this way."

"Well, I dun' know of anything that's any fitter; mebbe you do."

Caleb looked appealingly at his companions; they stood stiff and irresponsive. Hetty's eyes were sharp and watchful upon them all.

"Well, Hetty," said Caleb, "we've found a nice, comfortable place for you, an' I guess you'd better pack up your things, an' I'll carry you right over there." Caleb stepped back a little closer to the other men. Hetty, small and trembling and helpless before them, looked vicious. She was like a little animal driven from its cover, for whom there is nothing left but desperate warfare and death.

"Where to?" asked Hetty. Her voice shrilled up into a squeak.

Caleb hesitated. He looked again at the other selectmen. There was a solemn, far-away expression upon their faces. "Well," said he, "Mis' Radway wants to git somebody, an'—"

"You ain't goin' to take me to that woman's!"

"You'd be real comfortable—"

"I ain't goin'."

"Now, why not, I'd like to know?"

"I don't like Susan Radway, hain't never liked her, an' I ain't goin' to live with her."

" Mis' Radway's a good Christian woman. You hadn't ought to speak that way about her."

" You know what Susan Radway is, jest as well's I do ; an' everybody else does too. I ain't goin' a step, an' you might jest as well make up your mind to it."

Then Hetty seated herself in the corner of the pew near- est her tent, and folded her hands in her lap. She looked over at the pulpit as if she were listening to preaching. She panted, and her eyes glittered, but she had an immovable air.

" Now, Hetty, you've got sense enough to know you can't stay here," said Caleb. " You'd better put on your bon- net, an' come right along before dark. You'll have a nice ride."

Hetty made no response.

The three men stood looking at her. " Come, Hetty," said Caleb, feebly ; and another selectman spoke. " Yes, you'd better come," he said, in a mild voice.

Hetty continued to stare at the pulpit.

The three men withdrew a little and conferred. They did not know how to act. This was a new emergency in their simple, even lives. They were not constables ; these three steady, sober old men did not want to drag an old woman by main force out of the meeting-house, and thrust her into Caleb Gale's buggy as if it were a police wagon.

Finally Caleb brightened. " I'll go over an' git mother," said he. He started with a brisk air, and went down the gallery stairs ; the others followed. They took up their stand in the meeting-house yard, and Caleb got into his buggy and gathered up the reins. The wind blew cold over the hill. " Hadn't you better go inside and wait out of the wind ?" said Caleb.

"I guess we'll wait out here," replied one ; and the other nodded.

"Well, I sha'n't be gone long," said Caleb. "Mother'll know how to manage her." He drove carefully down the hill ; his buggy wings rattled in the wind. The other men pulled up their coat collars, and met the blast stubbornly.

"Pretty ticklish piece of business to tackle," said one, in a low grunt.

"That's so," assented the other. Then they were silent, and waited for Caleb. Once in a while they stamped their feet and slapped their mittened hands. They did not hear Hetty slip the bolt and turn the key of the meeting-house door, nor see her peeping at them from a gallery window.

Caleb returned in twenty minutes ; he had not far to go. His wife, stout and handsome and full of vigor, sat beside him in the buggy. Her face was red with the cold wind ; her thick cashmere shawl was pinned tightly over her broad bosom. "Has she come down yet ?" she called out, in an imperious way.

The two selectmen shook their heads. Caleb kept the horse quiet while his wife got heavily and briskly out of the buggy. She went up the meeting-house steps, and reached out confidently to open the door. Then she drew back and looked around. "Why," said she, "the door's locked ; she's locked the door. I call this pretty work !"

She turned again quite fiercely, and began beating on the door. "Hetty !" she called ; "Hetty, Hetty Fifield ! Let me in ! What have you locked this door for ?"

She stopped and turned to her husband.

"Don't you s'pose the barn key would unlock it ?" she asked.

"I don't b'lieve 'twould."

" Well, you'd better go home and fetch it."

Caleb again drove down the hill, and the other men searched their pockets for keys. One had the key of his corn-house, and produced it hopefully; but it would not unlock the meeting-house door.

A crowd seldom gathered in the little village for anything short of a fire; but to-day in a short time quite a number of people stood on the meeting-house hill, and more kept coming. When Caleb Gale returned with the barn key his daughter, a tall, pretty young girl, sat beside him, her little face alert and smiling in her red hood. The other selectmen's wives toiled eagerly up the hill, with a young daughter of one of them speeding on ahead. Then the two young girls stood close to each other and watched the proceedings. Key after key was tried; men brought all the large keys they could find, running importantly up the hill, but none would unlock the meeting-house door. After Caleb had tried the last available key, stooping and screwing it anxiously, he turned around. "There ain't no use in it, any way," said he; "most likely the door's bolted."

"You don't mean there's a bolt on that door?" cried his wife.

"Yes, there is."

"Then you might jest as well have tore 'round for hen's feathers as keys. Of course she's bolted it if she's got any wit, an' I guess she's got most as much as some of you men that have been bringin' keys. Try the windows."

But the windows were fast. Hetty had made her sacred castle impregnable except to violence. Either the door would have to be forced or a window broken to gain an entrance.

The people conferred with one another. Some were for

retreating, and leaving Hetty in peaceful possession until time drove her to capitulate. " She'll open it to-morrow," they said. Others were for extreme measures, and their impetuosity gave them the lead. The project of forcing the door was urged ; one man started for a crow-bar.

" They are a parcel of fools to do such a thing," said Caleb Gale's wife to another woman. " Spoil that good door ! They'd better leave the poor thing alone till to-morrow. I dun' know what's goin' to be done with her when they git in. I ain't goin' to have father draggin' her over to Mis' Radway's by the hair of her head."

" That's jest what I say," returned the other woman.

Mrs. Gale went up to Caleb and nudged him. " Don't you let them break that door down, father," said she.

" Well, well, we'll see," Caleb replied. He moved away a little ; his wife's voice had been drowned out lately by a masculine clamor, and he took advantage of it.

All the people talked at once ; the wind was keen, and all their garments fluttered ; the two young girls had their arms around each other under their shawls ; the man with the crow-bar came stalking up the hill.

" Don't you let them break down that door, father," said Mrs. Gale.

" Well, well," grunted Caleb.

Regardless of remonstrances, the man set the crow-bar against the door ; suddenly there was a cry, " There she is !" Everybody looked up. There was Hetty looking out of a gallery window.

Everybody was still. Hetty began to speak. Her dark old face, peering out of the window, looked ghastly ; the wind blew her poor gray locks over it. She extended her little wrinkled hands. " Jest let me say one word," said

she ; "jest one word." Her voice shook. All her cool-
ness was gone. The magnitude of her last act of defiance
had caused it to react upon herself like an overloaded gun.

"Say all you want to, Hetty, an' don't be afraid," Mrs.
Gale called out.

"I jest want to say a word," repeated Hetty. "Can't I
stay here, nohow ? It don't seem as if I could go to Mis'
Radway's. I ain't nothin' again' her. I s'pose she's a
good woman, but she's used to havin' her own way, and
I've been livin' all my life with them that was, an' I've had
to fight to keep a footin' on the earth, an' now I'm gittin'
too old for't. If I can jest stay here in the meetin'-house,
I won't ask for nothin' any better. I sha'n't need much to
keep me, I wa'n't never a hefty eater ; an' I'll keep the
meetin'-house jest as clean as I know how. An' I'll make
some more of them wool flowers. I'll make a wreath to
go the whole length of the gallery, if I can git wool 'nough.
Won't you let me stay ? I ain't complainin', but I've always
had a dretful hard time ; seems as if now I might take a
little comfort the last of it, if I could stay here. I can't go
to Mis' Radway's nohow." Hetty covered her face with
her hands ; her words ended in a weak wail.

Mrs. Gale's voice rang out clear and strong and irre-
pressible. "Of course you can stay in the meetin'-house,"
said she ; "I should laugh if you couldn't. Don't you worry
another mite about it. You sha'n't go one step to Mis'
Radway's ; you couldn't live a day with her. You can stay
jest where you are ; you've kept the meetin'-house enough
sight cleaner than I've ever seen it. Don't you worry another mite, Hetty."

Mrs. Gale stood majestically, and looked defiantly around ;
tears were in her eyes. Another woman edged up to her,

" Why couldn't she have that little room side of the pulpit, where the minister hangs his hat?" she whispered. " He could hang it somewhere else."

" Course she could," responded Mrs. Gale, with alacrity, "jest as well as not. The minister can havé a hook in the entry for his hat. She can have her stove an' her bed in there, an' be jest as comfortable as can be. I should laugh if she couldn't. Don't you worry, Hetty."

The crowd gradually dispersed, sending out stragglers down the hill until it was all gone. Mrs. Gale waited until the last, sitting in the buggy in state. When her husband gathered up the reins, she called back to Hetty: " Don't you worry one mite more about it, Hetty. I'm comin' up to see you in the mornin'!"

It was almost dusk when Caleb drove down the hill; he was the last of the besiegers, and the feeble garrison was left triumphant.

The next day but one was Christmas, the next night Christmas Eve. On Christmas Eve Hetty had reached what to her was the flood-tide of peace and prosperity. Established in that small, lofty room, with her bed and her stove, with gifts of a rocking-chair and table, and a goodly store of food, with no one to molest or disturb her, she had nothing to wish for on earth. All her small desires were satisfied. No happy girl could have a merrier Christmas than this old woman with her little measure full of gifts. That Christmas Eve Hetty lay down under her sunflower quilt, and all her old hardships looked dim in the distance, like far-away hills, while her new joys came out like stars.

She was a light sleeper; the next morning she was up early. She opened the meeting-house door and stood looking out. The smoke from the village chimneys had not yet begun to rise blue and rosy in the clear frosty air. There was no snow, but over all the hill there was a silver rime of frost; the bare branches of the trees glistened. Hetty stood looking. "Why, it's Christmas mornin'," she said, suddenly. Christmas had never been a gala-day to this old woman. Christmas had not been kept at all in this New England village when she was young. She was led to think of it now only in connection with the dinner Mrs. Gale had promised to bring her to-day.

Mrs. Gale had told her she should have some of her Christmas dinner, some turkey and plum-pudding. She called it to mind now with a thrill of delight. Her face grew momentarily more radiant. There was a certain beauty in it. A finer morning light than that which lit up the wintry earth seemed to shine over the furrows of her old face. "I'm goin' to have turkey an' plum-puddin' to-day," said she; "it's Christmas." Suddenly she started, and went into the meeting-house, straight up the gallery stairs. There in a clear space hung the bell-rope. Hetty grasped it. Never before had a Christmas bell been rung in this village; Hetty had probably never heard of Christmas bells. She was prompted by pure artless enthusiasm and grateful happiness. Her old arms pulled on the rope with a will, the bell sounded peal on peal. Down in the village, curtains rolled up, letting in the morning light, happy faces looked out of the windows. Hetty had awakened the whole village to Christmas Day.

THE REVOLT OF "MOTHER."

" FATHER !"

" What is it ?"

" What are them men diggin' over there in the field for ?"

There was a sudden dropping and enlarging of the lower part of the old man's face, as if some heavy weight had settled therein ; he shut his mouth tight, and went on harnessing the great bay mare. He hustled the collar on to her neck with a jerk.

" Father !"

The old man slapped the saddle upon the mare's back.

" Look here, father, I want to know what them men are diggin' over in the field for, an' I'm goin' to know."

" I wish you'd go into the house, mother, an' 'tend to your own affairs," the old man said then. He ran his words together, and his speech was almost as inarticulate as a growl.

But the woman understood ; it was her most native tongue. " I ain't goin'.into the house till you tell me what them men are doin' over there in the field," said she.

Then she stood waiting. She was a small woman, short and straight-waisted like a child in her brown cotton gown. Her forehead was mild and benevolent between the smooth curves of gray hair ; there were meek downward lines about her nose and mouth; but her eyes, fixed upon the old man, looked as if the meekness had been the result of her own will, never of the will of another.

They were in the barn, standing before the wide open doors. The spring air, full of the smell of growing grass and unseen blossoms, came in their faces. The deep yard in front was littered with farm wagons and piles of wood; on the edges, close to the fence and the house, the grass was a vivid green, and there were some dandelions.

The old man glanced doggedly at his wife as he tightened the last buckles on the harness. She looked as immovable to him as one of the rocks in his pasture-land, bound to the earth with generations of blackberry vines. He slapped the reins over the horse, and started forth from the barn.

"*Father!*" said she.

The old man pulled up. "What is it?"

"I want to know what them men are diggin' over there in that field for."

"They're diggin' a cellar, I s'pose, if you've got to know."

"A cellar for what?"

"A barn."

"A barn? You ain't goin' to build a barn over there where we was goin' to have a house, father?"

The old man said not another word. He hurried the horse into the farm wagon, and clattered out of the yard, jouncing as sturdily on his seat as a boy.

The woman stood a moment looking after him, then she went out of the barn across a corner of the yard to the house. The house, standing at right angles with the great barn and a long reach of sheds and out-buildings, was infinitesimal compared with them. It was scarcely as com-

modious for people as the little boxes under the barn eaves
were for doves.

A pretty girl's face, pink and delicate as a flower, was
looking out of one of the house windows.   She was watching three men who were digging over in the field which
bounded the yard near the road line.   She turned quietly
when the woman entered.

"What are they digging for, mother?" said she.   "Did he
tell you?"

"They're diggin' for—a cellar for a new barn."

"Oh, mother, he ain't going to build another barn?"

"That's what he says."

A boy stood before the kitchen glass combing his hair.
He combed slowly and painstakingly, arranging his brown
hair in a smooth hillock over his forehead.   He did not
seem to pay any attention to the conversation.

"Sammy, did you know father was going to build a new
barn?" asked the girl.

The boy combed assiduously.

"Sammy!"

He turned, and showed a face like his father's under his
smooth crest of hair.   "Yes, I s'pose I did," he said, re-
luctantly.

"How long have you known it?" asked his mother.

"'Bout three months, I guess."

"Why didn't you tell of it?"

"Didn't think 'twould do no good."

"I don't see what father wants another barn for," said
the girl, in her sweet, slow voice.   She turned again to the
window, and stared out at the digging men in the field.   Her
tender, sweet face was full of a gentle distress.   Her forehead was as bald and innocent as a baby's, with the light

hair strained back from it in a row of curl-papers. She was quite large, but her soft curves did not look as if they covered muscles.

Her mother looked sternly at the boy. "Is he goin' to buy more cows?" said she.

The boy did not reply; he was tying his shoes.

"Sammy, I want you to tell me if he's goin' to buy more cows."

"I s'pose he is."

"How many?"

"Four, I guess."

His mother said nothing more. She went into the pantry, and there was a clatter of dishes. The boy got his cap from a nail behind the door, took an old arithmetic from the shelf, and started for school. He was lightly built, but clumsy. He went out of the yard with a curious spring in the hips, that made his loose home-made jacket tilt up in the rear.

The girl went to the sink, and began to wash the dishes that were piled up there. Her mother came promptly out of the pantry, and shoved her aside. "You wipe 'em," said she; "I'll wash. There's a good many this mornin'."

The mother plunged her hands vigorously into the water, the girl wiped the plates slowly and dreamily. "Mother," said she, "don't you think it's too bad father's going to build that new barn, much as we need a decent house to live in?"

Her mother scrubbed a dish fiercely. "You ain't found out yet we're women-folks, Nanny Penn," said she. "You ain't seen enough of men-folks yet to. One of these days you'll find it out, an' then you'll know that we know only what men-folks think we do, so far as any use of it goes, an' how we'd ought to reckon men-folks in with Providence, an' not complain of what they do any more than we do of the weather."

"I don't care ; I don't believe George is anything like that, anyhow," said Nanny. Her delicate face flushed pink, her lips pouted softly, as if she were going to cry.

"You wait an' see. I guess George Eastman ain't no better than other men. You hadn't ought to judge father, though. He can't help it, 'cause he don't look at things jest the way we do. An' we've been pretty comfortable here, after all. The roof don't leak—ain't never but once —that's one thing. Father's kept it shingled right up."

"I do wish we had a parlor."

"I guess it won't hurt George Eastman any to come to see you in a nice clean kitchen. I guess a good many girls don't have as good a place as this. Nobody's ever heard me complain."

"I ain't complained either, mother."

"Well, I don't think you'd better, a good father an' a good home as you've got. S'pose your father made you go out an' work for your livin'? Lots of girls have to that ain't no stronger an' better able to than you be."

Sarah Penn washed the frying-pan with a conclusive air. She scrubbed the outside of it as faithfully as the inside. She was a masterly keeper of her box of a house. Her one living-room never seemed to have in it any of the dust which the friction of life with inanimate matter produces. She swept, and there seemed to be no dirt to go before the broom ; she cleaned, and one could see no difference. She was like an artist so perfect that he has apparently no art. To-day she got out a mixing bowl and a board, and rolled some pies, and there was no more flour upon her than upon her daughter who was doing finer work. Nanny was to be married in the fall, and she was sewing on some white cambric and embroidery.   She sewed industriously while her mother cooked, her soft milk-white hands and wrists showed whiter than her delicate work.

"We must have the stove moved out in the shed before long," said Mrs. Penn.   "Talk about not havin' things, it's been a real blessin' to be able to put a stove up in that shed in hot weather.   Father did one good thing when he fixed that stove-pipe out there."

Sarah Penn's face as she rolled her pies had that expression of meek vigor which might have characterized one of the New Testament saints.   She was making mince-pies. Her husband, Adoniram Penn, liked them better than any other kind.   She baked twice a week.   Adoniram often liked a piece of pie between meals.   She hurried this morning.   It had been later than usual when she began, and she wanted to have a pie baked for dinner.   However deep a resentment she might be forced to hold against her husband, she would never fail in sedulous attention to his wants.

Nobility of character manifests itself at loop-holes when it is not provided with large doors.   Sarah Penn's showed itself to-day in flaky dishes of pastry.   So she made the pies faithfully, while across the table she could see, when she glanced up from her work, the sight that rankled in her patient and steadfast soul—the digging of the cellar of the new barn in the place where Adoniram forty years ago had promised her their new house should stand.

The pies were done for dinner.   Adoniram and Sammy were home a few minutes after twelve o'clock.   The dinner was eaten with serious haste.   There was never much conversation at the table in the Penn family.   Adoniram asked a blessing, and they ate promptly, then rose up and went about their work.

Sammy went back to school, taking soft sly lopes out of the yard like a rabbit. He wanted a game of marbles before school, and feared his father would give him some chores to do. Adoniram hastened to the door and called after him, but he was out of sight.

"I don't see what you let him go for, mother," said he. "I wanted him to help me unload that wood."

Adoniram went to work out in the yard unloading wood from the wagon. Sarah put away the dinner dishes, while Nanny took down her curl-papers and changed her dress. She was going down to the store to buy some more embroidery and thread.

When Nanny was gone, Mrs. Penn went to the door. "Father!" she called.

"Well, what is it!"

"I want to see you jest a minute, father."

"I can't leave this wood nohow. I've got to git it unloaded an' go for a load of gravel afore two o'clock. Sammy had ought to helped me. You hadn't ought to let him go to school so early."

"I want to see you jest a minute."

"I tell ye I can't, nohow, mother."

"Father, you come here." Sarah Penn stood in the door like a queen; she held her head as if it bore a crown; there was that patience which makes authority royal in her voice. Adoniram went.

Mrs. Penn led the way into the kitchen, and pointed to a chair. "Sit down, father," said she; "I've got somethin' I want to say to you."

He sat down heavily; his face was quite stolid, but he

looked at her with restive eyes. "Well, what is it, mother?"

"I want to know what you're buildin' that new barn for, father?"

"I ain't got nothin' to say about it."

"It can't be you think you need another barn?"

"I tell ye I ain't got nothin' to say about it, mother; an' I ain't goin' to say nothin'."

"Be you goin' to buy more cows?"

Adoniram did not reply; he shut his mouth tight.

"I know you be, as well as I want to. Now, father, look here"—Sarah Penn had not sat down; she stood before her husband in the humble fashion of a Scripture woman— "I'm goin' to talk real plain to you; I never have sence I married you, but I'm goin' to now. I ain't never complained, an' I ain't goin' to complain now, but I'm goin' to talk plain. You see this room here, father; you look at it well. You see there ain't no carpet on the floor, an' you see the paper is all dirty, an' droppin' off the walls. We ain't had no new paper on it for ten year, an' then I put it on myself, an' it didn't cost but ninepence a roll. You see this room, father; it's all the one I've had to work in an' eat in an' sit in sence we was married. There ain't another woman in the whole town whose husband ain't got half the means you have but what's got better. It's all the room Nanny's got to have her company in; an' there ain't one of her mates but what's got better, an' their fathers not so able as hers is. It's all the room she'll have to be married in. What would you have thought, father, if we had had our weddin' in a room no better than this? I was married in my mother's parlor, with a carpet on the floor, an' stuffed furniture, an' a mahogany card-table. An' this is all the room

my daughter will have to be married in. Look here,
father !"

Sarah Penn went across the room as though it were a
tragic stage. She flung open a door and disclosed a tiny
bedroom, only large enough for a bed and bureau, with a
path between. "There, father," said she—"there's all the
room I've had to sleep in forty year. All my children were
born there—the two that died, an' the two that's livin'. I
was sick with a fever there."

She stepped to another door and opened it. It led into
the small, ill-lighted pantry. "Here," said she, "is all the
buttery I've got—every place I've got for my dishes, to set
away my victuals in, an' to keep my milk-pans in. Father,
I've been takin' care of the milk of six cows in this place,
an' now you're goin' to build a new barn, an' keep more
cows, an' give me more to do in it."

She threw open another door. A narrow crooked flight
of stairs wound upward from it. "There, father," said she,
"I want you to look at the stairs that go up to them two
unfinished chambers that are all the places our son an'
daughter have had to sleep in all their lives. There ain't a
prettier girl in town nor a more ladylike one than Nanny,
an' that's the place she has to sleep in. It ain't so good as
your horse's stall; it ain't so warm an' tight."

Sarah Penn went back and stood before her husband.
"Now, father," said she, "I want to know if you think
you're doin' right an' accordin' to what you profess. Here,
when we was married, forty year ago, you promised me
faithful that we should have a new house built in that lot
over in the field before the year was out. You said you had
money enough, an' you wouldn't ask me to live in no such
place as this. It is forty year now, an' you've been makin'

more money, an' I've been savin' of it for you ever since, an' you ain't built no house yet. You've built sheds an' cow-houses an' one new barn, an' now you're goin' to build another. Father, I want to know if you think it's right. You're lodgin' your dumb beasts better than you are your own flesh an' blood. I want to know if you think it's right."

" I ain't got nothin' to say."

"You can't say nothin' without ownin' it ain't right, father. An' there's another thing — I ain't complained ; I've got along forty year, an' I s'pose I should forty more, if it wa'n't for that—if we don't have another house. Nanny she can't live with us after she's married. She'll have to go somewheres else to live away from us, an' it don't seem as if I could have it so, noways, father. She wa'n't ever strong. She's got considerable color, but there wa'n't never any backbone to her. I've always took the heft of every- thing off her, an' she ain't fit to keep house an' do every- thing herself. She'll be all worn out inside of a year. Think of her doin' all the washin' an' ironin' an' bakin' with them soft white hands an' arms, an' sweepin' ! I can't have it so, noways, father."

Mrs. Penn's face was burning ; her mild eyes gleamed. She had pleaded her little cause like a Webster ; she had ranged from severity to pathos ; but her opponent employed that obstinate silence which makes eloquence futile with mocking echoes. Adoniram arose clumsily.

" Father, ain't you got nothin' to say ?" said Mrs. Penn.

" I've got to go off after that load of gravel. I can't stan' here talkin' all day."

" Father, won't you think it over, an' have a house built there instead of a barn ?"

" I ain't got nothin' to say."

Adoniram shuffled out. Mrs. Penn went into her bed-room. When she came out, her eyes were red. She had a roll of unbleached cotton cloth. She spread it out on the kitchen table, and began cutting out some shirts for her husband. The men over in the field had a team to help them this afternoon; she could hear their halloos. She had a scanty pattern for the shirts; she had to plan and piece the sleeves.

Nanny came home with her embroidery, and sat down with her needlework. She had taken down her curl-papers, and there was a soft roll of fair hair like an aureole over her forehead; her face was as delicately fine and clear as porce-lain. Suddenly she looked up, and the tender red flamed all over her face and neck. "Mother," said she.

"What say?"

"I've been thinking—I don't see how we're goin' to have any—wedding in this room. I'd be ashamed to have his folks come if we didn't have anybody else."

"Mebbe we can have some new paper before then; I can put it on. I guess you won't have no call to be ashamed of your belongin's."

"We might have the wedding in the new barn," said Nan-ny, with gentle pettishness. "Why, mother, what makes you look so?"

Mrs. Penn had started, and was staring at her with a curi-ous expression. She turned again to her work, and spread out a pattern carefully on the cloth. "Nothin'," said she.

Presently Adoniram clattered out of the yard in his two-wheeled dump cart, standing as proudly upright as a Roman charioteer. Mrs. Penn opened the door and stood there a minute looking out; the halloos of the men sounded louder.

It seemed to her all through the spring months that she

heard nothing but the halloos and the noises of saws and hammers. The new barn grew fast. It was a fine edifice for this little village. Men came on pleasant Sundays, in their meeting suits and clean shirt bosoms, and stood around it admiringly. Mrs. Penn did not speak of it, and Adoniram did not mention it to her, although sometimes, upon a return from inspecting it, he bore himself with injured dignity.

"It's a strange thing how your mother feels about the new barn," he said, confidentially, to Sammy one day.

Sammy only grunted after an odd fashion for a boy; he had learned it from his father.

The barn was all completed ready for use by the third week in July. Adoniram had planned to move his stock in on Wednesday; on Tuesday he received a letter which changed his plans. He came in with it early in the morning. "Sammy's been to the post-office," said he, "an' I've got a letter from Hiram." Hiram was Mrs. Penn's brother, who lived in Vermont.

"Well," said Mrs. Penn, "what does he say about the folks?"

"I guess they're all right. He says he thinks if I come up country right off there's a chance to buy jest the kind of a horse I want." He stared reflectively out of the window at the new barn.

Mrs. Penn was making pies. She went on clapping the rolling-pin into the crust, although she was very pale, and her heart beat loudly.

"I dun' know but what I'd better go," said Adoniram. "I hate to go off jest now, right in the midst of hayin', but the ten-acre lot's cut, an' I guess Rufus an' the others can git along without me three or four days. I can't get a horse round here to suit me, nohow, an' I've got to have another for all that wood-haulin' in the fall.   I told Hiram to watch out, an' if he got wind of a good horse to let me know.   I guess I'd better go."

"I'll get out your clean shirt an' collar," said Mrs. Penn calmly.

She laid out Adoniram's Sunday suit and his clean clothes on the bed in the little bedroom.   She got his shaving-water and razor ready.   At last she buttoned on his collar and fastened his black cravat.

Adoniram never wore his collar and cravat except on extra occasions.   He held his head high, with a rasped dignity. When he was all ready, with his coat and hat brushed, and a lunch of pie and cheese in a paper bag, he hesitated on the threshold of the door.   He looked at his wife, and his manner was defiantly apologetic.   "*If* them cows come to-day, Sammy can drive 'em into the new barn," said he ; "an' when they bring the hay up, they can pitch it in there."

"Well," replied Mrs. Penn.

Adoniram set his shaven face ahead and started.   When he had cleared the door-step, he turned and looked back with a kind of nervous solemnity.   "I shall be back by Saturday if nothin' happens," said he.

"Do be careful, father," returned his wife.

She stood in the door with Nanny at her elbow and watched him out of sight.   Her eyes had a strange, doubtful expression in them ; her peaceful forehead was contracted.   She went in, and about her baking again.   Nanny sat sewing.   Her wedding-day was drawing nearer, and she was getting pale and thin with her steady sewing.   Her mother kept glancing at her.

"Have you got that pain in your side this mornin'?" she asked.

" A little."

Mrs. Penn's face, as she worked, changed, her perplexed forehead smoothed, her eyes were steady, her lips firmly set. She formed a maxim for herself, although incoherently with her unlettered thoughts. " Unsolicited opportunities are the guide-posts of the Lord to the new roads of life," she repeated in effect, and she made up her mind to her course of action.

" S'posin' I *had* wrote to Hiram," she muttered once, when she was in the pantry—" s'posin' I had wrote, an' asked him if he knew of any horse? But I didn't, an' father's goin' wa'n't none of my doin'. It looks like a providence." Her voice rang out quite loud at the last.

" What you talkin' about, mother ?" called Nanny.

" Nothin'."

Mrs. Penn hurried her baking ; at eleven o'clock it was all done. The load of hay from the west field came slowly down the cart track, and drew up at the new barn. Mrs. Penn ran out. " Stop !" she screamed—" stop !"

The men stopped and looked ; Sammy upreared from the top of the load, and stared at his mother.

" Stop !" she cried out again. " Don't you put the hay in that barn ; put it in the old one."

" Why, he said to put it in here," returned one of the hay-makers, wonderingly. He was a young man, a neighbor's son, whom Adoniram hired by the year to help on the farm.

" Don't you put the hay in the new barn ; there's room enough in the old one, ain't there ?" said Mrs. Penn.

" Room enough," returned the hired man, in his thick, rustic tones. " Didn't need the new barn, nohow, far as room's concerned. Well, I s'pose he changed his mind." He took hold of the horses' bridles.

Mrs. Penn went back to the house. Soon the kitchen

windows were darkened, and a fragrance like warm honey came into the room.

Nanny laid down her work. " I thought father wanted them to put the hay into the new barn?" she said, wonderingly.

" It's all right," replied her mother.

Sammy slid down from the load of hay, and came in to see if dinner was ready.

" I ain't goin' to get a regular dinner to-day, as long as father's gone," said his mother. " I've let the fire go out. You can have some bread an' milk an' pie. I thought we could get along." She set out some bowls of milk, some bread, and a pie on the kitchen table. " You'd better eat your dinner now," said she. " You might jest as well get through with it. I want you to help me afterward."

Nanny and Sammy stared at each other. There was something strange in their mother's manner. Mrs. Penn did not eat anything herself. She went into the pantry, and they heard her moving dishes while they ate. Presently she came out with a pile of plates. She got the clothes-basket out of the shed, and packed them in it. Nanny and Sammy watched. She brought out cups and saucers, and put them in with the plates.

" What you goin' to do, mother?" inquired Nanny, in a timid voice. A sense of something unusual made her tremble, as if it were a ghost. Sammy rolled his eyes over his pie.

" You'll see what I'm goin' to do," replied Mrs. Penn. " If you're through, Nanny, I want you to go up-stairs an' pack up your things; an' I want you, Sammy, to help me take down the bed in the bedroom."

" Oh, mother, what for?" gasped Nanny.

" You'll see."

During the next few hours a feat was performed by this

simple, pious New England mother which was equal in its way to Wolfe's storming of the Heights of Abraham. It took no more genius and audacity of bravery for Wolfe to cheer his wondering soldiers up those steep precipices, under the sleeping eyes of the enemy, than for Sarah Penn, at the head of her children, to move all their little household goods into the new barn while her husband was away.

Nanny and Sammy followed their mother's instructions without a murmur; indeed, they were overawed. There is a certain uncanny and superhuman quality about all such purely original undertakings as their mother's was to them. Nanny went back and forth with her light loads, and Sammy tugged with sober energy.

At five o'clock in the afternoon the little house in which the Penns had lived for forty years had emptied itself into the new barn.

Every builder builds somewhat for unknown purposes, and is in a measure a prophet. The architect of Adoniram Penn's barn, while he designed it for the comfort of four-footed animals, had planned better than he knew for the comfort of humans. Sarah Penn saw at a glance its possibilities. Those great box-stalls, with quilts hung before them, would make better bedrooms than the one she had occupied for forty years, and there was a tight carriage-room. The harness-room, with its chimney and shelves, would make a kitchen of her dreams. The great middle space would make a parlor, by-and-by, fit for a palace. Up stairs there was as much room as down. With partitions and windows, what a house would there be! Sarah looked at the row of stanchions before the allotted space for cows, and reflected that she would have her front entry there.

At six o'clock the stove was up in the harness-room, the kettle was boiling, and the table set for tea. It looked almost as home-like as the abandoned house across the yard had ever done. The young hired man milked, and Sarah directed him calmly to bring the milk to the new barn. He came gaping, dropping little blots of foam from the brimming pails on the grass. Before the next morning he had spread the story of Adoniram Penn's wife moving into the new barn all over the little village. Men assembled in the store and talked it over, women with shawls over their heads scuttled into each other's houses before their work was done. Any deviation from the ordinary course of life in this quiet town was enough to stop all progress in it. Everybody paused to look at the staid, independent figure on the side track. There was a difference of opinion with regard to her. Some held her to be insane ; some, of a lawless and rebellious spirit.

Friday the minister went to see her. It was in the forenoon, and she was at the barn door shelling pease for dinner. She looked up and returned his salutation with dignity, then she went on with her work. She did not invite him in. The saintly expression of her face remained fixed, but there was an angry flush over it.

The minister stood awkwardly before her, and talked. She handled the pease as if they were bullets. At last she looked up, and her eyes showed the spirit that her meek front had covered for a lifetime.

"There ain't no use talkin', Mr. Hersey," said she. " I've thought it all over an' over, an' I believe I'm doin' what's right. I've made it the subject of prayer, an' it's betwixt me an' the Lord an' Adoniram. There ain't no call for nobody else to worry about it."

"Well, of course, if you have brought it to the Lord in prayer, and feel satisfied that you are doing right, Mrs. Penn," said the minister, helplessly. His thin gray-bearded face was pathetic. He was a sickly man ; his youthful confidence had cooled ; he had to scourge himself up to some of his pastoral duties as relentlessly as a Catholic ascetic, and then he was prostrated by the smart.

" I think it's right jest as much as I think it was right for our forefathers to come over from the old country 'cause they didn't have what belonged to 'em," said Mrs. Penn. She arose. The barn threshold might have been Plymouth Rock from her bearing. " I don't doubt you mean well, Mr. Hersey," said she, " but there are things people hadn't ought to interfere with. I've been a member of the church for over forty year. I've got my own mind an' my own feet, an' I'm goin' to think my own thoughts an' go my own ways, an' nobody but the Lord is goin' to dictate to me unless I've a mind to have him. Won't you come in an' set down ? How is Mis' Hersey ?"

" She is. well, I thank you," replied the minister. He added some more perplexed apologetic remarks ; then he retreated.

He could expound the intricacies of every character study in the Scriptures, he was competent to grasp the Pilgrim Fathers and all historical innovators, but Sarah Penn was beyond him. He could deal with primal cases, but parallel ones worsted him. But, after all, although it was aside from his province, he wondered more how Adoniram Penn would deal with his wife than how the Lord would. Everybody shared the wonder. When Adoniram's four new cows arrived, Sarah ordered three to be put in the old barn, the other in the house shed where the cooking-stove had stood. That added to the excitement. It was whispered that all four cows were domiciled in the house.

Towards sunset on Saturday, when Adoniram was ex-

pected home, there was a knot of men in the road near the
new barn. The hired man had milked, but he still hung
around the premises. Sarah Penn had supper all ready.
There were brown-bread and baked beans and a custard
pie ; it was the supper that Adoniram loved on a Saturday
night. She had on a clean calico, and she bore herself
imperturbably. Nanny and Sammy kept close at her heels.
Their eyes were large, and Nanny was full of nervous
tremors. Still there was to them more pleasant excitement than anything else. An inborn confidence in their
mother over their father asserted itself.

Sammy looked out of the harness-room window. "There
he is," he announced, in an awed whisper. He and Nanny
peeped around the casing. Mrs. Penn kept on about her
work. The children watched Adoniram leave the new horse
standing in the drive while he went to the house door. It
was fastened. Then he went around to the shed. That
door was seldom locked, even when the family was away.
The thought how her father would be confronted by the cow
flashed upon Nanny. There was a hysterical sob in her
throat. Adoniram emerged from the shed and stood looking about in a dazed fashion. His lips moved ; he was
saying something, but they could not hear what it was.
The hired man was peeping around a corner of the old
barn, but nobody saw him.

Adoniram took the new horse by the bridle and led him
across the yard to the new barn. Nanny and Sammy slunk
close to their mother. The barn doors rolled back, and
there stood Adoniram, with the long mild face of the great
Canadian farm horse looking over his shoulder.

Nanny kept behind her mother, but Sammy stepped suddenly forward, and stood in front of her.

Adoniram stared at the group. "What on airth you all

down here for?" said he.   "What's the matter over to the
house?"

"We've come here to live, father," said Sammy.   His
shrill voice quavered out bravely.

"What"—Adoniram sniffed—"what is it smells like
cookin?" said he.   He stepped forward and looked in the
open door of the harness-room.   Then he turned to his
wife.   His old bristling face was pale and frightened.   "What
on airth does this mean, mother?" he gasped.

"You come in here, father," said Sarah.   She led the
way into the harness-room and shut the door.   "Now,
father," said she, "you needn't be scared.   I ain't crazy.
There ain't nothin' to be upset over.   But we've come here
to live, an' we're goin' to live here.   We've got jest as good
a right here as new horses an' cows.   The house wa'n't fit
for us to live in any longer, an' I made up my mind I wa'n't
goin' to stay there.   I've done my duty by you forty year,
an' I'm goin' to do it now; but I'm goin' to live here.
You've got to put in some windows and partitions; an'
you'll have to buy some furniture."

"Why, mother!" the old man gasped.

"You'd better take your coat off an' get washed—there's
the wash-basin—an' then we'll have supper."

"Why, mother!"

Sammy went past the window, leading the new horse to
the old barn.   The old man saw him, and shook his head
speechlessly.   He tried to take off his coat, but his arms
seemed to lack the power.   His wife helped him.   She
poured some water into the tin basin, and put in a piece
of soap.   She got the comb and brush, and smoothed his
thin gray hair after he had washed.   Then she put the
beans, hot bread, and tea on the table.   Sammy came in,

and the family drew up. Adoniram sat looking dazedly at his plate, and they waited.

"Ain't you goin' to ask a blessin', father?" said Sarah.

And the old man bent his head and mumbled.

All through the meal he stopped eating at intervals, and stared furtively at his wife; but he ate well. The home food tasted good to him, and his old frame was too sturdily healthy to be affected by his mind. But after supper he went out, and sat down on the step of the smaller door at the right of the barn, through which he had meant his Jerseys to pass in stately file, but which Sarah designed for her front house door, and he leaned his head on his hands.

After the supper dishes were cleared away and the milk-pans washed, Sarah went out to him. The twilight was deepening. There was a clear green glow in the sky. Before them stretched the smooth level of field; in the distance was a cluster of hay-stacks like the huts of a village; the air was very cool and calm and sweet. The landscape might have been an ideal one of peace.

Sarah bent over and touched her husband on one of his thin, sinewy shoulders. "Father!"

The old man's shoulders heaved : he was weeping.

"Why, don't do so, father," said Sarah.

"I'll—put up the—partitions, an'—everything you—want, mother."

Sarah put her apron up to her face; she was overcome by her own triumph.

Adoniram was like a fortress whose walls had no active resistance, and went down the instant the right besieging tools were used. "Why, mother," he said, hoarsely, "I hadn't no idee you was so set on't as all this comes to."

Afterword

THE STORIES

For contemporary readers, Mary Wilkins Freeman's interest lies in her depiction of the lives of women in late nineteenth-century New England, for in the variety of those portraits she stands unsurpassed in American literature to her time. In some of these stories, Freeman portrays life for women alone; in others, Freeman's fiction analyzes bonds between sisters or close friends, and between mothers and daughters or women who become surrogate mothers, daughters, or sisters to each other. In several of the most dramatic stories, she depicts women in conflict with men, and in two of the stories included here, she examines life as men alone experience and view it. It would be impossible in a short space to analyze all of the stories in depth, but a few observations about each of them may help the reader to begin that task and to appreciate the collection's strength.

Freeman's first significant publication, "Two Old Lovers," establishes her interest in patterns and in the ways men and women separately live their lives. The story suggests that the habit of life in Leyden, rather than David Emmons's particular idiosyncracy, explains his slowness in asking Maria Brewster, his apparent lover of more than twenty-five years, to marry him. Beginning with a description of Leyden, in which the houses are "built after one of two patterns," the story creates a fictional world in which even the patterns of human lives are fixed. The men inhabit the world of the town's shoe factories during the day while the women stay at home and keep the cottages, and the shoe factories resemble clumsy angels "tempered with smoke or the beatings of the storms." Like the town itself, the "two old lovers" have both chosen a different pattern by which to live, and throughout, the story sets their lives in juxtaposition. Maria is stronger than David, and her affection is more "mother-like" than "lover-like." David, on the other hand, is compared to the poet Robert Herrick, and his courtship, prolonged even to his deathbed, partakes of the sixteenth century's idealization of the beloved rather than the "eminently practical" feeling Maria has for him.

Maria perceives both her need for a human kinship and David's need for mother-love, whereas David sees nothing. Therefore she thrives and he declines. The story focuses on a world in which mother-love is not absent but unrecognized. The clumsy angels—the shoe factories to which the men of Leyden turn for inspiration—become angels of destruction.[1] The men making shoes become so worn that their paths and those of the women do not cross. Even on his deathbed, David Emmons does not ask Maria to marry him but only says that he " 'allers meant to—have asked.' " Despite the overtones of romance, then, "Two Old Lovers" portrays the effects of an industrializing culture that has destroyed all but the idealized, courtly forms of love between men and women.

In subsequent stories, Freeman would turn to the lives of women in order to explore the nature of vision, affection, and human conflict obscured by her culture's insistence on divergent patterns of life for men and women. "An Honest Soul" presents a situation emblematic of that in which many women in Freeman's fiction find themselves. After the death of her hard-working parents, Martha Patch has struggled to eke out her survival alone, by taking in quilting and living frugally. The story anatomizes the seventy-year-old woman's pride, as she believes she has switched pieces for two separate quilts and in her confusion restitches them not once but twice. But the elderly woman's strength of will forms the backdrop for another drama—one that Freeman suggests is more significant to Martha's life and health than her want of food. For the house she inhabits—never completed in her father's lifetime—lacks both door and window in front; and living without a front window becomes symbolic of her life's burden.

Many women in Freeman's fiction lack front windows in a symbolic sense—focusing their sights on back views and domestic struggles in lieu of connection with the outside world, which Martha's idea of having a front window implies. Yet Martha contents herself with watching the progress of the grass—which, she thinks, grows much greener in the spot she can see from inside her house than elsewhere in the yard. The story implies a connection between that green grass and Martha's own transforming gaze; for despite her lack of a front window on the passing world, Martha Patch yet possesses a vision. When she lies collapsed in a sunbeam at the end of the story and a neighbor discovers her, the neighbor offers her husband's skill at carpentry in payment for needlework. Now Martha will have her front window, but the view that remains real for her is the one she has intensified by her own watching—the greener spot of grass. With or without a front window, the woman has found a form for vision.

Similarly, in "A New England Nun," Freeman portrays a woman who has managed to transform domestic ritual into vision. Living alone, Louisa Ellis possesses "the enthusiasm of an artist" in the way she keeps her house. When she reconsiders marriage to Joe Dagget and chooses to align herself against the values he represents, Freeman implies that nineteenth-century women were not left behind but, rather, chose to remain when the young men of the region went West, moved to cities, or like Joe Dagget tried their fortunes in Australia. Although "A New England Nun" has been read as a story about Louisa's sexual repression (because one of the fears she associates with marriage concerns Joe Dagget's threat to release her long-chained and reputedly vicious dog Caesar),[2] Louisa's greater fear seems to be that of losing not her virginity but her vision. When she discovers that Joe has become infatuated with a younger woman, she feels free to break off their engagement, and in the story's concluding image she becomes nunlike in her solitude yet "uncloistered" by her decision not to marry. She sees herself cut off from the "busy harvest of men and birds and bees," yet the vision she protects is more than compensatory for her celibacy. Her choice of solitude leaves her ironically "uncloistered"—and freer, in her society, than she would otherwise have been.

The desire to find a form for vision and to protect that vision establishes a sisterhood of sorts in many of Freeman's stories. Like "A New England Nun," "A Patient Waiter" epitomizes the historical position of the late nineteenth-century New England woman—Fidelia Almy waits in vain forty years until she dies for a letter from her departed lover—but specifically characterizes the nature of the vision as that of "mother's" legacy. For although Fidelia takes center stage in the story, her orphaned niece, Lily, who lives with her and whom she mothers, achieves the story's vision. Like her aunt, Lily has a departed lover for whose letters she waits in vain—until he writes announcing his plans to return just as Fidelia lies on her deathbed. The arrival of this letter seems to confirm Lily's own faith, but in witnessing the final shattering of her aunt's—when the latter arrives, Fidelia thinks her long-lost Ansel Lennox has written at last—Lily receives a vision that offers her a realistic perception of the "awful pitifulness" of life. The absence of mail for Fidelia evokes years of broken promise. Only in her death can Fidelia pass the post office on her way to the green graveyard without caring whether or not there is a letter for her. And amid all the "fair, wide possibilities of heaven," Lily loses her faith in Providence. In that loss, she discovers that the real sky—despite her imminent marriage to her own lover—yields no male but only her "dear, poor aunty." Fidelia's "faithful soul" could not force the heavens to fulfill their own promises, and in the image of mortality that her aunt's death leaves Lily, the young woman recognizes the depths of her loss: she regains her lover but loses the only mother she ever knew.

This story, and another from Freeman's first collection, "A Gatherer of Simples," may be seen as transitional fiction that bridges stories of women alone and the larger group of stories in which Freeman explores relatedness among women. In addition, more than any other story, "A Gatherer of Simples" invites the reader to explicate the title of *A Humble Romance* as a romance of the soil, in which the word *humble* derives from the Latin *humus*. For herbs, with their powers to heal and restore, provide the symbolism. The story explores what in Aurelia Flower's world is in need of restoration. The reader discovers that with the exception of Aurelia herself, the women in this story either lack mothers altogether or are deficient in their mothering. When Aurelia takes in an orphaned two-year-old girl and proves to be a successful mother, the reader is invited to consider the qualities that she possesses and other women do not, and that become inextricably linked with her herbalism.

"A Gatherer of Simples" portrays a world in which "mother" needs restoration but in which the idea of mother becomes, for Freeman, significantly associated with unconventionality. Both the physical description of Aurelia and her occupation as a healer establish her as an eccentric, and in her mothering, too, she is unorthodox. Unlike another mother in the story, Mrs. Atwood—who deliberately constricts her own daughter's life—Aurelia takes little Myrtie with her when she goes for herbs, the long voyage out that symbolizes her eccentricity. The story characterizes the nature of Au-

relia's paradise in an image: the mother-figure with a garland
over her shoulder caring in the "tender twilight" for her two
babies, the sleeping Myrtie and the sheaf of herbs. Her reputation as an "old yarb-woman," however, brings her close to
tragedy, when Myrtie's natural grandmother tries to take the
child away. Like Lily in "A Patient Waiter," Aurelia discovers
that Providence does not "provide" for women. She must act
on her own behalf, and when Myrtie runs away from her
grandmother, Aurelia unlawfully keeps her for the night. The
story ends in romance, clearly—when the grandmother dies
of a heart attack on the same night—but it is a "humble"
one in which Freeman expresses her vision. In the story's
closing lines, she suggests that it is the entire world for which
Aurelia is providing atonement—creating a pattern for Myrtie
to follow that will restore "mother." It is not, finally, Providence but women themselves who provide for other women.
In mothering Myrtie, Aurelia finds the "mother" in herself.

The search for "mother," or for a tie with another woman
that will allow them to replicate that experience in some
visionary way, links several of the protagonists in stories collected in this volume. "On the Walpole Road," from *A Humble
Romance,* is one of Freeman's best stories, as well as one in
which the narrator explores connecting links between women
who are related by blood ties or by surrogate motherhood and
sisterhood. The story's narrative frame depicts two women
trying to get home before a storm hits. On the way, the older
one, Mrs. Green, tells a story about her Aunt Rebecca's unhappy marriages to Uncle Enos and a man named Abner
Lyons. Several related stories embedded within the narrative
imply, by the story's end, that Mrs. Green and her younger
listener, Almiry, have found outside of marriage what Aunt
Rebecca could not achieve within it—a community of women.
For Rebecca (who once served as surrogate mother to Mrs.
Green), life became a tragedy of isolation from such a com-

munity. Forced by her own mother to marry Enos, then forcing her second husband Abner into a masculine role to which he is unsuited (androgynous by nature, he prefers to share domestic tasks), Rebecca perversely perpetuated the lack of sympathy between women and androgynous men, a sympathy that might have eased her alienation. By the story's end, Mrs. Green seems to be consoling the unmarried Almiry, and Freeman implicitly links the two women as surrogate mother and daughter.

Stories about sisters and sisterhoods serve as variations on the same theme. In "A Gala Dress," for example—another of Freeman's strongest stories—two women, Emily and Elizabeth Babcock, share a black silk dress, which means that they can never appear at church or social gatherings together. One sister trims the dress in black velvet; the other sister rips off the velvet and sews on black lace when it is her turn to wear the dress. In their secret sharing, the sisters approach the closest possible symbiosis, seeming to inhabit the same (dress) body. They practice this deception to hide their poverty from the town and from their closest neighbor, Matilda Jennings, who lives alone and who, in the sisters' eyes, belongs to an inferior social class.

In their treatment of Matilda throughout the story, Emily and Elizabeth Babcock limit the potential of their sisterhood to include other women—until, as a result of an accident at the Fourth of July picnic, the sisters and Matilda manage to confess their deepest secrets to each other. The story portrays their mutual discovery that in their impoverishment of spirit they have cut themselves off from deep friendship. When they offer Matilda the damaged though mended dress (after receiving a windfall inheritance of two new ones), they offer her much more than a garment. They reject their formerly exclusive "sorority" and extend the symbol of their own shared body to Matilda, in the process transforming the "coarse old

face" of their new friend with a "fine light," which the reader
of these stories will recognize as emblematic of the vision
that results from new relatedness between women in Freeman's fiction. The theme of "mother" becomes transposed in
this story about sisters, but the qualities of the vision are
familiar.

"Sister Liddy"—which Ann Douglas has called "one of the
most powerful short stories written in America" [3]—depicts
social conditions for New England women living in an almshouse that, with its inhabitants who have outlived their lives,
serves as a hollow echo of the world of women outside it.
Some of the women have come to resemble children, and at
least one of them is mad. They separately embody those traits
misogynistic convention has considered characteristic of
women—vindictiveness, vanity, and verbal cruelty. One of
them—the perennially silent Polly Moss—tells a story about
her Sister Liddy, who becomes a composite of everything the
old women have been but have lost, and everything they would
have wanted to be. Yet even though she seems to increase the
misery of the other women with her descriptions of Sister
Liddy's material wealth, at the same time she holds their
attention and transforms their present in a way that their
memories have failed to do. Her story actually gives them
more than it takes away. When at the end of the story Polly
confesses that Sister Liddy is only a fiction, Freeman implies
an unspoken kinship between Polly Moss and the young mad
inmate of the house.

The story points to the tragedy of a world in which women
cling to the remnants of material life to warm them rather
than to each other. Simultaneously, though, Freeman implies
that women can enrich the "almshouse" of their community
by beginning to disclose their deepest dreams, and by recognizing their mutual isolation—creating fictions of sisters where
none may exist but in which the desire for sisterhood may be
viewed as a symptom of health rather than insanity.

In "Up Primrose Hill," the most unconventional depiction of friendship between women in this collection, Freeman offers homoerotic ties as a variation on familial relatedness. The erotic overtones of the story exist in symbolic form but are unmistakable. In the two friends' discovery that a window in the old Primrose house has remained unfastened, and that if they want to do so they can easily, if stealthily, enter the house, Freeman creates an atmosphere of seduction, as Mrs. Daggett continues to insist that there is no "harm" in their entering, while her friend, Mrs. Rowe, "with many quavers" is finally persuaded. Once inside, Mrs. Daggett invites her friend to commit even further trespass, as they explore first the kitchen, with its interior pantry, in which they "taste" a small jar of quince sauce; then "the statelier and more withdrawn recesses" of the house; and finally a bureau drawer in one of the bedrooms. The "treasure" they find there, their subsequent fear of discovery when they hear the doorbell ring, and Mrs. Rowe's determination not to feel "ashamed" when she returns home all point to the mysteries of erotic, if sublimated, friendship between the two women. Subplots in the story juxtapose the women's friendship with conventional romance, and in the climactic moment in which all three plots converge, the Primrose house becomes the scene of a baroque parody of sexual comedy. With the belated return of Maria Primrose to take up residence once again in the old house, it seems likely that there will no longer be opportunities for Mrs. Daggett and Mrs. Rowe to experience the "harm" women's sexuality, the story implies, is capable of. Yet among the three variations on the expression of human intimacy Freeman offers—marriage itself, unrequited love, and the "guilty" friendship between the two women—only the third possibility seems likely to lead to peace. The story implicitly and mischievously answers Mrs. Daggett's own repeated question: " 'What's the harm, I'd like to know?' " It appears to have occurred to Freeman, whatever her own personal experience may have been, that where friendship between women is assured, there is no "harm" at all in a defiant intimacy.

The largest group of stories with a related theme explores the nature of female rebellion and portrays women in conflict with men, with social institutions, and with convention in its various forms. In two stories—"A Conflict Ended" and "The Revolt of 'Mother,' "—the male character manages, as a result of conflict, to conquer his own will, which is to dominate and destroy. Within a Puritan context, will was considered a masculine quality and heart, a feminine quality.[4] Puritanism emerges in Freeman's studies of men who commit themselves on principle or out of stubbornness to a course of behavior long after they might otherwise humanly reject that course. In "A Conflict Ended," where Marcus Woodman sits on the steps of the Congregational church each Sunday rather than cross the threshold to listen to a minister against whom he spoke out ten years earlier, and in "The Revolt of 'Mother,' " where Adoniram Penn has built sheds and cow houses and two new barns instead of the new house he promised his wife when they married forty years before, the male characters must undergo a change of heart before they can conquer their will or behave in a more human way.

"A Conflict Ended" is an important story in part because it anticipates Freeman's interest in will—which she would develop in *Pembroke,* her best novel—and in part because it establishes the necessary condition for a man like Marcus Woodman to capitulate. The story's female protagonist, Esther Barney, broke her engagement to Marcus ten years earlier when he refused to leave the church steps; but when Esther reverses New England patterns and calls on Marcus after ten years, suggesting that she might have been a little more patient with him, he responds in a parody of courtship by throwing himself at her feet. The social stigma she formerly rejected she now vows to live with, but when Marcus discovers that his new wife intends to sit on the church steps with him he asserts the "grand mien of a conqueror" and conquers his own will, refusing to allow Esther to experience the humiliation and stigma he himself has endured. It is significant that one of the catalytic events in the story is the death of Marcus's mother—had she lived, Esther realizes, she could not have called on Marcus. When Marcus leaves behind his church step, he crosses over from the world in which men exert their will into one in which Esther can replace his mother in creating tidiness and comfort in his life. He reveals himself to be a man just as cut off from "mother" as many of Freeman's women characters. Marriage itself may or may not be best for Esther but clearly is for Marcus; his refusal to allow his new wife to be humiliated makes it possible for him to triumph over the will—or, in Puritan terms, the "man"—in himself.

"The Revolt of 'Mother'" depicts conflict between Sarah Penn and her husband Adoniram—a man who has acted for forty years not out of principle but simply out of what he viewed as the strength of his position as a man in the house, and out of his own stubborn determination. As Foster describes him, "Through forty years his ego has gorged on the rich food of deference and respect."[5] And although Foster quotes Freeman, years later, as repudiating the story, when she claimed that "There never was in New England a woman like Mother," and that Sarah Penn would have "lacked the nerve" and the "imagination" to move into the barn,[6] the story itself establishes its conflict along lines of gender.

In one of the strongest moments in the story, Sarah tries to explain the irony of deference to her daughter:

> "You ain't found out yet we're women-folks, Nanny Penn.
> . . . You ain't seen enough of men-folks yet to. One of
> these days you'll find it out, and then you'll know that we
> know only what men-folks think we do . . . an' how we'd

ought to reckon men-folks in with Providence, an' not complain of what they do any more than we do of the
weather."

When she moves her family into her husband's new barn,
and he opens the doors expecting to tie up his horses where
his family newly resides, Sarah's "revolt" ends her subordina-
tion because she manages through her action what she could
never accomplish with words: she alters Adoniram's view of
her condition. The story compares the barn threshold to
Plymouth Rock, as Sarah herself remembers " 'our forefathers' " who " 'come over from the old country 'cause they
didn't have what belonged to 'em.' " Like "A Conflict Ended,"
however, this story ends in Adoniram's admirable capitulation.
When Sarah finds him weeping, she discovers that he has
undergone a change of perception. His last statement—in a
story that begins with " 'Father!' "—is sympathetic as well
as conciliatory: " 'Why, mother,' he said, hoarsely, 'I hadn't
no idee you was so set on't as all this comes to.' " Before
"mother's" revolt, he thought he was the only one who was
"set"; her action allows him to conquer his granitic inability
to feel, and he sits weeping with newly opened eyes.

The last action the Shattuck sisters in "A Mistaken Charity"
would seem capable of, as the story opens, is rebellion. Yet
their revolt is one of the most memorable in Freeman's fiction.
Two poor women, one of them blind, Harriet and Charlotte
live with their independence (and chinks in their roof) rather
than accept the town's charity. When a woman named Mrs.
Simonds launches her "new project" and has them moved to
an "Old Ladies' Home," Harriet asserts her lifelong habit of
independence. Refusing to be transformed from "unpolished
old women" into "nice old ladies," the two sisters run away
from the home and successfully escape back to their own
leaky-roofed cottage. In their action, they achieve their mo-

ment of greatest vision, characterized by blind Charlotte's insistence that she sees light again in the "chinks" that penetrate the double walls of her cottage and her literal blindness. The title of this story, like many of Freeman's titles, minimizes the struggle the story portrays. For Mrs. Simonds is more than "mistaken" in her charity; she is trying to change the mold into which the Shattuck sisters have cast their lives. The sisters must actively triumph over that "charity," or, as Charlotte expresses it, they " 'can't stay here no ways in this world.' " Finding a way to "stay" in the world, the Shattuck sisters, and all of Freeman's rebellious women, form their own cloister of "nuns" who create the world in their own image even as they appear to be fleeing from it.

When Freeman depicts women in conflict with institutions or with ministers and deacons who represent church and town for the descendants of Puritan New England, she writes some of her most intriguing stories, and among these I have included in the present collection "A Village Singer," "A Poetess," "Christmas Jenny," and "A Church Mouse." They have in common conflict between a woman protagonist and men who represent patriarchal values; the ministers in these stories object to what they view as women's defiant entrance into the worlds of music, poetry, folk medicine, and religion. The four stories, viewed together, present a comprehensive portrait of the barriers nineteenth-century New England women found against social acceptance whenever they deviated from conventional expectations.

"A Village Singer" has been the most frequently anthologized and deserves an even wider audience. Candace Whitcomb discovers how difficult it is for her community to perceive women as fully human when the members of her church congregation dismiss her as their soprano, making way for a younger woman to replace her in their choir. As an act of protest, on the Sunday the new soprano makes her debut

Candace disrupts the solo by playing her parlor organ and singing so loudly that she drowns out the "piercingly sweet" tones of Alma Way. The choir leader, Candace's sometime suitor, leads the outcry against her, but it is the minister who tries to convince her to stop her protest. In the scene of the interview between the minister and Candace, the woman reveals the hypocrisy of her congregation's "Christianity," makes it plain that they have applied a double standard to her (retaining the old choir director and the old minister while "retiring" the old soprano), and loses her "inborn reverence for clergymen." Yet Candace's "revolution" touches her deeply—as has her dismissal—and within a week she contracts the fever that brings on her death.

The interesting complication in the story concerns the relationship she develops with her rival, a woman engaged to marry her nephew. After presenting the reader with evidence that Alma Way herself has already begun to show the signs of aging, Freeman depicts a deathbed reconciliation between Candace and the younger woman. Candace asks Alma to sing for her, and in her response, she leaves her rival with what the reader can only interpret as a warning. When Alma finishes, Candace insists that Alma face the truth of her own singing. " 'You flatted a little on—soul,' " she tells her, reminding Alma of the inevitable decline of her voice as well as the congregation's potential dissatisfaction (in later years, Alma may find herself supplanted, in a church that accords old women less than full humanity). Freeman links the fever that brings on Candace's illness with her burgeoning vision, so that on her deathbed she achieves a kind of martyrdom, asking for forgiveness for her own actions and exemplifying the humanity her community must learn to emulate. She leads them to a meek sense of their own human insignificance, whether born women or men, even though her eyes follow everyone "with an agonized expression" because she fears being misunderstood even in her death.[7]

"A Poetess" portrays another old woman who, by the practice of her art, manages to offend the minister. In the previous story, Candace Whitcomb openly rebels against her congregation's treatment of her; in "A Poetess," Betsey Dole only hears third-hand that the minister has condemned her poetry as worthless, and she remains conventional in her external behavior, if eccentric, to the story's end. The contempt of men they respect brings both women to illness and quick death, however; and although Betsey Dole does not rebel, her final interview with the minister in the story's closing scene displays with even greater force than "A Village Singer" the pathos inherent in the woman artist's attempt to express herself and remain at peace with her society.

Throughout "A Poetess," Betsy is characterized as eccentric, as childlike and anarchic by temperament, and as someone who forgets to eat when she is in the middle of writing a poem. The conflict in the story comes about when Betsey writes an obituary poem for Willie Caxton and the dead child's mother has it published in a limited edition. By implication, Betsey has stepped over the line, threatening to rival the minister's own occupation, for she creates an alternative immortality for the child in her poem and also manages to console the mother more deeply than the minister did. Freeman's portrait of Betsey Dole hard at work on her poem as the light wanes is worth examining for its echo of decades of sentimental poetesses (like Mrs. Lydia Huntley Sigourney, famous in her time for her funerary prose and poetry [8]), as well as for its contribution in the story. When Mrs. Caxton reports back to Betsey that the minister has called her poem " 'jest as poor as it could be,' " Betsey gathers and burns all of the poems she has ever written and within two months' time has taken to her deathbed.

Like Candace Whitcomb, Betsey has a last confrontation

with her rival, for the reader learns that the minister considers himself a poet as well. And like Candace, Betsey triumphs at her death, even though the minister himself seems puzzled rather than enlightened by a request she makes. She asks to be buried with her sugar bowl containing the ashes of her poetry; and she asks the minister to promise that he will write " 'a few lines' " about her after she is dead. Thus, though she may not have achieved a reputation as a poetess, she knows that in death she will at least become a poem. The minister may deny the quality of her poetry, but he cannot in the nineteenth century deny the appropriateness of death as subject matter. Although she seems to acquiesce to the minister's greater talent as a poet, in reality she forces him to memorialize her on her own terms, implicitly rejecting his power to console her with religion by using the future tense to thank him—" 'I'll be much obliged.' " But "A Poetess" itself stands as Betsey Dole's lasting obituary, and the act of publishing the story both immortalizes the writer's ambition, which created all the trouble for Betsey in the first place, and asserts that fiction in the hands of women writers is a form of literary rebellion. The story champions the woman writer's right to excavate and display the ambition, pride, and power her sentimentalist predecessors felt forced to sublimate.

"Christmas Jenny" is representative of one particular genre Freeman would write in throughout her career—that of the occasional story, particularly the Christmas story.[9] *A New England Nun* alone contains four of these ("A Church Mouse" also ends on Christmas). But in spite of its ending, which apparently transforms a realistic story with an overlay of allegory into a mere fable of the Christmas season, "Christmas Jenny" is one of Freeman's most interesting works of fiction. Like Aurelia Flower of "A Gatherer of Simples," Jenny Wrayne is associated with growing things; she is called "Christmas Jenny" because she comes down from the mountain every year during Christmas week to sell evergreens. The story's conflict is the consequence of rumors that Jenny has caged and starved wild birds and rabbits and is mistreating a deaf and dumb boy at her cabin in the woods. During one of her absences, the minister and deacon enter her cabin un-invited, to be discovered by Jenny's closest neighbor down the mountainside, Mrs. Carey. In an interesting reversal of power, once the men enter Jenny's cabin, finding themselves in an interior world that resembles a grotto and is filled with wild creatures and evergreens, they lose the power of articulate speech. Once Mrs. Carey enters the cabin, she finds herself able to make an eloquent defense of Jenny, shames the men with the evidence of Jenny's veterinary skills, and earns the androgynous woman (who is also described as resembling a tree) new respect from the townspeople. The sexual symbol-ism of the men's violation of the absent Jenny's privacy is unmistakable, and the story rivals "Up Primrose Hill" in its portrait of links between Jenny's sexuality, vision, and rebel-lious eccentricity.

"A Church Mouse" represents the last of four confrontations in *A New England Nun* between solitary, anchorite women and the ministers of the churches, who control both secular and spiritual life in their villages. In "A Church Mouse," Hetty Fifield keeps her physical health after her confrontation with the minister, deacon, and other men in her congregation and at the same time wins a complete moral victory with the assistance of the minister's wife and other women in the con-gregation. In this way, it stands as Freeman's most powerful story of women's struggles to achieve equality and recognition from their communities.

Once again the story leaves the reader with a parable of the Christmas season. Yet the ending does not detract from the fierce portrait of vanquished patriarchy Freeman creates. The story opens with an argument between Hetty Fifield and the deacon of the village church. Caleb Gale is unwilling to contemplate allowing a woman to do something that has never been done before: "'I never heard of a woman's bein' saxton.'" By asserting her right as a charity case to a roof over her head, Hetty manages to move her stove and her bed with its sunflower quilt into the meetinghouse for one night—which stretches into several months, as she takes over the maintenance of the church and rings its bell, in every respect becoming its sexton. For a while, although her presence makes particularly the men in the congregation uneasy, they cannot find a way to evict her—until the Sunday they smell fumes from her dinner of boiled cabbage the evening before. The odor of cooking violates their sense of the Sabbath—on which, for the descendants of the Puritans, no one must work—and they gather force to turn her out of the meetinghouse. Freeman's description of the transformation Hetty produces in the physical appearance of the church is worth examining in detail: she hangs her worsted work on its walls and transforms its chimney corner into a hearth. The house of God becomes a human house, with Hetty its chief vestal priestess. When Caleb Gale and the other men try to evict her, however, they find themselves opposed by "mother" (Mrs. Gale) and the other women of the congregation, who object strenuously when the men threaten the door with a battering ram. With the young daughters of the congregation watching from the perimeter, the scene illustrates that the nature of man's most basic power over a defiant woman comes down to physical strength and symbolic violation of her person, or her privacy. Hetty transforms the meetinghouse window into her own pulpit—preaching an eloquent message on the rights of old women—and the story ends with her triumphant move into the minister's own cloakroom, which will become her permanent place of residence.

Only three of the fifty-two stories in *A Humble Romance*

and *A New England Nun* focus exclusively or predominantly on male protagonists, but two of these serve as interesting counterpoint to Freeman's studies of the lives of women. In "A Solitary," reminiscent of Hawthorne's "Ethan Brand," Nicholas Gunn has seceded from the human race. He has tried to shield himself against feeling by shunning human contact, until he encounters Stephen Forster, an apparently consumptive young man who turns to Nicholas for protection from the New England cold and who becomes the one person capable of bringing out Nicholas's suppressed humanity. Yet both Nicholas and Stephen occupy positions familiar to Freeman's women protagonists. Loneliness and alienation are not new emotions for women in the stories of *A New England Nun;* what strikes the reader as new is the way Freeman portrays men experiencing them. Stephen Forster begins to break down Nicholas Gunn's self-imposed alienation as his suffering takes on human qualities. The progression of Freeman's description of Stephen—from animal or hungry bird to human child— coincides with the transformation in Nicholas Gunn from Buddhist monk to male nurse. When Nicholas finally pulls Stephen in from the cold one desolate night, the reader finds him transformed from a "rough, loud voice" to a man capable of harboring, feeding, tending, and encouraging. By morning, Nicholas has completed his transformation, and like the male characters in "A Conflict Ended" and "The Revolt of 'Mother,' " Nicholas has conquered his man's will, becoming instead a maternal man and discovering that Stephen, overnight, has taken on the "helplessness of infancy." Stephen's alteration from wild furred animal to human infant parallels Nicholas's transformation into "mother," and Freeman's vision of the world becomes an androgynous one, in which even men can suckle each other.

Finally, in "A Village Lear," Freeman completes her study of the feminized male and the destructive effects, for either a man or a woman, in possessing the trappings of male will and power without the moderating effect of human affection and feeling—those qualities we associate with the concept of "mother." Literal sexual identity does not always indicate the quality of a person's character, and in "A Village Lear" Barney Swann's daughters, Ellen and Malvina, once possessed of their father's former wealth and property, demonstrate their fundamental lack of human affection. They, like Shakespeare's Goneril and Regan in *King Lear,* are daughters in name only.

Having given away all of his material possessions but a few trinkets, with which he hopes to barter for his family's love, Barney Swann's need for human affection begins to outstrip his ability to ensure the fulfillment of that need. His need becomes infinite, whereas male force (symbolized by the phallic connotations of Barney's trinkets: a stick of candy, and the watch chain sold to buy a gold-plated brooch) becomes illusory and of finite strength. Within the hut—his old shoe shop, to which he has been exiled by his daughters—Barney resembles a human version of Louisa Ellis's dog Caesar in "A New England Nun," and his drawer filled with "treasures" recalls the symbolism of the bureau drawer the two women friends discover in "Up Primrose Hill." Despite his abdication of the trappings of male power, Barney has managed to achieve a vision specifically female in its connotations. In the womblike hut he also becomes infantlike—a tragic development, because he not only fails to find the love he needs but discovers at the end of his life that he has never come close to satisfying even a part of his immense human craving. Unlike Lear's finding comfort in Cordelia's love at the end of his life, Barney's friendship with his neighbor Sarah cannot replace the loss of his own daughters and granddaughter. When Malvina loses patience with her failing father and announces her intention to tear down his shoe shop, she hastens his death.

Despite the many women characters in Freeman's stories

who resemble Ellen and Malvina in their lack of human feeling, it is significant that Freeman must create a man, not a woman, for her depiction of this unmitigated tragedy of human isolation. For women in Freeman's fiction have available to them, whether or not they recognize it, a community that sustains their spirit and validates their vision. Barney Swann does not naturally belong to this community, and even though he gives over the money and power that superficially make him male instead of female in his society he has the bad luck to have daughters who possess the worst qualities of men rather than the best qualities of women. His isolation, then, is unique in Freeman's early stories, partly because he is a man who suffers the powerlessness usually reserved for women and partly because he discovers the depth of human need without having the ability, characteristic of many women characters in Freeman, to look for a surrogate mother, daughter, sister, or, in Barney's case, granddaughter.

FREEMAN AND THE CRITICS

The measure of Freeman's success in creating an alternative vision of American culture may be gauged by critics' neglect during the last fifty years.[10] It has proven easier to ignore or minimize her work than to integrate it into prevalent thematic depictions of American literature. Perhaps this is why critics have tried to convince readers of her "local" rather than "universal" appeal.

Quite often a survey of critical opinion about an author's work becomes merely an academic exercise, but this is not the case with Freeman, for when we discover that there were critical voices capable of assessing her objectively during her lifetime, the neglect to which others, particularly since the fifties, have subjected her suggests that until recently we have been suffering a long period of cultural blindness.

The fact that Freeman wrote predominantly about women characters in her early work was viewed at one point as a limitation. Charles Miner Thompson praised her in 1899 yet added,

> the limitations of her environment determine the scope of her work, and they are unfortunately great. If we keep them in mind, the fact is not surprising that of the twenty-eight stories in *A Humble Romance* every one is told from the point of view of some woman,—and that there are very few which do not deal with one of those family or neighborhood quarrels which have been referred to as the staple of the women's gossip in small country towns.[11]

Edward Foster points out that most of the stories in *A Humble Romance* were originally written for and published in *Harper's Bazar,* a woman's magazine. As he succinctly expresses it, "a woman was writing for women." [12]

However, many of her contemporaries in the 1890s recognized her genius and wrote about her with respect and attention to detail. We can learn a great deal from these early critics—among them an anonymous reviewer of *A New England Nun,* writing for *The Atlantic Monthly* in 1891. The reviewer described the singular pointedness of Mary Wilkins's stories, writing that "the compression of these stories is remarkable, and almost unique in our literature." The writer also commented, "Of the genuine originality of these stories it is hard to speak too strongly. . . . Always there is a freedom from commonplace, and a power to hold the interest to the close." [13]

Thompson, writing after the publication of *Pembroke* (1894) and six additional volumes of Freeman's fiction, said retrospectively of *A Humble Romance:* "This book, which appeared in 1887, came with the force of a new revelation of New England to itself." He examined the strengths of Free-

man's artistry then added that this first book forms, together
with "its succeeding sister volume," *A New England Nun,*

> in a way a brief memorandum of Miss Wilkins' entire mes-
> sage to the world, which her later work, for the most part,
> only serves to amplify and make clear. When one begins to
> read the novels, the short stories assume almost the aspect
> of preliminary sketches of their scenes and episodes, for
> they are similar not only in substance, but in method.[14]

And in *Literature and Life,* William Dean Howells described the occasional pleasure he took at midday in New
England "in identifying this or that one-story cottage with its
lean-to as a Mary Wilkins house and in placing one of her
muted dramas in it." [15] For Howells, who elsewhere called
Wilkins's art "exquisitely realistic," [16] "one cannot know the
people of such places without recognizing her types in them,
and one cannot know New England without owning the fidelity
of her stories to New England character." [17] Although, as
Edward Foster points out in his biography, *A Humble Romance* "produced no sensation among American critics" when
it appeared in 1887, "the warmest commendation came from
the most distinguished critic," Howells, writing in his "The
Editor's Study" column for *Harper's Monthly.*[18] Howells con-
cluded his comments on the stories by writing,

> They are good through and through, and whoever loves the
> common face of humanity will find pleasure in them. They
> are peculiarly American, and they are peculiarly "narrow"
> in a certain way, and yet they are like the best modern
> work everywhere in their directness and simplicity.[19]

Such statements continue to ring true for readers in our
own time, and it is a pleasure for someone who has newly
discovered Freeman's fiction to find that he or she belongs to
a group of respectful admirers of her work from the past—

even if critics after the 1930s began to relegate her to the footnotes of literary history. Once or twice every decade during the last thirty years of Freeman's life, we find a commentator who assessed her strengths and placed her within the context of American literature. Some of their ideas are worth developing.

In 1905, for example, Paul Elmer More linked Cotton Mather, Nathaniel Hawthorne, and Mary Wilkins Freeman in a "regular progress," writing about Freeman that "the very genealogy of her genius shows that she has laid hold of an essential trait of [New England] character, and, indeed, it needs but little acquaintance with the stagnant towns of coast and mountains to have met more than one of the people of her books actual in the flesh." [20] Whether or not readers today would agree that her fictional towns were stagnant (as More describes their real-life models), Freeman's resemblances to Hawthorne and her fictional portraits of the pervasive effects of Puritanism on New England culture long after its waning as theology raise interesting questions for the reader and remain relatively unexplored by the critics.

As Perry Westbrook notes in his critical book on Freeman, "ever since the 1880's, Mary Wilkins has been recognized as the anatomist of the latter-day Puritan will." [21] In his 1899 essay, Charles Miner Thompson discusses the impress "upon her imagination [of] the awful power for evil of a perverted will," and describes this major theme in her work as that particular "keystone of New England character" inherited from the Puritans. He writes, "The old Puritans exercised their stubbornness upon a great issue; these country descendants, living in narrow ways and thinking narrow thoughts, exercise their stubbornness upon petty issues. That is the only difference . . ." [22] And Howells agreed, writing:

The life of New England, such as Miss Wilkins deals with, and Miss Sarah Orne Jewett, and Miss Alice Brown, is not on the surface, or not visibly so, except to the accustomed eye. It is Puritanism scarcely animated at all by the Puritanic theology. . . . A people are not a chosen people for half a dozen generations without acquiring a spiritual pride that remains with them long after they cease to believe themselves chosen.[23]

The study of the will, for Westbrook, involves characters who possess "overrefined consciences" or "sheer fixation" and who undergo "spiritual crisis," which manifests itself as general revolt and rebellion.[24] In an overstatement of the case, Westbrook writes, "Pride, whim, stubbornness, habit, sensitivity, indecision, rebelliousness, monomania plague Miss Wilkins' characters."[25] Westbrook finds related to the study of the will what he calls the "central theme" of Wilkins's village fiction, namely "the struggle of the individual toward self-fulfillment, whether in marriage, on the farm, in the pulpit, or in the schoolhouse."[26] And Thompson, in his analysis of the "abnormal" Wilkins characters from whom "we may learn what is the normal New England character," argued that the "contests of will . . . have their fine aspect in that they are almost always upon some question of personal dignity, or freedom, or point of ethical opinion."[27] Critical statements like these move us in the right direction toward understanding Freeman's fiction—particularly her early stories, where her study of individual rebellion takes center stage—but the statements are not accurate enough in one sense: by minimizing or ignoring the fact that almost all of the protagonists of Freeman's early fiction were women, the critics stop short of considering the extent to which the protagonists' experience as women in a patriarchal, Puritan society color their struggles toward self-fulfillment and characterize the nature of their personal rebellions.

Thompson's statements about the Puritans and their descendants have special relevance to Freeman's women protagonists. He writes, "These people are nonconformists to their backbones. They are fanatics or martyrs according to the point of view . . ." [28] But when we recall that one of the most famous Puritan nonconformists was Anne Hutchinson, and that the great majority of witches executed during the Salem trials of 1692 were women, gender plays an important role in Freeman's choice of nonconformists, fanatics, and martyrs as models for her village protagonists.[29] What critics have ignored or minimized in their treatment of Freeman's fiction, then, is the extent to which gender becomes a regional feature in Mary Wilkins's landscape, one that explains her fascination for the Puritans at the same time that it allows her to characterize post-Civil War New England with its preponderance of women inhabitants.

Finally, of course, her fiction must stand on its own, but the comments of her contemporaries remain a useful guide to her work and point the way to further study. As we read her stories, we need to reassess her strengths as the heir to Hawthorne in her exploration of Puritanism and the human will, as an innovator in the American short story tradition, and as one of the writers who gave New England a strong regional literature to the close of the nineteenth century. We certainly need to study in greater detail her portraits of American women's community and how late nineteenth-century New Englanders tried to reverse patriarchal structures of social organization they had inherited from their Puritan founders.

NOTES TO THE AFTERWORD

1. In its portrait of the factory town, "Two Old Lovers" prefigures Freeman's later interest, in novels like *Jerome, A Poor Man* (1897) and *The Portion of Labor* (1901), in depicting the role factories played in destroying the possibilities for Arcadian life in New England.

2. See David H. Hirsch, "Subdued Meaning in 'A New England Nun,'" *Studies in Short Fiction* 2 (1965): 124–36.

3. Ann Douglas Wood, "The Literature of Impoverishment: The Women Local Colorists in America 1865–1914," *Women's Studies* 1:1(1972): 25.

4. See Edmund S. Morgan, *The Puritan Family* (Boston: Trustees of the Public Library, 1956).

5. Foster, p. 93.

6. Foster, pp. 91–92; Foster's source is a statement Freeman made in the *Saturday Evening Post,* December 8, 1917, p. 25.

7. For a fuller discussion of this story, see my essay "The Humanity of Women in Freeman's 'A Village Singer,'" forthcoming in *Colby Library Quarterly.*

8. See Ann Douglas Wood, "Mrs. Sigourney and the Sensibility of the Inner Space," *New England Quarterly* 45 (1972): 163–81.

9. Nineteenth-century editors frequently "ordered" holiday stories, and Freeman regularly published Christmas stories in *Harper's Bazar.*

10. The most generous critics during that time have been Arthur H. Quinn, *American Fiction* (New York: Appleton-Century, 1936), pp. 324–30; Perry Westbrook, *Acres of Flint* (Washington, D.C.: Scarecrow Press, 1951), and his critical study, *Mary Wilkins Freeman*; and Edward Foster in his biography. Westbrook's *Mary Wilkins Freeman,* as one of its many strengths, merits the distinction of being the only study to deal, at least in passing, with everything Freeman ever wrote that was collected in her more than thirty volumes of fiction.

11. Charles Miner Thompson, "Miss Wilkins: An Idealist in Masquerade," *The Atlantic Monthly* 83 (1899): 670.

12. Foster, p. 71.

13. "New England in the Short Story," *The Atlantic Monthly* 67 (June 1891): 847–48.

14. Thompson, pp. 668, 672.

15. William Dean Howells, *Literature and Life* (New York: Harper & Bros., 1902), pp. 279–80.

16. William Dean Howells, *Literary Friends and Acquaintances* (New York: Harper & Bros., 1901), p. 118.

17. Howells, *Literature and Life,* pp. 279–80.

18. Foster, p. 64.

19. Howells, "The Editor's Study," *Harper's New Monthly* 75 (September 1887): 203.

20. Paul Elmer More, "Hawthorne: Looking Before and After," in *The Shelburne Essays,* second series (Boston: Houghton Mifflin, 1905), p. 180.

21. Westbrook, *Mary Wilkins Freeman,* p. 72.

22. Thompson, p. 671.

23. Howells, *Literature and Life,* p. 281.

24. Westbrook, pp. 42, 43, 51.

25. Westbrook, p. 46. Westbrook discusses these themes at length in chapters on *A Humble Romance* and *A New England Nun,* and in analysis of three related novels, *Jane Field* (1893), *Pembroke* (1894), and *Madelon* (1896).

26. Westbrook, p. 70.

27. Thompson, p. 671.

28. Thompson, p. 671.

29. Both Foster and Westbrook note that Freeman, like Hawthorne, traced a descendant to the Salem trials, a man named Bray Wilkins. Westbrook hypothesizes that although "unlike Hawthorne, Miss Wilkins took upon herself no burden of guilt for the mistakes of her ancestors, . . . her interest in Salem is clearly more than that of the objective historian" (p. 134). Whether or not this genealogy is correct, one of the ways in which Freeman manifested that interest was to write a play, *Giles Corey, Yeoman* (1893), based on the accusation, trial and execution of one of the few male witches—the only witch who was pressed to death for his refusal to plead either innocence or guilt.

Selected Bibliography

SELECTED SECONDARY MATERIALS

Both Edward Foster's biography, *Mary E. Wilkins Freeman* (New York: Hendricks House, 1956), and Perry D. Westbrook's critical study, *Mary Wilkins Freeman* (New York: Twayne, 1967), include extensive bibliographies. Westbrook's annotated bibliography of the most perceptive treatments of Freeman's life and work is particularly useful. In the bibliography that follows, I have confined myself to the most useful works not cited by either Foster or Westbrook.

Brand, Alice. "Mary Wilkins Freeman: Misanthropy as Propaganda," *New England Quarterly* 50 (March 1977): 83–100.

Crowley, John W. "Freeman's Yankee Tragedy: 'Amanda and Love,'" *Markham Review* 5 (Spring 1976): 58–60.

DeEulis, Marilyn Davis. "'Her Box of a House': Spatial Restriction as Psychic Signpost in Mary Wilkins Freeman's 'The Revolt of "Mother,"'" *Markham Review* 8:51–52.

Gallagher, Edward J. "Freeman's 'The Revolt of Mother,'" *Explicator* 27 (March 1969), item 48.

Hamblen, Abigail Ann. *The New England Art of Mary E. Wilkins Freeman.* Amherst, Mass.: The Green Knight Press, 1966.

Hirsch, David H. "Subdued Meaning in 'A New England Nun,'" *Studies in Short Fiction* 2 (1965): 124–36.

Kendrick, Brent L. "The Infant Sphinx: Collected Letters of Mary E. Wilkins Freeman," (diss., Univ. of South Carolina, 1981).

————. "Mary E. Wilkins Freeman," *American Literary Realism* 8 (Summer 1975): 255–57.

Pryse, Marjorie L. "The Humanity of Women in Freeman's 'A Village Singer,'" *Colby Library Quarterly* (forthcoming).

Quina, James H., Jr. "Character Types in the Fiction of Mary Wilkins Freeman," *Colby Library Quarterly* 9 (June 1971): 432–39.

Sherman, Sarah W. "The Great Goddess in New England: Mary Wilkins Freeman's 'Christmas Jenny,'" *Studies in Short Fiction* 17 (Spring 1980): 157–64.

Toth, Susan A. "Defiant Light: A Positive View of Mary Wilkins Freeman," *New England Quarterly* 46 (March 1973): 82–93.

————. "Mary Wilkins Freeman's Parable of Wasted Life," *American Literature* 42 (January 1971): 564–67.

Wood, Ann Douglas. "The Literature of Impoverishment: The Women Local Colorists in America 1865–1914," *Women's Studies* 1:1 (1972).

THE ADULT FICTION OF MARY E. WILKINS FREEMAN

A Humble Romance and Other Stories. New York: Harper & Bros., 1887.

A New England Nun and Other Stories. New York: Harper & Bros., 1891.

Jane Field. New York: Harper & Bros., 1893.

Giles Corey, Yeoman: A Play. New York: Harper & Bros., 1893.

Pembroke. New York: Harper & Bros., 1894.

Madelon. New York: Harper & Bros., 1896.

Jerome, A Poor Man. New York: Harper & Bros., 1897.

Silence and Other Stories. New York: Harper & Bros., 1898.

The People of Our Neighborhood. Philadelphia: Curtis Publishing Co., 1898.

The Jamesons. New York: Doubleday and McClure Co., 1899.

The Heart's Highway, A Romance of Virginia. New York: Doubleday, Page and Co., 1900.

The Love of Parson Lord and Other Stories. New York: Harper & Bros., 1900.

Understudies. New York: Harper & Bros., 1901.

The Portion of Labor. New York: Harper & Bros., 1901.

Six Trees. New York: Harper & Bros., 1903.

The Wind in the Rose-Bush and Other Stories of the Supernatural. New York: Doubleday, Page & Co., 1903.

The Givers. New York: Harper & Bros., 1904.

The Debtor. New York: Harper & Bros., 1905.

By the Light of the Soul. New York: Harper & Bros., 1906.

"Doc" Gordon. New York: Grosset & Dunlap, 1906.

The Fair Lavinia and Others. New York: Harper & Bros., 1907.

The Shoulders of Atlas. New York: Harper & Bros., 1908.

The Whole Family, A Novel by Twelve Authors (including Mary W. Freeman, William D. Howells, Henry James, et al.). New York: Harper & Bros., 1908.

The Winning Lady and Others. New York: Harper & Bros., 1909.

The Butterfly House. New York: Dodd, Mead & Co., 1912.

The Yates Pride: A Romance. New York: Harper & Bros., 1912.

The Copy-Cat and Other Stories. New York: Harper & Bros., 1914.

An Alabaster Box (with Florence Morse Kingsley). New York: D. Appleton & Co., 1917.

Edgewater People. New York: Harper & Bros., 1918.

The Best Stories of Mary E. Wilkins. Introduction by H. W. Lanier. New York: Harper & Bros., 1927.